GUARDIAN
ZHEN HUN

3

GUARDIAN
ZHEN HUN

3

WRITTEN BY

priest

ILLUSTRATED BY

Ying

TRANSLATED BY

Yuka, Shry, amixy

Seven Seas

Seven Seas Entertainment

GUARDIAN: ZHEN HUN VOL. 3

Published originally under the title of 《镇魂》(Zhen Hun)
Author © priest
English edition rights under license granted by 北京晋江原创网络科技有限公司
(Beijing Jinjiang Original Network Technology Co., Ltd.)
English edition copyright © 2024 Seven Seas Entertainment, Inc.
Arranged through JS Agency Co., Ltd
All rights reserved

Cover and Interior Illustrations by Ying

Seven Seas press and purchase enquiries can be sent
to Marketing Manager Lauren Hill at press@gomanga.com.
Information regarding the distribution and purchase of digital editions is available
from Digital Manager CK Russell at digital@gomanga.com.

Follow Seven Seas Entertainment online at
sevenseasentertainment.com.

TRANSLATION: Yuka, Shry, amixy
ADAPTATION: Ealasaid Weaver
COVER DESIGN: M. A. Lewife
INTERIOR DESIGN & LAYOUT: Clay Gardner
COPY EDITOR: Jehanne Bell
PROOFREADER: Jade Gardner, Pengie
EDITOR: Laurel Ashgrove
PREPRESS TECHNICIAN: Melanie Ujimori, Jules Valera
MANAGING EDITOR: Alyssa Scavetta
EDITOR-IN-CHIEF: Julie Davis
PUBLISHER: Lianne Sentar
VICE PRESIDENT: Adam Arnold
PRESIDENT: Jason DeAngelis

Standard Edition ISBN: 978-1-63858-943-3
Special Edition ISBN: 979-8-89160-850-4
Printed in Canada
First Printing: August 2024
10 9 8 7 6 5 4 3 2 1

TABLE OF CONTENTS

BONUS STORIES

APPENDIXES

ARC 4

SOUL-GUARDING LAMP

THE FIRST THING GUO CHANGCHENG did when he got home was pass out and catch up on some much-needed rest. When he eventually woke up many hours later, he made himself presentable and finally headed out to buy holiday gifts and visit his relatives' homes.

His first stop was his second uncle's house. After entering and greeting everyone, Guo Changcheng took out the red envelope containing the gift cards that Zhao Yunlan had given him. With the gravity of an official presenting an offering to the emperor, he announced, "Second Uncle, our boss said this is for my aunt and cousin to buy new clothes for the New Year."

Since Guo Changcheng's cousin had plenty of talent for spending money yet none for earning any, his second uncle had never seen a return on his investment before this very moment. Somewhat flattered but also shocked, his uncle took an astonished peek inside before handing the gift back to Guo Changcheng. "That's quite a bit. Let me give it right back to you—consider it red envelope money from me. It's odd, though. Lao-Yang isn't exactly known for his generosity, is he? Why is he giving out red envelopes this year?"

Baffled, Guo Changcheng said, "Who's lao-Yang?"

His second uncle stood and accepted a plate of dumplings passed to him. Casually, he asked, "Isn't that the surname of your boss at the Household Registry Department? Three characters—Yang something?"

Guo Changcheng was even more confused. "Our boss's surname is Zhao."

His second uncle heard but didn't really register the comment other than to think he must've misremembered. As he distributed chopsticks, he said, "Yeah, okay, if you say so. Either way, I heard he was the kind of stingy guy who always brings home the leftovers when he eats out. But then again, he has parents and children to take care of. It's understandable when he has to provide for a family. If he's treating you well, make sure you work hard for him. You're an adult now, so don't spend your paycheck all at once. Try to save a little. You need to learn to survive..."

The more Guo Changcheng heard, the more confused he got. Finally, he couldn't help interjecting. "Second Uncle, our boss isn't married."

"Impossible. His daughter's about to enter university. Just last month I was telling someone that he doesn't have it easy and that they should cut him more slack." It finally struck Guo Changcheng's second uncle that something wasn't adding up. "Wait, what did you say your boss's name was?"

"Director Zhao."

"Director Zhao? Which one?"

"Er... Director Zhao Yunlan from the Special Investigations Department?"

This elicited a dumbfounded stream of questions from his uncle. "The Special Investigations Department?! The one on 4 Bright Avenue? Zhao... Zhao Yunlan?"

"What investigations department?" His aunt had joined them at the table. "Aren't you at the Household Registry Department?"

"I work in the criminal investigation unit of the Special Investigations Department," Guo Changcheng replied.

"Criminal investigation...?" His aunt froze. Having watched him grow up, she knew what this poor child was made of. She turned on her husband at once. "What the heck were you thinking? How could a kid from our family join a criminal investigation unit? It's dangerous! Precarious! If he runs into a deadly case... Aiya!"

"I did no such thing!" Her husband's face radiated innocence. "The Special Investigations Department is its own unique entity. I certainly don't have the power to assign anyone there!"

Overflowing with worry, Guo Changcheng's aunt asked, "What does this department investigate? Surely not important high-profile cases?"

Guo Changcheng opened his mouth, but before he could speak, his second uncle rapped his chopsticks on the side of his bowl. "Keep your questions to yourself. Everything the Special Investigations Department handles is top secret. Don't make him slip up and say something he shouldn't. But this is truly bizarre! How did you end up *there*?"

Only now did Guo Changcheng finally process what he was hearing: his acceptance into the Special Investigations Department really had been a mistake all along, just as he'd suspected. Given his below-average intelligence and people skills, no relative with even a shred of self-awareness would've ever recommended him to such a prestigious position.

Guo Changcheng, passive introvert that he was, only ever told his family good news, leaving out the bad entirely. Every time he'd called to tell them how he was doing, it had always been the same report:

"I'm doing well." As a result, over six months had passed without them realizing that he ended up working in the wrong place.

Uncle and nephew stared at each other. The whole idea remained unfathomable no matter how Second Uncle thought about it. "And your Director Zhao didn't say anything about it? He just let you stay on and become a full-time employee?"

Guo Changcheng's chest swelled with pride. All his life, he'd had such a hard time meshing well with any group. He'd been bullied throughout school and lived in a constant state of anxiety and fear, as if walking on thin ice. Now, for the first time ever, he felt as though he'd managed to become part of a group...albeit a group that was far from normal.

4 Bright Avenue had a loyal black cat; gentle, attentive Wang Zheng; brisk, capable Zhu Hong; hilarious Lin Jing; patient Chu-ge, who was always willing to teach him what he didn't know; and above all, Director Zhao, who was like everyone's guardian. Yes, the situations they encountered were always dangerous and deeply strange, and yes, there was often overtime required, but with those people around him, how could he ever want to leave?

Their "guardian" Zhao Yunlan was awakened by the sound of his phone. His temples throbbed as if someone had punched a hole through them; now that he was awake, he somehow felt more exhausted than he had before going to sleep. He didn't know how long he'd been asleep, but his dreams had been a disjointed mess, constantly circling back to him blinding the divine dragon and toppling Buzhou Mountain. The images were seared into his mind.

He felt around his bedside table and then his phone was pressed into his hand. Without even opening his eyes, he picked up the call and offered some bullshit greetings. After a conversation in which he barely seemed to register who was calling or what he himself said in response, he reeled off a bunch of auspicious blessings and hung up, feeling even more drained. Burying his face back into his pillow, he whined, "My head hurts."

Shen Wei was beside him at once, holding him close in a supportive embrace. After carefully feeling his forehead, Shen Wei said, "You're a little warm. What brought this fever on so suddenly?"

"What do you think?" Zhao Yunlan's voice was weak. "Get me some antibiotics and fever meds, will you?"

Shen Wei blushed and obeyed without a word.

After choking down the handful of little pills Shen Wei brought him, Zhao Yunlan rolled up his pajama sleeves and abruptly launched himself forward, pinning Shen Wei down on the bed. Expression fierce, he demanded, "Did this lowly one serve you well last night, my lord?"

Quickly moving to support his waist, Shen Wei pulled Zhao Yunlan's gaping pajama top tightly closed around him. "Don't kick the blanket—you've let the heat out! Now you're going to catch a cold."

"Fuck colds." Zhao Yunlan pushed against Shen Wei's shoulder with one hand and grabbed his collar with the other. "Since my lord enjoyed himself, don't I deserve a little tip?" His tone had turned ominous.

Shen Wei let Zhao Yunlan press down against him as he gazed up into his eyes. From Zhao Yunlan's point of view, Shen Wei was practically begging to be ravaged. Courage gave birth to wickedness. Sitting up, he straddled Shen Wei and began peeling off his clothes. "If I don't take you today, I'll take your last name tomorrow—ow! Fuck!"

Instantly, Shen Wei's arms closed around him again. "What is it?"

"...My leg cramped up."

It was possible that Zhao Yunlan had been a tad calcium-deficient to begin with, and now, after all he'd been through the night before, his leg had decided that enough was enough. The cramping pain slowly migrated from his thigh down into his calf before finally settling into his foot. All Shen Wei could do was forcefully straighten the leg out and gradually smooth the abused muscles while Zhao Yunlan cursed up a storm.

At first, the pain was bad enough that Zhao Yunlan's features contorted into a grimace, making him bite down on a corner of the blanket, but eventually he calmed down. From the corner of his eye, Shen Wei glimpsed angry bruises under the edge of Zhao Yunlan's pajamas and gently massaged his stiff muscles in apology. Zhao Yunlan stopped kicking up a fuss and lay back without further protest, letting himself enjoy it.

His gaze shifted to the phone on the bedside table. After a while, he said, "That was Guo Changcheng's second uncle who called."

Shen Wei made a quiet sound of acknowledgment.

"I haven't really interacted with him, but we work in the same system, so I've heard some things. He's got a reputation for being smooth and clever and has a knack for handling people," Zhao Yunlan said, a little muffled. "His nephew's worked under me for over half a year, but the guy's never gotten in touch with me once. Now he calls out of the blue and invites me out for a meal. Do you think that's normal?"

There were so many unspoken rules dedicated to keeping up appearances, and Shen Wei's grasp on them was shaky at best. "What's the problem?" he asked.

"It's no way to handle things," Zhao Yunlan said. "My guess is that he only just found out that Guo Changcheng got assigned to the SID..." He trailed off, glanced at Shen Wei, and abruptly changed the subject. "Hey, I need to ask you something. Was I really the one who knocked down Buzhou and destroyed the Path to Heaven?"

Shen Wei froze, suddenly looking anywhere but at Zhao Yunlan. "Legend says that the Water God, Gonggong, was responsible for that."

"Oh." Zhao Yunlan lowered his eyes. Shen Wei was one of the gui, so if the gui hadn't been released until after the mountain fell, Shen Wei probably wasn't in a position to know what had really happened.

After a brief hesitation, Shen Wei asked, "What exactly did you see inside the Great Divine Tree?"

"Stuff from ancient times." Zhao Yunlan turned his head on the pillow. "I saw how you fell off a large rock into the water the first time we met. At the time, I thought you'd been dazzled by my beauty. That golden glow must've blinded you and the shock made you fall—ah!"

By that point Shen Wei's hands had reached Zhao Yunlan's waist, and hearing that had made him involuntarily press down too hard.

Zhao Yunlan hissed. "Are you trying to kill your husband?!"

Shen Wei rubbed the sore spot gently. He answered with surprising candor, as if the absolute physical intimacy they'd shared had loosened his tongue. "It's true. My heart was swept away the first time I laid eyes on you. I've never forgotten it for a single moment."

"Love at first sight, huh?" Zhao Yunlan flashed him a smug, lascivious smile. "Hey, you're supposed to have long hair, right? Take off your glasses and let your husband have a look."

Shen Wei obligingly removed his glasses. As he shifted back to his true appearance, a cascade of ink-black hair spilled across the bed.

Some men had an inexplicable obsession with long hair. Whether or not that was true of Zhao Yunlan, the sight of Shen Wei's hair tumbling down around him went straight to his id—a flawless example of the kind of thing he was into.

At first, he just gazed, struck speechless. Then he carefully reached out one greedy hand to caress a silken lock of hair. *This life was truly worth living.*

Shen Wei resumed massaging, working on Zhao Yunlan's shoulder while Zhao Yunlan cuddled up to his hair and fantasized.

His fantasies evaporated the moisture from Zhao Yunlan's waterlogged brain, clearing his mind enough that he could finally think. He curled his fingers into Shen Wei's hair. *If I looked after Chiyou's descendants because he entrusted them to me and watched generations of the Dragon tribe grow from tiny worms into huge divine beasts, could I really have been capable of blinding one of them and just letting it die in the collision? It would be like blinding Daqing now and using him as a tool. Could I really do that?*

Throughout reincarnation and rebirth, his souls were unchanging. Was it possible for him to become a completely different person? The thought of the radical fury he had witnessed in the Great Divine Tree kept running through his mind. It just didn't seem like something he would do. Was there any guarantee that what the tree had revealed was true? How much of what he'd seen was real? How much was false?

And who had wanted him to see those things?

Softly, Zhao Yunlan said, "Tell me more about what happened after we met in the grove."

Shen Wei paused before replying. "I didn't really understand anything at the time," he said, his voice low. "I only knew how good you were to me. You took me to see all the great mountains and rivers. We traveled all over, stopping here and there. But you kept saying how unfortunate it was that Nüwa hadn't yet mended the sky. You said that the unending torrents of rain had robbed even the great mountains and rivers of their beauty. I didn't mind, though.

They were still beautiful to me—the most beautiful sights I'd ever seen."

Zhao Yunlan's brow furrowed. "*Was* I good to you? I was the one who forcibly elevated you to godhood."

Shen Wei laughed. "There's no place for the likes of me between the earth and the sky. You brought me out of the Place of Great Disrespect to protect me, not to do me harm. I'm grateful to you for all of that. The time we spent together was all the life I needed; having had that, I would've died willingly."

"Shut up," Zhao Yunlan said. "Don't talk such nonsense."

Shen Wei leaned down and pressed a gentle kiss to Zhao Yunlan's temple, taking his hand.

Zhao Yunlan kept talking. "After Nüwa repaired the sky, I used the Four Hallowed Artifacts to seal the Four Pillars. Was that when I abandoned you...and died?"

Shen Wei froze. His grip on Zhao Yunlan's hand was suddenly painful.

"But why?" Zhao Yunlan mumbled to himself. "If I was the one who knocked down the Pillars of Heaven, why did I seal the Four Hallowed Artifacts? Did I do it for Nüwa?"

A hint of displeasure flickered across Shen Wei's face. For an instant, there was something almost ominous in his expression. Seeing it, Zhao Yunlan briefly set those questions aside. He touched Shen Wei's chin with a finger, tilting his head. "Don't be upset. I was just wondering. To me, you're much more beautiful than Nüwa.

"Now, little beauty, tell me how you seduced me with your youthful body and gorgeous face all those years ago. I want *all* the details."

The request struck Shen Wei as unbearably absurd. He took hold of the blanket and draped it over Zhao Yunlan, giving him a stern glare. But before this poor affronted gentleman could launch into a serious scolding, his gaze fell on Zhao Yunlan's neck with its constellation of love bites.

Shen Wei's ears flushed crimson. Unable to maintain the pretense of propriety in the face of this evidence, the only words he could squeeze out were, "...I'm going downstairs."

He swiftly got to his feet, grabbed the laundry slip from the table, and left to pick up the cleaning.

Zhao Yunlan pressed a hand to his still-sore waist. There were no words to describe everything he was feeling.

THE MAGISTRATE HURRIED into the Yanluo Courts to find the Qin'guang King, one of the Ten Yanluo Kings, waiting for him. Before the Magistrate could even begin to bow, the gesture was cut off by an impatient swish of one of the Qin'guang King's sleeves. "How did it go?"

The Magistrate offered a hasty recap of what had transpired on Kunlun Mountain. He smiled as he concluded, "After scaring away the Chaos King of the Gui, Kunlun-jun entered the Great Divine Tree alone. It didn't seem as though the Soul-Executing Emissary said much to him. My king, now that the Mountain God of the Great Wild has awakened, surely the Great Seal must—"

"Kunlun-jun's spirit may not truly be awakened," the Qin'guang King interrupted, expression heavy.

The Magistrate froze in place. "How could that be?"

The Qin'guang King hummed. "Zhao Yunlan is unspeakably cunning. He's deceived you more than once. Perhaps he simply managed to piece together enough to bluff and frighten the Chaos King of the Gui."

"But..."

"The Soul-Guarding Lamp remains unlit," said the Qin'guang King.

The Magistrate's expression changed at once.

"Shennong himself sealed Kunlun-jun's divine spirit within the Reincarnation Cycle," the Qin'guang King continued. "As long as the Mountain God remains within the cycle, his spirit will not be released. The legends spoke true: our little tricks won't be enough to awaken him." The Qin'guang King gave a low sigh. "It seems our only choice is to sacrifice this mortal body of the Mountain God."

The Magistrate fell heavily to his knees.

"We do what we must for the sake of all living beings."

Zhao Yunlan, having run into his father after returning to Dragon City the day before, decided to be prompt about calling and setting a time to properly introduce Shen Wei to his parents. And yet when the agreed-upon time came, he and Shen Wei arrived only to find that Zhao Yunlan's father was once again not home to meet them. Only his mother was there, left in the position of offering apologies and explanations.

Shen Wei, of course, was too good-tempered to mind, and for once Zhao Yunlan didn't say a word. They ate a quick meal at the family home and promptly left.

When Zhao Yunlan had first come back to the city, his mind had still been fully occupied by the past he'd seen within the Great Divine Tree. He hadn't even registered that something about his dad had been off. What kind of father, knowing full well that his son's gay lover was in the apartment above, would so coldly and haughtily say, as if he were some kind of gentleman, that "he's unprepared," and that they could "make proper plans at a later date"? It wasn't as if Shen Wei had been set up on a blind date with him. What was there to prepare for?

Clearly, his dad didn't want to see Shen Wei.

But why? Was he simply unwilling? Or was he too scared?

Before leaving after dinner, Zhao Yunlan went into his old room and got out a small wooden box. Curious, his mother asked, "Didn't you play with that as a kid? Why haven't you thrown it out? What are you taking it out for?"

Zhao Yunlan just waved dismissively at her. "Sharing childhood memories with my lover. You're half of an old couple who've long since grown tired of each other; you wouldn't understand."

Thanks to his annoying mouth, Zhao Yunlan was chased out of the house.

It just so happened to be Valentine's Day. Where the city's streets had been all but deserted during the Lunar New Year holidays, they were now bustling with life again. A girl selling flowers passed by Shen Wei and Zhao Yunlan, and she picked up a little something between them from how their shoulders kept bumping into each other. She greeted them with a smile. "Hey, cutie, do you want to buy a flower for the cutie next to you?"

"How many do you have?" asked Zhao Yunlan. "Enough for me to buy as many as I want?"

Giggling, she said, "As many as you need. I'm selling for a flower shop. If I don't have enough on me, I can go get more for you."

"In that case, I'll take five thousand for now—"

Shen Wei's hand clasped over his mouth, cutting Zhao Yunlan off. "I'm sorry," Shen Wei said, dragging him away. "He's just joking."

Zhao Yunlan struggled out of his grasp, managing to look back. "Hey, I'm in the middle of buying something...! Miss, wait!"

Yanking the car door open, Shen Wei stuffed him inside, leaving no room for argument.

"Don't you know anything about romance?" Zhao Yunlan exclaimed.

There was an ache in Shen Wei's stomach. "I think *you* know too much."

Zhao Yunlan was an expert when it came to squandering money. "When it comes to flowers, ordinary mortals buy nine hundred and ninety-nine of them to symbolize staying together forever. But us? We've been together practically the whole time since Pangu split the sky and earth. So really, it's frugal if we just take the saying 'five thousand years of Chinese history' and buy five thousand flowers for now. I want to cover the hood and trunk of my car with them to marry you into the family."

By this point, Shen Wei was almost relentlessly subjected to this kind of teasing. The fact that he hadn't yet exploded suggested that he was silently becoming more twisted inside.

He removed his glasses and wiped the condensation away, pretending for all he was worth that he didn't care about what Zhao Yunlan was saying. With tremendous effort, he kept up a banner of resistance and spoke with artificial calm. "Regardless, I should be the one marrying you into the family, shouldn't I? After all, just yesterday you said you'd take my last name."

That stopped Zhao Yunlan in his tracks, but he—a pervert to the bone—quickly recovered. He made a shameless pretense of stripping off his jacket. "Sure, I can work with your last name. Do you want to fuck right here in the car, husband? You don't need to do a thing—just lie back and enjoy. I'll take good care of you."

"Zhao Yunlan!" Shen Wei fumed.

"Present!"

Shen Wei practically slouched down below the steering wheel. "How... How can you be so *indecent*?"

Smiling radiantly, Zhao Yunlan put a hand on either side of Shen Wei's seat. "You call that indecent? You have no idea how indecent I can be."

Shen Wei's embarrassment finally turned into anger. His expression darkened as he grabbed Zhao Yunlan by the collar and pushed him away.

The look on his face made Zhao Yunlan shrink back. "I'm just joking."

"How many others have you joked with like this?" Shen Wei's voice seemed frozen, his words catching in his throat. His pale lips trembled. "Do you know how many times I've almost... I've..."

The rest of what he'd started to say was likely unfit for polite company. Shen Wei, ever proper, choked it back with difficulty. He looked as though he had swallowed a massive fishbone and it was firmly, painfully lodged in his throat all the way down to his chest.

Zhao Yunlan stayed utterly still. It suddenly began to sink in that while he had known Shen Wei for less than a year, Shen Wei had been watching over him for an unimaginable amount of time. *This* life would last only a few dozen years, but there had been the life before, and the one before that, and the one before that—hundreds of lives, one after another. From ancient times to the present, this man had silently watched over him as he was endlessly buffeted by the cycle of reincarnation. Again and again, Shen Wei had borne witness as Zhao Yunlan had been born, aged, suffered illness, and ultimately died. He had seen every love and every hatred Zhao Yunlan had ever known—none of it to do with him whatsoever, as if he was watching it all play out on screen.

Looking at it from that perspective, Zhao Yunlan was suddenly unable to breathe.

Shen Wei started the car without another word.

Zhao Yunlan suffered in silence for a while before he had to find something to do. So he opened the little box he had retrieved from his family home, which was full of the sort of junk kids liked to collect. He took out a small radio-like thing, then pulled a few screwdrivers of varying sizes from the toolbox he always kept in the car and started tinkering. His fingers were unusually nimble. It took only a moment's observation to determine that he had been one of those kids who secretly messed around with a lot of wires and caused fire hazards at school. Clearly, if it weren't for the fact that he was clumsy and liked buying new and shiny things, having a partner like him would probably mean never having a brand-new appliance in the house.

The fire that had erupted in Shen Wei's heart died as quickly as it had arisen, giving way to regret. Where others put up a facade around outsiders, then relaxed and revealed their true selves with an intimate partner, Shen Wei was the polar opposite. He was accustomed to firmly locking himself down in front of Zhao Yunlan, terrified of his true nature being even slightly perceived.

Even now that they had bared themselves wholly to each other, Shen Wei sometimes still had no idea how to speak to Zhao Yunlan. How could he, when he always felt so unbearably filthy and unworthy?

Zhao Yunlan silently kept himself busy with his tools, and finally Shen Wei couldn't keep from sneaking a glance at him while at a red light. Eventually Shen Wei asked, very lightly and cautiously, "What are you doing?"

Going along with Shen Wei's attempt to move past their argument, Zhao Yunlan responded as if he'd completely forgotten about it. With more excitement than he actually felt, he said, "This is a tracker I made when I was younger. It uses a wireless radio's signal receiver. Hold on, I just need to fix this loose connection and put in a battery..."

With a beep, the tiny screen—less than five centimeters across—came to life. A tiny, blurry dot appeared. The display was so dim that Zhao Yunlan had to cup it with both hands and lean down over it to see clearly. He adjusted the frequency slowly, then adjusted the placement of the dot and compared it to the hand-carved scale beside the screen. "Mm-hmm, the old man isn't far. He's obviously hiding from me. Let's turn back."

Shen Wei didn't know what was going on, but he still made a U-turn at the intersection, as instructed. Zhao Yunlan kept his head down over the little screen and gave directions.

Although Shen Wei probably couldn't have explained the concept of a "radio" to save his life, he still did his best to keep up the conversation. "What are we tracking?"

"My dad. I installed the signal in his phone. Even after all these years, he's still using the same one," Zhao Yunlan said. "I was still in middle school, so my technical skills weren't the best. The craftsmanship's kinda shoddy, so sometimes the voltage jumps, and it takes ages to adjust the frequency. It can also only pick up the signal at fairly close range."

Shen Wei reflexively put a hand to his own pocket, thinking of the phone he never touched. He sometimes even put the wrong side to his face when answering a call. If anyone ever tampered with it, he would have absolutely no way of knowing.

Zhao Yunlan noticed, of course. He crossed his legs and lit a cigarette leisurely. "Don't worry. As long as you don't go find yourself a pretty boy to cheat with, I won't put anything on you."

Shen Wei shot him a tremendously vexed look.

"Left turn here—yes, that teahouse ahead. I see my old man's car." Zhao Yunlan's voice was light and easy, but the darkness in his expression told a completely different story. "Someone has the gall to pretend they're my dad. I need to get to the bottom of it today."

Before the car even came to a complete stop, Zhao Yunlan had unbuckled his seat belt and jumped out, running up to the second floor with the ease of familiarity. Shen Wei locked the car and followed, half a beat behind. He didn't seem to be in much of a hurry. In fact, when he reached the bottom of the stairs, he took the time to nod at a waitress, maybe twenty years old, who was carrying some tea sets. For some reason, her hands shook at the sight of him. A teapot fell to the floor and shattered.

The man who wasn't Zhao Yunlan's father sat with his back to the doorway. At the sound of the teapot breaking, he turned around. Behind his glasses, his gaze was sharp, calm, and strangely far off. It seemed somehow ancient and completely at odds with Zhao Yunlan's dad's normal vigor.

Zhao Yunlan paused on the threshold, then strode into the room and shooed away the waiter, who was in the middle of a tea ceremony. He sat in front of his "father" and got straight to the point. "You're not my dad. Who are you?"

The man didn't respond. He kept his eyes on the stairway, face solemn, as Shen Wei approached. When their gazes met, the air nearly crackled.

Shen Wei nodded with utmost courtesy. "Uncle."

The lines on the man's face tightened. Age made his smile lines seem even deeper. Voice steady, he replied, "I wouldn't dare presume."

Shen Wei's answering smile was so light as to be nonexistent. Rather than taking a seat at the tea table, he sat in one of the spare chairs that were a few steps off to the side. He washed a new cup for himself, brewed the tea, and poured, going through the motions with the smoothness of passing clouds or flowing water. He kept his eyes lowered, sending a clear signal that he wasn't going to butt into the conversation.

"I wasn't in my right mind that day," Zhao Yunlan said. "Otherwise I would've taken one look at your eyes and realized you were a fake. My dad's driven by sheer ambition. His only goals are to be promoted and make more money. He puts on a show of being a refined gentleman, but it's completely obvious that he loves nothing more than authority and worldly prosperity. He's not remotely capable of the kind of serene expression I've seen you wear.

"I've called you 'Dad' a few times, but that won't be happening again. Now, where is he?"

The man glanced at Shen Wei, humming as he sipped his tea.

"Sir, I'm trying to be nice here before resorting to force, considering that you might be connected to Shennong—one of the Three Sovereigns." There was a limit to Zhao Yunlan's patience. Light gleamed in his hands as his speech quickened; the Soul-Guarding Whip flashed in and out of view between his palms. "Don't test me. If I need to protect my family, my politeness goes out the window."

"Your father is fine," the man said, finally breaking his silence. "I just come out and borrow his body occasionally, and I make sure he remembers the important things afterward. I've never caused him any problems. Don't worry."

"What are you, then? Don't tell me you're Shennong himself."

"No, no, I'm no one so mighty." His "dad" smiled. "I'm nothing but a stone mortar left behind by Shennong. During the Battle of the Creation of Gods, I hitched a ride. Through sheer fortune, I managed to successfully cultivate a consciousness. I've done many things to offend Kunlun-jun in the past, but I truly had no choice. My apologies."

"So what are you doing in my dad's body? Did you forge the memories I saw in the Great Divine Tree?"

The man's brows tightened. "Oh?" he asked slowly.

"I'm not some edgelord, and I'm not the Monkey King who turned the Heavenly Palace upside down." Zhao Yunlan drank the high-quality tea in one gulp, as if it were water. "Sure, I can be a little arrogant, but most of the time I'm pretty easygoing. If something drove me to rebel, it would have to be something as vast as the sky—something that filled me with the fury of the earth. But those things I saw in there? Those memories? I didn't relate to them at all. There's no way that was me. Besides, Kunlun was charged with all the mountains and rivers between the earth and the sky. He was the protector of every living spirit within those mountains. I've basically been an animal rights activist in all my lives. There's no way I'd ever blind a divine dragon for no reason."

His "dad" glanced at Shen Wei and nodded in agreement. "That makes sense."

Zhao Yunlan's gaze iced over. "I haven't yet asked why you used the tree to mislead me."

There was a long sigh. "Perhaps when Kunlun-jun can see through time, it will—"

"Cut the crap," Zhao Yunlan snapped, interrupting. "Speak plainly before I run out of patience. Don't piss me off. I don't care whose stupid bowl you are."

That unfamiliar gaze skimmed over him and landed on Shen Wei, who was idly flipping through a magazine. Then his father's body shuddered violently, eyes going blank. A moment later, different eyes looked back at him, and the man's aura had completely changed.

It was Zhao Yunlan's dad, having just undergone a complete

transformation, who was rubbing his own temples and looking back at him, brow furrowed. "What were you saying just now?" he asked, confused. "Sorry, I've been a little tired lately. I spaced out and missed what you said."

Zhao Yunlan immediately underwent his own transformation, turning from a threatening crime lord to a juvenile delinquent sitting behind bars. He wilted, then said humbly, "Dad...?"

His dad's forehead creased. "Mnh?"

That expression was far too familiar. To Zhao Yunlan, it plainly said, *If you have something to say, spit it out. If you have to fart, get it over with. You're my son, so I'll give you one minute to explain yourself. I'm tired and don't want to hear any bullshit.*

Under such dire circumstances, he could only drag Shen Wei into it as his shield. "It's just that we'd made plans, and you weren't home when we arrived. I noticed your car here, so I brought him over for you to see..."

"Something came up," his dad mumbled. "I'm here to see a friend." His gaze shifted uncomfortably to Shen Wei. There was a long silence while he assessed Shen Wei, but he ultimately found nothing to complain about. In the end, he had no choice but to offer a stiff, dry greeting. "I wasn't hospitable enough today. Please don't take it to heart, Shen-laoshi."

When dealing with anyone but Zhao Yunlan, Shen Wei was entirely comfortable, navigating social interactions with ease. He offered an appropriate response.

Zhao Yunlan took the chance to pull out a god-banishing talisman and secretly folded it into a triangle behind his back. He pushed it toward his dad. "Also, I was at the temple a few days ago, and I got you a blessed protective talisman. Don't open it. Just keep it with you."

With no sign of suspicion, his dad accepted the talisman...and absolutely nothing happened. Zhao Yunlan's brow furrowed. Had the stupid bowl run off, or was it so strong that even such a powerful talisman had no effect?

CHAPTER

·3·

I N THE END, Zhao Yunlan's one shot at evicting the stupid immortal bowl from his father's body hadn't worked, and he was left face-to-face with his actual dad and the full weight of paternal authority.

His father, unsurprisingly, was uncomfortable with Shen Wei's presence. And while the old man might've been able to endure some brief discomfort, it wasn't long before it had to become someone else's problem. Shen Wei, an outsider, was spared; Zhao Yunlan, the poor son, was not.

The scolding that resulted dealt a devastating blow to Zhao Yunlan's ego, especially with Shen Wei there to witness it. Back in the car, he muttered, "Other people get possessed by gorgeous fox demons, but *he* only managed to attract some stupid bowl. I'd bet the old man belonged to the Beggars' Gang[1] in a previous life, but he still has the gall to chew me out?"

"Don't worry," Shen Wei said comfortingly. "Shennong's entire lineage has always felt sympathy for humans. Doing anything to hurt mortals would be very out of character. Besides, didn't you put a tracker on him? I'll help you keep an eye on him too."

---

1   The Beggars' Gang (丐帮) is a large grassroots organization made up of beggars. It is common across many wuxia settings and noted for being a large, powerful group with an excellent information-gathering network. Its members traditionally carried bowls to collect coins when they begged on the streets.

Zhao Yunlan laughed, mildly embarrassed. "I can't ask you to do that. You haven't even married into the family yet, and your stupid father-in-law is already causing trouble for you."

It was as if he remembered only the carrot, not the stick. Apparently forgetting about Shen Wei's earlier anger, he went straight back to flirting. After all, it was Valentine's Day—the perfect time to go see a movie with Shen Wei. But instead, he dozed off right there in the car. The heat might've been turned up too high, making him unwittingly fall asleep...but even as he drifted into slumber, Zhao Yunlan was confused. He hadn't been *that* busy recently. Why was he so tired?

Maybe there was some truth to that common saying: one feels drowsy in the spring, feels tired in the fall, takes naps in the summer, and can never get enough sleep in the three months of winter.

But the sleep he fell into was restless, full of one disjointed dream after another. Someone seemed to be muttering in his ear, over and over: "You can't let go of eternity, you're unable to see through right and wrong, you can't differentiate between good and evil, and you don't understand life and death..."

After all those repetitions, Zhao Yunlan couldn't help wondering, *What exactly* are *life and death?*

The noise in his ears only intensified, growing from a mere clamor to a cacophony. Zhao Yunlan knew he was dreaming, but the knowledge didn't free him. He remained ensnared in the dream, as if he'd fallen into a bog that was swallowing him up. The more he struggled, the less he could breathe.

Then a bowl that smelled of something raw was pressed to his lips. Ignoring his struggles, the person holding it pried his mouth open and forced him to take the medicine. Zhao Yunlan resisted instinctively, trying to push the stuff back out of his mouth with his tongue. The person seemed to sigh. Then hands cradled his head, and soft lips pressed against his. A familiar scent momentarily quieted Zhao Yunlan's thoughts of protest, and the other person seized their chance to make him swallow the medicine.

Zhao Yunlan's eyes flew open as he started coughing and found himself already home in bed. Dazed, he watched as Shen Wei set down the bowl and brought him a cup of tea that was at the perfect temperature. Shen Wei ducked his head and touched their foreheads together. "Here," he said. "Drink this and rinse your mouth."

Zhao Yunlan accepted the tea. His heavy lashes were lowered, and a trace of cold sweat from his nightmare still beaded his forehead. In a single gulp, he drank the tea to the last drop before asking hoarsely, "Did I catch a cold? Why am I getting sick so easily lately?"

There was a curious pause before Shen Wei replied, "It's nothing. Your time within the Great Divine Tree took too much of your energy."

"Oh." After a long look, Zhao Yunlan continued, deliberately drawing out each word, "I thought maybe..." Shen Wei's spine stiffened, only for him to hear the dumbass conclude, with a bit of a lilting whine, "I was carrying your child."

Shen Wei didn't hurl the medicine bowl and teacup to the floor, but it was a close call. Crimson-faced, he stalked off, arms swinging in angry unison with his strides.

Zhao Yunlan had himself a good laugh, but when he took out his phone to check the time, he found an email from Wang Zheng— a new case for the Special Investigations Department.

There was a tourist town in a prefectural-level suburb about two hundred kilometers from Dragon City that advertised itself as the perfect spot for rest and recuperation. The town had a cluster of

vacation villas. Someone occupying one of the villas had report-
edly gone out to do their morning exercise and found a corpse in
the woods outside the neighborhood. The corpse's blue face was
contorted with alarm and fright, and its hands were locked around
the neck of a black dog. Both the human and dog had long since
gone cold.

Wang Zheng's email concluded with a professional reminder:
"It's almost the seventh day of the first lunar month."

Legend had it that the seventh day of the first lunar month was
the Day of the Humans—a day upon which, via occult methods
known among the common folk, one might borrow years off someone else's life. These so-called "borrowed" years would be added to
your own life span, thereby extending it.

One belief was that the blood of a black dog was required to
link the yin with the yang. The method involved writing down the
birth charts of both parties on a piece of paper with that blood,
clearly indicating the number of years to be borrowed. Then one
would weigh the paper down with incense on all four corners. If the
incense smoke rose straight up, undisturbed by any breeze, it meant
a passing reaper had accepted the bribe and would turn a blind eye
to this. After that, the paper was burned, and the ashes were fed to
the borrower to complete the ritual.

In older times, such a ritual might've been held when an elder fell
ill. A filial child of the family would voluntarily burn the incense to
show their willingness to lend their life. But these days, hardly anyone knew of these old customs and traditions, long since dismissed
as outdated relics of feudal times. In the modern era, anyone who
would attempt such methods was so terrified of dying that they'd
hire an amateur to perform a ritual to steal from someone else's life.
Any shaman conducting the ritual would be consuming their own

merits in exchange for money—and if the ritual was unsuccessful, the shaman might suffer backlash and bear the consequences on their greedy employer's behalf.

As a result, on the seventh day of the first lunar month each year, it wasn't unusual to find someone dead beside a black dog. It was certainly nothing new to the Special Investigations Department. Zhao Yunlan forwarded the email to everyone in the criminal investigation unit with instructions for someone to look into it when they were free.

Before he even finished typing out the message, Zhao Yunlan's eyelids felt practically glued together. He managed to cling to consciousness long enough to hit *"Send,"* then collapsed back onto the bed, falling asleep with the speed of losing consciousness. He was out cold before he could count even a single sheep.

The email arrived while Zhu Hong was meditating on the roof. She had her long snake tail out, trying to make sure the faint moonlight fell evenly on her entire body. That was the thing about northern cities: once winter arrived, most nights were foggy or snowy, and clear skies were few and far between. A night when the moon was bright and the stars were sparse was a rare commodity.

The email notification roused Zhu Hong from her meditative state. But when she opened her eyes, she found a man standing in front of her, facing away. She went utterly still. "Fourth Uncle?"

Fourth Uncle turned and looked down at her. "Back when you failed to pass your tribulation[2] and were injured by the divine lightning,

---

2   The heavenly tribulation (天劫) is a common aspect of many xianxia stories. Cultivation is a process that goes against the natural order of things, so sometimes the cultivators must pass a trial to ascend to a higher stage of cultivation or godhood. This trial usually requires the cultivator to withstand the strike of a divine lightning storm or another natural disaster, and failure can mean death or significant loss of cultivation and/or power.

I entrusted you to the Guardian's care. It was my hope that his fierce yang energy would provide you some protection. He's clearly taken good care of you."

As he spoke, he gestured with one hand. A small pavilion materialized on the rooftop, buffeted by the northwestern wind. There was a large tea tray of solid wood inside, which held a small stove that was heating a kettle. A little teapot already contained tea leaves. He waved at Zhu Hong. "Come."

Zhu Hong's tail shifted into legs. She quickly skimmed Zhao Yunlan's email, then said, a bit hesitantly, "Can we be brief, Fourth Uncle? The Guardian just notified me of a case..."

"Just a petty thief who tried and failed to borrow a few years of life," Fourth Uncle said without looking up. A stronger note of command entered his voice. "Sit down."

Fourth Uncle was the established leader of the Snake tribe. He had a kind face but a cold heart; it was difficult to ever know what he was thinking. Zhu Hong didn't dare disobey, and she instinctively sat a little straighter.

Picking up the kettle, Fourth Uncle poured the boiling water over the tea leaves. Shrouded within a cloud of steam, he spoke leisurely. "I primarily came to discuss something with you. Dragon City isn't an ideal place for focusing on your cultivation. I'm sure you don't need me to tell you that you haven't made much progress in the last twenty years."

With a careful glance toward him, Zhu Hong tentatively asked, "Fourth Uncle wants me to move to the countryside?"

Playing dumb, was she? Fourth Uncle decided to stop beating around the bush. With a light smile, he got to the point. "I meant that you should leave Dragon City."

Zhu Hong bit her lip. "But the Soul-Guarding Order—"

"Entrusting you to the Guardian's care placed you under his command, but you're no convict sentenced to serve your time within the Order. The Order has no power over you. You could leave right now and the Guardian wouldn't say a word."

Zhu Hong was beginning to panic. Her eyes darted around, as if a reason to stay would present itself.

"What, you don't want to leave him?" Fourth Uncle still seemed gentle and amiable. The smile tugging at the corners of his mouth was like that of a temple's bodhisattva, but his gaze was stern. "If you still consider me your elder, then heed my advice and come with me immediately. Besides, if you really had a place in his heart, I wouldn't be here acting like an annoying stick prying you two lovebirds apart. Do you really not know how the Guardian feels about you?"

There was nothing Zhu Hong could say.

Fourth Uncle rapped his fingers lightly on the edge of the table. "You've always been a smart kid. I don't need to spell out everything for you. You can figure it out."

Zhu Hong's poor phone hadn't been built to withstand a female yao's anxious grip. There was a *crunch* as the back plate popped off and a spiderweb crack spread across the screen.

Fourth Uncle pretended not to notice. He sat and sipped his tea, carefree and leisurely, not hurrying her.

After a while, Zhu Hong spoke again. "I'll bid him farewell in person after...after I wrap up this last case for him," she said quietly. "Is that okay?"

Well aware of the principle of not taking things too far, Fourth Uncle gave her an understanding nod. "A beginning and an ending, as it should be."

He then pulled out a small box and opened it to reveal a brilliant, iridescent pearl. "Here, take this water dragon pearl. If someone keeps it on their person, it turns misfortune to fortune and wards off water and fire. When you say your farewells to the Guardian, pass this along to him for me. He's taken care of you for many years, and our tribe is deeply grateful. This little thing really isn't enough to pay our respects."

Zhu Hong accepted the box, but before she could thank him, Fourth Uncle's silhouette flashed, and he disappeared.

The moon was just right, but with her heart now in such disarray, she was no longer in the mood for meditation. She looked down, plucked the SIM card out of the remains of her phone, and disappeared into the night.

Zhao Yunlan received Zhu Hong's text at midnight. *"Lin Jing and I are heading over,"* it said. *"Remember to pay us double for overtime."*

Shen Wei was a very light sleeper—so much so that Zhao Yunlan sometimes wasn't quite sure he could fall asleep at all. As a result, ever since Shen Wei had moved in, Zhao Yunlan had started setting his phone to vibrate at night and kept it under his pillow to avoid waking Shen Wei. But this time, he'd fallen asleep too quickly to tuck his phone away and was sleeping with it still in his hand.

When the phone vibrated in his palm, it silently jarred him awake. His first instinct wasn't to look at the text. Instead, he held his breath and turned over to see if it had woken Shen Wei up too.

The other side of the bed was empty and already cold to the touch. It was impossible to say how long Shen Wei had been gone.

Startled, Zhao Yunlan sat up and saw light coming from the kitchen. He groped around the floor for his slippers, but when he couldn't find whatever corner they'd been kicked into, he headed for the kitchen barefoot.

Shen Wei was facing away, doing something with his hands as Zhao Yunlan entered. A little clay pot bubbled on the stove. The faint smell of a medicinal decoction wafted from the pot, as if Shen Wei was preparing some grand dish that needed to be stewed overnight.

Zhao Yunlan rubbed his eyes and walked over, rolling up his sleeves. "What are you making? I'll help—" His voice startled Shen Wei, who dropped what he'd been holding.

What clattered to the floor was a knife, dripping enough blood that the clean white cabinets were spattered when it landed. Zhao Yunlan broke off mid-sentence, pupils constricting. In an instant, all trace of sleepiness was gone. Shen Wei had been...had been cutting into his *own chest*.

Shen Wei's face was white as a sheet. For a few seconds, one could have heard a pin drop in the silence.

Grabbing Shen Wei by the shoulder, Zhao Yunlan spun him around and tore his shirt open. The stab wound on his pale chest had already started to heal, but the surrounding skin and his pajamas bore telltale bloodstains.

Zhao Yunlan felt as if he were the one who'd been sliced open. Every tiny movement pained him. He carefully extended a finger, tracing it over Shen Wei's now-unmarred chest. After a small eternity, he hoarsely asked, "What's going on?"

When Shen Wei said nothing, Zhao Yunlan took hold of his collar. "I'm asking you what's going on! Talk!"

Shen Wei's lower back slammed heavily into the cutting board. Zhao Yunlan was genuinely furious. He suddenly understood how Shen Wei had felt back at the hospital, when he'd raised his hand and nearly struck Zhao Yunlan after he used the Ghost Army Summons. The anger lodged in his throat was suffocating.

"What have you been making me drink? Shen Wei! Fucking look at me when you speak!"

"Long ago...your left soul fire went missing, and your heart's blood became the Soul-Guarding Lamp's wick," Shen Wei responded, very low. "Your spirit was already weak. Your three souls were unstable. And for all that you forcibly elevated me to godhood, the fact remains that I was born from the Place of Great Disrespect. The gui are filthy and inauspicious. If you spend enough time in my presence, I'll start wearing you down. As I do, you'll become deficient in both qi and blood. Ultimately, I'll burn you out until there's nothing left."

Shen Wei dropped his gaze, hiding his ink-black eyes under lashes like crow feathers. Barely audible now, he said, "All those thousands of years ago, Shennong said that, as a King of the Gui, my life was fated to both begin and end badly. If you insist on protecting me and keeping me at your side, I'll inevitably kill you."

"So the 'medicine' I've been drinking has your blood in it... The purest blood from the tip of your heart." Zhao Yunlan's lips trembled. "That's your way of replenishing my 'lamp oil'?"

Shen Wei looked at him with a faint, soft smile. "Every part of me is dark, down to my very soul. Only the very tip of my heart is clean, and that's where I've kept you—where the blood runs red. I'll gladly use it to protect you."

It was Zhao Yunlan's turn to stare at the floor. After a while, he lifted his head and covered his eyes with a hand.

If Shen Wei didn't like him and kept him at a distance, Zhao Yunlan could either choose to keep pestering him or choose to back away gracefully. To advance or retreat were both reasonable options.

If Shen Wei lied to him, hurt him, or wronged him, Zhao Yunlan had the choice to either forgive him or walk out of his life forever. Once again, it was reasonable to either advance or retreat.

But Shen Wei had woven him into his web, and Zhao Yunlan was unable to scold him, curse at him, or hate him...and equally unable to accept his actions.

Zhao Yunlan's silence stretched on for a long time. Finally, he grabbed a thick jacket off the large coatrack in the foyer, bundled it around himself, and walked out the door without a backward glance.

It turned out there was a kind of love that was like a knife to the heart.[3]

---

3   From Life and Death Are Wearing Me Out, *a novel by Mo Yan.*

HAVING COORDINATED THEIR PLANS, Zhu Hong and Lin Jing arrived at 4 Bright Avenue to ask Wang Zheng for an official SID car before the sun rose. They walked in and were greeted by the unexpected sight of their boss, who hadn't been answering his texts, curled up asleep on the sofa. He was wearing pajamas, and an unfamiliar heavy wool coat was draped over him.

Daqing was crouched in front of the sofa, washing his paws with great satisfaction. A plateful of bones from tiny dried fish sat before him.

Zhu Hong turned up the thermostat. "Why is he sleeping here?" she asked quietly.

Lin Jing had swelled up over the Lunar New Year, as though inflated like a balloon. He rubbed his chin, which now looked mochi-soft, and said, "Something must be up if he's not going home during the holidays. My guess is he's either being forced into an unwanted marriage, or he's been forced into a breakup."

Zhao Yunlan looked up at that. He had a tremendous case of bedhead, there were heavy bags under his eyes, and he was clearly enraged at being woken up. "Fuck off!" he snarled, his sinister gaze cutting right through Lin Jing.

Lin Jing only sighed. "Who on earth could handle a man like our boss? Director Zhao, if your hardworking wife made you breakfast and woke you to eat it, would you talk to her that way too?"

The fake monk just *had* to mention the one subject Zhao Yunlan least wanted to discuss. Zhao Yunlan reached up and grabbed a tiny bonsai from the cabinet next to him, then hurled it at Lin Jing. There was a loud smash as it hit the wall.

Daqing and Zhu Hong exchanged glances at this outburst. Even Lin Jing was momentarily frozen in place. But it was his careless talk that had caused the trouble, so he had no choice but to find a broom and sweep up the mess. "Amitabha," he murmured. "May the pieces bring peace."

Daqing sprang up onto the back of the sofa. "Hey, are you okay?"

Zhao Yunlan flung himself back down and buried half of his face in the coat, which actually belonged to Shen Wei—he'd left in such a rush that he'd been halfway to the office before he realized he'd grabbed the wrong one. Traces of the owner's lovely, clean scent still lingered on the collar, but...

"I'm fine," Zhao Yunlan muttered. "Lin Jing, don't worry about that. I'll sweep it up later. I didn't mean to take everything out on you. Just let me lie here for a bit, and you guys can carry on with whatever you're supposed to be doing."

Daqing's whiskers quivered. Zhao Yunlan reached a hand out from the coat and tousled the fur on Daqing's head, then gave the fat cat's rump a somewhat perfunctory pat. "When you have time, go find out exactly where that *Record of Ancient Secrets* book came from."

"Ordering your cat grandpa around?" Daqing groused. "Where's my red envelope? Where's my lucky money?"

Eyes closed, Zhao Yunlan dug through Shen Wei's coat pocket.

He took out a handful of small bills, grabbed hold of the cat's neck to tuck the money under his collar, and waved him off as if sending a beggar on his way. "So shameless. Even if you printed off your own mountain of lucky money,[4] there'd never be enough to do any good for someone your age. Hurry up and leave."

Daqing snarled and made to sharpen his claws on the coat, but Zhao Yunlan managed to reach out and block him just in time. Daqing retracted his claws the moment they touched warm human skin, but they still left white marks on Zhao Yunlan's arm.

What kind of stupid coat couldn't even be used for sharpening his claws? After a dumbfounded moment, Daqing ran off in a huff. He felt as though Zhao Yunlan, the huge asshole, was tossing money at him the way one drops it into the fare box on a bus.

There were countless rules and traditions surrounding the Lunar New Year, and since most of the SID staff weren't human, they all had their own ways of spending the holiday. As a result, their break usually lasted until at least the fifteenth day of the Lunar New Year, which meant that 4 Bright Avenue was empty and quiet for a change. Thanks to Shen Wei, Zhao Yunlan's chest ached with the weight of his frustrations, so he opted to just sink back into his dreams and sleep some more.

It was late morning when he woke in the silent office. Dizzy and disoriented, he got up—and froze when he looked down. In his hurry to get out of the apartment, he hadn't even stopped to put on socks, only noticing once he was outside that he was only wearing leather shoes and it was a little cold.

But here were the short boots he normally wore, set tidily by the sofa with a pair of thick knit socks stuffed into them. A full set of

---

4   Lucky money (压岁钱), literally "keep the age (sui岁) down money," sounds like "keep the evil (sui祟) away money."

ironed clothes lay on the arm of the sofa, with underwear tucked into the innermost layer. His phone, wallet, and keys were on top of the clothing.

The only thing missing was a coat of his own. The obvious conclusion was that Shen Wei wanted Zhao Yunlan to keep *his*.

A voice spoke up. "Shen-laoshi brought all that over for you. I wanted to wake you, but he didn't let me."

Zhao Yunlan pinched the bridge of his nose. Zhu Hong was seated at her desk, idly surfing the web to kill time. "Where is he?" he asked.

"He left."

Zhao Yunlan's voice was hoarse when he spoke again. "Where did he go? What else did he say?"

"He said, 'It's cold out, so you should go straight home after work. I'll be at my own place, so don't worry about running into me.'" Zhu Hong parroted the message precisely. "Then he left. I guess he went home. Why did you guys decide to get in a fight during the New Year?"

Zhao Yunlan didn't reply. He knew exactly what Shen Wei meant by his "own place," and it wasn't Shen Wei's apartment, like Zhu Hong assumed. But even the thought of it made him feel like his heart was being run through with knives.

It wasn't something he could discuss with anyone else, though. A stiff nod was the only answer he could give. He pulled on his socks and grabbed the clothing, then went to the bathroom to get changed.

He washed up hurriedly, then rested his palms on the edges of the sink. After staring down at the snow-white ceramic for a while, he plunged his face into the frigid water. For a time, he didn't dare think of Shen Wei. He'd never cared for anyone like this before, with such intensity that just thinking of the other person hurt as if his heart had been gouged out.

Eventually, he'd been gone so long that Zhu Hong started to get worried. She came and knocked on the door. "Director Zhao? Are you all right?"

Zhao Yunlan made some sound of acknowledgment. Looking at his reflection, he wiped the water off his face and shaved off the stubble. He carefully cleaned himself up so that he looked human again, then straightened up and walked out. Even if his heart ached until it burned, what would that solve? Nothing.

He ordered breakfast at the cafeteria and silently sat down to eat. It wasn't until his stomach was full that some warmth came back to his frozen, numb limbs. Finally, he gave Zhu Hong a confused look. "Why did you come to the office?"

"The original plan was to take the train and go check out the black dog and the corpse with Lin Jing today."

"So why didn't you go?"

"I was a little worried about you, so I told him to go on his own."

Zhao Yunlan wiped his mouth, stood, and cleared away his tray. "What's there to worry about?" he asked calmly. "If you've got nothing to do, you can go home."

Zhu Hong didn't say anything or show any sign of leaving. When Zhao Yunlan strolled back to his office and turned on his computer as he would on any other day, Zhu Hong followed him in.

"Why are you still following me?"

"What exactly is wrong?" she countered.

Zhao Yunlan took a pack of cigarettes and a lighter from his drawer. "Nothing's wrong," he said lightly.

Zhu Hong wasn't having any of it. "Oh? Then why did you spend the night sleeping here instead of at home?"

"Oh, that." Zhao Yunlan sucked in a mouthful of white smoke, not letting even a wisp escape. "We just had a small argument last night."

"Bullshit," Zhu Hong retorted, arching a brow. "Don't act like we're all blind. You treat that Shen guy like a treasure. If you two had some small fight over nothing, you would've run back to him ages ago. You'd be kneeling on a motherboard and writing a ten-thousand-word apology letter, not here feeding me your crap."

Zhao Yunlan had nothing to say to that.

"Did he mistreat you?" As Zhu Hong spoke, her eyes shone with terrifying brightness, as if a nod from Zhao Yunlan would make her hunt Shen Wei down and swallow him whole.

Zhao Yunlan flicked ashes from his cigarette. "Lately you've been gossiping more and more. Early menopause or something?"

Sad and angry, Zhu Hong said, "What does it matter? Either way, the person I like doesn't like me back."

Zhao Yunlan knew exactly what she was getting at, but what could he say? He decided to take the coward's way out: he found a briefcase, stuffed his wallet and phone inside, and went to leave without even turning off his computer.

Zhu Hong, dead set on not letting him go, was right on his heels. "Where are you going?"

"I've got an appointment with a higher-up in the ministry." He glanced over at Zhu Hong. "Don't follow me."

Ignoring him, she followed him out the front door, and when he unlocked his car, she immediately claimed the passenger seat and fastened her seat belt. "I'm going too," she said, resolute.

Utterly exhausted, Zhao Yunlan sighed. "Can you please show me some mercy, ma'am?"

Zhu Hong looked away and ignored him.

They faced off for what seemed like an eternity before Zhao Yunlan crumbled. Reining in his temper as best he could, he put out his cigarette and got in.

He was silent the entire ride. Zhu Hong snuck a few glances at him but saw only his handsome, cold profile. Gradually, she started to fidget and resorted to small talk. "Which higher-up are you meeting?"

"Xiao-Guo's second uncle," Zhao Yunlan said. "Speaking of which, it's fine if I bring you along. Afterward, I want you to find out who meddled and got Guo Changcheng transferred to our department."

"'Meddled'?" she asked, confused. "Someone meddled with xiao-Guo? Why? How could he benefit anyone?"

Zhao Yunlan didn't reply. The truth was, he had his suspicions: that the bowl possessing his dad had used his dad to do it.

As for *why*, though? It was a total mystery. Guo Changcheng was a true mortal. Looking back through his family tree, there hadn't been a single cultivator in eight generations. Sure, he had an abnormally high number of merits, but what else was special about him?

If it was at all possible, Zhao Yunlan wanted to regain Kunlun-jun's powers and true memories. Failing that, he at least wanted to know what was up with all these lies among truths, shrouded in layers of mystery, and learn what had motivated it all. He couldn't act rashly without seeing the full picture.

Shen Wei... The name alone overwhelmed Zhao Yunlan with worry. It was as though a flame was burning in his heart, steadily eating away at his energy, but he had to hold it in—and not only that, he had to seem outwardly peaceful while he was at it, as if he had everything under control.

He'd noticed at times that if he was just sitting there and no one else was around, his brow would furrow subconsciously. The same scene kept unfolding in his mind, no matter where he was or what he was doing: in some cold, dreary place, without a single beam of light or sign of life, Shen Wei was half swallowed by an endless darkness. Helpless to do anything but look up, Shen Wei desperately strained to glimpse the emerald seas and azure skies, but they were beyond him. His vision couldn't pierce the unending, absolute blackness. Sooner or later, inevitably succumbing to disappointment and despair, Shen Wei was slowly sucked away into the darkness...

Zhao Yunlan jolted awake as someone abruptly nudged him. He found his heart racing and his forehead beaded with sweat.

Zhu Hong was the one who had nudged him. Expressionless and a little unhappily, she said, "We're here."

He sat stock-still for a moment before realizing that he had been dreaming. He'd had a few drinks with Guo Changcheng's second uncle, and Zhu Hong had driven them back. He didn't know when he'd nodded off.

Zhu Hong sat motionless. "What were you dreaming about? What made you cry out for Shen Wei so heart-wrenchingly?"

Having already lost control, Zhao Yunlan didn't want to betray anything else. He pretended not to hear.

"Yunlan," she said suddenly, and he waited, watching as she pulled a little box from her pocket. She opened it and took out the water dragon pearl, which she had strung on a red string and finished with a lucky knot. "My fourth uncle asked me to bring you this. He said it's to thank you for all the years you've assisted the Snake tribe. And I... Soon, I'll probably have to leave with him."

"Leave?" Zhao Yunlan was taken aback. "Leave to go where?"

"Oh, probably back to the tribe." Zhu Hong forced a smile. When Zhao Yunlan didn't reach out for the pearl, she hung it around his wrist. "It's really from my fourth uncle, not me. Water dragon pearls are sacred within my tribe. Where would I get the authority to give it away? It offers protection from water and fire, and it will keep you safe." She swallowed. "If... If there's anything else you need me to do, now's the time. There's not much I can do for you anymore."

Zhao Yunlan was silent for a while. Finally, he nodded. "It's for the best. Dragon City is too noisy. It's not a suitable place for you yao to cultivate. Going back to your tribe isn't a bad idea. Once you're there, stay away from crowds and people. You'll get into less trouble that way. Your fourth uncle is powerful, so you should learn from him. You have such a bright future ahead of you. Who knows, maybe you'll be the Snake tribe's next chief."

He spoke as if he was getting his affairs in order before death, so calmly that it made her heart ache. Zhu Hong found her real feelings tumbling out of her mouth. "Director Zhao, just give me the word. One word and I'll sever all ties with my tribe and follow you to the end, through hell or high water."

It was as if she'd handed her whole life over on a silver platter, leaving her scared of Zhao Yunlan's response, but also anticipating it. However, a declaration of love was never guaranteed reciprocation. In the end, Zhao Yunlan still wouldn't meet her eyes.

"What do you mean?" he asked. "You and I have known each other for years, and we don't have any grudges against each other. Why can't I wish you well? As long as you're doing well, that's what matters to me."

The light in Zhu Hong's eyes flickered out.

Zhao Yunlan had already gotten out of the car.

WHEN DAQING SAW FIRST Zhao Yunlan and then Zhu Hong enter the office, he jumped onto a table, carrying *Record of Ancient Secrets* in his mouth. He ignored the weird vibe between the two of them and set the book down. "This book absolutely stinks of death. I did some research. As I expected, it came from Antiques Street."

Zhao Yunlan picked the book up and brushed his hand over the cover, wiping the cat's saliva away. "Antiques Street, huh?"

Antiques Street was true to its name. It was full of shops dedicated to all manner of antique objects and artifacts—even if most of them were fakes. Every once in a while, a burial object that had been illegally unearthed from a grave site would pop up. But this copy of *Record of Ancient Secrets* obviously came out of a modern printer—not exactly "relic" material. So the "stink of death" Daqing had mentioned had to be due to something else.

One little shop down at the end of Antiques Street not only sold a variety of superstitious objects but also guarded the pagoda tree at its entrance. This tree was a transportation hub linking the realms together; for example, anyone going from the Mortal Realm to the Yao Market, or from the Mortal Realm to the Netherworld, had to pass through there.

The pagoda tree's leaves reached up into the Mortal Realm, while its roots sank down into the Huangquan. It was an awe-inspiring plant, neither mortal nor ghost.

"So you're saying this book came from the Netherworld?" Zhao Yunlan asked. At the black cat's nod, he continued, "Who bought it and brought it here?"

The cat licked his paws. "No idea. I can't find a record of the purchase. Perhaps the previous Guar—"

"Impossible." Zhao Yunlan flipped through the book, which had neither an ISBN nor any publication details. "Looking at the printing and typeset quality as well as the age of the paper, it was printed in the nineties at the earliest. There's no way it's older than I am now."

"In that case, it must be a black-covered book," said Daqing.

A "black-covered book" was one that had been purchased by a book buyer who could work only at night, obtained through certain means from somewhere other than the Mortal Realm.

Daqing flipped the book open with a paw. As soon as he pressed his paws down on the paper, mysterious dark mist suddenly swirled through the pages. "Whoever smuggled it in here was very careful. Nobody noticed it on our end."

Books at the Special Investigation Department were meticulously organized. The spine of each book had been marked with color-coded labels and special barcodes, which was why Sangzan was able to shelve them correctly despite his illiteracy. Given that, how had this book about ancient gods wound up among the books about Nüwa's creation of humans and how she had repaired the sky? Was it pure coincidence, or had someone predicted that Zhao Yunlan would be looking up that information?

As night fell, Zhao Yunlan finally gave in and called Shen Wei, but what answered was a cold, robotic female voice: "The number you have dialed is not in service..."

One day apart is akin to the passing of three autumns. He stared blankly at his phone screen for a while, savoring the bitter taste of that idiom, until Daqing came over and nudged his elbow impatiently with an extended paw. "Now's not the time to dwell on your love life. If you want to go to Antiques Street, let's go."

Zhao Yunlan picked up the cat and walked out. As he set foot outside, he saw Zhu Hong already waiting silently by the car. He opened his mouth to speak, but Zhu Hong beat him to it. "Do you think I'm degrading myself, following you around after what happened earlier?"

After a beat, Zhao Yunlan said, "I was just going to remind you to wear your down jacket."

The atmosphere was intensely awkward as the two humans and the cat drove to Antiques Street in the middle of the night. They followed the familiar path to the pagoda tree, where they found two pale white paper lanterns hanging at the entrance of the little store. Each lantern held a pea-sized light, and the lanterns themselves were so weather-worn that it was nearly impossible to make out what was written on them. With some effort, the words "Soul-Guarding" were just barely discernible.

Zhao Yunlan suddenly tapped the black cat perched on his shoulder. Keeping his voice low, he asked, "What exactly does the 'Soul-Guarding' in 'Soul-Guarding Order' mean…?"

"Guard the souls of the living, bring peace to the hearts of the dead, atone for crimes done in life, and complete the unfinished cycle." Daqing's glance was heavy with judgment. "It's written right on the back of the Soul-Guarding Order, isn't it? Are you blind?"

For once, Zhao Yunlan didn't offer a snappy comeback. Instead, he mumbled, "But why is the order Kunlun-jun left behind called 'Soul-Guarding'?"

Why not "Mountain-Guarding," "Sea-Guarding," or "Monsters-and Demons-Guarding"?

And what exactly was the "life and death" Shennong kept mentioning in his dreams?

Zhao Yunlan couldn't figure it out. His heart was heavy as he stepped into the pagoda tree. Following the trunk all the way down would take one to the banks of the Huangquan.

The Huangquan Road ran down the center of the Huangquan River. Paved with long stone slabs, the narrow path sloped upward, like the legendary Path to Heaven. The air was so cold there that it seemed the river itself should be crusted with ice. Anyone setting foot on it hardly dared to breathe for fear of startling the resentful souls sharing the road. Those dull-eyed souls shuffled along, shepherded by reapers. All around them, the waters of the Huangquan swirled and gurgled; occasional bubbles broke the surface, as though something could burst up from the depths at any moment.

Little oil lamps stood on either side of the road, similar to streetlights. There was one of these "soul-guarding lamps" every three meters or so, each giving off a tiny glow that cast long shadows. Spider lilies bloomed in vivid red, coloring the path in clusters.

Some time back, Zhao Yunlan had read a travel diary that mentioned these "soul-guarding lamps" that served to light the way for the dead. The length of the Huangquan Road depended on how many indelible memories were carved into an individual's heart. The glow of those lamps cleansed a soul of everything that connected them to the Mortal Realm. By the time a soul reached the Naihe Bridge and had had everything from this life and the ones before washed away with a bowl of Mengpo Soup made from the waters of the Wangchuan River, they were ready for the next life.

Zhao Yunlan couldn't help bending down to study a soul-guarding lamp. Four words were engraved neatly at its base: Life Begins at Death.

Suddenly, something seemed to flash before his eyes. There was an abrupt and excruciating pain in his heart, as though someone had reached in and torn a piece out.

Zhu Hong steadied him from behind when he stumbled. Barely audible, she murmured, "What's wrong?"

Zhao Yunlan's face was deathly pale. He swallowed, choking down the blood welling up in his throat. Pressing a hand to the left side of his chest, he shook his head. "Nothing. Let's keep moving."

When they reached Ghost City, Zhao Yunlan took out a few Leaves of Illusion. The three of them each tucked one into their mouth—a leaf in the mouth would keep them from smelling like living beings and thus keep the city's little ghouls from realizing that they were alive. In addition to ghostly immortals and souls waiting for reincarnation, some of Ghost City's residents were unable to move on and be reincarnated, either because they were still clinging to something or because they had sinned and were there serving their time. Once in Ghost City, they would remain for hundreds or thousands of years. Their obsession with life was beyond the comprehension of a living person.

Once, when Zhao Yunlan had been inexperienced and arrogant, he'd come to the city in pursuit of a living soul who had entered it accidentally. Ultimately, he'd been unable to retrieve it. Instead, he'd witnessed how the little ghosts in the city had swarmed and mobbed the soul, sucking it dry. The reapers had needed to call in reinforcements to quell the violent unrest.

Zhao Yunlan had still been young at the time. After returning to the Mortal Realm, he'd had nightmares for a whole month and came close to being permanently traumatized.

The fact that the living could write "What joy is there in life, and what fear in death"[5] was probably because the writer no longer remembered how it felt to die. The dead yearned for life as fervently as a drowning person yearned for air; it was instinctual and impossible to contain.

Zhao Yunlan's thoughts ran away from him again, and what surfaced was: if this was what became of humans, then what about the gui, who were born deep below the surface? What about Shen Wei...? Shen Wei's harsh treatment of himself bordered on abuse. He seemed absolutely unwilling to take his own nature into account. Thousands of years, tens of thousands of years enduring such endless yearning... How could he have done that to himself?

Zhu Hong, on the other hand, had never been to Ghost City before. When she glanced uneasily at Zhao Yunlan, he came back to himself. "No matter what happens, don't spit out the Leaf of Illusion," he cautioned quietly. "Enough ants can kill an elephant. These little ghouls are way harder to get rid of than you'd think."

She nodded hurriedly.

Still worried, Zhao Yunlan shot her a look. "By nature, snakes lack yang energy. This is no place for you. Maybe you should wait for me outside."

"No. Don't be racist." Zhu Hong shook her head firmly. To be honest, she didn't know what good her presence could do, but she couldn't help feeling a bit more at ease if she kept him in sight, wherever he went.

Daqing jumped down from Zhao Yunlan's shoulder and led the way. Black cats and black dogs were all beings of both tremendous yin and tremendous violence. Any little ghouls who laid eyes on one would instinctively give them a wide berth, so having a black cat

5   A line adapted from the writing of 4th century BCE philosopher Zhuangzi (庄子).

along was like having a police car to clear the way. It made sneaking into Ghost City easy as pie.

As it was neither the first nor the fifteenth of the lunar month, Ghost City seemed somewhat desolate. At the intersection, a life-dealing crone squatted by the entrance with a basket by her feet. She hunkered down at the roadside, her beady, murky yellow eyes following the occasional passing ghost, like an old person trying to eke out a living selling their wares in the Mortal Realm. She looked pitiful enough that Zhu Hong couldn't help but give her a second glance. The crone noticed and immediately broke out into a wide smile full of yellow teeth. "Come buy some life," she called. "Come buy some life."

The crone's voice was hoarse and shrill, like tiny metal pieces scraping against bone. Zhu Hong broke out all over in goosebumps.

Zhao Yunlan dragged her away at once. "Don't look," he muttered. "That crone has a bad reputation. She only sells duds."

In spite of herself, Zhu Hong asked, "What does that mean?"

"If you eat her longevity cake, it's not your natural life span that gets extended. Lying in bed in a vegetative state is also a kind of longevity. Got it?" Zhao Yunlan wrapped his coat tighter around himself and popped the collar. He lowered his voice even further. "Keep your eyes on the road. Don't look around too much. In a no-man's land like this, if your eyes linger, they'll mark you as a target. Don't make trouble."

Zhu Hong didn't dare look around after that. She just walked forward, determined to stay focused.

After passing through the long streets of the market, they came to an end and saw a small thatched cottage. A white paper sign on the door read "Welcome," written in black ink.

The hut was unmistakably in disrepair, but hanging by the door were two white lanterns that bore the words "Soul-Guarding," just like the little shop on Antiques Street.

"The book most likely came from this store," the black cat said, looking back at them. "This family reincarnates once every sixty years, the yin alternating with the yang. The person in the yang realm guards the entrance to the Huangquan by the pagoda tree while the person in the yin realm minds the general store in Ghost City."

Zhao Yunlan entered first. The decrepit door creaked and opened easily when he pushed on it. He took a small mirror from his wallet and stuck it on the door before going inside.

A little girl's voice rang out from within. "'With a bright mirror to light the way, little ghouls don't enter,'" she recited. "This honored guest knows the rules well. Where do you come from?"

Zhao Yunlan raised his chin, signaling to Zhu Hong to close the door. Someone lifted the curtain inside, and a little girl sporting pigtails walked out. She didn't stand even waist-high on him, and her face was frighteningly pale. Her cheeks were bloodred with cinnabar, her black-bean eyes seemed somehow morbid, and her lips were a deep crimson. She wore an old-fashioned cotton coat.

The result went far beyond not being cute; on the contrary, the effect of a child's voice coming from that face was flat-out terrifying.

Zhao Yunlan didn't beat around the bush. He took out *Record of Ancient Secrets*, pressed a Soul-Guarding Order down on it, and squatted so that his eyes were at the same level as the girl's. "I have something to ask you, if you could please do me a favor."

The little girl's gaze fell on the Soul-Guarding Order. Clearly and with no trace of inflection in her voice, she said, "So it's the Guardian blessing this place with his presence. How's my older brother?"

"You're too kind. Your brother's doing well. Just a couple of days ago, I had someone send him a few pounds of cured meat for the New Year," Zhao Yunlan said politely. "I came today to ask if this book was purchased from your fine establishment."

The girl took the book. Even from a palm's length away, the chill emanating from her body was palpable. Wherever she touched the book, a trace of frost lingered. She flipped through a few pages and nodded. "Yes, this came from my store."

She turned to the last page, revealing a gray seal in the most inconspicuous corner. If one looked closely, the words "General Goods" were just barely discernible. The little girl pointed at it and said, "This is our store's private seal."

Immediately, Zhao Yunlan asked, "Could you look up who bought this book and brought it into the Mortal Realm?"

As he spoke, he took a stack of spirit money from his bag and ignited it with his lighter. Her eyes shone as she inhaled the scent, and she broke out into a stiff smile. "The Guardian is kind. Please come in and have a cup of tea while you wait."

The two people and the cat followed her into the dilapidated general store, where she poured them all tea. Zhao Yunlan lifted the cup and smelled it, going through all the motions of tasting it even if he couldn't actually drink. Common sense dictated that living souls weren't to eat or drink anything that came from below the Huangquan.

The little girl brought out an ancient thread-bound book from behind the table and skimmed through it, one page at a time. "Ah, here we are."

She looked up at Zhao Yunlan with a smile. "I forgot to ask, what noble name should I use to refer to the current Guardian?"

"My surname is Zhao." Zhao Yunlan's brow furrowed as a bad feeling came over him. "Just Zhao Yunlan is fine."

"This is right, then." The little girl pushed the giant account book toward him.

The buyer's name was clearly recorded: Renwu year, fifteenth day of the seventh month, Guardian, Zhao Yunlan.

·6·

FOR A MOMENT, Zhao Yunlan just stood there, rooted to the spot. He didn't immediately dismiss what he was seeing. Finally, he said, "Remind me which year Renwu was?"

"The last Renwu year was 2002," the black cat replied. "The one before that was sixty years earlier—well before you were born. What were you doing in 2002?"

"I was struggling to stay on top of my secret duties as Guardian and going to class at the same time." Zhao Yunlan thought for a moment. "Between school and that side job, I was drowning. I was about to give up on university and just go work as some phony medium, but my dad stopped me. That was the year that he found the long-abandoned Special Investigations Department from some connections and got me installed there.

"Actually, hang on—was it really my dad who did that? Or was it..."

"Huh?" Daqing, still in the dark about what Zhao Yunlan had learned, was confused.

"I'll fill you in after we get back," Zhao Yunlan said. He turned to the little girl running the general store. "How do you verify a buyer's identity? You don't just let them write down whatever they want and take their word for it, right?"

An enigmatic smile crossed the child's stiff face. A seven- or eight-year-old girl with the expression of a powerful old woman from a wuxia novel might've been funny in any other context, but here in Ghost City of the Netherworld, the effect was a bit creepy. "I keep clear, accurate accounts here, of course," she said. "Every buyer's full name and identity are checked against *The Book of Life and Death*. Does the Guardian have any doubts?"

Zhao Yunlan gave it some thought but realized he wasn't going to learn anything else from her. He put the book away. "Do you remember what the 'me' who came and bought that book eleven years ago looked like?"

A corner of her deep-red lips curved up. In a meaningful tone, she said, "A moment ago I couldn't remember, but now that the Guardian mentions it, it's coming back to me. Looking at you again, I've only just realized that you're a past visitor who's returned. If the Guardian hadn't mentioned it, I wouldn't have realized that it's been eleven years since then."

Zhao Yunlan went very still as he processed what she was hinting at: that the Zhao Yunlan who'd originally bought the book had looked much the same as he looked now.

Deep in thought, he lowered his head for some time before saying, "Many thanks." He turned and walked out, with Zhu Hong close behind him.

The girl called out lightly from behind the counter, stopping him in his tracks. Her crisp childish voice dropped so low that it sounded unutterably ominous. "I'll be a busybody and offer a word of caution. It's possible that the Guardian could suffer a bloody disaster in the next few days. You'd do well to take extra care."

Zhao Yunlan showed very little reaction. Zhu Hong, on the other hand, quickly asked, "A bloody disaster? What do you mean by that?"

The little girl only stared at them with her black, almost plastic-looking eyes. Zhu Hong moved as if to rush forward and ask more questions, but Zhao Yunlan stopped her. He gave the girl a nod and pulled Zhu Hong away.

"Wait!" Zhu Hong exclaimed. "She just said..."

"The only reason she said anything at all is that I sent her brother some cured meat during Lunar New Year. How big a favor do you think a few pounds of meat can buy?" Zhao Yunlan walked swiftly out of the store, glancing at Zhu Hong. "Even if she dared to say more, I wouldn't dare hear it. Courtesy and manners don't apply in Ghost City. Sometimes there isn't even logic. You can't judge the dead the same way you judge the living. Why do you think the Netherworld has them cordoned off here in this no-man's land? Remember, it's not good to be indebted to the dead."

"Why are you suddenly telling me all this?" Zhu Hong asked.

"I'm trying to teach you. I've never had many girls working for me; you're few and far between. I never wanted to force any of you to do legwork or interact with weirdos. But now I don't think that was the right move," Zhao Yunlan said quietly. "I never thought about you leaving one day. If I'd realized, I would've given you more chances to learn and train. Remember, without practical experience, it wouldn't matter if you cultivated until you're equal to the Goddess Nüwa herself. You'd still be just some technical analyst working for me, and you'd never earn the respect of your milky-eyed elders who refuse to die."

Zhu Hong's nose and eyes reddened simultaneously.

"Shhh, keep the leaf in your mouth. Save your tears. When our whole department gets together for your farewell party, you can cry all you want. Ghost City is no place for it."

Pushing Zhu Hong behind him, Zhao Yunlan abruptly stopped talking. At some point, what seemed to be some sort of...person...had appeared by the general store's door, squatting on the long stone slabs.

He or she or it was bald, with arms so long they went past its knees. Squatting on the ground, it looked like a hairless baboon. Its neck was nearly thirty centimeters long—long enough that if it lowered its head, its chin could touch its belly. It looked up at Zhao Yunlan, face splitting literally from ear to ear in a sudden smile. It stood and extended its neck, its head spinning 180 degrees. What had been the back of its head was now the front, revealing the classic ferocious features one expected from a horror story cryptid. It flung itself toward them.

Zhao Yunlan had already drawn his gun, finger on the trigger. Just as he was about to shoot, the double-faced ghost came to a sudden stop in midair and fell to the ground. The double-sided head spun around again, facing them with the creepy smile. The smile exposed two yellowing front teeth with a gap between them.

The ghost studied Zhao Yunlan, head swinging, and broke out into a fit of giggles as it rocked back and forth.

Zhao Yunlan didn't want to cause any trouble while they were here. Keeping his gun trained on the ghost, he signaled Zhu Hong to walk the other way. Keeping their distance from it seemed like the best plan.

When the double-faced ghost saw that they were trying to leave, a hissing noise came from its throat. "Humans and ghosts belong on separate paths," it said. "Humans and ghosts belong on separate paths!"

The words landed like a blow to the heart. Zhao Yunlan instantly thought of Shen Wei. Expression darkening, he snapped his head around and stared at the giggling ghost. With ice dripping from his voice, he said, "I've been exercising restraint here because I don't want to burn bridges with the Netherworld, but you guys keep taking a mile when given an inch."

The double-faced ghost's smile eventually vanished. It tilted its head, staring at him with its creepy face. Finally, Zhu Hong couldn't take it anymore. She tugged on his sleeve. "Director Zhao, let's go."

Veins stood out on Zhao Yunlan's gun hand. Just as he was about to take a step, the ghost suddenly spoke again. "Do you want humanity or inhumanity? You must choose. Do you want to walk the Mortal Realm or tread the paths of ghosts? You must choose. Do you want the world above or the abyss beneath? You must choose."

Its voice grew in volume until it was piercingly loud. The words "You must choose" spread like waves through the cold, bleak streets of Ghost City, echoing everywhere. It lingered in his ears like an inescapable interrogation.

Countless ghosts and souls peeked out between dilapidated shingles, cracked rocks, and the ground itself. Their peering eyes gleamed with an eerie light as they whispered among themselves. With Zhu Hong accompanying him, Zhao Yunlan had to tread with more caution than he otherwise might. Forcing the fury in his heart back down, he started to lead her away.

The double-faced ghost's head spun again, and its ferocious features now faced forward. Its voice rose into a scream that cut the air like an owl hooting at night. "Live souls here! There are live souls here!"

The words were like water poured onto hot oil—a sizzle that became a conflagration. Zhao Yunlan opened fire, shooting right through the ghost's head. The special bullet immediately ignited beneath its skin, turning the creature to ash from the shoulders up.

But it was too late. The words "live souls" had summoned mobs of little ghouls, their faces empty but voracious. They descended like a hunger-crazed pack of wild dogs, eyes burning with absolute, insatiable *need*. Even the black cat, whose fur stood on end, wasn't enough to ward them off.

Cursing under his breath, Zhao Yunlan blew the head off one of the ghosts at the head of the pack. The dead soul disappeared with a hysterical scream, but the others were completely undeterred. Not a single ghost spared a glance for their comrade, soul shattered beyond repair. They had lost all capacity for fear or reason.

The streets that had been so empty were teeming now. More and more ghosts crawled out of unbelievable places, their numbers swelling.

Zhao Yunlan was insufficiently armed, as he had only come to investigate a mystery. In no time at all, he was out of bullets. A massive python appeared at his side as Zhu Hong shifted into her true form, lashing out at the swarming ghosts and swallowing four or five in a single bite. But the stream of souls was endless. Some ghosts even climbed onto her, biting at her hard scales. She thrashed violently, flinging them away and striking at them with the weight of her tail, as wide as an adult's waist.

But there were just too many of them. Opponents like the Yanluo Kings were easy to avoid, but wave after wave of little nuisances added up to big trouble.

The crazed ghosts were like jungle leeches, desperate to drain the living of their flesh, their blood...their life itself. Four or five swarmed Zhu Hong and were thrown down, only to rush her yet again. One even stepped on the snake's vulnerable spot, seven inches down from her head, and tore off a scale with its long nails.

An instant later, a fierce wind swept past. A palm-length dagger sheared through the head of the little ghost who was holding the bloodied scale. Even as the ghost disappeared into the wind, it still craned its neck and stuck out its tongue to try and get a taste of the fresh blood and flesh.

Zhao Yunlan, knife in hand, gave the tip of Zhu Hong's tail a light tug. "Shrink down a little! Hurry!"

He slashed the knife out horizontally, reducing a row of ghosts to dust. He quickly drew his arm back, and despite the danger, took two seconds to strip off his coat and hug it to his chest.

The way he treasured the coat might've looked funny, but knowing the reason, Zhu Hong couldn't laugh. She contracted down into a far smaller snake, only the width of a finger, and slithered into Zhao Yunlan's sleeve. There, she coiled herself around his wrist. Zhao Yunlan bent down and grabbed hold of Daqing, the ragged furball.

Raising a wind-borrowing talisman in one hand, he lit it with the last True Flame of Samadhi in his lighter. Vast gales and ferocious flames surged into existence, wind and fire reflecting each other. The city erupted with screams as the inferno descended. Zhao Yunlan didn't dare waste a single moment. Shielded by the True Flame, he beat a hasty retreat to the exit, racing toward the gates…only to arrive and find them inexplicably shut.

Zhao Yunlan whipped around and saw that the vicious ghouls, ravaged by starvation, had managed to swallow some of the raging True Flames. All the ghouls who had gorged themselves on the fire transformed into wingless bird people. Stomachs distended, they flew into the sky, where they exploded. It was a scene straight out of hell—and yet the remaining ghosts' appetites were unaffected. Drawn like moths to the flames, they rushed at the True Flames of Samadhi in waves, somehow managing to bite the stream of fire in half!

Daqing gave a few yowls, reflexively clawing at Zhao Yunlan's hair. "Fuck! What do we do?!"

"What choice do we have?" Zhao Yunlan rubbed at his arm, where a ghoul had left three bloody scratches. "We'll just have to force our way through."

The True Flames were starting to weaken and dwindle, the stream of flame breaking into segments. And then, out of nowhere, the Soul-Guarding Whip appeared, and with a crack, tore fiercely through the lifeless sky above Ghost City.

As soon as Zhao Yunlan had the whip in hand, a strange energy gathered there—unfamiliar at first, but less so by the moment. The power felt as though it had always been his, as if it was part of him.

Something deep inside him was stirring, quickly awakening.

A sudden blow struck the closed gates behind him. A figure clad entirely in black strode through the resulting person-shaped hole without so much as lowering his head. He grabbed Zhao Yunlan by the hand that held the whip, and the whip curled back onto Zhao Yunlan's arm. Zhu Hong, still coiled around his wrist, caught the whip in her mouth.

A long blade materialized in the newcomer's hand and shot out, aimed with ruthless will. A great boom annihilated nearly half the city's inhabitants. The stone slabs lining the streets began to shake and whir; countless resentful ghosts shattered under the blade.

He threw an arm around Zhao Yunlan's waist, all but dragging him out of the city through the hole in the gates and speeding away. In the blink of an eye, the ghouls and their territory were far behind them.

Zhu Hong, shocked and delighted, resumed her human form as soon as they reached safety. "My lord Emissary!"

Her great savior, the Soul-Executing Emissary, dismissed her gratitude with a wave. Stiffly, he addressed Zhao Yunlan. "Why are you here?"

The expressionless mask Zhao Yunlan had been maintaining, calm to the point of creepiness, finally gave way. Utterly exhausted, he let go of Daqing, letting the fat cat drop to the ground. Then, with no concern for their surroundings, he wrapped his arms around the black-cloaked figure, who was feared and revered by all, and pulled him into a hug. In a hoarse rasp, he said, "Just come home."

Poor Zhu Hong, having only just returned to human form, wasn't quite steady on her feet yet. The shock of what she was seeing knocked her on her ass.

CHAPTER 7

HAND SHAKING, Zhu Hong pointed at the Soul-Executing Emissary. "He... H-he... He's..."

"He's Shen Wei," Daqing supplied, feeling rather superior. He looked at Zhu Hong, now sprawled on the ground, and cleaned his claws. Only pretending to be outwardly calm, he graciously gave the girl next to him a moment to begin reconstructing her shattered worldview.

The Emissary's hood fell back and revealed the elegant, refined features of Professor Shen—features that seemed wildly out of place in the current circumstances. After some time, he gently pushed Zhao Yunlan away, only to grab him by the wrist, brow furrowing at the sight of the scratches left by the little ghoul. Grip tightening, he opened his other hand and made a snatching motion. Impossibly thin threads of black emerged from the wounds and dispersed into the air. The gouges on Zhao Yunlan's arm began to heal at once.

Not wanting to speak too much, Shen Wei avoided Zhao Yunlan's gaze and gave Zhu Hong a brisk nod. "Let's leave this place first."

But before they could go, a group of reapers came rushing toward them, followed by the Magistrate, huffing and puffing. The Ten Kings' butts might've been welded to their thrones, given their unwillingness to do anything but throw their weight around. All the actual work, errand running, and generally thankless tasks inevitably landed on the Magistrate's plate. The panting old Magistrate directed the reapers to repair the city gates and contain the ghouls. There was even a clerk standing off to the side, wiping sweat from his face as he took inventory of everything. Ghosts of all kinds within the city had fallen beneath the Soul-Executing Blade; few were left standing.

Shen Wei and Zhao Yunlan turned to leave, both tacitly ignoring the sudden bustle. Zhu Hong and Daqing hurried to keep up. Mopping at his forehead, the Magistrate shouted from behind them, "My lord! Great Immortal! Please wait!"

Shen Wei turned back, wordlessly lifting a brow.

"Every... Every soul in Ghost City, whether they're here to atone for sins or to await reincarnation—they must all be accounted for. M-my lord, you..."

"I what?" Shen Wei asked, voice gentle and dangerously mild. "I can't kill them?"

The Magistrate was unable to summon a response.

Smiling, Shen Wei turned his head to the side. Without his glasses, there was something demonic about his eyebrows. The smile he wore could've chilled anyone down to the marrow. Tucking both hands into his pitch-black sleeves, he kept talking, his tone almost humble. "Lord Magistrate, despite my low birth, my unworthiness, and how little my life has amounted to, before today I've heard of nothing in existence that the Soul-Executing Blade cannot or should not sever. But if my actions have inconvenienced you in any way... Well, you have my sincerest apologies, of course."

The Magistrate shuddered and forced his face into a wooden smile. "Of course, of course."

After a long look and a frigid smile, Shen Wei pulled Zhao Yunlan away.

Somehow, Shen Wei's expression seemed a bit unfamiliar to Zhao Yunlan; it might've been because he'd never seen this over-bearing side of Shen Wei before. Once they'd covered a bit of ground, he looked back at the Magistrate, who stood where they'd left him, dabbing his cold sweat. "What was the Netherworld trying to do? Use that double-faced ghost to stop us? What good would that do them?"

Shen Wei's smile disappeared. Head lowered, he said nothing.

"Shen Wei!" Zhao Yunlan grabbed him. "Don't play dumb. I'm telling you to just come home with me! Say *something*!"

Until they'd reached the pagoda tree beside the Huangquan, Shen Wei held his silence. "You should go," he said, very quietly. Having shed his hostility and coldness, he seemed tired. "It's not good for the living to spend too long in the Netherworld. If you keep delaying, you'll fall ill upon your return."

Zhao Yunlan let go of him and stopped moving. Shen Wei stood right in front of him, unwilling to turn around and face him.

Teeth gritted, Zhao Yunlan snarled, "I want to fucking drag you home and handcuff you so that you'll stay put."

With his back still turned, so Zhao Yunlan couldn't see, Shen Wei suddenly smiled as though he'd just heard the most stirring, heartfelt romantic declaration the world had ever known. Even the trace of gloom in his eyes turned gentle, as if about to melt.

"If I leave with you, will you take the medicine?" he asked.

"Fuck off!"

Now, finally, he turned around and faced Zhao Yunlan. There was a quiet sigh before he said, "I'm one of the gui, Yunlan. No mat-ter what Kunlun-jun did for me, no matter what...you made of me all those years ago, they're all empty titles. My nature is that of a gui. From their first breath, the gui were inauspicious. At the dawn of

Chaos, it was even said in the Mortal Realm that the mere sight of a gui foretold a horrible death and an eternity without peace."

Zhao Yunlan gazed back at him, fighting to contain the restless fury in his heart. "I don't believe in that shit. Just come home with me, and we can figure everything else out from there. Even if we can't be together, you have to at least be somewhere I can see you every day, so I can rest easy..."

"Where you can see me," Shen Wei echoed, very low. His narrow lips twitched as if trying to quirk up but managed only a bitter smile. After a while, he said, voice still soft, "Yunlan, I beg you, stop tormenting me so. In all my existence, my greatest regret is my carelessness in becoming entangled with you and lacking the self-control to keep from making mistake after mistake. I... I think perhaps I'm simply not good enough. I'm too weak and lack the necessary willpower."

A sudden suspicion made Zhao Yunlan throw himself toward Shen Wei, reaching out to grab hold of him...but his hands closed on empty air. Still facing him, Shen Wei retreated with such swiftness that he seemed to become only a streak of black shadow. As he disappeared before Zhao Yunlan's eyes, all that lingered were his final words, which also faded further and further into the distance. "I won't be accompanying you any longer. Hurry and leave."

The word "leave" resounded again and again—a repeated blow to the eardrums, like an inauspicious curse.

There was a moment when Zhu Hong thought Zhao Yunlan was about to cry. But in the next instant, he'd brutally quashed it; the only remaining evidence was his reddened eyes.

Staring in the direction where Shen Wei had vanished, Zhao Yunlan told Zhu Hong, "You go back first." His voice was very calm. "Take Daqing with you. Oh, right—you said you were leaving.

Do you know when, exactly? If so, let me know beforehand, and Wang Zheng can plan—"

Zhu Hong interrupted him. "Director Zhao, what's happening?"

Zhao Yunlan waved, not wanting to say more. "Nothing. Get going."

"Go where? I'm not going anywhere!" Zhu Hong raised her voice. "Why did he... Shen... The Soul..." She sighed in frustration. "Whoever he is, why did he say that? Why can't you guys be together? What medicine is he forcing you to drink? Why—"

Daqing jumped onto Zhu Hong's feet. From his seat there, he looked up at Zhao Yunlan. "There's an ancient saying that humans and ghosts belong on separate paths, but in all my years, I've never seen two people so truly desperate to be together despite being separated by yin and yang. Some truths have existed since the beginning of time: water will always flow downward, and the dead will always suck the life from the living. It may just be the natural order of things. It's so easy for a living being to lose their life, and so hard for it to be returned. It can be returned only if one willingly offers up a part of themselves that's connected to their very spirit. As a King of the Gui, he was born to stand among the sages. He most likely doesn't have an inner core as the yao do, so...the only option left is blood from the very tip of his heart, right?"

Zhao Yunlan, for all his extroversion, was hard to read. If he didn't want to show his joy or sorrow, his face would never betray him.

A breath caught in Zhu Hong's throat. But a glance at Zhao Yunlan showed that the man still hadn't moved or spoken. His expression was calm, and the reflection of the Huangquan on his face made it as pale as snow, but not even a trace of vulnerable melancholy was visible.

At first, Zhu Hong didn't know what to say. But people's hearts are unavoidably biased, and her heart held only Zhao Yunlan.

She seemed to feel his every emotion as if it were her own. Zhao Yunlan still hadn't said a word, but the more Zhu Hong thought about it, the more frustration she felt on his behalf. Finally, under the double weight of his sadness and her own, she yelled, "He's setting you up to be in the wrong!"

Zhao Yunlan's gaze finally shifted and landed on her. "What was that?"

"He's deliberately setting things up so you're the one in the wrong!" she said indignantly. "If he hadn't sent you mixed signals to begin with, would you have chased him for so long for no reason? You're not the son of the emperor; if he hadn't oh-so-reluctantly given in, would you have forced yourself on him? On the *Soul-Executing Emissary*? As if someone that powerful could be forced into anything!"

Zhu Hong's bold accusations made the black cat sway and slide off her feet. It seemed to him that her shattered worldview had been reassembled in record time. The cat was in awe of her ability to take a blow and come back swinging. It was as if she didn't even realize that she was talking about the Soul-Executing Emissary—the same man who, once upon a time, she'd feared so much that she'd been scared to even open his letters.

The more Zhu Hong spoke, the angrier she got and the more her heart ached. She just couldn't let it go. "He obviously seduced you on purpose and then strung you along and played hard to get. He's just a fucking cocktease! If he can't be with you, why didn't he say so in the first place? He's obviously forcing...forcing you to..."

Zhao Yunlan took the last cigarette from the pack in his pocket, lighting it with a flick. After slowly exhaling a puff of white smoke, he asked mildly, "Forcing me to do what?"

For a second, Zhu Hong didn't have an answer, but then a light bulb went off in her mind. "Forcing you to be unable to leave him!"

she blurted. "Forcing you to feel like you could never bear to give up on him, until he's all you can see and nothing else matters! The way I see it, his intentions have been sketchy right from the start!"

Laughing lightly, Zhao Yunlan touched Zhu Hong's shoulder and steered her toward the pagoda tree. "Okay, now that you've got that all out of your system, hurry and leave."

"Are you even listening to me?!" Zhu Hong asked, stamping a foot.

Zhao Yunlan's smile evaporated. He looked down, flicking his cigarette. "Do you want a gold star for that emotional insight, silly girl? You really don't know when to stay in your lane. Don't you know what 'outsiders shouldn't meddle in private affairs' means? He's mine. If the two of us have a problem, it's between us, no matter who's in the wrong. An outsider criticizing him in front of me is no different from slapping me in the face. Me, I can't be bothered to take this seriously, but anyone else would've lost their temper long before now. That's enough talk, so hurry and go. Head home and get some good sleep. You've worked hard these last few days, so I'll make sure to pay you holiday overtime."

Zhu Hong's voice was shaking. "Me? I'm an outsider?"

"Obviously." Zhao Yunlan side-eyed her. "Three's a crowd in a relationship, you know."

"You asshole!"

Zhao Yunlan spread his arms helplessly. "How am I an asshole?"

Zhu Hong could no longer avoid a truly clichéd question. "In your eyes, how exactly is he better than me?"

Daqing, who had witnessed the entire scene, covered his face with his paws and came to the realization that he actually quite enjoyed melodramatic moments worthy of evening soap operas. His feline standards had tragically fallen.

All Zhao Yunlan could do was sigh. "You're gentle, kind, pure, and beautiful, plus you're a girl. You're better than him in every way."

"Then why not me?"

After giving it a moment of thought, two dimples blossomed on Zhao Yunlan's cheeks. "I must be blind. The same goes for you, actually. Look, I'm a chain-smoking drunk. I'm annoying. I talk too much. I have a shitty temper. At best, I can pretend to be tender and considerate for about three days before I blow my cover. I'm great at wasting money, and I'm no help at all on the everyday-life front, but I'm great at causing trouble. My own mother stopped being able to cope with me and kicked me out ages ago. Why is a beautiful woman like you so hung up on me?"

Zhu Hong looked at him, tears brimming in her eyes. "You're friend-zoning me!"

"I guess." Zhao Yunlan's eyes slid half closed as he savored the last puff of his cigarette. It smoldered between his fingertips. "True story: I'm too lazy to even wash my socks. I buy seven or eight pairs and wear them all once, and then I shake them out, sort them by how bad they smell, and wear them again. Then I finally stuff them into the laundry bag and send them off to be washed. Rinse and repeat, ad nauseam. Every so often a sock goes missing, so its partner ends up among the mismatched. I didn't start wearing them in pairs until after Shen Wei moved in."

As he spoke, the small smile lurking at the corner of his mouth couldn't quite be contained. A trace of tenderness shone through. "Sometimes I don't have the first clue how he stands me. You probably can't even imagine how good he is to me.

"Listen. Going forward, whether you go back to your tribe or decide to come back to us, you're always welcome. But let's agree on one thing: we're not bringing this up again, all right? The streets are full of men better than me. Don't you think it's foolish to forsake the forest and hang yourself to die on a single ugly tree?"

As he spoke, he stubbed out the cigarette, which had burned all the way down. Taking advantage of his height, he put a hand on Zhu Hong's head and ruffled her hair. "What future could you have with a shameless gay guy like me? Come on, goddess, I'll let you spit on me to clear out the bad luck and release all your anger. Throw the fuckboy card in my face. Say you're too good for me and don't want me anymore. How's that?"

Zhu Hong finally couldn't hold back her tears. As they streamed down her cheeks, she swallowed the lump in her throat and said, "Shameless gay is right. Only ghosts would ever like you. Who but a ghost would ever want you?"

When Zhao Yunlan thought about it, what she was saying made a lot of sense; her choice of words almost seemed to wish him and Shen Wei a happily ever after. He smiled at her. "Of course only a ghost would like me."

Then he reached out with a foot and nudged Daqing's belly with a toe. "Now head back together, you guys. Be careful on the way."

Having said that, Zhao Yunlan stepped onto the Naihe Bridge without a backward glance. He went right over the railing, landing gracefully on the deck of a boat and scaring the faceless ferry ghost. Zhao Yunlan patted the ghost's shoulder. "Hey, bro, can I get directions? I wanna go to the Great Seal. How do I get there?"

The ferry ghost's face was white as a sheet. Without a word, he jumped right into the Wangchuan River. Not even a bubble came up after he went under, perhaps because he didn't need to breathe.

Zhao Yunlan, seeing that his words had scared a ghost into jumping ship, couldn't help rubbing his nose. He sat there on the ferry and contemplated his situation.

"Thousands of zhang below the Huangquan, below the Huangquan..." He stared down into the calm Wangchuan below him, struck by a sudden thought. He folded Shen Wei's coat neatly and set it down in the boat. A weak spirit popped its head up from the water, wanting to reach out and touch it. Without sparing a glance, Zhao Yunlan said, "That garment belongs to the Lord Emissary. Are you hoping some of his divinity will rub off on you?"

Frightened, the spirit plunged headfirst back under the water and disappeared.

Zhao Yunlan rolled up his sleeves and pant legs and plunged into the river. In the distance, a woman and a cat cried out in surprise, while the shock that struck the wandering spirits in the water sent ripples spreading out.

The Wangchuan waters were bone-chillingly cold. Everything in the Netherworld felt like it had just been taken out of the fridge. Zhao Yunlan's watch, Clarity, emitted a gentle luminescence in the water. He looked further down and decided to dive as far as he could and head back up when he ran out of air.

Right at that moment, the water dragon pearl around his neck suddenly glowed a brilliant white as a huge air bubble formed, surrounding him completely. Zhao Yunlan tried letting go of the breath he was holding and was delighted to find that he could breathe again. Unafraid, he dove further down.

He traveled downward for some unknown amount of time. The pure white glow of the ferry boats was no longer visible. Pitch-black water spread infinitely above and below him. Clarity, now essentially a flashlight, kept radiating its glow, but its ticking had stopped. It was as though time itself had stopped existing for him.

The swimming spirits around him gradually faded away. After a while, even the water was motionless, seeming to stagnate.

There was no light, no sound...nothing. Zhao Yunlan's own heartbeat had become very loud, pounding like the beat of a drum. Even covering his ears would do nothing to block out the sound.

After a while, even Clarity's light started to dim, and he gradually found himself enveloped by the absolute darkness. He sank and sank, with no idea how long he had been descending. It felt almost as if this wasn't an absence of light but some sort of new blindness that had come upon him.

UNEXPECTEDLY, the first familiar face Chu Shuzhi saw when he arrived back in Dragon City was Guo Changcheng.

Finally being freed of his shackles and reclaiming the belongings that the Netherworld had confiscated from him all those years ago had put him in a great mood. As a result, he'd found a wild burial mound and gone there to spend a few days of his Lunar New Year break in seclusion. But when he received Wang Zheng's email about Zhu Hong's plan to leave the SID, he immediately bought a standing-room train ticket [6] and raced back to Dragon City, joining the throngs of people headed back after the holiday.

The train station was bursting at the seams with activity. Chu Shuzhi walked around a bit, trying to find a taxi. What he found instead was Guo Changcheng, bent practically double under a huge woven bag. Guo Changcheng was hunched so far forward by the weight that his body almost formed a circle as he slowly inched along.

A single glance was enough to tell anyone that Guo Changcheng was unaccustomed to physical labor. Beneath the giant bag, he looked like a snail burdened by the weight of the world. No one who passed by could help looking back at him.

---

6   Train ticket without a seat reservation.

Who knew what was in that bag, but as Chu Shuzhi watched, its contents forced a tiny split in the sturdy-looking nylon exterior. A woman selling corn on the roadside even kindly called out, "Hey, young man! Your bag's about to split!"

Guo Changcheng looked back, but his burden was too heavy. Worse, when he turned, he wasn't paying attention to what was underfoot and tripped over a wheel of a young woman's rolling suitcase. Flustered, Guo Changcheng stumbled, trying to catch himself. Before he could even apologize, a young man beside the girl with the suitcase gave him a shove. "Watch where you're going!"

From the start, Guo Changcheng had been unsteady on his feet. When he stumbled this time, the immense structure atop his back collapsed completely and its contents spilled out. A mind-boggling array of things clattered to the ground: pots, bowls, ladles, basins, food and clothing wrapped in plastic bags, and weirdest of all, a large wooden cutting board that was sixty centimeters across and eight centimeters thick. He'd practically been carrying a miniature Walmart on his shoulders.

The guy who'd pushed him had likely also just fought his way out of the crowded train station, which might have accounted for his incredibly short temper. He *tsk*ed, brow creasing with contempt. He took one look at Guo Changcheng's worn gray clothes and mistook him for someone from the countryside, coming back to the city to do factory work. A tremendous sense of superiority joined the feeling of loathing, leading him to deliver a sharp lecture as he pulled the girl away. "How stupid are you to bring so many things with you when you know there'll be crowds like this? What if you break someone's suitcase? Can you afford to replace it?"

Guo Changcheng apologized again and again, scrambling to pick up his things. The nylon bag that had so valiantly given its life had burst open at both ends. Guo Changcheng was sweating all over from the stress. But just then, a pair of bony hands interceded, deftly tying the ends of the bag together in a double knot. Having turned the bag into a cloth basket, Chu Shuzhi loaded all the items into the middle and lifted it with one hand, holding the vast collection of odds and ends as easily as if the bag were empty.

"Chu-ge!" Guo Changcheng exclaimed, looking up. If he'd had a tail, it would've been wagging hard enough to resemble an electric fan. From his perspective, the Corpse King was a savior who'd descended from the Heavens.

Chu Shuzhi ignored him. Eyes locked on the rude youth, who hadn't gone far, and while still holding the huge nylon bag in one hand, he called out, "You there! Get the fuck back here right now and apologize."

When Chu Shuzhi's face took on that dark, menacing expression, he looked especially terrifying. He radiated the ominous ferocity of a criminal willing to throw away his own life. The young man, who had been so arrogant and domineering just moments ago, puffed himself up to seem as intimidating as possible, trying to hide his fear of Chu Shuzhi behind bluster. "What do you want?"

Just as Chu Shuzhi was about to approach the man, Guo Changcheng caught his hand and stopped him. "Chu-ge, Chu-ge, let's go. I didn't see her. It was my fault." Keeping hold of Chu Shuzhi's ice-cold hand, he smiled uneasily at the couple. "It was my fault," he repeated.

The two people in front of them walked away, cursing...and completely oblivious to the great danger they'd narrowly escaped.

Chu Shuzhi turned back and rolled his eyes at Guo Changcheng— there was clearly something wrong with the kid's brain on top of his terminal case of blind virtue. How was someone with absolutely no sign of either a temper or a spine even human, never mind a hot-blooded young man?

Annoyed, Chu Shuzhi tugged his hand out of Guo Changcheng's grip and pointed at the bag. "Is your family so poor that you have to come out here during Lunar New Year and sell stuff?"

"No, I'm taking these things to someone. I wasn't expecting the bag to break halfway." Guo Changcheng followed him eagerly, then was overcome with embarrassment. "Let m-m-me carry it. It's not far."

Chu Shuzhi impatiently avoided the grasping paws and furrowed his brow. "Lead the way."

Guo Changcheng obediently took the lead, jogging along. Passing through the street in front of the station and making quite a few turns into a little alleyway, they wound up in a shadowy area of the prosperous city. Dilapidated single-story houses awaited them there, and further in, there was a ponytailed female student sweeping in a doorway. At the sight of Guo Changcheng, she called out a joyful greeting. There was a Winter Break Volunteer tag from a university hanging around her neck.

Always a bit flustered when interacting with girls, Guo Changcheng bowed his head unnaturally low. In a mosquito-thin voice, he managed, "Hello."

The sharp-eyed girl caught sight of the large bag in Chu Shuzhi's hand. She set her broom aside at once and pushed the door open for him. As they walked in, she asked Guo Changcheng, "Did you register already? Did you print it out? We have to post it online and tag everyone to thank them."

Nodding hurriedly, Guo Changcheng pulled out a bundle of printouts. There were at least seven or eight pages, detailing exactly what had been donated by whom and recording the donors' information: street addresses, phone numbers, online IDs, and email addresses. The donations were an eclectic variety of things, ranging from different amounts of cash to cabbage—a large and strange collection indeed.

As it turned out, this was a winter break volunteer movement called "Helping Our Elders and Children," a joint effort by several universities and social organizations in Dragon City. Guo Changcheng was involved with a facet of the movement that focused specifically on helping impoverished old people who were no longer able to take care of themselves for various reasons. Each group of volunteers was responsible for providing long-term care to a few elderly folks.

Guo Changcheng's weak communication skills meant he wasn't the best companion for the elderly or adept at raising donations, so he worked hard to do some of the heavy lifting. He'd spent this break serving as a delivery man.

Chu Shuzhi set the stuff down and then commandeered Guo Changcheng's car, driving them both to 4 Bright Avenue. Guo Changcheng's palms had been rubbed raw by the nylon bag. He sat in the passenger seat and silently cleaned them with a wet wipe.

For once, Chu Shuzhi was feeling chatty. "You really do try to take care of everyone, huh? What's the plan? Delivering all of humanity from torment?"

Confused, Guo Changcheng just stared at him with his naive eyes.

"Does your family know you're doing all this?" Chu Shuzhi asked, shaking his head.

"I've never brought it up."

Chu Shuzhi didn't really understand him. "Did you burn incense on the first day of the Lunar New Year, then? Wishes tend to come true for people like you."

Guo Changcheng shook his head again. He was completely satisfied with his life as it was. What could he possibly wish for other than his friends' and family's health? And right now, his friends and family all seemed happy and safe. He felt it was best not to bother the bodhisattvas unnecessarily.

Chu Shuzhi couldn't help glancing over at him while waiting for a green light. Guo Changcheng wasn't tall, strong, or handsome. No one was going to accuse him of having attractive features or of catching anyone's eye in any way. He didn't even own a single item of brand-name clothing; everything he wore was probably a hand-me-down from who knew how many lifetimes ago. He was basically the kind of person you could drop into a crowd and never find again. His absolute lack of confidence meant he didn't have even a shred of charisma.

But when he simply sat down in silence, his peaceful expression held a kind of indefinable, innate zen. Guo Changcheng was just a mortal moving through the world, eating and drinking. He had no clue what cultivation was. He couldn't read a word of the Buddhist texts, and out of all the bodhisattvas and arhats of the world, he only knew two: Guanyin and Rulai.[7] And even that much was only thanks to the popular television drama *Journey to the West*.

Despite all that, Chu Shuzhi had the sense that Guo Changcheng was quietly cultivating *something*, wholly on his own.

It wasn't luck for this life, or merits for the next, and Chu Shuzhi's keen perception and his own cultivation gave him only a vague feeling. He couldn't put a finger on exactly what it was. No, he couldn't know what Guo Changcheng was thinking while doing

---

7   Guanyin (观音), called the Compassionate Bodhisattva or Goddess of Mercy, is the primary protector of the heroes in Journey to the West. Rulai (如来) is the Chinese name meaning Tathāgata, which may indicate one of several Buddhas, here likely Siddhartha Gautama, and refers to having transcended mortal concerns.

so many good deeds, but he couldn't help feeling discomfort deep down. It felt like a sort of outrage, or a sense of indignation.

All things being equal, shouldn't the fact that the kid's merits were a meter thick grant him a life of safety and happiness? Why had he been born with such ill luck overshadowing him? Everyone knew merits and sins were bullshit when it came to *The Book of Life and Death*, but did the Netherworld really need to flout it so blatantly?

Chu Shuzhi stopped talking, and his fanboy, Guo Changcheng, lacked the courage to start a conversation on his own. The two of them drove the rest of the way to 4 Bright Avenue in silence.

At this point, night had fallen. Virtually the entire staff, both alive and dead, were in the criminal investigation unit when Chu Shuzhi and Guo Changcheng walked in.

The first thing Chu Shuzhi noticed was that every single person's eyes were completely blank, as though his coworkers had been collectively struck by lightning. Before he could ask what had happened, Wang Zheng turned to face them. Voice shaking, she asked, "Chu-ge, did you know that Shen-laoshi...th-that Shen Wei... is the Soul-Executing Emissary?"

Chu Shuzhi froze for just a moment but replied calmly. "What won't that dumbass Zhao Yunlan do? Where is he? Realized he's in way over his head and ran off?"

Off to the side, Daqing meowed and said, "He jumped into the Wangchuan River."

"Broken heart?" Chu Shuzhi asked. "What, did he off himself?"

Daqing and Zhu Hong's initial rush of panic had worn off by this point, leaving them mostly calm. Zhu Hong knew that Zhao Yunlan was wearing the water dragon pearl—she'd put it on him just before the trouble started—and that it would protect him from suffering any harm from water. If she was just a little more inclined to be suspicious, she would almost think that her fourth uncle had known something in advance.

"I'm guessing he went to find the Emissary," she said.

Chu Shuzhi's gaze swept across the room. The only other person absent was Lin Jing, who was currently out of town. He stuffed his hands in his pockets and leaned back against the office door. "Let's start by each sharing exactly what we know. Things have been too chaotic recently. Let's pool our information..."

And then he paused abruptly, expression turning to one of horror. It sent everyone else's nervousness through the roof. "What is it, Chu-ge?"

"Wait—*Shen Wei* is the *Soul-Executing Emissary*?" Chu Shuzhi's face had gone green. After another moment, he mumbled, "I've teased him so much!"

Evidently, sometimes one was crowned the King of Calm only thanks to a delayed reaction time.

While all that was happening, Zhao Yunlan had long since lost all sense of space and time. He was as blind in the waters of the Wangchuan as he'd been within the Great Divine Tree, but the experience was completely different. An indescribable pressure made him feel as though his temples were being squeezed together; nausea and exhaustion that felt much like a blood sugar crash slowly filled his torso. His heart seemed on the verge of beating out of his chest, and the pulse pounding in his ears was almost unbearably strong and rushed. He didn't dare move his head too much for fear of simply passing out.

Just as he was on the brink of collapse, Zhao Yunlan saw a trace of light.

The light was dimmer than the glow of a single firefly, but to eyes so thoroughly accustomed to darkness, its brightness was downright piercing. He shielded his eyes, irresistibly drawn to that faint light.

As he drew closer, he realized that it was a massive ancient tree. The branches seemed to stretch on endlessly and the trunk might've been hundreds of meters in diameter, but the tree was withered. Its dried, twisted branches held not a single leaf. It had the coarse texture of something that had weathered many eons.

Zhao Yunlan's very spirit shook. Was he looking at the Ancient Merit Tree itself?

He forced himself to stay alert as he followed the tree's trunk nearly a kilometer down. Eventually, he saw the ancient tree's roots, and then his feet, after so long floating downward, finally touched ground.

His first move was to walk around the Ancient Merit Tree in a huge circle, which brought him face-to-face with an old stone tablet. The faint glow of the tree was enough that Zhao Yunlan could clearly see the words carved into the stone—in a script he had never laid eyes on before, yet was somehow able to read.

It read, "The Imperial Skies and Houtu. The unearthly Land of the Gui. The Place of Great Disrespect."

A name burst from his lips. "Nüwa..."

His voice rippled out like a stone dropped in water, then dispersed like a sigh. In response, something stirred in the darkness. Entranced, Zhao Yunlan reached out and touched the edge of the tablet.

White light flowed into his brain, and for a second, he could see nothing at all. His gaze seemed to pierce time itself, coming to rest on a beautiful woman with a serpent's tail, her long hair trailing on the ground. His heart flooded with a sense of familiarity, springing

from the very source of his life: the recognition of both a mother and an elder sister.

Her voice sounded near his ear, both familiar and strange. "Kunlun, what if Shennong was wrong?" she asked. "What if we were all wrong?"

Wrong? Shennong? What had Shennong done?

"But...we can no longer turn back," she continued.

What...? Wait!

He thought he glimpsed tears in the woman's eyes. Face filled with a bottomless sorrow at her imminent departure, she spread her arms toward him. Zhao Yunlan reached out...

Only for her to shatter into countless shards before he could touch her, like an image projected into the air.

"No..." Zhao Yunlan's mouth opened instinctively, but no sound emerged.

In the next instant, the stream of time flowed around him. Zhao Yunlan seemed to find himself in some unknowably distant past, unsure whether he was Kunlun-jun or a mortal who lived thousands of years later. And he *remembered*...

He kept watch over the pitch-black opening of the seal, sitting against the large stone tablet as he meditated. When boredom struck, he simply stared at the Ancient Merit Tree and spaced out for the whole day. Later, a lovely but unsettling youth would always be close at hand—an ever-present shadow.

At first, Kunlun-jun ignored him, but finally he broke down and said, "We're in your territory now. Why are you still following at my heels?"

The youth's response was immediate and straightforward. "Because I like you."

Kunlun-jun had spent his existence being told that he was absurd and impudent, day in and day out. Presented with the opportunity to say it to someone else, he seized his chance. "How impudent," he scolded, despite not being angry at all.

The young King of the Gui just looked back at him in confusion, with no idea how he was being impudent.

For years and years, Kunlun-jun had been standing guard over the seal, bored out of his mind. He kept teasing. "What do you like about me, then?"

The young King of the Gui's desire for Kunlun-jun was plain as day, for he was yet unmarred by principles and morality. "You're pretty," he said bluntly. "I want to hide you away and hold you every day."

Kunlun-jun couldn't take his eyes off the fearless little king. He wasn't offended; on the contrary, he was amused. "What the hell?" he cursed, jokingly. "What are you even going on about?"

The young King of the Gui didn't understand why Kunlun-jun was looking down on him. But he thought Kunlun-jun would not say anything without reason, so he dropped his gaze in shame.

Kunlun-jun gestured broadly. "Come, let me teach you about morals and justice, you unenlightened little thing."

BACK WHEN CHAOS had first settled, the great sage
Shennong had personally descended to the Mortal Realm,
where he tasted hundreds of herbs and saved many lives.
He had become an old herbalist, spreading his teachings among
humanity. Kunlun-jun had joined the crowd a handful of times and
listened, and now he regurgitated what he'd heard back to the young
King of the Gui. His retellings made sense only half of the time, as
he was mostly doing it to dispel the boredom. But the young king
was utterly ignorant and hung on every word that came out of
Kunlun-jun's mouth. To him, Kunlun's bullshit was the truth of the
world.

Slowly, a sort of mutually reliant affection took shape there at
the maw of hell.

The young king's infatuation with Kunlun-jun didn't fade, but he
had the innate capacity to feel embarrassment and shame. Listening
to Kunlun-jun taught him that it was inappropriate to proclaim
those feelings aloud, so he tucked them away in his heart. Instead,
he searched every day for ways to make Kunlun-jun happy. But
alas, no matter how he tried, there was a limit to his imagination.
There simply wasn't anything fun to be found in the Place of Great
Disrespect, with its thousands of li of barren land that boasted not
so much as a single blade of grass. The entertainment options were

limited to capturing two low-level youchu and watching them fight and tear at each other, until one devoured the other.

This "entertainment" didn't appeal to the young King of the Gui, however, so how could it have been enjoyable for Kunlun-jun?

The young king went to the great effort of collecting a front tooth from each of thirty-six youchu, which to his mind represented the thirty-six glorious mountains that began at Kunlun. He then braided strands of his own hair into a string and strung the teeth together into an extraordinary necklace, which he gave to Kunlun-jun.

Kunlun-jun's expression when he accepted these thirty-six teeth was very strange—even stranger than the necklace itself. It was as if he had a toothache and wanted to wince from the pain but was instead forcing his features into a peculiar smile, thanking the little king through gritted teeth. From his reaction, the young king concluded that he probably didn't like it very much. Either way, Kunlun-jun didn't wear it a single time, and if the little king mentioned it, he invariably changed the subject.

But the little king's life was so bland and uninteresting that he couldn't think of anything else.

Then one day, while sitting on a huge protruding root of the Ancient Merit Tree, the young king remembered his fleeting glimpses of the Mortal Realm. "There's a kind of flower that looks like a bell," he said suddenly. "They come in all sorts of colors. If you get close and smell them, they have a very light fragrance."

Kunlun-jun tilted his head to look at him. "Mn?"

The simple, candid youth's face lit up with yearning. "They're so pretty. If I braided a chain of them, you'd like it, wouldn't you?"

After a silence, Kunlun-jun said, with what might've been a smile, "As long as I'm standing guard here, not a single gui can leave. Have you been trying to get on my good side so you can escape to the Mortal Realm?"

Realizing that Kunlun had misunderstood his intent, the young King of the Gui quickly shook his head.

Seeing how flustered he was, Kunlun-jun couldn't resist teasing. "Oh? Why, then?"

Because... The young king met that teasing gaze steadily, but he didn't know what to say. The unfamiliar emotion surging and leaping in his chest seemed impossible to express. He felt that if he gave voice to the admiration he felt, the words would only come out coarse and unrefined. And even then, he might not be able to convey even a fraction of what was in his heart.

He became frantic. Unconsciously, his nails extended into claws. Frustration turned his expression both glum and aggressive.

As people have said, once one was born into the world, most of the pain one endured—other than the hardships fate had in store— came from thinking too much and reading too little. Books were handed down by wise sages throughout history, but these sages of the distant past were born in the time of Chaos. Lacking books to read or anyone to teach them anything, they could do nothing but stumble down their paths, full of questions for the world. It must've been an agonizing, anxious time, when one lacked even the knowledge of how to share one's feelings with their beloved.

But Kunlun-jun laughed out loud. Hooking a gentle finger under the youth's chin, Kunlun-jun softly kissed his beautiful, clear forehead, then soared up into the tree's branches.

The young king sat frozen in place for some time. There was no trace left of his aggressive aura. A blush spread from his cheeks to his chin and ears. Eventually, he stood up numbly, as though drunk;

even his legs were like jelly. Mind empty, he toppled down from the Great Merit Tree's massive root.

Having been born a gui—even if he had somehow grown up completely differently from the rest of his kind—all he had ever seen and heard were the bestial, lustful copulations of lower-level youchu. The concept of a kiss was wholly new to him. Now, having experienced it, he felt enveloped by a cage of warmth, drifting lightly in midair.

Not even in the waters of the Wangchuan could he float so freely.

With no warning at all, the young King of the Gui turned and ran silently into the Great Seal, darting straight into the Place of Great Disrespect.

Dozens of years passed during which he didn't show his face a single time. When he finally appeared before Kunlun-jun once again, he seemed to have grown up a little. He was slightly taller, nearly matching Kunlun-jun's height. The soft lines of youth had become more defined. Only his brows and eyes, beautiful as a painting, seemed unchanged.

He stood before Kunlun-jun, cradling a ball of radiant golden fire in his hands.

Kunlun-jun looked at it. "This is..."

"The soul fire from your left shoulder that was scattered within the Great Seal. I've spent fifty years gathering its flames." Holding it with tremendous care, the young king rubbed his face against it, not wanting to be parted from it. Then he held it out to Kunlun-jun. "I'm returning it to you."

The smile at the corners of Kunlun-jun's lips gradually faded. Finally, he looked at the young man and asked, "And what do you want from me?"

"That..." The young king didn't know what to say. He had no idea how to express what he ached for. Finally, he pointed timidly at his own forehead. "That... Can you do it again?"

Kunlun-jun studied him for a long while. Under his intense gaze, the boy didn't seem to know what to do with his limbs. Then, suddenly, Kunlun-jun reached out and tilted his chin up. But this time it was the young king's lips that he kissed, ever so gently; he then took the boy's hand with a light squeeze, guiding the young king's long fingers closed around that ever-gleaming ball of soul fire.

"I hold all the world's famous mountains and rivers in my hand, but what of it? They're nothing but a bunch of rocks and wild waters. Of all that I am, the only part worth anything may be my heart. If you want it, it's yours."

With that, everything fell into place for the young King of the Gui. For the first time, he knew that there was a way to refer to the thing he yearned for so deeply but had been unable to voice. Its name was "heart"—a single word with the power to doom someone forever.

The gui were not living beings, but in that instant, he could almost hear his own nonexistent heartbeat.

"This too—if you like it, you can keep it." Kunlun-jun patted the back of his hand. "My heart's blood formed the wick of the Soul-Guarding Lamp, and my body became the Lamp itself. Since only my primordial spirit is here guarding this place, I have no need for this. Do you still have the tendon I gave you?"

The youth nodded hurriedly.

"Take it out and let me see," Kunlun-jun said mildly.

The young king pulled open his primitive garments and withdrew the tendon from inside the innermost layer.

"Do you know what this is?"

The youth paused in confusion.

"It's my spine."

The little king's hand shook, almost dropping what he was holding. Kunlun-jun took his wrist lightly. Through his hand, the Mountain God of the Great Wild gently smoothed over the tendon he'd ripped from his own body. "I grew out of Kunlun Mountain, and before that, the axe of Pangu. My bones and muscles are connected to the veins of Kunlun, a pillar of the sky. Shake it, and the sky will change."

As he spoke, he swiftly shaped a series of complicated hand signs with his fingers. The divine tendon was transformed into a stream of golden light that, guided by his fingers, drove straight into the King of the Gui's forehead. In an instant, the youth seemed to hear the passing of millennia, accompanied by the sound of ten thousand great mountains rising.

It was as though he suddenly stood atop an indescribable peak, from which he was watching over everything. Every mountain and every stream was plainly visible to him; under his eyes, they rose from the ground or sank with a great rumble, both the endless trickles and the surging torrents.

Woven into it all was Kunlun-jun's voice: "From this day forward, all ten thousand mountains will heed your command. The nature of your birth as a gui is difficult to shake off, but this tendon has made you at least half-divine. You can now freely wander the Three Realms. I won't restrict you any longer."

The youth's heart started beating wildly, driven by the suspicion that something more was about to happen.

"I won't!" His own voice broke him out of the illusion of mountains and rivers and brought him back to reality. "You're here. I'm not going anywhere."

"I won't be able to stay much longer," Kunlun-jun said softly, looking at the thousands of zhang of endless water from the Wangchuan. "I'm just a fragment of my primordial spirit. I can't leave, nor can I stay much longer. Lately, I've started to feel like it's about time."

Panicked, the young King of the Gui demanded, "Time for what? Where are you going?"

"I'm not going anywhere," Kunlun-jun replied calmly. "I'm about to die."

"Impossible! How can gods die?"

"Of course we can die. Pangu, Fuxi, Nüwa, Shennong...they all died, didn't they?" Kunlun-jun said. "Now it's my turn."

Hearing this, the young King of the Gui stood rooted to the spot. Then his expression turned fierce. "If the Great Seal didn't exist, if you hadn't sealed the Four Pillars in Nüwa's place, if your body hadn't turned into the Soul-Guarding Lamp, you wouldn't need to die, right? Then I'll cut down this tree and rip this damned seal apart!"

The young king was sometimes like a round little puffball of a wolf. He both looked and behaved much like a puppy. If you reached out and smoothed his fur, he would roll over obediently and expose his belly for petting...but his mouth still held fangs. If he wasn't careful, those fangs would bare themselves and plunge into someone's throat, sealing their fate.

Long before this, Kunlun-jun had accepted that the young king's feral nature would be hard to tame. Unbothered, he put a hand on his head and gently said, "To live forever and never die... Child, a rock that exists in a vacuum will last forever, but it's still just a rock, understand? Shennong said, 'If one doesn't die, doesn't perish, one cannot become a god.' I used to think he was spouting bullshit, but now, I'm finally starting to understand..."

The little King of the Gui shook his hand off. The last thing he wanted was to know what Kunlun-jun had understood. "Don't you *dare*!"

Kunlun-jun spread his hands, which had begun to look a little transparent. Shocked, the raging youth grabbed hold of them, nervously turning them over as though it was the only way he could confirm that Kunlun-jun was still there. Not giving up, he said, "What if I cut down the Ancient Merit Tree?"

Kunlun-jun laughed. "Now that you've inherited the power of the Mountain God of the Great Wild, you can cut down even the Great Divine Tree if you want. The Ancient Merit Tree is nothing."

"Then I can break apart the Great Seal and chop up the stupid stone that woman left behind, can't I?"

Again, Kunlun-jun laughed. "You can, but I might die faster that way."

"I can..." The young king couldn't find the words. "I can kill all the people in the world!" he snarled. "I can slaughter every living thing. I can strip every trace of green from the mountains and block even the smallest stream from flowing. I can litter the ground with corpses until there's no sign of life for thousands of li."

Kunlun-jun lifted a brow as he teased, "Wow, that powerful?"

The King of the Gui tightened his grip on Kunlun-jun's hands. "You're not allowed to die! I can do anything! There's nothing I wouldn't do!"

"Shennong was right about another thing." Kunlun-jun's expression turned stern and cold. "I should've killed you long ago and prevented any future troubles."

The young king pursed his lips and glared back stubbornly.

But then Kunlun-jun smiled again, warm as the first gurgling waters of a brook once winter's ice thawed, reflecting the green of life budding along its banks. "Ah, I'll quit frightening you. Listen, ever since Shennong borrowed the soul fire from my left shoulder—or no, ever since the Great War of Gods and Demons and Nüwa's creation of humans, or maybe even as far back as Pangu splitting the earth and sky—all of this was predestined. I was destined to die right here, right now. Even if you bring the sky and earth together again, you won't accomplish anything but making it so that I die in vain. You can't stop anything."

The rims of the young king's eyes reddened.

"You don't understand," said the Mountain God of the Great Wild. "What we call 'fate' isn't some divine constraint. It's a single moment when you're confronted with tens of thousands of possibilities. In that instant, you can ascend to the Heavens or descend into the earth, but in the end, there's only one path you'll inevitably choose. I didn't understand it when I was younger either, but when you grow up, you'll probably understand too."

The truth of his own powerlessness finally sank in for the young king. All his gifts were for slaughter, destruction, and devouring. All the Realms had shaken when he came into existence; ghosts and gods alike feared him. And what use was any of it?

The one he cherished most was still going to slip through his hands.

As Kunlun-jun watched, the youth's expression of murderous intent crumbled. The young king hadn't yet learned how to contain and suppress the emotions in his heart. Once his sheer shock began to fade, tears took its place; the little king broke down in wretched sobs.

Kunlun-jun looked at him with an almost loving sympathy and a pang of regret. *It's a pity I'll never see the great beauty into which this little beauty will grow.*

Thousands of years of wind, frost, rain, and snow passed in the blink of an eye. Everything was the same, but the people were gone.

Zhao Yunlan let go of the Rock of the Great Seal with a jolt. Suddenly, he realized someone was behind him, and they laughed lightly. Zhao Yunlan immediately pulled out the Soul-Guarding Whip and turned, pressing his back against the stone. Warily, he looked at Ghost Face, who was but ten steps away.

Ghost Face looked him up and down in turn, shaking his head. A smile broke out on his mask. "I've heard that all of Nüwa's memories are contained within. What did you see?"

Zhao Yunlan scoffed. "Why would I tell you?"

Ghost Face approached slowly. Mimicking Zhao Yunlan, he put a hand on the stone tablet. "Tens of thousands of years ago, he and I were twin Kings of the Gui. There was no difference between us. And yet somehow, he managed to gain Kunlun-jun's—your—favor. Now, millennia later, one of us is within and one of us is without. One of us rots in jail and one holds the keys."

The upturned corners of the smile fell. Ghost Face lowered his voice, pausing after each word. "But the Great Seal is about to fall apart. That's why I can come and go as I please. In the end, everything must die, and you are no exception. Kunlun, if my idiot brother hadn't ambushed you all those years ago and confined your primordial spirit—if he hadn't forced you into the Reincarnation Cycle to become a lowly mortal, relegated to living one life after another—you would have dissipated into *nothing*, just like the rest of the primordial gods. In this world, nothing can last forever. The only constants are death and Chaos."

As he spoke, he touched Zhao Yunlan's face with one ice-cold finger. The sigh that escaped him was almost a groan. "But 'death' itself was set ablaze by your soul fire, bringing us into existence... things that are neither living nor dead. Isn't that such a fascinating coincidence?"

Zhao Yunlan's brow furrowed. He tilted his head slightly, avoiding Ghost Face. By this point he'd heard too many versions of how he'd lost his soul fire to know which account was true. "Didn't Shennong borrow my soul fire? How did it appear later in the Place of Great Disrespect? And what do you mean, it set death itself ablaze?"

This line of questioning seemed to throw Ghost Face for a loop. His mask went blank for an instant, as though he didn't understand what Zhao Yunlan was asking. Then realization dawned. He flung his head back in wild laughter. "Ha ha ha ha ha ha! So that's how it was! And here I thought he was so pure and innocent! What a virtuous facade he put up, when really—"

He was cut off by the Soul-Executing Blade slashing down at him, wielded with enough hostility to split him in half. Ghost Face took flight and dodged, but the blade's momentum drove even Zhao Yunlan back a few steps.

"Shen Wei?" he exclaimed.

Shen Wei reached to grab him, face set with willingness to kill. "How could you come alone to a place like this? Have you lost your mind?!"

But before his hand could reach Zhao Yunlan, Ghost Face appeared out of nowhere and blocked him. Turning into a puff of black smoke, he slammed into Zhao Yunlan's chest, managing to keep Zhao Yunlan from wielding his whip. He then immediately transformed into countless wisps of black smoke, cocooning Zhao Yunlan inside as he let out a maniacal laugh.

Then the laughter stopped abruptly. The smoke dissipated as Ghost Face resumed his usual form...but Zhao Yunlan was gone.

Seeming astounded, Ghost Face quietly said, "Someone took him away. But who?"

HEN GHOST FACE'S BLACK MIST swallowed Zhao Yunlan up, it had felt like having a sack yanked down over his head. Once he finally managed to get free of it, he realized he had somehow teleported and had no idea where he was.

If nothing else, it was clear that he was no longer beneath the Wangchuan River. The world around him was nothing but white. Coiling his whip, he started walking, trying to find his way. Then, as he squinted against the blinding whiteness, he saw a lonely figure walking ahead in the far distance.

Zhao Yunlan was tall and had long legs, so he quickly caught up. The distant silhouette turned out to belong to a short old man whose height barely reached Zhao Yunlan's chest. His spine was curved like a cooked shrimp, and he had a basket on his back—the kind often used by people from the Yunnan-Guizhou Plateau. Taking a peek inside, Zhao Yunlan saw that it was empty. And yet the old man moved as if carrying hundreds of kilograms, too weighed down to even lift his head. He walked onward with his face toward the ground and his back facing the sky.

Zhao Yunlan reached out and put a hand under the basket to help support it. "Is it that heavy?" he murmured.

Finally, the old man stopped and wiped his dripping forehead.

He looked up, revealing a tanned, aged face—not unlike that of the old man holding water in Luo Zhongli's famous oil painting *Father*. He gave Zhao Yunlan a weary smile. "Come," he said. "Follow me."

"Where are we going?" Zhao Yunlan asked. "Where is this? Who are you?"

The old man didn't answer. He dropped his gaze back down and struggled forward like a decrepit ox pulling a plow. The empty basket dug into his shoulders. Sharp old collarbones peeked out below his collar.

"Are you the one who brought me here?" Zhao Yunlan sighed. "Why? I finally managed to catch my wife, and you interrupted and ruined it before I got a single word out."

With a small smile, the old man listened to his griping but didn't explain or respond.

Zhao Yunlan wasn't discouraged. "What are you carrying in the basket?"

There was still no reply. The old man just continued at his own pace, singing under his breath. "Guard the souls of the living, bring peace to the hearts of the dead, atone for crimes done in life, and complete the unfinished cycle..."

His voice droned on, spitting out the words as though he were chanting, repeating the phrase again and again. His tone was reminiscent of those people in the past who'd chant "This family is awarding 120 silver taels" while tossing spirit money during funeral processions.

Zhao Yunlan was getting more suspicious by the moment. The whip in his hand transformed into the Soul-Guarding Order, red words on black paper. He rolled it up like a cigarette and put it in his mouth, holding it there as he patiently followed the old man. But they'd been walking for such a long time now, and there was still no end in sight. He had the sudden feeling that he was walking on a road to Heaven.

That rang a bell. Path to Heaven... Wasn't *Buzhou* the Path to Heaven?

Hadn't Buzhou Mountain already fallen?

Just as he had that thought, a sigh came from somewhere in the void. Something crystallized in Zhao Yunlan's mind. Staring at the old man, he blurted, "Are you Shennong?"

Once again, the old man's footsteps stopped. Slowly, he turned back and looked at Zhao Yunlan, not saying a word. Every muscle in Zhao Yunlan's body tensed.

Ever since he'd confirmed that the "memories" he'd seen within the Great Divine Tree were fake, a suspicion had lurked in his mind. It wasn't as if just anyone could even go to the peak of Kunlun Mountain, never mind tamper with the Great Divine Tree itself. He could count the number of people who'd be capable of it with one hand. Since then, he'd pored over those memories countless times. The parts that had to do with his left soul fire were particularly unclear, and the parts that related to the fall of Buzhou Mountain were especially clunky and forced.

So who was lying to him...?

Shennong seemed like the most obvious candidate. What Zhao Yunlan had seen inside the Tree had shown Shennong consistently appearing at exactly the right time, coolly overseeing events at a distance from start to finish. At first glance, Shennong's righteousness seemed unquestionable, but after reviewing it carefully, it seemed clear to Zhao Yunlan that something wasn't right. Those memories had told a complete story. If any one person in that story hadn't played their part, things would've ended differently; that meant all their actions were directly connected to sequences of events that could be explained. Any one person, except Shennong. If Shennong hadn't been part of the story, it still would've started and ended the same way. Nothing would have changed.

Later, Zhao Yunlan had seen Shennong's stone mortar possessing his dad, and when Zhao Yunlan heard Ghost Face say that Shennong had borrowed his soul fire, it had seemed as though he'd unintentionally let something slip. Those things seemed to confirm Zhao Yunlan's suspicions. But most of all, he now kept coming back to Nüwa's vague, confusing words in the Great Sealing Rock: "Shennong was wrong."

Zhao Yunlan clenched his fist. "So was it you who tampered with the Great Divine Tree or not?"

The old man still said nothing, but worry entered his expression. For an instant, Zhao Yunlan felt like he heard the wind blowing on Buzhou.

Without warning, the snowy white world shattered, admitting a piercing bright light. Zhao Yunlan quickly shielded his eyes. Then, vision blurred by tears, he realized that he had somehow arrived in the Mortal Realm.

He assessed his surroundings, which immediately felt both familiar and...not. It took him a few minutes to recognize where he was.

It was the ice cream shop on the corner that tipped him off. Zhao Yunlan's eyes went wide. He was near his childhood home! That old ice cream shop had closed ages ago, and the spot had been a small hot-pot restaurant for five or six years now.

At first, he was completely at a loss. He bought a bowl of shaved ice with the meager change he had on him and ate it, staring at the prominent "2002" on the calendar on the shop wall. He stuck out like a sore thumb among a group of middle school girls, the shaved ice crunching between his teeth. He looked exactly like someone the mafia had sent to collect protection fees in exchange for not smashing the store.

Somehow he had returned to the year 2002!

The whole thing was like being in a dream, or like watching some shoddy movie that abruptly changed scenes: one minute the protagonist was up in the sky, the next they were underground, and then finally they managed to get back to the Mortal Realm, only to be transported eleven years into the past.

Zhao Yunlan suddenly glimpsed something in his peripheral vision. Through the shop window, he saw a familiar car driving out of the neighborhood: the old car that had held countless childhood memories—the car that his father had heartlessly replaced!

Dropping his half-eaten shaved ice on the table, Zhao Yunlan bolted out of the shop with the speed of someone catching their spouse with their secret lover. He flagged down a taxi, digging out his tattered work ID and brandishing the police badge in front of the driver's eyes. "I need you to follow that car! Stay close!"

The driver had never imagined he'd have the chance to chauffeur a 007. Thrilled by this once-in-a-lifetime chance, he stomped on the gas. The car shot forward like a racehorse, nearly sending Zhao Yunlan sprawling in the passenger seat.

Ahead of them, his father drove to Antiques Street, with its alley full of shops where cars weren't permitted. From a hundred meters away, Zhao Yunlan watched as his father parked on the roadside and went into the alley, face hidden by the kind of large sunglasses celebrities wore to avoid paparazzi.

"Sir, stop here! Here!" Zhao Yunlan's eyes were glued to his father's silhouette. He fumbled for his wallet, only for the driver to righteously refuse to let him pay.

"Please don't waste any more time!" Zhao Yunlan exclaimed. "Take this! I'm about to lose him!"

The driver only saluted and gave him a vigorous handshake. In a resonant voice that clearly wasn't about to take "no" for an answer, he said, "Comrade, go. I won't take your money. I want to serve the people!"

Zhao Yunlan lost another moment to speechlessness, then decided not to push harder to be polite. He decisively flung himself out of the car.

Eleven years ago, Antiques Street had been far less regulated. The narrow alleyway held tons of roadside stalls, hawking anything from jewelry and jade to ancient paintings and calligraphy. Anything you could imagine could be found there, authentic or fake. Either way, the place bustled with activity.

Hiding his tracks, Zhao Yunlan dry-swallowed a yellow paper talisman. It was one of the ones he'd drawn back when he was blind; he'd sold all the good ones, so the only ones he still had on him were defective. Up ahead, Shennong's mortar was clearly the one piloting his father's body. Zhao Yunlan kept his distance, afraid that the inferior talisman wouldn't be able to hide him completely.

As a result, he turned a corner just to find that he'd already lost him.

Zhao Yunlan peeked cautiously into every shop but didn't see his quarry anywhere. Then his gaze landed on the pagoda tree that was linked to the Netherworld.

Having no other choice, Zhao Yunlan took a deep breath and headed down the Huangquan Road for the second time that day, itching to kick that stupid bowl spirit a new asshole. Walking on the Huangquan Road wasn't a pleasant experience for a living being. Even a hoodlum like Zhao Yunlan, who'd venture outside without socks in the dead of winter, really couldn't endure the bone-piercing, gloomy cold.

His "dad" waited on the road for some time, rubbing his hands idly. His brows drew tighter and tighter together. It seemed as though he was waiting for someone.

Zhao Yunlan didn't dare just appear out of nowhere, but the long, thin path of the Huangquan Road offered nothing to hide behind. His only option was to curl in on himself and hide within the pagoda tree, which left him feeling stuck between the yin and yang realms.

He was just hitting the point where half of his body was about to go numb when a familiar figure approached along the road from the other direction. It was someone who drew every eye, if only because not a single ghost dared linger wherever he passed. Even the reapers, who were doing their utmost to feign calm, couldn't help lowering their heads and giving him a wide berth. From a distance, the effect was almost like the Red Sea parting before Moses.

With just one look, Zhao Yunlan immediately felt deeply awkward—as anyone would in his shoes, realizing that their "wife" had privately met up with their dad eleven years ago. Shen Wei was wearing the Soul-Executing Emissary's long cloak, face fully concealed. He stopped five paces away from Zhao Yunlan's father and said not a word. The chill clinging to him was even more piercing than the desolate Huangquan.

Zhao Yunlan's "dad" stopped pacing and rubbing his hands. It was as though the two men were competing to see who could hold their silence longer. The atmosphere was suffocating as they stared each other down.

Finally, it was Zhao Yunlan's "father" who cracked. "The evening newspaper that Yunlan brought home had my lord's scent on it."

Shen Wei snorted with cold laughter. It was so unlike anything Zhao Yunlan had ever heard from him that he could almost suspect that the black-cloaked man wasn't Shen Wei at all but the passive-aggressive Ghost Face.

Zhao Yunlan's father's body might have been possessed by an impressive soul, but it was still mortal flesh. After only a short time on the Huangquan Road, his lips had already started to turn purple from the cold. At a close glance, he even seemed to be shivering slightly, but there was no trace of weakness in his tone. "Don't forget what you promised my master when you insisted on sending Kunlun-jun's soul into the Reincarnation Cycle."

"Oh?" Shen Wei finally spoke. "I merely glimpsed him from afar. When he passed by, I avoided him. Even if you have no faith in my character and fear that I'll go back on my word, do you not believe in the sage Shennong's golden contract?"

His voice now sounded as courteous and mild as usual, but Zhao Yunlan was used to detecting the subtleties in other people's tones. Those few words held unmistakable disrespect and mockery.

"Then what's happening with the Great Seal?" Zhao Yunlan's "father" demanded. "Why would the Great Houtu Seal come loose?"

"The original Great Fuxi Seal lasted only a few hundred years before the Pillars of the Sky fell and broke it, after which it was repaired. Ever since Nüwa descended, the Great Houtu Seal has remained for thousands of years. Truthfully, it's held up longer than expected," Shen Wei said icily. "Even dripping water can wear through rock eventually. The Great Seal is weakening because its time has come to an end. Preventing that is beyond anyone's power, including mine."

"The Great Houtu Seal was created with Nüwa's life and is filled with Kunlun-jun's care and hard work. Of course I wasn't implying you'd do something to it that you shouldn't, but what if it were to truly collapse? What will you do then?"

"Yes," Shen Wei replied lightly. "What *do* I plan on doing? I'm an utter fool, but I finally understand what the ancient sages used to say: 'If one doesn't die, doesn't perish, then one cannot become a god.' But when I stop and think about it, I was never a god respected and worshipped by all."

"Don't you even entertain the notion that on the day the Great Seal collapses, you'll no longer be bound by Shennong's contract. If my son—"

The sentence broke off unnaturally, like speakers malfunctioning halfway through a movie. Zhao Yunlan's "father" opened and closed his mouth, but there was no sound.

Even with Shen Wei's face hidden by black mist, Zhao Yunlan could feel that he was smiling. Leisurely, Shen Wei said, "Your son? You've really gotten into your role, haven't you? Do you think your 'son' would accept you as his father if he knew you gave up being a carefree immortal to descend to the Mortal Realm and possess a human who just happened to be his father? Do you suppose he'd see you as friend or foe?"

There was a gurgling in the silenced man's throat. He clutched at his own neck, eyes bulging, but he couldn't make a sound.

Entirely unbothered, Shen Wei watched for a bit. Finally, he gave a light laugh and waved. It was as if Zhao Yunlan's "dad" had been punched. He stumbled back a couple of steps, barely managing to stay upright. "You..."

Shen Wei gathered up his long sleeves. With a slight nod, he said, "Please watch your words. Some things are better left unspoken, even if it's something everyone knows, don't you think? The ancient sage Shennong was well respected. I too respect him greatly, of course.

But respect only goes so far. If he still walked this earth, he and I would always be in opposition; we would never come to peace under the same sky. I never took the Three Sovereigns themselves seriously, much less Shennong's treasured mortar. You haven't yet cultivated to Shennong's level of power, have you?"

As the man stood trembling from head to toe, Shen Wei mildly continued, "I'd rather not do anything crass. I'm willing to stand here and speak calmly with you, with the hope that you can learn to conduct yourself properly from now on. Don't overreach or meddle in too much. If there's nothing else, I won't be sending you off."

Without another glance, Shen Wei turned and walked into the Wangchuan River, heading deeper into the Huangquan.

Zhao Yunlan was all but paralyzed with shock. Why had Shen Wei and Shennong refused to come to an accord under the same sky...?

No wonder Shennong's medicine mortar had fled without a word of explanation that day—he'd been too afraid to speak in Shen Wei's presence! How could Zhao Yunlan's delicate, scholarly, easily bullied lover also turn out to be a terrorist who'd put a gag order on Zhao Yunlan's fake dad?

And also...what was Shennong's golden "contract"?

If Shennong had been the one to borrow Zhao Yunlan's left soul fire...if the past that Zhao Yunlan had seen in the Great Sealing Rock was true...then how had his soul fire come to end up with the gui?

If the memories in the Great Divine Tree were really Shennong's invention, what was he trying to hide?

Zhao Yunlan's "dad" was approaching, so Zhao Yunlan hastily scrambled up the tree and hid between the lush leaves and branches. He only peered out once the man had disappeared into the distance.

He then descended back down the Huangquan, thinking hard

as he stared in the direction Shen Wei had gone. Somehow, he still doubted that this was real. He was starting to get used to being lied to; at the rate things were going, he was going to become paranoid and suspect that *everything* was a lie.

A light bulb suddenly went off in Zhao Yunlan's head. Remembering that *Record of Ancient Secrets* was rolled up in his breast pocket, he quickly took it and opened it...only to find the book blank. Its cover and pages were all empty. Not a single word of text remained.

Zhao Yunlan's gaze dropped. Eleven years ago—2002—just so *happened* to be the legendary Renwu year he'd heard so much about.

If what he'd just seen was real, then what if he headed to the general store at the end of Ghost City and bought *Record of Ancient Secrets*? Would that be the copy that would appear at 4 Bright Avenue in eleven years?

CHAPTER 11

THAT DAMN BOOK—what if he *didn't* go buy it? What if he just dumped this roll of blank pages into the waters of the Wangchuan?

Zhao Yunlan acted on the thought the moment it entered his mind, flinging the blank paper into the Wangchuan River. It landed with a splash and slowly began to sink. He stood there waiting for a good, long while, but no one came to fine him for littering.

If everything he had experienced here was what had really happened in the past, then if he didn't go buy *Record of Ancient Secrets*, the Special Investigations Department wouldn't have a copy of it in eleven years' time. He wouldn't be able to learn the secrets that had enabled him to deduce what had happened after Nüwa created humans and became Houtu. It was possible that, just to be safe, he wouldn't have even gone up Kunlun Mountain, in which case the Merit Brush could've ended up anywhere. He wouldn't have seen what he'd seen inside the Great Divine Tree, and none of what came after would've happened. As a result, he might not have plunged into the Huangquan, and even if he *did* happen to make his way here somehow, he wouldn't know that Shennong's mortar was occupying his father's body. In that case, he might just go home and visit his mother, not caring in the slightest why his father had stepped out. Of course, *that* would mean he wouldn't flag a taxi to follow his dad...

Taken all together, it would mean he wouldn't be here now on the Huangquan Road, pondering the stupid question of whether or not he should go buy that book...because that book wouldn't even exist.

According to the famous grandfather paradox, this would be impossible unless he'd entered a parallel universe, as good old Einstein had said. In other words, if he made a different choice and disturbed time and history, he'd find himself in a completely different parallel world.

Unless...

Stopping his pacing, Zhao Yunlan closed his eyes. The only thing he could hear was the murmuring of the Wangchuan; the fathomless Netherworld seemed as silent as an abyss. He found himself suddenly thinking of what he'd heard in the Great Houtu Seal—words that had come from Kunlun-jun's own mouth. "What we call 'fate' isn't some divine constraint. It's a single moment when you're confronted with tens of thousands of possibilities. In that instant, you can ascend to the Heavens or descend into the earth, but in the end, there's only one path you'll inevitably choose."

Zhao Yunlan's breathing gradually slowed. He knew perfectly well where his thoughts were trying to go. He desperately wanted to know if Shen Wei and the mortar possessing his father's body had truly met behind his back eleven years ago, if the conversation he'd overheard between them had really happened, if there truly was a contract between Shen Wei and Shennong that he didn't know about, and if there was another side to Shen Wei, one completely different from his righteous, gentlemanly appearance.

And on top of all that... Did Shen Wei really not know that the Netherworld had been using him all this time? If he knew, how could he not care? Or did he have something else planned...?

Half a minute later, Zhao Yunlan slipped a Leaf of Illusion into his mouth to block his own living scent and strode off toward Ghost City.

The little owner of the general store still looked only seven or eight years old, and she didn't seem at all surprised to see him. Even when Zhao Yunlan asked specifically for *Record of Ancient Secrets*, she merely quoted the price in spirit money before bringing out the giant account book and asking him to write down his name. When he obliged, there was a white flash, and the word "Guardian" appeared before his name, along with the date.

This time, no one in Ghost City noticed that one of the living was walking among them. Zhao Yunlan escaped successfully and headed straight home with his new acquisition. As stealthily as possible, he flipped over the fence and crawled through the window into his own bedroom.

The Zhao Yunlan and Daqing of eleven years ago weren't there. There was only a computer and a pile of random university English final study guides on the desk. On one page, someone had commented "dog shit" in a distinctive chicken-scratch scrawl. Zhao Yunlan couldn't help touching a light finger to those inelegant words, smiling in spite of himself. It felt like looking in a mirror and seeing his own reflection from back when he was still in his edgy teenage phase.

He turned away and lifted the baseboard of his bed, revealing the space where he'd once hidden all sorts of books about folk legends, myths, and the occult, along with cinnabar, yellow paper, and other tools. To keep this new addition to his collection from standing out, he treated it the same way all the other books had been. He grabbed a stack of old wall calendars from the drawer, tore out a page from the middle, and deftly wrapped the cover of *Record of Ancient Secrets*.

On this new snow-white cover, he began writing in small print, *"Nüwa created humans, repaired the sky..."*

He intended to write "Nüwa created humans, repaired the sky, and then turned into Houtu. Fuxi used the yin and yang Bagua to create the Great Seal. Shennong sacrificed his godly status, turned into a human, and tasted every herbal medicine. Gonggong and the divine dragon struck down Buzhou in anger"—a rough summary of everything in the book that would be useful to him in the future. But he'd only written a few words when there was a noise from the hallway.

Quickly dropping the book, Zhao Yunlan closed the baseboard compartment, clumsy enough in his hurry that he nearly caught his hand in it.

The person in the hallway had sharp ears. There was a knock, and then his mother's voice, as it had sounded eleven years ago, called out to him, "Little asshole, you home? What are you doing, making so much noise?"

Zhao Yunlan's throat bobbed, but he didn't dare answer. The next knock was harder. "Zhao Yunlan?"

All Zhao Yunlan could do was pitch his voice higher and let out his best attempt at a meow.

"The cat?" his mother muttered. "But it only comes home after dark. Why's it back so early today? Is it pregnant? I said ages ago that we should've gotten it spayed."

Zhao Yunlan kept his mouth shut, relieved to have fooled his mom. He exhaled and was about to finish writing on the book when he heard a car outside. He carefully pulled the curtain aside and glanced out to find that his dual-personality father was back.

He was a tough nut—harder to fool than his mother. Making a split-second decision, Zhao Yunlan stuffed the book into his messy library of eleven years ago and nimbly jumped out the window. He landed silently on the grass and looped around in the opposite direction from the approaching car. He'd successfully broken into and escaped from his own house.

From there, he cut through the residential compound and reached the main road, only to be at a loss for where to go next.

Then the ground shook violently beneath him—an earthquake? But no, everyone he could see looked perfectly calm, and the buildings all sat in place, steady as fortresses. Not a single speck of debris fell. As Zhao Yunlan concluded that it was only *his* world that was spinning, his surroundings melted away, and the ground vanished beneath his feet.

He looked up again and found himself back on that empty white path, standing before the old man he suspected of being Shennong.

Grabbing the old man's collar, Zhao Yunlan demanded, "Tell me what's—"

The old man finally spoke, cutting him off. In a strange accent, he said, "Do you know what 'death' is?"

Zhao Yunlan's brows knit tightly together. Seconds passed as he met the old man's gaze, and then he tentatively offered a textbook answer. "Death is the cessation of a body's vital signs?"

"Then what are the ethereal and corporeal souls?" rasped the old man. "What are the six paths of reincarnation?"

He quickly regrouped and gave a philosophical explanation. "Then death is the end of one life and the beginning of another."

The old man smiled and continued questioning him. "What, then, are the gui? What is the Place of Great Disrespect?"

Zhao Yunlan's patience ran out. "All right, what would *you* say it is?"

A blinding light suddenly burst from the old man's eyes, so bright that it was briefly frightening. He grabbed Zhao Yunlan's arm, holding on so tightly that his fingers seemed on the verge of tearing right through the flesh. "Did you forget? In truth, Kunlun, death is—"

He spoke like some doomed extra in a TV show—the kind who sobbed interminably and choked out a single clue but didn't manage to actually name the murderer before finally dying. This particular old man, however, was cut off and cut cleanly in half right before Zhao Yunlan's eyes. The blade that killed him descended with overwhelming power, slicing him in two as one might split a melon. When the blade, wrapped in a bitter cold energy, struck snowy ground, a trench nearly a meter deep was left in its wake; the ground itself trembled from the blow.

The dead man was somehow still on his feet, his bisected face forever frozen in that expression of indescribable fervor.

Zhao Yunlan instinctively stepped to the side to avoid the meter-high spray of blood. Throat working hard, he slowly looked up at Shen Wei.

"Are you all right? Hurry and come with me." Shen Wei reached out as he spoke, only to see Zhao Yunlan's pupils constrict minutely. He looked down at his own hand, as bloodied as a butcher's. Withdrawing it uneasily, he roughly wiped it on his cloak, but no amount of wiping made it feel clean. He made no further attempt to touch Zhao Yunlan; instead, he tucked both hands into his sleeves, as if to avoid contaminating him. Voice tight with restraint, he said, "You vanished in front of me just now. I..."

Zhao Yunlan finally snapped out of it. He strode over and seized Shen Wei's hand. Shen Wei shuddered violently and tried to pull away, but Zhao Yunlan only held on tighter.

"You're Shen Wei from eleven years later? Quick, how many drunken trysts have we had?" he asked.

Any possible answer seemed like a waste of breath. Rather than reply, Shen Wei reached out again, this time ripping the water dragon pearl from Zhao Yunlan's wrist. In his hand, the pearl acted like cold water hitting a hot pan: there was a sizzle and a plume of black smoke as it transformed into a scale. Zhao Yunlan's eyes widened. He moved to take a closer look, but Shen Wei flipped his hand over and the scale disappeared.

"Wait—wasn't that the water dragon pearl?" Zhao Yunlan asked. "What was that just now? It looked like it came from some kind of reptile, not a fish. Was it from a snake?"

"You kept it on your person without even knowing what it was." Shen Wei's voice betrayed an abominable mood. "Not to mention, it...it came from someone else's body. Doesn't that strike you as unclean?"

Zhao Yunlan looked at him, baffled.

Shen Wei, fully aware that his jealous anger was unreasonable, could only hold Zhao Yunlan's gaze for a few moments. Unable to take it anymore, he turned away. A huge hole appeared behind him, as though the air had been ripped open. He pushed Zhao Yunlan's head down and shoved him into it.

A cascade of light flowed before Zhao Yunlan's eyes, accompanied by the sense of being surrounded by a vast amount of water. Forgetting that he could not, in fact, breathe underwater, he didn't manage to hold his breath in time. *Shit!* he screamed silently, bracing himself to choke. But the instant his body touched the water, hands turned his head, and a soft tongue gently pushed his lips apart. Air filled his lungs.

With Zhao Yunlan in tow, Shen Wei swam upward at tremendous speed. Every time Zhao Yunlan began to run out of air, Shen Wei would pass him another breath. It took no more than four or five breaths before they broke the water's surface. Zhao Yunlan thought about how long it had taken him to dive down, how he had nearly fallen asleep in the process; he now knew what it meant to be as swift as the wind.

Shen Wei picked him up and set him in a ferry, not sparing a single glance for the trembling ferryman cowering in the corner. He tilted Zhao Yunlan's chin up. "The living must not drink the Wangchuan waters. Did you choke? How do you feel?"

Zhao Yunlan wiped his face and reflected carefully on what seemed to have been an extraordinarily short journey. "I feel like I was riding a torpedo."

When Shen Wei let go of him, Zhao Yunlan fell back heavily, nearly capsizing the ferry. His legs were still a bit weak, perhaps because he'd just come up out of the water. There was a splash beside them as the faceless ferryman finally leaped into the water, sheer terror getting the better of him.

Startled, Shen Wei hurriedly reached for Zhao Yunlan's arm. "What's wrong?"

But even with Shen Wei's help, Zhao Yunlan didn't get up. So much time in the Wangchuan waters had left his hands pale and puffy, too soft and weak to exert any force. One hand nearly slid out of Shen Wei's grasp. He had been under the Huangquan for too long. His eyelids closed heavily as he pillowed his head against the side of the boat. "I'm dizzy," he moaned, through lips drained of color.

"I'm taking you back immediately." Shen Wei tried to help him up, but Zhao Yunlan, either because he didn't want to cooperate or because he truly had no energy left, kept slipping back down. Shen Wei made a valiant attempt to carry him in his arms...but Zhao Yunlan was no girl with a pliable body. He was a man around Shen Wei's height, making him difficult to carry. It was easier when he was simply unconscious, but at this moment, Zhao Yunlan clung to consciousness just enough that he kept squirming out of discomfort. Shen Wei came perilously close to losing his grip on him entirely. Ultimately, he had no choice but to carry Zhao Yunlan on his back.

"Don't forget the coat," Zhao Yunlan mumbled next to his ear.

"Coat? What coat?"

Just then, a little ferry ghost emerged from the water and dragged another ferry over. This one held a carefully folded coat, not an edge out of place. Shen Wei hesitated, but what could he do but bring it along?

Once Shen Wei had carried Zhao Yunlan all the way home on his back, he laid him down gently on the bed. He took a step toward the bathroom to start running a hot bath, only for Zhao Yunlan, who'd seemed to be at death's door, to spring up as though he'd just received a shot of adrenaline. He shoved Shen Wei down on the bed. "Where do you think you're going?"

Belatedly, Shen Wei realized he'd been duped. "So you're fine?"

Zhao Yunlan's eyes curved with silent laughter. "I'm not fine. It's very serious. My wife ran away from home." He sighed. "Babe, stop running off. You're so gullible; what if you get trafficked?"

Shen Wei was practically fuming with rage. He pushed Zhao Yunlan away, unsure how to even begin to express his fury. Finally, he fell back on cursing. "You're full of shit!"

Wreathed in smiles, Zhao Yunlan pulled Shen Wei's coat over and hugged it to his chest like a throw pillow. He rolled all over the bed, still smiling, and then, right in front of Shen Wei, he buried his face in the coat and inhaled deeply. "Aiyou, you're swearing. It's lovely! Do it again."

To Shen Wei's mind, he was clearly behaving like a pervert. Shen Wei reached out to grab his own coat. "Give me that!"

But Zhao Yunlan, a champion at rolling around in bed, continued to do so almost maniacally. Still clinging to the coat, he said, in a sleazy voice, "No. If I give it back, what am I supposed to jack off to?"

Shen Wei, both embarrassed and angry, had no answer. Whatever thought had flashed into his mind turned his cheeks scarlet.

Zhao Yunlan looked up and said, very seriously, "You look like you really want to murder your husband."

Kneeling on the bed, Shen Wei threw himself forward and caught a corner of the coat. He started to pull, and Zhao Yunlan continued to roll...right off the edge of the bed. To no one's surprise, he hit the floor with a thump.

After a moment—with the bed between them and each of them holding a corner of the coat—they both broke out into laughter.

Zhao Yunlan finally sat up, clinging to the edge of the bed. "Hey, I want to ask you something."

Shen Wei lowered his eyes and looked at him.

As if they were having an idle conversation, Zhao Yunlan asked, "Is the Great Houtu Seal about to kick the bucket? What're you planning to do?" Shen Wei stared, caught by surprise, and Zhao Yunlan continued, "Are you hoping that I'll stay with you, then die with you?"

On top of the bedding, Shen Wei's hand curled into a tight fist. But Zhao Yunlan's smile was pure and true, without a hint of shadow or deceit.

"Actually, I kind of get it now." Zhao Yunlan's soft voice struck Shen Wei's ears like a thunderclap. "The 'death' Shennong keeps mentioning is 'Chaos,' right? You didn't let him finish, but I could tell."

As he spoke, he climbed up onto the bed and went to Shen Wei, gathering him close. Shen Wei was completely rigid in his arms.

Still soft, Zhao Yunlan said, "You've never asked me for anything; I don't even know how to suck up to you. But the truth is, if there's anything you really want, you could just *tell* me, and as long as I have it... So why lie to me?"

Shen Wei didn't make a sound. Zhao Yunlan slowly lowered his head, touching and lifting Shen Wei's chin. To Shen Wei's eyes, his gaze seemed tinged with helplessness and desolation.

"Look at me," Zhao Yunlan said. "I want you to personally tell me each and every single thing you did. I don't want to waste my brain cells on wild guesses. Shen Wei, I care for you. I don't want to second-guess you. Sometimes overthinking things can damage a relationship, but I'd rather not learn the truth from someone else. I've already shifted my boundaries for you time and again, and demeaned myself just as often, but if you keep doing this..." Zhao Yunlan paused before continuing, voice steady, "I'll really be angry with you."

Zhao Yunlan's expression was calm. There was no sign of his usual bursts of temper in his voice, nor any trace of aggression. His lowered eyes held none of their usual sparkle. For a second, his face was that of the high and mighty Mountain God of the Great Wild in Shen Wei's memory, as if Kunlun had returned.

Utter terror boiled up in Shen Wei's heart. From the moment of his birth, he had looked at the world with disdain, with no comprehension of fear. But at this moment, he was wracked with it.

He knows, Shen Wei thought. *Despite all my machinations, he found out.*

At the pinnacle of his fear, there was an instant in which the King of the Gui was gripped with the temptation to follow his natural instincts and slaughter the person before him. He could solve this problem the way the rest of his kind would: simply and violently.

Then, once Shen Wei had consumed every last morsel, they would be one in flesh and blood. Nothing would remain in all the world that could threaten him so; no longer could anything make him tremble at the possibility of losing the one he loved.

But Shen Wei was no longer the young King of the Gui from thousands of years ago, whose open heart had been a blank slate. Ruthlessly, cruelly, he had crushed his own instincts and nature underfoot, contorting himself into the kind of gentle, righteous person Kunlun-jun had once described.

Restraint had long since been carved into his very bones.

Shen Wei's face, pale to begin with, looked more and more as if it were made from snow. Not a hint of color touched his cheeks. An unspeakable chill bloomed in his heart, like a clear, silent stream. It was unaggressive, but in an instant, it had spread throughout his body. By the time Shen Wei came back to himself, his limbs were numb.

But Zhao Yunlan waited for him with endless patience—as if he had reserved every drop of patience he had in this life for Shen Wei.

Zhao Yunlan sank his fingers into Shen Wei's hair, carefully combing through it. For some time, he couldn't have said what he was feeling. His fingers curled unconsciously around the soft locks, suddenly remembering that day when Shen Wei's long hair had spilled all over his bed.

Such unparalleled elegance. It might've been a lifetime ago.

His mind wandered for a while longer. His heart was a melting pot of emotion, impossible to settle. Rationally, he knew he was dealing with a grave matter, but he was too lazy to think too hard about it. Perhaps sometimes, when faced with a dilemma, one might wish for time to stop, freeing them from the need to move forward or look back. Then they could stay in the same spot, deluding themselves.

But all the clocks of the world kept ticking. Time stopped for no one.

Zhao Yunlan closed his eyes, then opened them again. He moved the desk chair, placing it in front of Shen Wei, and dragged the coffee table between the two of them. Then he went into the kitchen and unearthed a dusty tea set from the depths of his cupboard. This man, who ate the type of instant noodles that came in bowls just so he could avoid doing dishes, actually spent twenty minutes washing the tea set—every last piece of it, clumsily yet meticulously, as if he needed to busy himself with something to calm down.

Washing done, he placed the solid wood tea tray on the coffee table, set the water to boil in the small kettle, and got out a tin of tea from under the coffee table. "Is Iron Goddess okay?" he asked.

Shen Wei could not have cared less whether the tin held Iron Goddess or Mud Bodhisattva. He just kept staring at Zhao Yunlan, following with his eyes as Zhao Yunlan went to the kitchen and washed every cup. It seemed as though looking away, even for a single moment, might cause Zhao Yunlan to vanish from his sight.

Not having received an answer, Zhao Yunlan silently warmed the cups with hot water, rinsed the tea leaves, and placed the first cup of tea before Shen Wei.

Steam and the tea's delicate fragrance filled the air, but alas, no one was in the mood to appreciate it. Shen Wei reflexively accepted the tiny cup, which held no more than a mouthful; his hand trembled so hard that half of its scant contents spilled. He looked down only when he felt the burn. Forcing his hand steady, he sat stiffly for a long time before finally raising the cup to his lips. He tossed it back as if it were his last drink before going to his death. "How did you find out?" he asked hoarsely.

"The memories in the Great Divine Tree were intricately made—*very* intricately." Zhao Yunlan cocked his head, as though listening to the sound of the water boiling. "They carefully strung together nearly everything I knew at the time and got my feelings all stirred up. But there were also enough flaws that, after I calmed down, I immediately knew something was wrong."

Shen Wei's face was empty. When he was expressionless, his composed brows were beautiful to the point of seeming other-worldly—breathtaking enough to steal one's soul.

"I should've realized ages ago that it would be stupid for someone to try misleading me by planting fake memories in the Great Divine Tree. It would've been stupid for *anyone* because you were with me at the time. If I got suspicious about anything, I would've asked you about it, and if your answers didn't match what I'd seen in the tree, obviously you're who I'd believe.

"By extension, you're the only person who could've planted the fake memories," Zhao Yunlan continued softly. "You listened to what I said when I tried to trick Ghost Face on the peak of Kunlun Mountain earlier on, and from that, you deduced what I already knew. Right?"

After a brief silence, Shen Wei answered honestly with a small noise of affirmation. Things had gone far enough that attempting either shameless denial or a desperate cover-up would disgrace his status. The best choice now was to face the truth head-on.

Zhao Yunlan looked him straight in the eyes. "Fabricating so much in such a short amount of time just shows how capable you are. I can't believe Ghost Face has the audacity to call himself your twin. I don't think you two are remotely similar, other than in looks. Your intellect alone is worlds beyond his."

Shen Wei simply maintained his upright posture, as though meditating.

"Naturally, when I began to realize that there was something fishy about the memories in the Great Divine Tree, my first suspect was Shennong. People who could tamper with the tree were few and far between, and in your story, you made sure to shine a spotlight on Shennong as a special character. Later, speaking with Shennong's mouth, you deliberately said all that stuff about time, life, and death. Was it because you guessed that as soon as Shennong's mortar noticed something, he would come out and try to use that to remind me?" Zhao Yunlan laughed bitterly. "And he did exactly that. You even got that right. You're capable *and* your luck is decent."

"Yes," Shen Wei admitted, after an even longer silence.

"I treasure you so much," Zhao Yunlan said. "I really... In all my life, I've never had feelings like this for anyone." His expression twisted for just a second as he spoke, as if slipping out of his control. But he reined it in in a heartbeat, as though it had been a trick of the light. "I didn't want to doubt you. Even as I was doing my best to get to the bottom of those exquisitely crafted, sketchy memories, as I was trying to guess who was deliberately misleading me, I never even considered that it might be you."

Shen Wei's expression was so stoic that it looked as if he might ascend at any moment, but the veins on the back of his hand suddenly stood out.

"The second time I felt like something was wrong was in front of the Great Sealing Rock." Zhao Yunlan lowered his voice. "Most of the memories inside were of times we had spent together. Nüwa only appeared for a moment to say a few vague words. They were very interesting words—carefully crafted to hint at the tragedy that unfolded back then, and that the tragedy happened because of Shennong."

Zhao Yunlan exhaled lightly before continuing. "But this time, your luck wasn't as good, because then I bumped into Ghost Face.

Unknowing, he said something to me: 'all of Nüwa's memories are contained within.' How could those few words be *all* of Nüwa's memories? I was enough of a mess at that moment that I didn't realize the implications. I even asked what my left soul fire had to do with Shennong. And Ghost Face's reaction to *that* seemed to suggest that I was missing something I should've known. He laughed out loud about it, but you interrupted before he could say anything else. Now that I think about it, he probably realized that you'd even tampered with the memories within the Great Sealing Rock—although I'm guessing that this time, you weren't making stuff up. You just cherry-picked the truth."

By now, it was nearly dusk, but they didn't turn on the lights. As it got steadily darker, Shen Wei blended into the dimness like some emotionless god in a temple.

"But I *still* subconsciously discounted you as a suspect, even though my instincts had already pointed me in the right direction. Naive of me, huh?" Zhao Yunlan sighed. "And then, while I was carrying all those suspicions about Shennong, I met that old man— that *was* Shennong, right?"

"No. Shennong is long dead." Shen Wei finally spoke. "That's just an apparition he left behind."

"No wonder he could smile so joyfully even while being split from head to toe," Zhao Yunlan marveled, reaching a hand out toward Shen Wei. "The water dragon pearl—that scale, I mean—can I have it back now?"

Shen Wei brought out the scale that had been the water dragon pearl and placed it next to the tea tray.

Zhao Yunlan picked it up with two fingers, studying it closely as he turned it over. "It looks like a snake scale. Is it from Fuxi or Nüwa?"

"Nüwa," Shen Wei said.

"Nüwa's scale! No wonder the Snake Tribe worshipped it as something sacred. It took me back to eleven years ago, to where I followed Shennong's mortar down to the Huangquan Road, and where I saw you. You and the mortar in my dad's body had a whole conversation, and it sounded like you two really didn't get along. I thought you were behaving like someone I didn't know at all. I didn't want to believe any of it was real, but I felt like it had to be. So I went to buy a book in Ghost City—the same one I tried to find the source of a few days ago, the one the shopkeeper at that general store told me I had purchased myself eleven years ago. And, as I expected, that book's existence proves that everything I saw was real."

Shen Wei looked up at him.

"The book's called *Record of Ancient Secrets*. I'd read it before going to the peak of Kunlun Mountain. If it weren't for that book, I might've never gone up the mountain." Zhao Yunlan began speaking more slowly. All of a sudden, he was itching for a smoke.

He fell silent and tapped his lighter gently on the table. A tiny flame shot up. The moment he lit the cigarette, the sound of its paper burning seemed unusually loud.

"I had the book on me at the time, but when the water dragon pearl transported me back eleven years, the book was suddenly nothing but empty pages because another copy already existed in that time—the exact same one." He paused. "Right, I still haven't asked—how did you bring me back, anyway?"

"The Soul-Executing Blade can cut through anything." Shen Wei extended a finger and gently tapped Zhao Yunlan between the brows. Reflected in Shen Wei's eyes, Zhao Yunlan saw a golden light flash on his own forehead. "Your soul bears my mark. Given enough time, I can always find you. That...*Record of Ancient Secrets*, what happened to it?"

"I threw the copy I had on me into the Wangchuan of eleven years ago," Zhao Yunlan said. "On the one hand, Shennong was reminding me to be careful of you; on the other, he told me something. Not whatever he wanted to say at the end there, but what he'd been hinting at the moment the water dragon pearl took me away. He'd been hinting at the word 'cycle.'"

When Shen Wei said nothing, Zhao Yunlan continued. "So I bought the book. Many years later, I discovered it. Reading it put certain suspicions in my mind. When I tried to find its origin, I found out that *I'd* been the buyer, after which I was sent back eleven years, which was when I really bought that book. It's a cycle where the beginning is the end.

"But having left that cycle, *Record of Ancient Secrets* disappeared. It's stuck in there forever. The people on this huge globe can never reach the edge. The paths winding around a fixed circle are endless. In the cycle of reincarnation, one lives to die, and dies only to live again. There is no real difference between life and death, so there is no true 'death,' and that also corresponds to Fuxi's concept of the Bagua."

Shen Wei suddenly dropped his head, unable to keep from laughing at himself. "You don't need to say any more. I understand."

Zhao Yunlan turned aside and blew a smoke ring.

"By that point, you already knew that Shennong couldn't have been the one to plant the crudely constructed fake memories in the Great Divine Tree. The primordial gods truly were as powerful as one would expect. They knew what happened five thousand years before and what would happen five thousand years later. Back when he left behind his shadow, Nüwa's scale, and the dictated *Record of Ancient Secrets*, he'd already predicted everything that would happen here and now. Each link connects perfectly to the next; the end is an echo of the beginning. Such is the work of the head of the Three Sovereigns," Shen Wei murmured. "I truly cannot compare."

Zhao Yunlan squinted within the white smoke. Picking up the teapot, he poured another cup for Shen Wei. "No, you're just different people with different points of view. The 'me' in the Great Divine Tree—the one who raised the banner in revolt, the one whose heart was choked with all that grief, anger, and rebellion—none of those emotions were mine. They were yours, weren't they?"

Without thinking, Shen Wei picked up the little zisha cup, brought it to his nose, and sniffed. Whatever he managed to glean from the scent only made him laugh helplessly. "It's a shame I wasn't born earlier and missed out on that Great Battle of Gods and Demons."

Zhao Yunlan lifted the kettle and added hot water to the teapot. "So after telling all those lies and sending me on such a wild-goose chase, can you finally tell me the truth now?"

Quietly, Shen Wei asked, "Do you really want to hear it?"

Zhao Yunlan gave him a long, hard look. "Nothing that comes from your lips, whatever it might be, could ever make me hate you."

G UO CHANGCHENG'S PHONE wouldn't stop vibrating. The number on the call display wasn't just unfamiliar—it was *weird*. It didn't look like it belonged to a cell phone or a proper landline, and there were a lot of inauspicious fours[8] in the first few digits. It struck Guo Changcheng as probably being a telemarketer. The serious things his colleagues were discussing were mostly over his head, but he still wanted them to see that he was doing his best to understand, so he ignored the phone and let it keep vibrating away.

Even after the conversation had been going on for a while, the team hadn't reached any conclusions, but Chu Shuzhi made a fuss over Fourth Uncle's water dragon pearl. Chu Shuzhi spent most of his time in graves, and he walked the path of necromancy; he didn't exactly have a sunny disposition. He was occasionally a little dark, and what was more, he was a genuine conspiracy theorist.

"Your fourth uncle definitely knows more than he's letting on," Chu Shuzhi said decisively. "Why else would he try to take you away at a time like this, and at the same time tell you to give the water dragon pearl to Director Zhao?"

Zhu Hong's brow creased, and she crossed her arms in front of her chest. Everyone else, humans and ghosts alike, went silent.

---

8   Four (四, sì), which sounds like "death" (死, sǐ), is an unlucky number.

Then lao-Li, who worked at the gatehouse during the day, suddenly spoke up. "Actually, I... I have some information." Everyone turned toward him, and he gave an embarrassed smile, seeming a bit ill at ease from the sudden attention. "I'm just an old bachelor. I don't have much to do after work, but I like to go to Antiques Street and play xiangqi and drink tea with some old pals. The other day, I heard a chess buddy mention that in the last few days, the snakes he worshipped at home to protect the house had all left. They wouldn't even eat any of his offerings. Apparently, it's happening in other households too. It seems like the Snake tribe wants to completely vacate the city."

Zhu Hong went very still. "That... My uncle didn't tell me that."

"It's not just the Snake tribe," Daqing said. "Think about it. Spring's almost here, but do you see so much as the shadow of a crow around? Those Crow tribe bastards—the second there's even a whiff of trouble, they flee faster than rats." On the word "rats," Daqing unmistakably wrinkled his nose in an expression of extreme contempt; to a cat, perhaps the word "rat" could apply to everything worthy of contempt.

"My fourth uncle, he..." Zhu Hong paused, the furrow in her brow deepening. Fourth Uncle had raised her. In her heart, there was basically nothing Fourth Uncle couldn't do. She had never seen him struggle in any situation. It seemed like as long as the Snake tribe had him, the sky would never come crashing down.

She understood that he probably hadn't mentioned anything to her because he was afraid her feelings for Zhao Yunlan ran too deep. If everything was fine, perhaps she would've simply left, having realized that she had no chance with Zhao Yunlan. But now that she knew he was in danger, how could she possibly just leave with her tribe?

But...how serious must the situation be for Fourth Uncle to be relocating the entire tribe?

Everyone in the office felt as if they were lost in a heavy fog; of them all, only Daqing had a faint gut feeling. From the Netherworld's abnormal behavior to that strange book from eleven years earlier, everything seemed to vaguely point back to the events of the primordial past—that sky-toppling, earth-shattering era when the gods fell to nothing.

Zhao Yunlan's style had always been to work smarter, not harder. He had a remarkable gift for gathering people together but wilted the moment anything required him to actually work. That loafer bossed the less lazy around; honestly, he'd try to order around anyone he could. Sometimes, when he felt too lazy to even read a subordinate's investigation report, he'd park his ass in his chair and make them read the report aloud.

And yet whatever Zhao Yunlan was facing at this very moment—or rather, what the Soul-Guarding Order was facing—he was keeping it all close to his chest rather than asking his subordinates to investigate a few details here and there. He most likely knew that even if his team did get involved, they'd be nothing but cannon fodder. He wanted to carry this burden himself.

The black cat, understanding Zhao Yunlan's intentions, found an excuse to interrupt everyone's wild guessing. "Xiao-Guo, your phone's about to explode from all that vibrating! Aren't your hands numb? Answer the call." Addressing everyone else, he continued, "How about this? This kind of speculation isn't going to get us anywhere. Day shift, go home and rest. As for the night shift, Sangzan and Wang Zheng will head to Director Zhao's place together and see if he's back. If he hasn't returned before sunrise, I'll go back down the Huangquan Road to look for him. And if that doesn't work... Well, there's no shame in asking the Netherworld for help once in a while."

Having said all that, Daqing leaped onto the table. With the serious air of a deputy director, he issued one more order. "Zhu Hong, give Lin Jing a call in a bit. Ask him whether he's on the train yet and when exactly he'll be back."

"Oh, okay," Zhu Hong responded, then reached out to pet his fur and scratch his chin. Daqing instantly went from an overbearing, aggressive King of Beasts to a lazy kitten. Comfortable and relaxed from the scritches, he leaned on his front paws and started purring.

There were a few suppressed snorts from the onlookers. Daqing's head snapped up, and he swatted Zhu Hong's hand away with his claws. "What impudence! Men and women mustn't openly touch in broad daylight! I'm male! Show some respect!"

Off to the side, lao-Li subconsciously rubbed the bone ring on his finger. Kissing up a little, he said, "Daqing, you've been so busy all day. Would you like some dried fish? I fried some yesterday at home…"

Daqing tried to act disinterested, but his pricked-up ears betrayed him. Eventually, he extended a paw and permitted lao-Li to tote him away, with the attitude of an empress dowager waited on by a servant.

Guo Changcheng finally picked up the call that had been harassing him so persistently. Cheap, domestically made phones were very loud; the voice yelling from the other end of the line was audible from two steps away. Whoever it was had a thick, heavy accent and spoke with nearly gravity-defying speed. Guo Changcheng listened politely until the person finished, then weakly said, "I'm sorry, I didn't catch that… Could you repeat it…slower?"

There were a few seconds of silence, followed by a sudden heart-wrenching sob from the other end.

It might've just been the garbage quality of Guo Changcheng's phone, but there was something unique about the sobbing. It spread like waves from the phone through the entire office. Chu Shuzhi, about to pack up and leave, abruptly turned back. He snatched Guo Changcheng's phone, switched it to speaker, and set it on the desk.

Guo Changcheng froze up. Chu Shuzhi raised a finger to his lips and kept listening carefully, then grabbed a pen from the holder and wrote on a sticky note: *"That's a ghost crying."*

Goosebumps erupted all over Guo Changcheng's body.

Chu Shuzhi whispered quickly, "Tell her to stop crying. Ask what's wrong."

Guo Changcheng did his best to calm the caller down, and after a long time, the crying eased as the person tried her best to speak through the tears. In accented Mandarin, she said, "Guo-laoshi, do you still remember me? Three years ago, when you were teaching here, you visited my home. My daughter's name is Cui Xiuyun. I served you a bowl of vegetable tofu."

This time, Guo Changcheng finally understood what was being said. After a brief moment, it came back to him. "Ah! Of course I remember! Hello, Cui Xiuyun's mom!"

She started sobbing again. "Xiuyun disappeared."

The young girl he'd met three years before would've been fifteen or sixteen by now—not really young enough to be considered a lost child. Guo Changcheng asked, "How could a girl her age disappear? She didn't run off into the mountain to play by herself, did she?"

Fascinated, Chu Shuzhi looked at him. It struck him that when Guo Changcheng spoke to people in need, he spoke more naturally, and his words flowed more smoothly.

The woman on the line kept breaking into tears again as soon as she got anxious, and once she started crying, she went back to speaking in dialect. Communicating with her was like a chicken talking to a duck. Guo Changcheng was dripping with sweat before he finally grasped the situation.

The girl's father made some money working out of town, and he'd bought her a cell phone. It wasn't a good, imported brand, but by local standards it was still considered quite fancy. The sheltered girl quickly lost herself in her new smartphone and learned to go online, where she made a few uncouth friends. One such friend had made the long trip to meet her and said they could take her to Dragon City and find her a job. It hadn't taken much to trick the foolish girl and lure her away. The only thing she'd left for her family was a note.

"Ask if she can leave and come to Dragon City," Chu Shuzhi instructed.

Guo Changcheng did as he was told, and the woman became a bit evasive. "I... I can't leave the village," she said. "I... I'm a bit sick..."

Chu Shuzhi understood. If she was unable to leave her place of death, this was a low-level earthbound spirit.

Guo Changcheng tried again. "Is there anyone else at home?"

"Just an old granny... Guo-laoshi, please, you're the only one I know in Dragon City. Please help me out. Help me find her. My girl is so young. She doesn't know anything about the world..."

Dragon City was massive, crammed full of people and cars. Finding a single person was like looking for a needle in a haystack, and who even knew what the girl might look like now, after three years—three years during which puberty had struck, even. It was entirely possible that Guo Changcheng wouldn't recognize her even if she was right in front of him.

Chu Shuzhi shook his head and wrote, *"Don't agree to it."*

The living should never casually agree to a ghost's request. Superstitions about it abounded. If you took on the task and were unable to follow through, you'd only bring trouble on yourself.

But by the time Chu Shuzhi finished writing, Guo Changcheng had already responded. "Of course, Xiuyun's mom. Don't worry. I promise to find her and bring her back!"

The tip of Chu Shuzhi's pen dragged across the paper, leaving a long mark. But just as he was about to scold Guo Changcheng and say how disappointed he was, Guo Changcheng glowed white with his merits—and they seemed to change color. For just an instant, a flame-like orange flash passed across his entire body.

Shocked, Chu Shuzhi grabbed Guo Changcheng's shoulder. Guo Changcheng hung up the phone and gave him a confused look.

"N-nothing. I must've been mistaken," Chu Shuzhi mumbled. Having reconsidered the situation, he set his bag back down. "How do you plan to find her? I'll help you."

Right around then, Wang Zheng and Sangzan, the two ghosts who had been sent to Zhao Yunlan's apartment, arrived. They knocked politely, but when there was no sound from inside, Wang Zheng led Sangzan right through the door. There were no lights on, but the coffee table had been moved. Both the chair and bed seemed to have been sat on, and the fire was still on for the kettle, which had nearly boiled dry. There was no one to be seen.

Sangzan leaned over and examined the abandoned tea tray, turning off the stove without needing to be told how. "They tame back, then loft again," he concluded. "The poo of them loft before dork."

Setting out tea indicated a long discussion. What had they talked about...?

At dusk, after Zhao Yunlan had said those words to Shen Wei—words almost as solemn as a vow—Shen Wei just gazed at him for a while, as though drowning in Zhao Yunlan's eyes. Finally, softly, he agreed. "All right."

But then he only stared into the curling white steam rising from the teapot. There was something faintly lost about his expression. As he started reflecting on his tens of thousands of years of memories, the weight of his great age seemed to settle on his shoulders.

"I... I don't know where to start," Shen Wei said at last. He exhaled lightly and held out a hand to Zhao Yunlan. With a sad smile, he said, "Why don't you see for yourself?"

Zhao Yunlan thought he had every reason to keep his guard up around Shen Wei, but before his brain could catch up, he took the proffered hand. Shen Wei's grip closed hard on his hand, yanking Zhao Yunlan toward him. It made Zhao Yunlan feel like they were about to crash into each other; he instinctively made a grab for the bed frame to stop his own momentum, but his fingers passed right through it, as if nothing were there.

In the next moment, he seemed to fall into something. He stumbled, but gentle hands caught hold of him.

Zhao Yunlan opened his eyes wide, but he couldn't see anything at all. He could only clutch the hands that were steadying him. "Shen Wei?" Shen Wei made a quiet, wordless sound of acknowledgment.

Despite the absolute darkness, there was nothing tranquil about their surroundings. There was a sound like howling, shrieking wind, but Zhao Yunlan couldn't feel even the faintest breath of moving air. He fell silent and listened intently. It somehow sounded like both a wail and a roar. It rose and fell, sometimes nearby and sometimes distant. Eventually, Zhao Yunlan couldn't resist asking, "What *is* that?"

Shen Wei's grip tightened on his hands. "Wait a second."

Before the sound of his words faded, the entire world suddenly brightened. There came the far-off, agonized cry of a dragon. The ground started to shake. Next, a ball of fire like the sun itself fell from the sky. Its heat was scorching. The shift from extreme darkness to extreme brightness made Zhao Yunlan's eyes burn with tears, but he endured the pain of it, refusing to close them.

He felt rather as though he was seeing the creation of the world.

When the tremendous fire struck, it splintered into innumerable shards. The sparks reflecting off the ground looked like flakes of gold, creating the sense that one was stepping on the Milky Way. The staggeringly beautiful display of light and colors was enough to steal the breath from their lungs.

Then, from beneath the fragments of flames, countless hands reached up, as if sprouting from the mud. Slowly, beings emerged, adjusting their shapes as they grew to roughly the height of a man and climbed out of the muck.

They had no creator. Their life came solely from the mud and silt.

No one taught them how to live or how to procreate. Their stumbling became walking and then running as they learned to move across the vast ground that was strewn with shattered light. And then, out of pure instinct, they learned to kill and consume one another.

These were the gui, born in the crack between light and darkness.

Where the ball of flame had initially landed, a huge fire burned. The mud beneath it swelled, gradually forming into a large flower bud. The bud grew larger and larger as the fire atop it dwindled, and finally, the last of the flame was completely swallowed by the "bud" of mud. All at once, every one of the gui—the running, slaughtering, feeding gui—stopped what they were doing and looked in that direction.

There was a sudden crack, and then a clattering as the "flower bud" shattered open into several petals, like ceramic shattering in the kiln.

Two pitch-black figures stretched out from within. The nearest gui was inexorably drawn toward them and consumed before it could even struggle. The figures fed and fed, and the more gui they consumed, the more clearly defined they became. Heads, necks, torsos, limbs, facial features, and even hair gradually took shape.

The mud Nüwa had flicked so casually, the gui born from mud... It seemed as though all things born from the mud were being driven by some unexplainable force, moving in the same direction as they grew—exactly the same as the sages and gods.

Or perhaps it was that the gods and sages, born from the earth and the sky, had come into existence in the same way.

"That was my soul fire that just fell, right?" Zhao Yunlan asked. "And...that's you and Ghost Face growing from the flower?"

"Yes, that's us. At the time, you were protecting the wu and the yao, as Chiyou had charged you." Right by his ear, Shen Wei's voice was low and calm as he explained. "No one could have known that only a few dozen years after the first War of Gods and Demons, the Water God Gonggong and Emperor Zhuanxu would start the second War of Gods and Demons. The Water God was close with the Dragon tribe, so they formed an alliance with the yao. Then Houyi from the East found Fuxi's bow, gathered Chiyou's former subordinates, and ganged up with the wu. The wu, the yao, and the humans were all dragged into the war. The fighting couldn't be stopped.

"Order had yet to be established," Shen Wei continued. "It hadn't been long since Nüwa first created humans. She could only watch as they reproduced, wave after wave, and died, wave after wave. Before she turned into Houtu, the Netherworld didn't exist, so there were no such things as 'life,' 'death,' or 'reincarnation.' To those who lived in those days, death was death. As Shennong said, 'death' meant a return to the Chaos—returning to the empty Place of

Great Disrespect. Naturally, everyone feared death, especially those who died with resentment. They refused to close their eyes and go, so they were caught between life and death, their souls remaining forever in the world.

"During both Wars of Gods and Demons, the vast amount of blood spilled formed rivers. The souls that refused to leave hung in the air, endlessly wailing. They refused to let go or disappear. During the day, they suffered under the blistering sun. Some of them melted beneath it and returned to Chaos. Others hung on and were able to recover slightly during the night, only for the torture to resume the next day."

Shen Wei fell silent, gazing at the place of his birth. After a while, he continued, "That's when Nüwa knew that her act of creation wasn't worthy of merits. It was a sin. She gave humans resplendent but short lives, as weak as a spring flower. And after that short life, they had to experience all the suffering of the world: the pain of being burned by the sun, the pain of their restless souls having nowhere to go, and the pain of being pursued by death every day of life."

He glanced at Zhao Yunlan. "Some say that babies cry when they are born because they are one step closer to death. All of that is why Shennong, whose godhood was lost by then, had no choice but to borrow your soul fire. He wanted to use the Mountain God's soul to safeguard all the resentful spirits who had died from battle and lessen their suffering, that they might find peace sooner. That's why the wooden plaque you wound up leaving behind was called the 'Soul-Guarding Order.'"

The crack overhead grew and grew until it was large enough to reveal a sliver of the sky. Soft, faint moonlight filtered down. Out of nowhere, Zhao Yunlan was gripped by the feeling that Buzhou Mountain was about to fall completely.

Shen Wei resumed his explanation. "It just so happened that Shennong passed by Buzhou Mountain, carrying your soul fire that was meant to deliver all living things, just as Gonggong was riding the divine dragon straight for the mountain. The divine dragon's tail brushed against Shennong and knocked your soul fire from his hands. And then, coincidentally, it landed in the Place of Great Disrespect at the foot of Buzhou Mountain."

He paused, then gave a cold laugh. "Of course, it was you who told me all of this. I don't know how true it is. Perhaps it really was a coincidence, or perhaps Shennong did it deliberately. Who can say?"

Right then, Zhao Yunlan saw two figures land in the Place of Great Disrespect, which was now exposed to the Mortal Realm: Kunlun-jun and Shennong. After all, this was Shen Wei's memory. Everything was from his point of view.

Through Shen Wei's eyes, Zhao Yunlan watched as the handsome— beautiful—young Mountain God of the Great Wild peered around curiously. There was even some innocent childishness to his face.

Kunlun-jun seemed a bit lost as he stared at the ground, which seethed with monsters and devils. "What are these?" he asked.

"They are part of the natural order," Shennong replied.

S HENNONG GRABBED HOLD of Kunlun's wrist. His aged, murky eyes were fixed on the naive yet savage gui as he walked forward. He was already very old. Kunlun-jun could only lean slightly forward and carefully support him. The faintest shadow crossed Kunlun-jun's face when he looked down at Shennong. Old age meant Shennong was close to death.

Though Kunlun-jun had never experienced old age or death, he could smell the frightening scent of decay clinging to the old man.

"You heard my last discussion with Nüwa, I take it?" Shennong asked.

Kunlun-jun's brow wrinkled. "Who'd be interested in your debates? Just tell me what we're supposed to do now. I can't believe you're even mentioning Nüwa. If she knew you'd accidentally burned through the Great Fuxi Seal, you'd be lucky if she didn't try to hunt you down! And doing it with *my* soul fire means you're bringing trouble down on my head too."

"She wouldn't do that," said Shennong. There was a passive-aggressive note in the noise Kunlun-jun made in response. Then Shennong coughed, and even his cough sounded old. "Life and death are serious matters," he said. "All life fears death, and one shouldn't joke about it. But if you can jump out of the cycle of life and death, then you'll have no more need to fear."

"I'm standing right here and not jumping anywhere." Kunlun-jun's tone was haughty. "Nor do I need to be afraid. I think *you're* the one who should be frightened. But I should tell you that the Great Divine Tree has borne fruit. Only two fruits have ripened in the last century. I gave one to my furball and saved the other for you. It'll extend your life by another hundred years."

"Thank you, but I don't fear death." Shennong smiled. "Ah, little Kunlun, you don't understand. If one doesn't die, doesn't perish, then one cannot become a god. Perhaps once we're all dead, you'll understand."

Kunlun-jun rolled his eyes and glanced around, as if hoping to find something to stuff into Shennong's yammering mouth.

"There will be hope, though." As they were about to leave, Shennong took another long look at the gui, who carpeted the ground. "If life could spring forth from even this most barren of places, surely nothing remains impossible."

Kunlun-jun was steadying him as they crossed the uneven ground, but upon hearing this, he turned back to look at the two gui closest to them. One was holding the other's head and gnawing on it. The Mountain God of the Great Wild furrowed his brows again. "What kind of shitty life is this? I think you're just senile. You should be thinking about how you're going to explain all this to Nüwa."

With that, Kunlun-jun and Shennong left the Place of Great Disrespect.

Shen Wei, who'd watched in silence, tugged on Zhao Yunlan's hand. "Let's go." As they followed Kunlun-jun, Shen Wei said, "With your intellect, I imagine you already knew what Shennong was thinking back then. You just disagreed, thinking it was a wild fantasy."

Zhao Yunlan gathered his thoughts. "Okay, so...Shennong wanted to create the Reincarnation Cycle. That way, as long as souls still existed, they could enter the six paths of reincarnation, where life would become death and death would become life. That was what he meant about standing outside of life and death, right?"

Shen Wei gave a light laugh. "Shennong wanted to use the darkness beneath the Great Seal to separate out the yin and yang on the edge of true death, thereby creating the Reincarnation Cycle."

"But he obviously didn't succeed," Zhao Yunlan said. "If he had, Nüwa wouldn't have died for the Great Seal."

"Do you know why he failed?" Shen Wei stopped walking. A peculiar smile appeared on his face, and he continued before Zhao Yunlan could answer. "He couldn't create the Reincarnation Cycle because there is only emptiness in Chaos. The gui born from Chaos don't have souls."

Great evil. A soulless being...

"We are nothing but physical manifestations of Chaos—violence incarnate. From the lowest to the highest among us, from the cradle to the grave, all we can do is instinctively consume and plunder. The craving for the freshest flesh and blood drives us." For the first time, Shen Wei realized that he felt a kind of pleasure in saying it aloud. It was the kind of enjoyment someone might feel when squeezing their own wound or cutting into their own flesh with a knife. "And me...because you elevated me to divinity by force, I became an anomaly—neither human nor god, neither devil nor ghost. In all the world, I alone was entirely unlike anything else in existence."

Zhao Yunlan couldn't say anything.

Since the moment Zhao Yunlan had revealed that he knew Shen Wei was lying to him, Shen Wei had felt as if a lump of ice had sunk down into his heart. There it stayed, unable to go up or down; it had left him deeply chilled on top of his struggle to keep everything bottled up inside. But now, having said all that, he felt a miraculous sort of lightheartedness.

"We *are* Chaos," he said. "Chaos that can walk and move through the world. What Ghost Face said to you wasn't wrong either: death itself came to life thanks to a single flame and birthed us—these supposed 'living things' that are neither alive nor dead. What an interesting coincidence." Shen Wei's smile faded. He glanced over his shoulder at Zhao Yunlan, voice almost gentle. "But you—without the faintest regard for your own life, you had to come and provoke me. Do you know what you've lured in? Do you realize how dangerous this is?"

Zhao Yunlan slung an arm around him from behind. "C'mon, get to the point. Less of this bullshit."

Through the embrace, his body heat flowed into Shen Wei. It felt like the first sip of warm porridge after being frozen to the very bone. It was enough to make one tremble.

Shen Wei was silent for a while. Before he continued, he reached up and grasped Zhao Yunlan's hands in front of his chest. "Buzhou Mountain collapsed. The sky fell and the earth sank, thus unexpectedly ending the war between the humans, the yao, and the wu. The endless rain pouring from the hole in the sky washed over the resentful spirits floating in midair and struck the ground, from which nothing grew. And billions of gui climbed out of the abyss... all of which you must have seen in the Great Divine Tree.

"Actually, the day of my birth should've been the first time I saw you. But you were standing too far away, unwilling to take even a single step closer to me—as though I were something filthy. My eyes hadn't fully opened yet, so all I could see was the vague shadow of a green robe."

Shen Wei shut his eyes. Gently, longingly, he rubbed his cheek against Zhao Yunlan's hand. "But from birth, I was more ferocious than my brother. I had consumed more of our brethren than he had. At that point, I could already hear, and could vaguely understand, what you and Shennong were saying...so right from the beginning, I knew exactly what I was. Later, I searched the world for you, resisting the temptation of the flesh and blood of the living. I ate only the things that crawled out of the ground—other gui, which I felt were just as disgusting as I was.

"I searched for you because I desperately wanted to ask you what life is." When he said this, Shen Wei felt Zhao Yunlan's grip on him tighten. "But then when I finally met you at the edge of that grove, when you were about to climb up Penglai... As soon as I saw you, the words all died on my tongue."

"Why did I want to ascend Penglai at the time?" Zhao Yunlan asked hoarsely.

"Of the three great divine mountains of the Great Wild, Buzhou had already fallen, and Kunlun was the forbidden place of gods, closed to all mortals. That left Penglai as the only one that could shelter and protect the living beings on earth...but not all. There were too many of them. Of the humans, the wu, and the yao, the mountain could hold only two. The rest of them would have to wait for Nüwa to prepare the Stones of Many Hues and repair the sky. Their fate was up to the Heavens." Shen Wei suddenly stopped for a moment. "'Up to the Heavens.' I despise that phrase."

"Then wouldn't they start fighting each other?"

"Shennong originally thought that, as the Mountain God, you would be biased toward the wu and the yao, casting humans aside," Shen Wei said. "He wanted to personally lead Zhuanxu up the mountain to see you, but you surprised him. You set up an array at the foot of Penglai Mountain. It was a simple altar holding Chiyou's head, right in the middle of the path up the mountain. The yao had always worshipped Chiyou as their ancestor, so they immediately knelt to pay their respects. And the humans, having had the Yellow Emperor, Xuanyuan, at their helm, also worshipped Chiyou as a war god. Therefore, Zhuanxu had the humans stop and stand behind the yao with their heads lowered in respect. Only the wu ignored it completely. In their hurry to claim a spot on the mountain, they offered neither respect nor worship. They walked past Chiyou's head as if it wasn't there, and the moment they passed by, Chiyou's head vanished and the true path up the mountain materialized. The wu, having already gone past, were deceived by illusion and trapped in the abyss below the mountain."

That, then, was why the yao sang about the fall of Buzhou Mountain. That had been their chance to overtake the wu. They finally had a solid place on the land of the Great Wild, on equal footing with humans...even if it didn't last more than a few years.

"You took me with you, and we walked across the Great Wild, which was filled with wailing," Shen Wei said. "From Kunlun Mountain to the peach blossom grove, and from the grove to Penglai Mountain, I watched you save people, slaughter gui that were feeding upon humans, and get dragged into the war between the different races. We gui had always viewed each other as things to be consumed. We had no sentiment for our own kind. Back then, I didn't understand anything. I didn't understand what they were fighting about. I just thought it was wasteful that you killed without eating. And all the while, you became more and more silent.

"Come, let's go up the mountain." Shen Wei turned and wrapped an arm around Zhao Yunlan's waist. Lights blurred across Zhao Yunlan's vision, and an instant later, they arrived at the foot of Penglai Mountain. With one leap, Shen Wei took Zhao Yunlan up to the peak.

From that great height, no lightning could be seen. There was only the sky, so dark and heavy that it seemed about to fall. Layers of mist billowed off the ceaseless rain, carrying an indescribable stench.

There, at the peak, Zhao Yunlan saw Nüwa. She was alone among the clouds, long snake tail extended behind her. Below, Kunlun-jun and the young King of the Gui watched her from afar. At this point, Kunlun-jun looked nothing like he had when first visiting the Place of Great Disrespect with Shennong. He was skinnier now, making his already-pronounced features seem ever wearier. His gaze, however, was bright and resolute; his eyes were like burning torches on his gaunt visage.

Nüwa turned, worry written across her beautiful face. "Kunlun, what if Shennong was wrong?" she said. "What if we were all wrong?"

Kunlun-jun's hands were tucked into his sleeves. His sleeves and sash billowed wildly in the fierce wind. "If we're wrong, we're wrong," he said serenely. "In that case, we'll atone with our lives and die for the cause. Then, when the Great Wild once again gives rise to a stronger, more powerful person like Pangu, he will learn from our mistakes and finish what we couldn't."

Nüwa sighed, her brows relaxing. "You're right. Shennong was wrong once, and I hope he won't be wrong a second time, but...even if he was, we can no longer turn back. You've grown up so much, truly. It makes me feel that even after I die, I can safely entrust this piece of land to you."

The mere words of the primordial gods held power. No sooner had she spoken than Kunlun-jun felt the immense pressure crash down upon his shoulders. But he didn't move an inch. Not even the King of the Gui behind him noticed anything wrong.

Kunlun-jun extended a palm to catch the rain falling from the sky, carefully feeling the crushing weight of the heavy sky and earth pressing down on him.

"I recently came to understand something, actually," he said. "Humans are so weak and small. They can never be free of the three worms—greed, rage, and delusion. Their six senses are tainted. They're stupid and nearsighted, violent and drawn to conflict. Why were such great merits bestowed upon you for creating such useless things? Why do the Heavens keep choosing humans over and over?" Kunlun-jun squinted into the sea of rolling clouds in the distance and the Stones of Many Hues hidden among them. "Now I understand. Humans are what most resemble the Heavens, the Earth, and us."

"How so?" Nüwa asked.

"From the moment they're born, humans know that they will die. Each day brings them one step closer to death, whether they be heroes or cowards. Dozens of years vanish like smoke at a snap of the fingers, after which every single one meets the same end. It's as though they were born to die," Kunlun-jun said softly. "But look. Every day that they are alive, they struggle fiercely for warmth, food, power, riches, love, another day to live—anything you can think of. They escape from the jaws of death countless times only to perish in their final struggle, completely exhausted."

"I don't understand what you're saying." Two voices spoke as one, as the young king by Kunlun-jun's side and Shen Wei by Zhao Yunlan's side opened their mouths at the same moment. To Zhao Yunlan's ears, the youth's bright, clear voice and the man's richer, lower timbre formed a strange duet. He had the sudden sense that it was he himself standing there. He and Kunlun-jun bled together in his mind.

Fully formed words appeared on his tongue, leaving his mouth without his volition. His voice overlapped with Kunlun-jun's from thousands of years ago. "Sealing the gui away was indeed unjust, but when the wu were trapped and washed away by the flood, the sin of their destruction fell upon me. I bear the guilt, but my conscience is clear. If the Reincarnation Cycle and eternal life that Shennong spoke of can't be achieved—if we've failed, if we're wrong, if we've created an even greater disaster...then it was simply a failed attempt in our continued struggle. If we all die, new gods will still come. They'll be the next to struggle for eternal life, just like us—even though we know there's no such thing as eternity, much as how all humans will eventually die."

Kunlun-jun suddenly turned to look at the young King of the Gui behind him, and then his gaze swept past him. It seemed to come to rest on Zhao Yunlan, several millennia in the future. Even though he knew Kunlun couldn't see anything, Zhao Yunlan still felt as though he was looking back into his own eyes across the chasm of time.

"If 'death' is Chaos, then 'life' must be endless struggle." The corners of Kunlun's mouth turned up into something that was almost a smile. The ghost of dimples showed on his face. But if his smile was like that of a child, his eyes were those of an old man. "Nüwa, go ahead. With me here, you don't need to worry about anything you leave behind."

As he heard the entire conversation at last, Zhao Yunlan finally understood how Shen Wei had cherry-picked from such a compassionate, lamenting speech and given it a completely different flavor.

Nüwa gave Kunlun-jun a long look. The stones flashed, and a stream of brilliant, iridescent rocks flew into the sky, where they collided with the thick, heavy clouds. There came a great roar and an alarming explosion of thunder and lightning. All the humans and yao on the mountain bowed down and prostrated themselves at once.

The thunder continued for what seemed like ages, but finally it stopped. Several months passed before the sky cleared, but auspicious clouds eventually appeared, and the sun revealed itself once more, shining down on the wasted, scorched earth.

From her place in the sea of clouds above Penglai, Nüwa had disintegrated. Her three ethereal souls formed the new Great Seal, her body turned into Houtu, and her seven corporeal souls landed in the thousands of mountains and bodies of water. Thin blades of grass grew from the cracks in rocks, revealing the green of new birth.

At some point, Shennong, old and doddering, had climbed up to the peak. "I'm leaving too," he told Kunlun-jun. Then he fell to the ground, body turning rigid in death. His divine spirit, so long suppressed within a human body, whistled as it flew into the ground and became the Reincarnation Cycle. Something seemed to draw the souls that wandered in the air night and day, and they followed after him.

The earth gently quaked, steadied by the Mountain-River Awl. The Reincarnation Dial atop the Three-Life Rock began to spin, and the Merit Brush floated above the Ancient Merit Tree. As it rose out of the thousands of zhang of the Wangchuan's waters, every soul now had a record of their merits and sins.

"One last thing," Kunlun-jun said softly. The sky above him was suddenly covered in dark, heavy clouds. Lightning flashed, as though divine retribution was about to crash down upon them. "My soul fire set the Place of Great Disrespect alight. Its flame spurred the gui out of the mud, yet I left them to their own devices rather than caring for them. I decided all on my own whether the gui should live or die. It truly is a great sin. But there is one last thing I need to do."

As Zhao Yunlan watched, Kunlun-jun extracted his heart's blood and turned it into a wick while his body became a lamp. He suddenly felt like he had always known that these things had happened—not just from the Great Divine Tree or the Rock of the Great Seal but from living through them himself. It was as though he had briefly forgotten them and now remembered.

Thus was the Reincarnation Cycle created. Life and death became a circle, and life and death were no more.

Kunlun's primordial spirit left his body; the mighty mountain winds swept past the little King of the Gui, who was crying himself sick. Then they both went down to the Huangquan River to guard the gate of the Great Seal.

Zhao Yunlan turned to Shen Wei. "And then what happened? Why did you say Shennong was your sworn enemy?"

Shen Wei was slow to answer, looking in the direction that the despondent little King of the Gui had gone. Finally, he murmured, "Actually, I have great respect for Shennong. He was truly more like a god than you or Nüwa."

"Wait." Zhao Yunlan raised a hand to stop him, brow furrowing as he thought. "This is all your fault for not being honest with me. Your lies are all over the place, but there's a glimmer of truth in every direction. Trying to make sense of it is giving me a headache. Let me get this straight. When Nüwa created humans, Kunlun, my past life, was a little dumbass with zero filter who was barely out of diapers. I said there was something in the mud of creation, so Nüwa realized that humans had inherited the three worms—greed, wrath, and delusion—from the mud they were made from. Is that when Nüwa foresaw the inevitable Great War of Gods and Demons that would be brought about by humanity?"

Shen Wei nodded. "Yes."

"Later, Nüwa called Fuxi over. The two of them built the Great Fuxi Seal that suppressed the flames in the ground, and that's how the Place of Great Disrespect came to be," Zhao Yunlan continued. Then his tone changed. "Oh, right, I wanted to ask. Legend says the two of them were a couple. Is that true or false?"

"...True," Shen Wei answered.

"Wow, sometimes gossip gets it right! Okay, after the Fuxi Seal was created, everything was peaceful for a few short years, but the Great War of Gods and Demons happened anyway, which was the Yellow Emperor versus Chiyou. As they fought, Chiyou realized he was about to lose, so his spirit left his body and went to Kunlun Mountain to find Kunlun-jun. He begged Kunlun-jun to take care of his underlings—the wu and yao—but since Kunlun-jun was the type who's too lazy to rotate the ring of flatbreads around his neck to eat the next one, he didn't want to deal with that. Unfortunately, the god kneeling and kowtowing up the mountain every step of the way like he was worshiping heaven and earth was just a little too much, and also, Kunlun-jun had a stupid gluttonous cat that unknowingly licked some of Chiyou's blood. That meant Kunlun-jun had to come out and return the favor, and he finally agreed.

"By the way, that stupid troublemaker of a cat is Daqing, right? God-fucking-dammit! I always knew that damn fatty was going to fuck shit up for his father!"

"In the first Great War of Gods and Demons, Kunlun-jun was able to preserve both the wu and yao. He gave them a place to live and cultivate and looked after them for many generations. But the peace didn't last very long before the second War of Gods and Demons began. This time, it was an internal conflict between the Yellow and Flame Emperors. The Water God, Gonggong, and Zhuanxu, descendant of the Yellow Emperor, faced off against each other, while Houyi tried to take advantage of how chaotic everything was. The Three Realms descended into messy conflict, and the wu and yao were dragged into it once again. Since there were more humans, wu, and yao around this time than there had been before, more of them died, providing Shennong with more specimens. Shennong reached two conclusions: that death is Chaos, and that the souls who are not content with Chaos cannot find peace and are therefore in more pain. Humanity—Nüwa's creation—lived unhappy lives and died in pain, so Shennong and Nüwa discussed ways to break away from death forever. That's when Shennong thought of reincarnation."

There was an edge to Shen Wei's laugh. "Perhaps it was simply because he himself had become mortal and had to face a mortal life: short like a cicada, born in the spring and dying in the fall. Perhaps it was only because *he* was afraid of death."

Zhao Yunlan shook his head. "Later, in the name of 'soul-guarding,' Shennong asked for the soul fire from my left shoulder. But when he passed by Buzhou Mountain, he unfortunately got caught in the crossfire when Gonggong carried out the world's first suicide bombing, and he dropped the fire."

"I think he did it on purpose." Shen Wei scoffed. "He was just afraid of not being able to justify it to Nüwa, so he found an excuse. He wanted to set up reincarnation deep beneath the surface from the very beginning."

"Okay, you can let go of your grudge. He's already suffered retribution." Zhao Yunlan pulled out a cigarette and lit it, squatting down on the ground. Like a large monkey, he rested his arms on his knees and carelessly polluted the air at the top of the divine mountain.

"Then, after the accidental creation of the gui, Shennong realized you were missing something: you didn't have souls. Not only was it impossible to build the Reincarnation Cycle on top of you, but as soon as the Great Seal opened even a crack, you'd go to the surface and bring ruin upon all living things. The sky leaked and the earth sank, so the gods collectively brought the living up onto Penglai. The wu were abandoned because they forgot the hand that fed them while the humans and the yao survived. Nüwa repaired the sky and turned into the earth; Shennong's body died of old age as his spirit turned into the Reincarnation Cycle; Kunlun gave the blood of his heart to seal the Four Pillars and then finally gave up his divine form and sent his primordial spirit to keep watch over the Great Houtu Seal. I think I get it now."

Zhao Yunlan had been constantly busy before and after the New Year and hadn't had time for a haircut. His hair had gotten a little long, almost covering his ears. The mountain breeze blew the messy hair on his forehead over his nose bridge. Shen Wei bent down and brushed his hair back. Quietly, he asked, "What do you get?"

"You were so young then. Since I was watching over the Great Seal, there's no way I would've let you run off. Why did I give you Kunlun's divine tendon?" Zhao Yunlan grabbed Shen Wei's wrist and looked up. "It was because Shennong wanted to kill you, right? I wanted to save you, and that was all I could do. I was hoping that if one day I was gone, I could pass the power of ten thousand mountains on to you."

"This time you guessed wrong. He didn't want to kill me. He wanted to obliterate all the gui. Shennong couldn't believe that soulless beings could possibly exist in the world. Without a soul, how could one be considered alive? But since he was the one responsible for the gui's existence, he couldn't escape the blame. He wanted to 'fix' his mistake." Shen Wei began to tremble. "If you hadn't given me your tendon... If you hadn't... You wouldn't have left me so soon."

Zhao Yunlan chuckled. "It would've happened sooner or later."

"If I had a little more time, maybe—"

"The little beauty has grown up into a great beauty. What can you possibly do, even now?"

Shen Wei was speechless for a moment.

"Then what happened?" Zhao Yunlan asked.

"Then I confined your primordial spirit and went down to the Reincarnation Cycle to plead with my enemy, Shennong," Shen Wei said. "He was the only one I ever begged for anything... At that point, the Reincarnation Cycle already had its own order, and the Netherworld had just been established with its own set of rules. I begged him to let you into the Reincarnation Cycle like a mortal. That way, even though you would never remember me, you would still *exist*. But he wouldn't do it. He said primordial gods could not enter the cycle because it was his own primordial spirit that was supporting it. It could accept all sorts of souls—humans, yao, gods, demons—but it would not be able to hold the true Mountain God...unless he sealed all your divine powers himself and washed your souls completely clean, turning you into a mortal. If he did that, Shennong's own primordial spirit would fade away too...like exchanging one life for another. His life for yours."

"What did you agree to that made him do that?"

"I swore to protect the Great Houtu Seal forever. As long as I existed, the Seal would exist too. If the Seal broke, then I would meet my death along with the rest of the gui." Shen Wei's fingers were ice cold. "And...for all of eternity, I could never see you again. If I couldn't help myself, then I would drain your life force and you would die, your souls shattering into a million pieces."

Shen Wei suddenly shook off Zhao Yunlan's hand, reaching up to caress his face. Then he grabbed Zhao Yunlan's chin, forcing him to look up. Pausing after each word, he said, "I kept this promise for thousands of years. Now that the Great Seal is almost broken, I'm at the end of my road. I originally wanted to come and go quietly, but because of a simple coincidence—because of *you*—it was all for naught. From that night when you truly belonged to me... No, from that day when you told me, for the second time, that you wanted to give your heart to me, I... I could never let you go again.

"The greed in my heart is bottomless. My inner demons drove my actions. I deliberately placed fake memories in the Great Divine Tree to mislead you; I let you see me extracting my own heart's blood for you; I left you so that you would come down to the Huangquan River to find me, then led you to see the edited version of memories in the Great Houtu Seal...and all of it to make you feel too much guilt to ever leave me, to make you joyfully and wholeheartedly choose to die with me."

Shen Wei's hands grew colder and colder. The higher his emotions spiked, the tighter his fingers became. His grip on Zhao Yunlan's chin was painful.

"Even now, even after you have seen through every lie, I'm still forcing you." Shen Wei's voice was very, very low. "Will you choose to die with me and return to Chaos for all eternity? Or would you rather I strip away your memories of this life, so that you would never know or remember me, leaving not a single thread of connection between us?"

Since Zhao Yunlan was unwilling to be deceived, these two paths were finally laid out clearly before him.

"You're not allowed to think it over," Shen Wei said. "You must answer me now."

Gazing into Shen Wei's eyes, Zhao Yunlan took hold of Shen Wei's wrist. Abruptly, he asked, "How long will the Great Seal hold out? Will there be enough time for me to live out my tiny mortal life? Will I be able to care for my parents in their old age and send them off?"

Shen Wei didn't seem to comprehend. His face and lips were as pale as snow. The only hint of blood anywhere in his features seemed to be in the veins of his eyes. After a long time, his entire body swayed. As though waking from a dream, he grabbed Zhao Yunlan's shoulder. "What... What did you say? Explain yourself. What do you mean...?"

Zhao Yunlan reached out and gently stroked Shen Wei's hair. "Such a heavy heart, full of such heavy calculations..." He sighed. "You sure are hard to take care of. Come on, we're going home."

Wide-eyed, Shen Wei could only stare at him. Then he flung himself at Zhao Yunlan, pulling him close.

The world spun around him, and Zhao Yunlan had the feeling of familiar ground beneath his feet. There was a sharp sound, as though someone had landed wrong and accidentally knocked over one of the little teacups on the coffee table by the bed, splashing its remaining bit of water on the floor.

But no one cared.

Shen Wei roughly pressed Zhao Yunlan down on the bed, tearing at his clothes almost violently.

"Hey, wait!" Zhao Yunlan grabbed Shen Wei's hand. "I'm not drinking your blood."

"It's no worse than a mosquito bite to me."

"That's all well and good for you, but it's nowhere near the same to me." Zhao Yunlan pushed him off and tried to feel for the bedside light, but his arms were almost immediately pinned. Shen Wei's tongue flicked over his Adam's apple, and Zhao Yunlan panted quietly, unable to hold it in. "Stop messing around."

"Even if I dug out my entire heart, I won't die at once. I'd still survive longer than the Great Seal." Shen Wei's voice was terribly low. The scorching heat of his breath caressed Zhao Yunlan's collarbones with each word. "I did consider it at the time—would it be more effective to cut out my heart for you? But I was afraid you'd be too badly frightened, so I only let you see my blood being drawn."

After a silence, Zhao Yunlan said dryly, "Thanks so much for remembering that I'm a scaredy-cat."

Shen Wei leaned in closer, kissing the corner of Zhao Yunlan's lips. His tall, straight nose rubbed against Zhao Yunlan's face, and their fingers tangled together as he pressed their half-naked bodies closer. "None of that matters. Yunlan, with only a few decades left, let's spend our lives together like mortals, all right?"

In the final darkness before dawn, their eyes met. As if bewitched by Zhao Yunlan's gaze, Shen Wei dropped a tender kiss on his lips, gentle and lingering.

After coming back to himself, Zhao Yunlan reciprocated with even more enthusiasm. He reached under Shen Wei's clothes and slid his hands around Shen Wei's waist. "Spending our lives together is a nice thought, but I need to lay down some rules for my husband."

He tightened his grip on Shen Wei's waist, moving to push him to the side and flip them over...and nothing happened.

It was as if Shen Wei weighed thousands of kilograms, but Zhao Yunlan distinctly remembered picking him up before. Shen Wei definitely weighed the same as a normal human! Zhao Yunlan was perfectly capable of lifting him with his own two hands!

Didn't you just say you wanted to live like mortals? Do you really need to bully a mortal like this?!

GUO CHANGCHENG HAD ACCEPTED a ghost's request on impulse, but now he was anxiously pulling his hair. "But how are we going to find her?"

After scrolling through his phone for a while, he found a large group photo in which none of the faces were really in focus. Next, he spent five minutes thinking and finally came up with a simple, if rough, idea. "How about I crop the photo and post a missing person bulletin online and in the paper?"

"That would give the kidnapper plenty of time to sell her to a wholesaler and for them to resell her at retail," Chu Shuzhi said. "My advice? Go look for her at Walmart. It'd be faster."

Guo Changcheng gave him a completely lost look.

"Fine, fine, tell me her address," said Chu Shuzhi. "Let's figure out how she'd get from there to Dragon City."

Guo Changcheng rattled off the province and administrative region. "Of course she doesn't live in the city," he clarified. "She lives in Cui Village, under the jurisdiction of a middle-of-nowhere county. It's one of about a hundred villages in that county. To get to Dragon City... Um, she could walk to the county, then take the eight-hour bus from the mountain to the Administrative Center, then take a train..."

"The train's unlikely," Chu Shuzhi interrupted. "They'd need to check her ID for a train ride. And even if the kidnapper would actually choose the train, we don't even know if she's got an ID to begin with. She wouldn't exactly steal her household registry book and run off with it."

As he spoke, Chu Shuzhi turned his computer on and started checking online long-distance bus schedules, looking for buses that ran between the prefecture-level city Guo Changcheng had mentioned to Dragon City. He also looked up the route. "Almost all the buses from that direction take National Highway 220, and the trip takes about thirty hours. If that kid ran away yesterday, she'll probably be arriving in the city soon."

Guo Changcheng's eyes shone. "Right! Chu-ge, you're so smart! If we go wait at the highway exit, maybe we'll run into her."

Chu Shuzhi glanced at his wrist and saw that it was almost 11 p.m. How long would they have to wait? He thought to himself that there must be something wrong with Guo Changcheng; seeing how elated he was, Chu Shuzhi couldn't help but rain on his parade. "Human trafficking isn't our jurisdiction. Can't you just go home and sleep? You don't think before you speak! And now you've just casually agreed to a ghost's demands..."

Guo Changcheng picked up on the complaint in his tone. Caught off guard, he rubbed his sleeves uneasily. "Chu-ge, how about... How about you go home and rest? I can just drive over on my own. Thank you for your help. I never would've thought of the bus route thing myself."

It was all so annoyingly submissive that Chu Shuzhi's temper flared, and his expression darkened. Guo Changcheng's instincts told him that he'd done something wrong, so he immediately bent over to apologize. "And I'm sorry you had to help me carry stuff today! I really am. How... How about I treat you to dinner when you're free?"

With a *hmph*, Chu Shuzhi picked up his jacket and walked out. Guo Changcheng lagged behind, not saying anything. When Chu Shuzhi reached the door and saw that Guo Changcheng wasn't following, he glanced back. "What are you waiting for?" he demanded. "Aren't you the one who wanted to find her? Get your ass in gear!"

Guo Changcheng instantly blossomed from a frost-wilted eggplant to a freshly watered sunflower and eagerly ran after him. The duo drove Guo Changcheng's car to the highway exit to wait for a bus with a license plate from the girl's home province. If they saw one, they'd pull it over and conduct a search among the passengers.

They spent the entire night staking out the highway exit.

Lunar New Year was over, but spring hadn't yet made its way to Dragon City—or at least spring temperatures hadn't. In the mornings and evenings, it was still below freezing outside, and spending time out there would quickly turn someone to ice. Under the circumstances, Guo Changcheng and Chu Shuzhi had little choice but to stay huddled in the car.

Sitting in the vehicle quickly made Guo Changcheng sleepy. More than once, Chu Shuzhi saw his chin droop almost to his chest, but each time, Guo Changcheng would suddenly shake himself awake, briskly rub his face, and get out of the car to glance in both directions. Once he verified that no buses had passed by, he'd let out a sigh of relief, wrap his coat tighter around himself, and take a quick stroll around in the night wind, hoping to wake himself a little. He only returned to the car to warm up after his entire body felt numb.

Somehow, Chu Shuzhi didn't find it annoying to see him constantly getting in and out of the car. He just watched pensively.

In general, the Corpse King spent very little time focused on Guo Changcheng, so until now, he hadn't fully realized that something felt off. There was what Daqing had said: Guo Changcheng was quiet about his good deeds, never drawing attention or looking for any kind of reward, and as a result, his merits increased exponentially. But even given that, how old was Guo Changcheng? Barely twenty? And yet he was covered in more merits than you could see through. Collecting that many should've required saving the world seven or eight times.

At that moment, another long-distance bus approached. As soon as it was close enough to see its license plate, Guo Changcheng vaulted out of the car as if he'd been flooded with adrenaline. He grabbed his ID and stood in the middle of the road, waving his arms to stop the vehicle.

"Tch, so naive," Chu Shuzhi mumbled. Keeping an eye on Guo Changcheng's back, he called Daqing. "Hey, night cat, you're still up, right? If so, I have something to ask you."

Daqing was in the middle of a dream. In it, he was floating on the ocean, holding and munching happily on a huge whale that would surely be enough to keep him fed for six months or a year. But he'd only taken two bites when the leviathan suddenly launched itself out of the water, splashing him in the face with bitterly cold water.

Jolting awake, Daqing found that Sangzan was holding a chilly receiver to his face and beaming. "Cat slutterer, phone."

At this point, Sangzan was clearly aware that "slutterer" was a rude word. He'd completely stopped saying it ages ago...except with Daqing. Sangzan, the troublemaker, kept cheerfully saying it to the cat, and even managed to pronounce it more and more like "slut."

The "cat slutterer" looked up, extremely cross. He pressed his ear to the phone, only to hear Chu Shuzhi's voice. "Fuck off, old corpse," Daqing grumbled. "Are you looking to die?"

Chu Shuzhi wasn't about to let him get away with his bad habit of spewing insults every time he opened his mouth. "You fall asleep as soon as you finish eating. If you're not careful, you'll be in a new weight class by the end of the year. By then, not even a dog would be attracted to you, never mind a little female cat. Aren't you afraid of high cholesterol, high blood pressure, and diabetes, old man?"

The cat slutterer gouged his claws into the desk, leaving a row of marks. Sangzan watched calmly and then floated away, hugging his books to his chest.

"If you have something to discuss, hurry and spit it out. If you don't, I'm dismissing the court. Chu Shuzhi, what do you want in the middle of the night?"

"I just wanted to ask, have you ever seen orange merit?"

"Of course," Daqing huffed. "Red, orange, yellow, green, blue, indigo, and purple—I've seen all the colors of the rainbow. When you collect all seven, you can summon Shenron to perform the acrobatic trick of tying himself into a bow in midair."

"I'm being serious." Chu Shuzhi lowered his voice, glancing out at the parked bus. "Most of the time it's white, not orange, but then sometimes it flashes like flame, as if it's on fire..."

Daqing turned serious. "Fire? Where did you see this?"

"On Guo Changcheng."

"Impossible," Daqing said decisively. "I'm familiar with what you're talking about. That's no small amount of merit—it's huge. Do you know what great merits entail? You can't earn them no matter how many old ladies you help across the street or how much you donate to a few mountain-region schools. These days, all living beings' merits and sins are written in *The Book of Life and Death*, meaning they're all recorded by the Merit Brush, made from the Great Merit Tree. Great merits are on a completely different level. I've never seen it myself, but I've been told that back when Nüwa created humans, she appeared to be surrounded by fire. *Those* are great merits blessed by the Heavens."

Chu Shuzhi froze. Guo Changcheng was already getting off the bus. Even from this distance, he was clearly hanging his head in dejection—another dead end, most likely.

Lowering his voice, Chu Shuzhi quickly asked, "And you're *sure* xiao-Guo is human?"

"Mmph. Of course he's human," Daqing said. "Wang Zheng even has a copy of his ID."

"I want to find his proof of birth, the kind that says, 'x year x month x day, a live male infant was born'—the kind you get from a hospital," said Chu Shuzhi.

"Huh?" Daqing exclaimed. "Holy shit. Humans are such weirdos. They have something like that?!"

"Enough bullshit. I'm in the middle of something, so I have to go. Remember to look into it for me." Chu Shuzhi hung up just before Guo Changcheng got in the car.

He seemed a little wilted. Despite the answer being obvious, Chu Shuzhi asked, "No luck, huh?"

Guo Changcheng nodded in confirmation.

After a moment, Chu Shuzhi carefully said, "It's possible that I was wrong. Maybe they *would* take the train, or even wait there longer instead of heading here right away. Maybe we should go home for now?"

Staying up all night made Guo Changcheng's already slightly slow brain seem even more sluggish. He rubbed his face forcefully, then said in a very small voice, "Sorry, Chu-ge, how about... How about you take the car and head home? Once I've found her, I'll take a taxi home."

"What, are you planning to stand out here all night and freeze to death?" Chu Shuzhi gave it a moment's thought. "Don't worry. You made a promise to a ghost, but it's fine. I can handle an earthbound spirit with no cultivation."

Shaking his head resolutely, Guo Changcheng turned to get out of the car. The instant his back was facing Chu Shuzhi, Chu Shuzhi pulled his hand out of his pocket where he'd been hiding it and slapped a talisman onto the back of Guo Changcheng's neck. "What are you?" he snapped. "Why are you possessing this mortal?"

Guo Changcheng's limbs felt like they'd been filled with lead. He wanted to turn back and ask Chu Shuzhi what was going on, but his neck was completely stiff; no matter how he tried, he couldn't move it. His awareness seemed to float out of his body. From a peculiar third-person perspective, he found himself staring at his own laughably positioned body and Chu Shuzhi's serious expression.

Chu Shuzhi frowned, looking up at Guo Changcheng's soul where it floated in midair. That was a genuine mortal soul, and it corresponded perfectly to the body. There was nothing out of the ordinary. In other words, the soul he'd smacked out of the body with his talisman was truly Guo Changcheng himself.

"So you really are Guo Changcheng?"

Floating there, Guo Changcheng wanted to say, "Chu-ge, what are you doing?" But when he opened his mouth, it was as if he'd been muted... Or no, it was like he was in a vacuum where sounds couldn't travel. He had made a sound, but he could only hear his voice through his body. Once the sound left his mouth, it couldn't go anywhere.

Chu Shuzhi hesitated, then reached out and removed the talisman. Guo Changcheng felt a huge pressure as an extremely bony hand pressed right down on his soul. It was an awfully strange feeling; Guo Changcheng couldn't help shivering. Then the sensation of floating was suddenly gone, and his body seemed so heavy that it was almost unfamiliar.

Trembling, he looked over to meet Chu Shuzhi's scrutinizing gaze.

Guo Changcheng's reaction time was always a little slow, but by this point he understood that his soul had just left his body. According to his understanding, "soul leaving body" was no different from "death"—which to him meant that Chu Shuzhi had nearly killed him with a talisman. He cowered back against the car door. "Ch-Chu-ge... W-what's this about...?"

"Are you human?" Chu Shuzhi asked.

Guo Changcheng gaped at him, not at all sure if Chu Shuzhi was being literal or insulting.

Chu Shuzhi tried again. "Let me put it like this: Do you have memories of your parents?" Guo Changcheng nodded, and Chu Shuzhi said, "Apologies. I know about your family. I'm so sorry for your loss." There was no sincerity in his tone. "But I have to ask, were you born to those parents? Can you prove they were your birth parents?"

Emotional intelligence wasn't Chu Shuzhi's strength. That shortcoming specifically presented itself in the fact that, despite knowing how to talk to people, he chose not to. He thought that was cool, and besides, he was too lazy to make the effort. If this had been Zhao Yunlan he was dealing with, he would've had his ass whipped by now.

But Guo Changcheng was a coward. The question made him feel a little weird, but he didn't show any signs of anger or annoyance. He even considered it carefully before answering, "I look a lot like my uncle and grandpa did when they were younger. My grandpa has kind of high blood pressure, which my dad inherited, and now I'm starting to show early signs of it too. So I think they were my birth parents."

"Then were any of your ancestors cultivators?" Chu Shuzhi asked.

"Ancestors?" Guo Changcheng paused, confused. "My family doesn't keep a family tree. At most, I can go back four generations. Before the Republican era, they could've come from anywhere as refugees."

Even if Guo Changcheng did have some ancestor with special lineage, the last three generations were all mortals. At this point, it was obvious how diluted that blood would've become by now. But if what Chu Shuzhi was seeing wasn't something Guo Changcheng had inherited, then the only remaining explanation had to be who he'd been in a prior incarnation...but the Corpse King couldn't see anything unique about Guo Changcheng's soul.

Just then, the headlights of a bus swept across them. Guo Changcheng immediately forgot about his freakish out-of-body experience and grabbed Chu Shuzhi's arm. "Chu-ge, bus! Bus!"

Chu Shuzhi paused and set his questions aside for the moment. "Okay, go."

Guo Changcheng stumbled out of the car. The last bus that had passed by had been from the girl's province, but by some great coincidence, this one was too. Guo Changcheng waved to stop the bus, boarded, and showed the driver his ID. Then he recited his prepared lines about needing to inspect the passengers, much as though he were reporting the news.

Routine inspections happened occasionally during the holidays, so the driver took it in stride. He turned and yelled to the busload of passengers, voice ringing out like a bell. "Wake up! Wake up! Everyone, please cooperate with the inspection! He's checking your IDs!"

Chu Shuzhi had initially stayed back with the car, but for some reason, his heart skipped a beat at that moment. Many people who cultivated had something of a sixth sense. He got out of the car and walked over just in time to see a tiny, skinny girl of fifteen or sixteen get off the bus behind Guo Changcheng. She was dressed in a dirty tracksuit, and she held her head so low that her chin nearly touched her chest.

"This is her?" Chu Shuzhi asked.

Guo Changcheng nodded. "The person who took her is still in the—" But before he even finished speaking, there was a clang as someone jumped out of the bus.

In reality, there was no proof that the guy had kidnapped the girl. After all, she'd just been quietly riding the bus and had left with Guo Changcheng voluntarily. It might've been a guilty conscience that made the kidnapper make a break for it as soon as he heard the word "police."

But he didn't even make it a few steps before he suddenly tripped on something and fell randomly on his face. He got up and made another attempt to flee, only to hit the ground face-first again. When it happened for a third time, Chu Shuzhi, the "People's Police," finally strolled over and grabbed him by the collar. Cold metal clamped down on the man's wrists.

Of course, due to his unique work situation, the Corpse King had never actually used handcuffs before. Unfamiliarity with this particular aspect of the job meant it took him some time to successfully lock the cuffs.

Chu Shuzhi looked back just in time to see Guo Changcheng speaking to the young girl in soft, hushed tones, explaining that she shouldn't have run away from home by herself. Then Guo Changcheng called the number the girl's mother had used, completely forgetting that the woman was now a ghost. "Hello? Auntie? Don't worry, we found your child. We'll arrange for someone to bring her back tomorrow."

After that, he passed the phone to the girl as though it was the most natural thing in the world. "Your mom's out of her mind with worry! She called me in the middle of the night and asked me to find you. Here, speak to her."

The girl was going through her teenage rebellion stage. She'd recognized Guo Changcheng, but to her, he was just some teacher or playmate who'd taught her for a month during a summer break in middle school. Her current attitude toward him wasn't great to begin with—she seemed disobedient and disinterested and had probably ignored everything Guo Changcheng had said to her... until now.

At his last few words, she went utterly still. Then she looked up at him suddenly and, moving like a marionette, accepted the phone with shaking hands. "H-hello...?"

The person on the other end of the line was silent for a moment, but then, via electromagnetic waves, the familiar village dialect reached her ears despite the barrier of death. "Cui-er?" It really, truly was her late mother's familiar voice.

Tears immediately began to stream down the girl's face. "Mom—!"

Through the phone, her mother said, "Don't cry, Cui-er. Don't cry. Listen to Guo-laoshi and come home tomorrow. You've gone too far for Mom to keep up. When I can't see you, I get worried..."

There, at the entrance to the national highway entering Dragon City, a young girl in an old school uniform finally started to wail, piercing the vast, hazy night with a grief beyond words.

Chu Shuzhi wasn't good at dealing with these situations. He'd meant to just capture the kidnapper and go, but when he unintentionally glanced at Guo Changcheng again, he once more saw that thick, heavy glow of merit, gleaming like firelight.

This time, the "firelight" seemed even brighter. For an instant, Chu Shuzhi thought something on Guo Changcheng's body was burning. He rubbed his eyes firmly, and when he looked up again, the light was already gone.

CHAPTER 15

A S THE SUN PEEKED over the horizon, signaling that the little ghosts of 4 Bright Avenue were off work for the night, a worried Daqing made his way to Zhao Yunlan's place, plump body swaying as he ran. Upon arriving, he jumped onto the window ledge in the hallway and launched from there, pouncing fiercely at Zhao Yunlan's door. His forepaws pressed the doorbell with perfect precision.

Button pushed, Daqing turned into a squashed-flat pancake of a cat and slid down to the floor.

The doorbell rang.

When Zhao Yunlan was home alone, he sometimes played games with earphones in. To make sure he didn't miss it when someone was at the door, he'd chosen a particularly earth-shattering tone for the bell. At a single push of the button, the soul-stirring song "The Hottest Ethnic Trend" played in its entirety, loudly enough to be heard from outside.

But this time, even after the song had played for a while, there was still no answer. Were they still not back?

The black cat paced anxiously before the door and unconsciously started chasing his own tail, turning into a black tornado on the spot. Not about to give up, he decided to try again. He sprang. Just as his front paws latched onto the hallway window ledge and his back legs flailed in midair while he struggled to pull himself up, the door opened from within with a faint *click*. Startled, the cat lost his grip and slipped off.

He rolled where he landed, looking over with widened round eyes. Upon seeing who had answered the door, he lost his freshly regained balance. His paws slipped on the shiny floor, and his heavy jowls quivered from the fall. But then, very circumspect, Daqing sheathed his claws and sat up properly. Chest puffed out and stomach sucked in, he meowed lightly. "My lord."

With a flick of Shen Wei's fingers, the interminable doorbell went silent. Daqing couldn't help holding his neck up stiffly. He swallowed with great difficulty as his gaze happened to fall on Shen Wei's clothes—clothes that seemed far too familiar. That shirt was unmistakably Zhao Yunlan's!

Zhao Yunlan, the absolute weirdo, liked to wear his sleeves rolled up. He always made a point of asking the laundry workers to iron his shirts with the sleeves that way so they would fold neatly. All unwilling, Daqing found a whole sequence of events popping into his head. First, the two would have taken off their clothes, and then... And then...

The black cat lowered his large round head, trying to get his mind out of the gutter.

"What is it?" Shen Wei asked.

"Oh, I... I just came to see if Director Zhao was back or not. We've all been so worried about him since he jumped into the Huangquan."

Very quietly, Shen Wei said, "He's back, but he's resting now. If you need something, you can leave a message with me. I'll pass it on once he wakes up."

Daqing immediately grasped the situation and began to make a quick retreat. "Ah... I won't disturb you any longer, then. There's nothing important. Please just remind our boss to write up our work schedule for the new year and our department's New Year speech. That's all. Don't let me keep you. I'll be on my way."

"Wait a moment." Shen Wei's smile seemed a little embarrassed. Politely, he said, "I have a favor to ask of you..."

Daqing, sensible cat that he was, darted back at once. Head raised high, he said, "Just say the word."

Ten minutes later, the door to the breakfast shop downstairs was pushed open by an outrageously fat cat. The cat's face was much too round, and his eyes were almost completely obscured by the fat, giving him a somewhat vicious look. A waitress nearly tripped over him and started yelling at once. "Hey! How did this cat get in?! Get it out! Hurry and get it out!"

The large black cat raised his head, leveling a contemptuous gaze at her. Then he jumped right onto the service counter and knocked on it with his front paw. Astonished, the cashier behind the counter watched as the cat spat out a piece of paper. The cashier shakily opened the note, which turned out to read, in very tidy handwriting, *"Half a liter of soy milk, one basket of steamed buns, three fried dough sticks. Please put them in a sturdy bag. You'll find the money on the cat's neck. Please take what's needed and put any change back in the same spot. Thank you."*

The cashier looked up, trying to locate the cat's neck by sight. The cat rolled his eyes and lifted his head, revealing a collar beneath his double chin. The cashier found 30 yuan tucked in there, hidden under the plush fur.

"Everyone, look at this!" The cashier's voice rang out loudly. "This is incredible! Even cats know how to buy things now!"

Daqing, who had to endure being stared at by everyone present, was so mortified and furious that he yearned for death. These stupid humans!

The sound of the door woke Zhao Yunlan. He opened his eyes. "Who...?"

"Your cat." Shen Wei closed the door. "He came to see you. I asked him to go buy breakfast. Sleep a little more."

As he spoke, he gently nudged Zhao Yunlan back into the blankets before tucking his hands back in. Then he bent down and kissed Zhao Yunlan on the forehead; with a fingertip, he smoothed out Zhao Yunlan's brow, furrowed from awakening. Once Zhao Yunlan's breathing was even again, Shen Wei walked to the window and looked at the plants on the windowsill, which were half-dead with neglect. He cupped a pot with his hands, and milky white light radiated from his palms.

The sickly plant responded like the earth tasting sweet rain after a long drought. It quickly became fresh and radiant. Its stem straightened. Soon it stood, graceful and elegant once more.

Shen Wei quietly washed the spray bottle, then carefully misted the leaves.

Most residents of Dragon City were already back at work, and the streets were once again busy at rush hour. Through a crack in the curtains, Shen Wei glanced outside. At the far reaches of the busy world, even further than the sky's edge, a wisp of black drifted up from beneath the ground. But one glance was all Shen Wei spared it. Seeming to turn a blind eye, he looked away again and carried on with his task. The Great Seal was about to break, but there was an unfamiliar tranquility in his heart. His entire body felt lazy and relaxed, as though even dying at that very moment would be no big deal.

It was nearly noon by the time Zhao Yunlan woke again, this time awakened by the fragrance of the hot soy milk that Shen Wei had placed by his bedside. He stared at the creamy drink for a while, then suddenly rolled over and sat up. "What did you say this morning? You told Daqing to do what?"

Shen Wei, wearing glasses while he looked through a handwritten lesson plan, calmly said, "Buy breakfast."

Dumbfounded, Zhao Yunlan just sat there with an indescribable expression, possibly imagining Daqing wandering the streets as the protagonist of *Nobody's Boy: Daqing*. Then he gave his head a firm shake. He rested his elbows on his knees, pressed his hands to his forehead, and started to laugh.

"What's so funny?" asked Shen Wei.

"I was just thinking how I've done well in the romance department for half my life, only to be defeated and sealed beneath your mountain, like the Monkey King sealed under Wuzhi Mountain. You're so powerful, Comrade Shen Wei."

Zhao Yunlan's voice dripped with sarcasm, but at whose expense was unclear. Either way, Shen Wei pretended not to notice. He kept smiling virtuously.

"Aiyou, babe. Please, I'm begging you. Drop the act or at least stop acting like that. My mind can't take it." Shen Wei's innocent facade was making Zhao Yunlan's teeth ache. He went to the bathroom to wash up, one hand pressed to his waist, and slammed the door behind him.

Afterward, as Zhao Yunlan was about to take out his frustrations on his food, Zhu Hong called.

"Hello? Director Zhao? Daqing says you're back. Are you all right?"

"Mnh." Zhao Yunlan bit into half a fried dough stick. "What's up?"

"Remember how Lin Jing went to check on that life-borrowing case? His ticket back was for last night. I was going to call him after midnight and see where he was, but his phone was out of range. At first I thought it was because the signal's so bad in the mountains from all the tunnels there, but that train arrived on time hours ago and he still hasn't shown up. And when I called just now, I still got a 'not in service area' message."

Zhao Yunlan's chewing slowed. "And he hasn't contacted the office?"

"No."

"Hm..." Zhao Yunlan's brow creased.

The Special Investigations Department's rules stated that, whether they were just evaluating a case or officially starting an investigation, no one worked alone. There always had to be at least two people. Daqing counted, of course. On the rare occasion when special circumstances forced someone to act solo, they had to contact the office at least twice a day to keep everyone advised of their location.

Lin Jing might not be the most reliable when it came to the little things, but he very rarely messed up anything important. He wouldn't spontaneously decide to go AWOL.

Zhao Yunlan hung up and took his own stab at calling Lin Jing but unsurprisingly got the same message. He pulled out a Soul-Guarding Order and wrote Lin Jing's name on it with a chopstick dipped in soy milk.

The Soul-Guarding Order acted like a compass. First it wavered from left to right, then settled on one direction. A fine thread of red extended slowly from Lin Jing's name, but the further it reached, the duller the color grew. By the time it reached under the table, the line had turned nearly gray.

Then it snapped.

Shen Wei, who had been immersed in his lesson plan, looked up and exchanged a glance with Zhao Yunlan. Then he bent down and picked up the broken string. At that light touch, it crumbled away like ash.

Shen Wei withdrew his hand and carefully sniffed his fingertip. "He should be fine for now. There's no scent of death or anything foul. He's still alive. You just can't reach him. Try not to worry."

Zhao Yunlan stuffed the last bun into his mouth without really tasting it, then took a notebook from beneath the table. For all that his life was a completely chaotic, slovenly mess, he was surprisingly precise when it came to time management. There were three labeled dividers sticking out from the notebook: "urgent," "important," and "complete."

The last section was blank. He'd clearly been in a state of terrible worry and busyness recently, with no time for anything unimportant.

The handwriting resembled that of a surgeon who was jumping up and down while riding on a rocket, but with great difficulty Shen Wei was able to read the only two items written under "urgent." The first item was his own name, and the second read "Figure out how to evict that stupid bowl from Dad's body." The "important" category held a lengthy list of work-related things, some long and some short. Zhao Yunlan added a check mark next to "Shen Wei," then added a third item under "urgent": "Find Lin Jing ASAP."

Zhao Yunlan kept writing as he spoke. "Lin Jing is actually descended from Bodhidharma.[9] To be honest, none of my other people have a better or cleaner pedigree. Plus, he looks powerful and formidable enough that even his selfies work to ward off evil. He's dependable. He wouldn't stir up shit for no reason. To be honest,

---

9   A legendary monk who came to China from the west in the 5th or 6th century, considered the founder of the Chan school of Mahāyāna Buddhism.

he's normally the one I trust the most. In a simple life-lending case like this, I can't help wondering if something fishy's going on, so I have to go take a look. Are you coming?"

Shen Wei had been too preoccupied lately with his own plans to pay attention to what the people in the Soul-Guarding Order were busy with. Hearing this, he finally raised his gentle gaze from his own checked-off name on the notebook. A trace of a smile curved the corner of his mouth. There was no sign that he minded Zhao Yunlan writing his name as messily as a dog who'd been given a pen. "Hmm? Life-borrowing?"

Zhao Yunlan brought up Wang Zheng's email on his phone. "This is it. Could the Great Immortal please take a look for us?"

Fossil that he was, Shen Wei had never used a smartphone before. His eyes swept over what Wang Zheng had written, and then he looked carefully at the photos of the scene. Being unused to touchscreens, he was unfortunately unable to figure it out even after a few attempts.

With a glance at Zhao Yunlan, who was currently gulping down his soy milk, he said, "Look away for a second. Don't peek."

Holding his palm above the phone screen, Shen Wei made a grabbing motion. The photo of the victim floated out of the screen, hovering in midair like a 3D projection. The visual effect was viscerally shocking. For a moment it was like the corpse, with its eggplant-purple face, was lying right there on the dining table.

Curiosity had kept Zhao Yunlan from obediently looking away, and now he was reaping what he had sown. He choked on a mouthful of soymilk, nearly spitting it all out onto the face of the corpse. This was a stellar example of feudal era superstitions triumphing over modern technology.

Shen Wei carefully examined the corpse's face, then reached out to "pinch" the eyes. It was as if he'd turned the very air into a 3D touchscreen, enabling himself to zoom in and out on different parts of the image!

"He may not have died from a life-borrowing spell backfiring." Shen Wei pointed at the corpse's eyes, now magnified to the size of one's palm. "Look at his eyes."

"I *just* ate..." Zhao Yunlan held his stomach in agony. Following Shen Wei's fingertip to the massively magnified eye, he saw that, upon closer inspection, the death-dilated pupil seemed to contain a person's reflection. Zhao Yunlan froze, pressing down on Shen Wei's hand. "Can you zoom in more?"

Shen Wei shook his head. "It's just a photo. If I zoom in further, it won't be clear anymore."

"Mm. That's fine." Zhao Yunlan grabbed a tissue from beneath the table and briskly wiped his mouth, then peeled a sticky note from the back of his notebook. He roughly sketched out the shadow's shape. "Still better than our shoddy moonlighting tech analyst could do."

"Who's that?" Shen Wei asked casually.

"Zhu Hong."

The dining table's leg creaked, dragging harshly against the floor. Zhao Yunlan felt a chilly gaze land on the back of his exposed neck. Pretending not to notice, he leaned over the table and carefully traced out the thing reflected in the corpse's eyes with a gel pen. But with his back to Shen Wei, he secretly smiled to himself.

"People used to say that a killer needed to destroy their victim's eyes after the deed was done or else the victim would retain the silhouette of the last person they saw, allowing the police to solve the crime," Zhao Yunlan said, still tracing. "But that's obviously impossible. If it were true, criminal investigators wouldn't need anything but eyeballs to solve cases. Looks like that particular rumor

didn't sprout from nothing, though. Sometimes stories spread in the Mortal Realm for a reason. What's the shadow in the eyes of the dead, then?"

When Shen Wei said nothing, Zhao Yunlan looked back at him, eyes smiling. "Hmm?"

Shen Wei's dark expression made it abundantly clear that he was displeased over Zhu Hong's name coming up. After a few more seconds of silence, he replied coldly. "The bodies of those whose souls are taken by reapers have clean eyes. But if someone's life had yet to reach a natural end and their soul was stolen by something or someone from beneath the Huangquan, the body's eyes will reflect the shadow of their attacker's origin."

"Mm... Then what do you think this is?" Zhao Yunlan asked.

"How would I know?"

"Oh? What's wrong? Unhappy? Jealous?" Zhao Yunlan looked like a cat who'd gotten the cream. "I love it when other people are jealous. Won't you let this lord see?"

Shen Wei answered with silence.

"You used to keep up a facade, like a god among men who was above mortal desires. I'm tired of watching you pretend. I get tired on your behalf just from watching." Zhao Yunlan casually stuck his sticky note on the back of one of Shen Wei's lesson plan drafts. "Come, Adonis, there's a scanner beside the computer on the desk. Scan this for me and send it to the office. Tell them to find out as much as they can before I get there."

Shen Wei accepted it, only to wind up standing stiffly in front of the computer. After turning it on, he just stared at the contraptions in front of him. This "god among men" essentially only knew how to do two things with computers: turn them on and off and deliver PowerPoint presentations that other people had prepared for him.

Everything else was his TA's job. He wasn't even sure which device was the printer and which was the scanner.

Zhao Yunlan suddenly came up behind Shen Wei. Wrapping his arms around Shen Wei, he guided his hands through the steps, starting with putting the sketched outline into the scanner. That done, he deliberately blew into Shen Wei's ear under the noise of the machine. "You should've said something if you didn't know how to use it. Why didn't you ask your husband to teach you?"

Shen Wei refused to grant Zhao Yunlan a response.

Laughing, Zhao Yunlan copped a feel, squeezing Shen Wei's ass. Shen Wei's face and ears flushed red, but before he could get mad, Zhao Yunlan sidestepped and flipped the calendar on the desk over. He tapped on the email and password written on the back. "You at least know how to do this, right? Find the category that says 'Coworkers' in the contacts and send the scanned image to them."

Next, Zhao Yunlan called 4 Bright Avenue. "Wang Zheng? You're still awake? Thanks for your hard work. Make sure the curtains are closed tightly—yes, I know. Something's happened to Lin Jing. I'm sending an image over to you, so make sure everyone at the office gets a look. Ideally, someone can figure out what it is. Get lao-Li to prepare two cars. We're leaving for the crime scene in half an hour."

At that moment, the ground below the city shook slightly, gently swaying the pendant light in the room. As soon as the tiny earthquake passed, an email notification chimed on both ends of the phone call.

"Hold on, Director Zhao," Wang Zheng said. "There's an email from Lin Jing."

On his side of the call, Shen Wei turned to look at him. "The person you're looking for seems to have sent an email."

"Don't hang up," Zhao Yunlan told Wang Zheng.

Lin Jing had sent a cell phone video of himself.

He was a selfie king, endlessly admiring himself, so he had superb filming skills. But in this video, the camera shook constantly. Lin Jing was breathing harshly, and the screen was jostling. He seemed to be running. Then the camera cut to Lin Jing's face. His mouth opened and closed, but there was no sound.

Brow creased, Zhao Yunlan lip-read with great difficulty. "I...lost my voice, I can't...hare—hear very well... My fungers...no, fingers are stiff. I have...a bad feeling."

Lin Jing's hand shook, and the camera moved away from his face, pointing toward the buildings across from him. He was at the wellness resort where the life-lending case had occurred. At first glance, the little houses were all beautiful, but Zhao Yunlan realized at once that something was off about them.

At that moment, they heard the sound of Lin Jing tapping on the back of the phone. The sound was very loud and a little piercing. It showed just how deathly silent the entire resort was.

In front of the camera, Lin Jing wrote in the air, "It's deserted. Not one person's here." Zhao Yunlan noticed that the second joint of his finger was stiff, as unbending as a rock, with a weird blueish-gray hue appearing on it. Then Lin Jing paused. He pointed the camera at his face, then at his ear, and shook his head. Expression solemn, he took out his Buddhist prayer beads, closed his eyes, and started reciting scriptures to force himself to calm down.

Next, Lin Jing's eyes flew open, a stunned look crossing his face. He narrowed his eyes with great effort. The camera shook furiously, and then the video ended.

"At the end there, he probably realized he was losing his vision and hurried to send the video," Zhao Yunlan said. "With his vision going, maybe he made a mistake and scheduled it instead. That could be why we're only seeing it now. Or..."

"Or for some reason, the email was unable to send until now," Shen Wei finished.

Zhao Yunlan turned to look at him. Their gazes met, and then, in unison, they both said, "The earthquake just now."

No sooner had they spoken when the vague shaking came once again. Just as during the aftershock of a normal earthquake, footsteps and people's voices could be heard in the hallway. Zhao Yunlan's apartment was a bit high up, so the shaking was probably more pronounced up there. When a second quake happened, people had started to run out in a panic.

Laying a hand on the wall, Zhao Yunlan carefully assessed the tremors. "Does this 'earthquake' seem a little weird to you? Like it's not the Earth's crust vibrating. It feels more like...trembling."

Shen Wei said, "It seems to be coming from the Netherworld."

Zhao Yunlan loaded his gun with special bullets and sheathed his talisman-inscribed dagger under his pant leg. He pulled all the money out of his wallet, stuffing it randomly into his pockets, and filled the wallet with a thick stack of talismans. Finally, he pulled out a thin carved piece of wood from the drawer: the true Soul-Guarding Order, made from the bark of the genuine Great Divine Tree. The words "Soul-Guarding Order" burst into eye-catching sparks the moment it touched Zhao Yunlan's skin.

"Let's go," he said to Shen Wei, cramming the Soul-Guarding Order into his pocket.

Twenty minutes later, they arrived at 4 Bright Avenue and collected a few coworkers. In two vehicles, they all raced to the spot where Lin Jing had run into trouble.

Dragon City was less than three hundred kilometers from the scene of the incident—four hours by highway. Between the mountains and the hot springs, it was a classic location for a wellness resort. The villages that had been nearby had all been relocated so as not to mar the glorious scenery. Day after day, the only people who came through here were service workers or employees who were making purchases for the business.

The resort was too quiet—practically a ghost town. There was a large delivery truck parked randomly in the middle of the road at the entrance. It still had its full load of fresh fruits and vegetables, with no sign of anything missing...except the driver. The driver's door was open, but there was no one to be seen.

"Lots of service workers must come here from the nearby villages every day," Zhao Yunlan said. "Xiao-Guo, take the second car to the town police station and ask our colleagues there if they've received any missing-person reports in the last few days."

Guo Changcheng was already keenly aware of the resort's creepiness. Just standing there was making his legs shake uncontrollably. Director Zhao was clearly protecting him by asking him to leave, which made him sigh in relief, but for some reason, his heart seemed to jump even further up into his throat.

"Zhu Hong will go with you," Zhao Yunlan added.

Zhu Hong wasn't like xiao-Guo, so easily ordered around. She objected immediately. "I'm not leaving! I'm sticking with you! I'm not going anywhere!"

Zhao Yunlan got out a cigarette and put it in his mouth. "What, disobeying orders before you even officially resign?"

"I..."

Leaving no room for argument, Zhao Yunlan got back into the car and closed the door. "Lao-Chu, get in this one."

Zhu Hong stood rooted in place, glaring furiously at Zhao Yunlan.

Chu Shuzhi waved at her from inside the other car. "Get moving. Director Zhao's plan makes sense. You won't be much help here, and xiao-Guo might not be able to communicate very well. Help him out."

Before Zhu Hong could say anything else, that asshole Zhao Yunlan had already slammed his foot on the gas and was driving away.

"**A**SSHOLE!**"** Zhu Hong bent down and picked up a rock, hurling it after the car. As a female snake yao, she had impressive strength, and when it came to smashing things, she was particularly gifted—accurate, steady, and merciless. There was a clang as the rock struck the trunk of Zhao Yunlan's official SID car, chipping off some paint.

But—maybe because it wasn't his own car—Zhao Yunlan didn't care at all.

Zhu Hong's phone vibrated in her pocket. She checked it and found a text from Chu Shuzhi, which read, *"Director Zhao told me to tell you that the fine for vandalism will come out of your monthly bonus. Keep throwing rocks if you want, but once you run through your bonus, your pay will get docked. Take it easy unless you want to leave without a penny."*

Her new phone's life was cut short. It died in her hand with a crunch as she roared, "Zhao Yunlan, you *fucking asshole!*"

Panicked, Guo Changcheng only stared at his treasonous, insubordinate coworker. He was too afraid to breathe a word.

Zhu Hong turned and glared at him with red-rimmed eyes. "What are you looking at?! Let's go!"

Guo Changcheng obediently trotted after her, only to meet the full force of her rage again as she took it out on him. "What kind of man are you?! Get in the driver's seat! Have you ever seen a man make a woman drive?!"

Driving a car wasn't like entering a public restroom. He'd never heard of any gender-related rules about it. Since she was clearly being unreasonable, he responded with honesty. "Zhu-jie, technically, you're not a wom—"

Zhu Hong's expression was dark and threatening, like a king cobra darting its forked tongue out before landing a deadly strike. Guo Changcheng instinctively sensed the danger he was in and crawled into the car, too scared to let out so much as a fart.

But then Zhu Hong hesitated. Instead of getting in, she slammed the passenger door shut and dismissed him. "Fuck off by yourself. I'm going to go find Zhao Yunlan."

It all happened without Guo Changcheng ever having a chance to voice a single full-fledged opinion. Swift as the wind, Zhu Hong was already gone.

Daqing and Chu Shuzhi, riding along in Zhao Yunlan's car, weren't having a good time either, due to the presence of the esteemed deity in the passenger seat. Now that they knew Shen Wei was the Soul-Executing Emissary, neither the Corpse King nor the old cat could take their usual innocent joy in teasing anyone they could get their hands on.

Thanks to the bizarre atmosphere, they drove all the way to the main entrance of the resort in complete silence. Upon arriving, they saw the grandiose words "Spring Harbor Resort" carved in marble relief on a sign in the beautifully designed flowerbeds. Somehow those carved words seemed impossibly bleak because of either the material itself or the overcast skies.

There were two security booths and two entrances at the gate with the roads blocked on either side to keep cars from entering. Off to the side was a card reader that allowed residents to come and go on foot, but its light was off. Evidently, the power had been cut.

Zhao Yunlan parked at the entrance and then glanced at his phone just in time to see the final flicker of signal disappear completely.

The security booth's window was open for some reason. A small package sat on the window ledge next to a notebook and an uncapped pen. There was a peculiar layer of dust covering both the ledge and the things on it. Zhao Yunlan put on some gloves and picked the notebook up to take a careful look. It turned out to be a record of packages that the guards had accepted on behalf of the residents. Each one was recorded before they were passed on to their recipients, who had to sign for them.

The most recent entry was dated just the day before. It read, "Unit 10A, Mr. Li, pack—" cutting off mid-word. The person writing had been interrupted too abruptly to even finish.

Closing his eyes, Zhao Yunlan could practically see the scene playing out. The courier handed the package through the window and then accepted the notebook, meticulously recording the package's information. Halfway through the word "package," something had happened.

But what?

If the stuff was still here, where had the people gone?

Walking over, Shen Wei swiped a finger through the dust on the ledge. He rubbed it between his fingers and then said, "It hasn't been here long."

"The dust?" Zhao Yunlan asked. "You can tell from just that? How?"

Shen Wei dusted his hands off. "With most types I wouldn't be able to tell, but this is human ash that collected here within the last two or three days. It's still very fresh."

Zhao Yunlan had no response.

Shen Wei had delivered the information with the same offhand tone he might use to say, "This milk is fresh from the cow."

Looking a little shocked, Zhao Yunlan closed the notebook and packed it securely in an evidence bag. Thank goodness he'd already sent Guo Changcheng away—if this sight had scared the poor boy half to death, they all would've suffered ten thousand volts...

"You're sure this is bone ash? It doesn't look like it to me."

"It's not the kind from a crematorium," Shen Wei explained. "You know the saying 'grind someone's bones to dust and scatter their ashes'? This individual might've been standing right here when their body disintegrated instantaneously. Their bones were shattered into this fine powder and landed here."

Chu Shuzhi had also made his way over to them and asked, incredulously, "Then where's the rest of them?"

"Incinerated." Shen Wei adjusted his glasses. "Flesh and blood can't withstand as much pressure as bones, so they rarely leave any traces."

Chu Shuzhi chose his next words carefully. "It sounds as though my lord knows how these people died...?"

Shen Wei gave a polite nod. Humbly, he said, "I'm not terribly knowledgeable, but I do happen to know a little in regard to this. In the ancient past, after Gonggong knocked down Buzhou Mountain, the sky burst and the earth split. The gui surfaced in the Mortal Realm for the first time, dripping with the ruthlessness of their birthplace thousands of zhang below the Huangquan. When that happened, every human and beast within a ten-li radius turned to dust in a heartbeat, just like this, and within one hundred li, not a single blade of grass grew."

As he spoke, he pointed at the landscaped flowerbeds beneath the entrance sign, still lush even in the depths of winter. "Those ornamental flowers are unaffected. They're probably artificial."

"But this place is less than ten li across," Zhao Yunlan pointed out. "There are two large pine trees right there by the entrance—way closer than a hundred li away."

"Because of that, I think," said Shen Wei, pointing. The other two looked in the direction he was indicating.

At the resort's entrance was a little garden surrounded by reception areas. Rather than a single building, reception was divided between several small buildings of different heights. They were arranged in a purposeful circle around the garden, like an excellent privacy screen.

"Look," Shen Wei continued. "The central pond is shaped like petals, and the waterway extends outward and just so happens to connect all the small buildings around it."

Chu Shuzhi usually liked to play the big shot, but at this moment, his attitude was considerably grounded and humble. "If I may say so, my lord—that's the Five-by-Five Plum Blossom Array, isn't it?"

"It is indeed. Chu-xiong is well-versed in these matters." Shen Wei nodded. "The Plum Blossom Array is commonly used to protect the home and ward off evil. Thanks to its presence, the yin energy was trapped inside by the array. As it was unable to get out, it would've only affected this little path by the entrance at most. If a crudely constructed Plum Blossom Array was enough to hold it off, that suggests to me that the Great Houtu Seal remains intact for the time being. This is most likely just a small leak here. Once it's fixed, it'll be fine."

Chu Shuzhi and Daqing didn't know what the Great Houtu Seal was, and Shen Wei spoke so calmly that he might've been talking about a button having fallen off a shirt—a few easy stitches and it would be back in place. They started to relax.

Zhao Yunlan, on the other hand, gave him a thoughtful glance. To anyone who didn't know better, Shen Wei generally came across as someone who was always composed, who knew his limits and never crossed the line...but in reality, not a single thing about him was *inside* the line. Zhao Yunlan was fairly confident about what was actually going on here: Shen Wei had already gotten what he wanted, and as a result, he was probably completely at ease now. He might not care at all about the Great Houtu Seal at this point; Zhao Yunlan suspected he might not even care about his own life or death.

"I suppose the Netherworld must be in complete chaos right about now." Shen Wei smiled as he spoke, then realized he was perhaps letting his schadenfreude show a little too blatantly. As that was a bit ill-mannered, he wiped the smile off his face and quietly cleared his throat. "No matter. Everyone, follow closely behind me."

Chu Shuzhi and Daqing deserted their boss at once, opting instead to stick close to the boss's mighty "wife."

Meanwhile, Zhao Yunlan had a vague sense of foreboding. At first, when he'd casually handed this life-lending case off to Lin Jing, he hadn't given it too much thought. But thinking back on it...wasn't "life-lending" what had set off the Reincarnation Dial case?

And the Reincarnation Dial was in Ghost Face's hands.

The Great Seal was weakening. It could still hold back most of the gui, but it could no longer contain the Chaos King of the Gui. Three of the Four Hallowed Artifacts had already appeared, and while their side didn't have possession of the Reincarnation Dial, they had both the Mountain-River Awl and the Merit Brush.

Trouble was, the Four Pillars were like four legs: not all four needed to be destroyed to bring down the entire Seal. If the gui could knock out two of the four legs, that would be enough.

The critical question, then, was the location of the Soul-Guarding Lamp. But who had the first clue as to where the mysterious lamp of legend might be?

As they headed in through the pedestrian walkway by the main gate, the thick stench of death hit them in the face. Daqing's fur stood on end. The Soul-Guarding Whip surreptitiously twined down Zhao Yunlan's arm, its tip peeking out near his wrist. With his other hand, Zhao Yunlan felt for the little dagger hidden in his sleeve.

From Zhao Yunlan's perspective, the Spring Harbor Resort was essentially a dangerous trap. Lin Jing's video hadn't shown him going inside. Lin Jing's level of caution and care meant there was no way he'd go into such an ominous, menacing environment alone without contacting the team first.

Something must've misled or even coerced him, stripping him of his senses before he even set foot inside. Even as a direct descendant of Bodhidharma himself, Lin Jing still wouldn't be able to withstand the force of the brutality erupting from thousands of chi below the Huangquan River when the Great Seal cracked open.

Wouldn't it be easier to just kill him directly, though? Who were they trying to lure here by keeping him...? The Soul-Guarding Order? Shen Wei?

The charming little path was completely empty. Every building was eerie and vacant, inhabited by not even the shadow of a ghost. Somewhere along the line, Shen Wei's black robes had manifested, and in response to *something*, the Soul-Executing Blade was already in his hand. The footfalls of three people and a cat seemed unusually loud on the empty path; the carrying sound only contributed to the indescribably creepy atmosphere.

The setting sun hung on the horizon, but its light was no longer a warm reddish orange. A dull, bloody red reminiscent of the color on the cheeks of paper dolls at funeral stores, it gave off a chilly glow. The light dragged their shadows on the ground, turning their silhouettes disturbingly long and dark.

Zhao Yunlan gave the black cat a sudden nudge away with his foot and took a huge stride forward. Before he even turned, he was already holding his dagger up to the middle of his back. There was a tooth-grinding clang as youchu fangs met the steel blade. The youchu lost a few teeth, and a crack appeared in the steel.

With all his weight on one foot, Zhao Yunlan was about to pivot and strike the beast again when sheer horror suddenly spread across the youchu's face. Its hideous form was sucked into Shen Wei's palm like a deflating balloon. Countless bells rang out at once in the distance as a black mist rose half a meter high on the little resort's clean roads.

There was a sharp yowl as the black cat shot up to Zhao Yunlan's shoulder. Pustule-ridden hands were reaching up from below the ground!

Youchu had climbed onto the roof at some point, materializing the way zombies would suddenly appear behind people in the movies. There was a whoosh as one jumped down and clamped huge claws down on Chu Shuzhi's head. The youchu opened its mouth to bite down. In an instant, Chu Shuzhi's stick-thin hand turned as hard as stone and, as if competing with the gui to see who was crueler, he punched directly through the youchu's throat. It staggered back a few steps, then toppled to the ground. Before it even breathed its last, countless other gui of even more bizarre shapes threw themselves at it, devouring it down to the last scrap in the blink of an eye.

Still more gui climbed out of the ground, each uglier than the last. The corner of Shen Wei's eye twitched. He had been born a gui, and his deep-rooted loathing for his own kind only deepened as they dared to appear in front of Zhao Yunlan. He drew his blade.

Zhao Yunlan hurriedly said, "Shen Wei, hold on. This doesn't seem like—"

But it was too late. The Soul-Executing Blade grew several meters, effortlessly cutting down countless gui. Shen Wei's expression was glacial. With a flip of his wrist, the blade pressed down with thousands of tons of pressure, far too sharp for anything to block. He split the thick black mist beneath the resort with one swing, and it dispersed before disappearing entirely. Then the blade struck the ground, opening a long, narrow crack dozens of meters deep. A bloodcurdling scream rang out. Shen Wei glared viciously down into the fissure. "Get the hell out here!"

With the astounding force and lightning speed of his attacks, it wasn't until then that Zhao Yunlan, who was not even five steps away, finally managed to grab his arm and hold him back. "This doesn't look like the Great Seal breaking! I think it's some distorted kind of Ghost Army Summons! Don't do anything rash!"

Laughter echoed from all around them before he was even done speaking. "Yes," a voice said. "Too bad the Guardian's brain and mouth aren't as fast as the Lord Emissary's blade."

The crack Shen Wei had opened started to break further apart. Shen Wei caught hold of Zhao Yunlan and held him close; Chu Shuzhi and the black cat landed on the other side of the rapidly widening gap. In no time at all, it was too wide to even see the people on the other side.

There was a muffled grunt from Shen Wei as his hand, which had a firm hold on Zhao Yunlan, seemed to be dragged away. A ball of black mist wrapped around his arm with the stickiness of cobwebs.

CHU SHUZHI's last text message sat on Guo Changcheng's screen, urging him to stay away from the resort no matter what happened, and more importantly, to prevent anyone else from going there.

Guo Changcheng tried to call him and tell him that Zhu Hong had run off, only to find that the call wouldn't go through. He tried sending messages and leaving voicemails, but they too got no response, as if they were rocks sinking to the bottom of the ocean.

It was as though everyone else in the world had disappeared, leaving his poor little self behind, helpless and alone and at a complete loss about what to do. Guo Changcheng pulled the car over on the roadside, where he hemmed and hawed for a good, long while before finally gathering enough courage to follow the GPS into the nearest town.

Once there, he made a beeline for the local police station, but well before he reached it, he could see a huge crowd clustering around the building's entrance. They were completely blocking the road. Guo Changcheng honked once, but no one paid any attention. An old lady was leaving the station, leaning on someone who was helping her. Her hair was pure white, and she seemed unsteady on her feet. Even with someone holding on to her, she managed to trip and stumble, falling against the hood of Guo Changcheng's car.

Alarmed, Guo Changcheng got out of the car at once. The old woman's friends and family scrambled to help her back up, as did the police officer who had followed her out. Their voices rose in a great clamor, and the old lady started crying loudly, as if none of them were there. Her sobs only got the crowd more worked up. Guo Changcheng heard one angry voice declare, "I have no clue what cops these days even do. According to them, they're not responsible for this, they're not responsible for that, and they can't solve anything. Why does the country even bother keeping them around in that case?"

"Exactly!" exclaimed someone else. "Just look at this poor lady! It's been just her and that one son for so long. They depend on each other. If anything happened to him, would she even be able to go on?"

This tactless question hit the old woman right where it hurt most. Her weeping became even more hysterical.

The officer who had followed her out was a young woman around the same age as Guo Changcheng. Like him, she looked like a recent graduate...but at the moment she was also representing the government, which meant all of the questions and pointed fingers were aimed at her. Face red and at a complete loss, she said haltingly, "We have to follow procedure. An adult must be missing for over forty-eight hours before..."

Angry cursing drowned her out at once. "Rules and procedures are set in stone, but people aren't!" someone cried. "The missing might still be alive now, but you guys want to wait forty-eight hours! Anything could happen to them in forty-eight hours! It would be too late! Their corpses would be long cold by then! But you're still not going to do anything? Young lady, ask yourself, what's the difference between your inaction and murder?"

The young officer thought that was all perfectly reasonable and made sense, but the fact remained that this was a small local police station with limited manpower. What was more, rules were rules. No matter how reasonable *she* thought the crowd's requests were, she couldn't just go against regulations. She was overcome with frustration. Tears began to swim in her reddened eyes.

The whole thing was quickly giving Guo Changcheng a headache. The crowd was saying all sorts of things and all talking at once, as worked up as a pitchfork-wielding mob. Then the old woman who was still crying on the hood of his car suddenly passed out, eyes rolling back in her head.

Guo Changcheng hurriedly pushed his way through. "Excuse me—sorry—please make way."

He pulled his work ID and keys from his pocket. Flustered, he tossed his ID to the woman's friends and family. "Take my car and drive her to the hospital!"

The relative who'd caught his badge stared at it. "Huh?"

Guo Changcheng looked at what they were holding. "Oh! Sorry, wrong thing. Take these."

He quickly traded the car keys for his ID, which he then handed to the female officer beside him. "Comrade, can you take me to your supervisor? It's urgent."

She looked at his ID in confusion, then suddenly straightened up. "Are... Are you the higher-up from Dragon City?"

"No, no, I'm not a higher-up. My office sent someone here two days ago to investigate a death. Your station should already have all the paperwork. But our colleague went missing yesterday. Our boss is already at the crime scene. He told me to come here and check in with you guys." Guo Changcheng finished speaking and wiped his brow, which had gotten sweaty despite it being the dead of winter.

Then, with rare competence, he asked the crowd, "Are you all here
to file reports? All for missing people?"

Many people nodded.

"Oh..." he said. "Oh, so how did they go missing?"

It was like he'd poked a hornet's nest. The whole crowd exploded
into speech at once; the wall of noise was like five thousand ducks
simultaneously yelling at the top of their lungs. The overwhelming
noise almost made Guo Changcheng pass out. He pressed a hand
firmly against his pants pocket, afraid that his fear of people would
activate the little stun baton in his pocket and accidentally hurt the
innocent crowd.

But to his own surprise, he didn't feel as afraid as he'd expected.

That was just how Guo Changcheng was. Whenever he wanted
to ask others for help, he felt like a tremendously ignorant nuisance.
Naturally, that made him afraid of whomever it was, and that grew
into a fear of all communication, whether speaking aloud or even
just making eye contact. But at a time like this, when he realized that
the people in front of him required *his* help, his words always flowed
far more smoothly.

It was as if he'd been born to do this.

A light bulb went off in Guo Changcheng's head. He waved his
hands abruptly and spoke over the noisy crowd. "I can't hear what
you're all saying. Let's take it slow, okay? When I ask a question,
can you please answer by raising your hand? First question: Does
your missing friend or relative work at Spring Harbor Resort? If yes,
please raise your hand."

Everyone's hand shot up at once. Beside him, the officer's eyes
widened. All the racket earlier must have left her ears ringing,
making her unable to focus on anything beyond the fact that adults
couldn't be reported missing until they'd been gone for forty-eight

hours. She hadn't made the connection that this could be a single, very serious case.

Guo Changcheng composed himself. He was getting a clearer idea of how to proceed. Next, he asked, "Anyone who's certain that their friend or relative went missing *at* the resort, please keep your hand up. If you're not sure, please put your hand down, okay?"

A few hands wavered and were lowered, only to be hesitantly raised again.

A middle-aged man spoke up. "Boss, can I say something?"

"I'm not the boss..." Guo Changcheng sighed. "Never mind that. Please go ahead, sir."

"My little sister waitresses at a restaurant at the resort's reception halls. She's only nineteen. She never came home after work last night, and we couldn't reach her. She's very responsible—she's never stayed out all night without a reason before. The entire family is worried sick. We all went out and searched for her in the middle of the night, and we went back and forth along her route to work a bunch of times. And then my dad and cousin disappeared too! When we couldn't reach them by phone either, I came to make a report." The man's eyes were bloodshot, but he tried his best to keep his voice steady, wanting to remain as calm as possible. "Boss, a young girl is one thing, but two grown men? What could possibly happen to them? My dad's seventy years old. Even if this were a human trafficking case, who'd traffic someone's old man?"

The entire crowd agreed that it was the same story for them. Everybody who had a missing loved one was as anxious as a cat on a hot tin roof, and they all tried to push closer to Guo Changcheng to say a bit more about their own situation. They were all desperate for an explanation from him. He looked far too young to be entrusted with this situation, but in their eyes, Guo Changcheng had essentially become their savior—and they all wanted a piece of this savior to dispel their worries.

What with all the jostling and shoving, a woman holding a child was pushed to the ground. The three-year-old in her arms started wailing loudly. Someone nearby yelled, "Don't push! We're all worried here!" while someone else screamed, "Watch out for the child! Don't step on the child!"

Guo Changcheng felt dizzy. *If only Zhu Hong-jie were here...* he thought. *If only Director Zhao were here.*

What should he do?

They had so much faith in him. They were counting on him to take care of things here. He'd had this job for six months, and this was his first time in charge of a situation all by himself. How could he fail to live up to their expectations and screw this up?

If it were Director Zhao, what would he do? If it were Chu-ge, what would he do?

He couldn't let these people go to the resort. It was too dangerous. Guo Changcheng suddenly took two steps forward and stood on the curb. "Everyone! Everyone!"

The crowd quieted.

He held his work ID up high. "I'm here from the Special Investigations Department in Dragon City. We specialize in very important, serious cases. Our boss has already rushed to the scene with our very best elite personnel, and he sent me here to explain the situation to you all.

"We haven't found any signs of your loved ones yet, but we also haven't had terrible news. We are already doing absolutely everything we can to search for them. Right now, the best thing you can all do to help is to cooperate with the comrades here at the police station while they record all the details. Just absolutely *do not* go anywhere near the resort. If you do, you'll make things harder for the rescuers, who'll have more trouble finding the victims."

He had never spoken so much in a single breath before. In that instant, Guo Changcheng felt like he wasn't fighting alone.

His heart felt warm and toasty, as if a flame were burning within him. Cupping his hands together, he bowed to everybody around him. "Thank you, everyone. You have my word that we will do our very best. Now, can I ask you all to line up and head inside to make your reports?"

At first, the crowd just stood there and stared at each other. But then, incredibly, they started lining up noisily. Slowly, order prevailed. Following directions from the young female officer, they successfully formed a line and filed inside.

Guo Changcheng, however, stood frozen in place for a long while, unable to believe that he had actually done it.

The other members of the SID weren't having it so easy. Shen Wei, entangled in the black mist, was suffering from a renewed case of bullheadedness and flatly refusing to let go of Zhao Yunlan no matter what. He had the Soul-Executing Blade between his teeth, and the blade's icy glint made his lips look scarily pale. He angled his head around to turn the blade on the mist.

Zhao Yunlan grabbed the blade from Shen Wei's mouth. "Give me that." He took the blade, completely unique in all the world, and slashed at the black mist wrapped around Shen Wei's arm. But beneath the blade, the substance felt like quicksand and was barely dented by the fierce weapon, never mind cut.

Shen Wei held Zhao Yunlan even tighter. "That's the power of Chaos. It's the only thing the Soul-Executing Blade can't cut through. Nothing will work but to cut my arm off. Do it quickly!"

Zhao Yunlan ignored him and carefully sheathed the blade. Then he got out a paper talisman of the Soul-Guarding Order. With a snap of his fingers, a small spark burst forth, and he sent the blazing talisman shooting straight into the mist...

...And the talisman disappeared. Not a speck remained.

"Cut off my arm!" Shen Wei yelled.

Zhao Yunlan acted like he didn't hear him. Next, he took out the true Soul-Guarding Order, carved from the Great Divine Tree itself, which he had brought along specially.

Alarmed, Shen Wei said, "You can't—"

But before Shen Wei could finish speaking, Zhao Yunlan proved that actions were faster than words. The Soul-Guarding Order, made from the wood of the Great Divine Tree, began to burn. The flame rose a third of a meter into the air, burning an unnatural red. The black mist ensnaring Shen Wei's arm finally shrank back in fear.

Regaining the use of his arm, the first thing Shen Wei did was grab the burning Soul-Guarding Order. Still holding Zhao Yunlan close, he dodged around the swamp-like mist. A pool of clear spring water welled up in his palm, extinguishing the fire on the Soul-Guarding Order, but half of the words were already burned off. Only the right half of the characters were still legible. The words on the back—"Guard the souls of the living, bring peace to the hearts of the dead"—were entirely gone.

The pair beat a hasty retreat from the area. Expression dark, Shen Wei said, "Don't you realize that you don't actually belong in the Reincarnation Cycle? That your status as Guardian essentially grants you protection? This was carved from the Great Divine Tree's bark, and you...you..."

Any time Shen Wei wanted to curse, his mind tended to go blank.

He repeated the word "you" a few times but was unable to come up with anything better than a refined "You squandering fool!"

Behind them, the black shadow kept giving chase. It was as thick as ink that was impossible to dilute, and wherever it passed, nothing remained. The shadow swallowed *everything*...almost as though it could swallow even emptiness itself.

It was true Chaos.

Neither man had ever imagined a day when they'd cut such a sorry figure, fleeing fast enough that they must've surely exceeded the speed limit of life and death.

Even running for his life, Zhao Yunlan found the time to roll his eyes at Shen Wei. "*You're* the squandering fool here, ready to cut off your arm or dig out your heart at the least provocation. Do you think you're a gecko?"

"I'm not arguing with you." Shen Wei wrapped Zhao Yunlan in his arms, and the huge black cloak of the Emissary billowed around them like a dark cloud soaring into the sky. His feet left the ground, but he stayed low—still holding Zhao Yunlan—and traversed dozens of meters in a heartbeat. Then he gently touched down and dove straight into the crack in the ground, swift as a black swallow.

Faint tremors shook the ground once again.

From even deeper down, a huge group of reapers, with their penchant for terrible timing, burst forth. Reapers were always either late when they shouldn't be or rushing forward when they were supposed to be delaying. But the moment this bunch appeared, over half of them were swallowed up by the all-consuming black shadow.

The Magistrate yelped. However, as he was about to dive back into the ground without a word, Ox-Head and Horse-Face, standing on either side, pulled him back out like a radish. "My lord, you can't. The underground is not a hiding place."

Just like that, a mismatched assortment of reapers also joined team "Run for Your Life," contributing absolutely nothing useful in the process.

Shen Wei suddenly leaped back out of the crack in the ground, shoving Zhao Yunlan forward. Zhao Yunlan followed his cue and let the momentum carry him forward a dozen or so meters. He steadied himself with his hands on the ground, then stood. Shen Wei, meanwhile, had levitated into the air. He formed a seal with both hands and silently recited an incantation from some distant time as the black shadow closed in, bit by bit.

Just as the shadow was about to touch the hem of his robes, a piercing white light erupted from the seal in Shen Wei's hands.

His timing was impeccable. The shadow lurched to a stop right in front of him, and then, shuddering violently, it was slowly sucked into the white light.

Everyone held their breaths.

It wasn't long before the all-encompassing shadow was fully drawn into the increasingly blinding white light. The cold sweat gathering on Shen Wei's face finally dripped down his cheek. The Magistrate fell back onto the ground, and Zhao Yunlan let out a breath, slowly relaxing his fist, which had been clenched tightly enough to leave crescent marks from his nails in his palm.

The white blaze started to shrink in Shen Wei's hand. The situation seemed to be coming under control.

And then, all at once, everything changed.

With no warning, a figure appeared behind Shen Wei as though he had ripped the air open. Ghost Face, who had been lying in wait for some unknown amount of time, thrust an icicle over a meter long through Shen Wei's back—right into his heart.

Before the Magistrate and the others realized what was happening, a long whip snapped out, curling toward Ghost Face like a venomous snake. There was a *whoosh* as it kicked up a fierce gust of wind, vicious enough to hurt where it touched bare skin. The nearby reapers felt like they'd been collectively slapped in the face, cheeks burning with pain where they were exposed to the air. As one, they turned their faces away and backed up as the whip wrapped precisely around Ghost Face's neck.

The Magistrate was so filled with woe, he was on the verge of vomiting. Five hundred years earlier, when the Great Seal had first shown signs of weakening, the Netherworld had taken charge and gathered forces from all over to discuss the matter. Back then, a single call from the Netherworld had been enough to gather hundreds of immortals from all over, each one of them staunchly righteous. Every sentence they uttered was about "the people" and "the world," so passionate were they about sacrificing everything for the Great Seal. But in the wake of the battle atop the peak of Kunlun Mountain, those people had disappeared en masse, as if by mutual agreement.

It was understandable. The road of cultivation was endlessly long. One had to face difficulties and dangers others could not fathom and endure loneliness beyond that of ordinary individuals. Perhaps one in a million had the natural talent, and those who were determined and willing to walk the lonely path, who didn't look for instant success or give up halfway, were rarer still. But beyond all that, no matter how great one's innate gift or how hard they worked, they still needed luck. Without it, success could slip right through one's fingers at the last moment. Who wouldn't prioritize self-preservation, having gone through such hardship just to get where they were? Who would rush to the front just to be cannon fodder?

If the Great Seal hadn't been damaged, and thus pushed the Netherworld to the front lines to bear the brunt of the impact, the Magistrate would've also preferred to stay far, far away. He was just a puny little Magistrate! Even the Ten Kings of the Yanluo Courts were betting that the Soul-Executing Emissary's pride would keep him from stooping to settle scores with them, thereby allowing the Netherworld to get away with all their petty machinations. But who among them would dare to truly go head-to-head with a King of the Gui from primordial times?

The Emissary alone was enough to scare them out of their wits, never mind the emotionally unstable Ghost Face.

The Magistrate's expression was complicated as his gaze landed on Zhao Yunlan. Cowards filled their ranks. Perhaps only those true primordial gods and demons from before Chaos had shattered could have hearts large enough to set aside their own lives for the greater good. Zhao Yunlan might be a mere mortal now, but he still dared to wrap his whip around the King of the Gui's neck without a moment's hesitation.

As beings without honor, flitting about like flies as they fought for survival, it was impossible for them to understand the kind of incisive passion that gambled life and death in a single instant. It was hard for them to imagine the moment of trudging forward, like a moth to the flame, in the face of tens of thousands of enemies. Above all, it was hard for them to measure up to the Great Wild of the distant past, when the sky and earth first parted and there was nothing to fear.

And yet...Kunlun-jun had disappeared into the Reincarnation Cycle. How *dare* this man, Zhao Yunlan, who was clearly no more than a silver-tongued mortal, not be terror-stricken or panicked?

Was the soul alone enough, even washed clean again and again by countless journeys through the Reincarnation Cycle? Even after losing the authority and power of the Mountain God...?

The three of them were in a stalemate. The veins of Shen Wei's forehead pulsed as he forced his fingers closed. The white light vanished within his fist, taking all the Chaos around them with it.

Black smoke like spider silk suddenly flowed from the icicle buried in his chest, wrapping him within an enormous cocoon.

Ghost Face still held the other end of the icicle in one hand, and he had managed to slip his other hand between the whip and his throat before the whip had wrapped around his neck entirely. Hovering in midair, the King of the Gui met the eyes of the fearless mortals in the distance. He saw a hard light in Zhao Yunlan's eyes, burning even brighter than the soul fire that had once brought light to the entire Place of Great Disrespect.

"If the Soul-Guarding Order hadn't been damaged," Ghost Face rasped, voice hoarse and broken, "my neck might be missing a layer of skin right about now. *Tsk*, how unfortunate."

Squeezing the words out from between his teeth, Zhao Yunlan said, "Let. Go. Of. Him."

"Him? He and I were born as twin Kings of the Gui. You know, even though circumstances left us so incompatible, I still had no desire to hurt him. *He* was the one who drove me to it, every step of the way." Pausing between each word, Ghost Face continued. "If you want him, fine. Bring me the Soul-Guarding Lamp in exchange."

Who the fuck even knew what a Soul-Guarding Lamp *was*?

Zhao Yunlan's handsome face clouded over. "If you were smart, you'd jam an icicle in my chest too. Otherwise, I'll make sure you never have a moment's peace for all eternity."

Through broken peals of laughter, Ghost Face replied, "If you were Kunlun-jun, I'd gladly die here today if it meant ending your existence, but..."

He quivered once, violently, and the Soul-Guarding Whip, which no longer had the Great Divine Tree's protection, shattered into innumerable fragments. The force of it cut Zhao Yunlan's palm open to the bone. "My dear Guardian, you truly have nothing to fear from me." Ghost Face sighed. "I'm grateful for your soul fire, and thanks to *his* influence, I can't help but...like you a little. There's no harm in letting you live."

There came another sharp laugh. Black mist filled the air, and just like that, both Ghost Face and the cocooned Shen Wei were gone.

THE PALM OF ZHAO YUNLAN'S HAND was a bloody mess. Eventually, unable to stay silent any longer, the Magistrate cleared his throat. "Ah... Guardian, you..."

Zhao Yunlan twitched as though the Magistrate's voice had startled him awake. When he glanced over, the corners of his eyes angled upward. There was an unutterable, inauspicious redness there. His pupils held the terrifying darkness of the abyss, and his thick lashes cast a bottomless shadow over his eyes.

For a moment, the Guardian seemed like a complete stranger to the Magistrate, whose skin broke out in goosebumps under his gaze.

"I need to ask a favor, Lord Magistrate," Zhao Yunlan said quietly. "Would you please take me to see the real Reincarnation Cycle in the Netherworld?"

It was best for the doer to undo his own handiwork. It was Shennong who had sealed Kunlun-jun's primordial spirit before becoming the Reincarnation Cycle. If Zhao Yunlan wanted to awaken Kunlun's spirit, going there was probably his best bet.

When the Magistrate didn't reply, Zhao Yunlan asked, "What, I can't go?"

Quickly, the Magistrate stammered, "I... This humble one expected the Guardian to inquire about the Soul-Guarding Lamp..."

"The Soul-Guarding Lamp?" Zhao Yunlan raised his left eyebrow so minutely that it might've been only a slight twitch. The fingers of his left hand were pressed unconsciously against his wounded right palm; blood stained his fingertips crimson. Alarmed and frightened, the Magistrate watched him, but Zhao Yunlan simply lowered his gaze and said, "Please lead the way."

"Director Zhao!" A woman's voice rang out behind him. Without turning, Zhao Yunlan recognized that it was Zhu Hong speaking.

"Mnnh." Zhao Yunlan showed no sign of anger or other emotion. He might've even completely forgotten that her presence meant she was disobeying a direct order. "If you see Chu Shuzhi and Daqing, tell them to keep looking for Lin Jing," he told her. "There's something I need to do. I'll be back."

"Where are you going? I'll go with you!"

Zhao Yunlan leveled an expressionless look at her. "No need. Having you along would just hold me back. You should train for a few more years first, little snake."

Steam was practically coming out of Zhu Hong's ears. "'Little snake'? *I'm* a little snake?! What are you, then? In my tribe, someone your age would still be nibbling their eggshells, you mortal brat!"

The corners of Zhao Yunlan's lips quirked into a cold smile as he left.

He didn't look back.

Lin Jing, meanwhile, was meditating—or at least he was doing his best to. After his senses had begun working properly, he'd realized someone had kidnapped him. He had no idea where he was, but he could tell he was leaning against a huge rock. Beside the rock was a giant towering tree, so tall that its crown couldn't be seen from the ground. Torrents of water seemed to be cascading all around him, but some sort of invisible dome surrounded him and protected him from drowning...at least for now.

He was also surrounded by youchu. The creatures pressed around him on every side, salivating. Just looking at them made Lin Jing quiver. All he could think to do was close his eyes and chant scriptures, but he'd barely uttered two lines when he realized that Buddhist scriptures only seemed to aggravate his neighbors. A ruckus broke out among the youchu, who began to roar and showed no sign of stopping.

With a gulp, Lin Jing forced a sad attempt at a smile. "U-um, I only just got here. I didn't know we had a rule against reciting scriptures. K-kindly forgive me. I'll correct my ways at once."

The youchu nearest to Lin Jing greedily came even closer. It raised its nose and sniffed hungrily at his scent of fresh flesh and blood.

Lin Jing was about to cry. "I haven't bathed in three days! Comrade, be mindful of your manners!"

The youchu's mouth gaped open, preparing to bite—only for a more humanlike youchu to suddenly grab the back of that one's neck, reacting to the gall of it daring to claim food for itself. This higher-ranked youchu twisted its fingers, separating the inferior youchu's head from its body. The head hung there, dangling like a grotesquely shaped wind chime.

The one that had casually killed its own kin tore an ear from the corpse and gobbled it up without even a splash of soy sauce or vinegar. Then it generously threw the corpse a short distance away. The corpse was immediately swarmed by youchu, which descended on it as if it were a holiday feast. Less than half a minute later, barely even a scrap remained of the dead youchu's skin or bones.

Gawking, Lin Jing murmured, "My Buddha is merciful. Please reflect on your table manners, benefactors."

His "benefactors" howled at him in unison, undoubtedly interested in practicing their table manners on him.

Lin Jing wiped cold sweat from his forehead. "Please, by all means, do as you wish."

Just then, a sharp whistling sounded in the distance. All the youchu—the gui—instantly fell silent. Fear twisted their expressions. They fled like fog blown away by the wind—and indeed, Lin Jing felt a strong wind blow past him.

In the next moment, someone was hurled down from above and pinned in place on the trunk of the strange adjacent tree. Four pitch-black manacles immediately sprouted from the tree and locked themselves around the person's limbs.

A second look showed Lin Jing that the person had a meter-long icicle buried in his heart, which meant he was as good as dead. Lin Jing was about to look away, unable to bear the sight, when the person's eyes opened...and suddenly Lin Jing recognized him.

Shocked, Lin Jing cried out in a ragged voice. "Shen-laoshi!"

Even with his forehead dripping with cold sweat and constant tremors running through his body, Shen Wei was courteous. He gave Lin Jing a slight nod.

Lin Jing rushed to the edge of the invisible dome. "What's happening? Shen-laoshi, why are you here? Who hurt you?"

Shen Wei's lips trembled, but he was unable to speak. Far off, someone *hmph*ed. A black shadow flashed in front of Lin Jing's eyes, and Ghost Face landed like a giant bat.

Ghost Face stood before Shen Wei, gleefully drinking in the sight of him. And then, slowly, he took off his mask.

Lin Jing gasped. "W-why are there *two* Shen-laoshi?!"

But upon closer inspection, the now-unmasked "Shen-laoshi's" skin was slightly paler—abnormally pale, in fact. It was a white that

bordered on blue, as though he had been soaked in formaldehyde. The skin tone was cold, somehow carrying resentment and yin energy. It made his face, which should have been so handsome, seem like a piece of skin draped over a skull.

To Lin Jing, it was as though this other person was some sort of unfortunate imitation. Perhaps this was someone who'd gotten plastic surgery to look like his boss's so-called wife—surgery by someone rather unskilled, that was. There was no question that this person was the ugly bootleg version.

The bootleg slowly opened his mouth. "I'm a sentimental person, but you forced my hand. I have no choice but to kill you, my brother."

As he spoke, his eyes sparkled with a strange light, as though he was both reluctant and yearning at once. The Chaos Kings of the Gui had entered the world as twins, neither superior to the other. But only Shen Wei had received Kunlun-jun's protection; he alone had attained divinity and now stood unaffected by the Great Seal...

"If I consume you, do you think I could break through the whole Seal?"

Even nailed to the Ancient Merit Tree, Shen Wei still laughed at him. The laugh was weak but mocking. "What, has your scheme with the Four Hallowed Artifacts failed already? What happened to the Reincarnation Dial? Did it turn into an ordinary rock in your hands?"

Ghost Face's eyelid twitched violently. He slapped Shen Wei across the face, and his brother's head snapped to the side with the force of it. The blow broke the skin inside his mouth on his gritted teeth.

Shen Wei spat the blood out, then said, "The Reincarnation Dial was made from the Three-Life Rock, and the Three-Life Rock and the Ancient Merit Tree are each connected to one of every person's seven corporeal souls. They are connected through the souls of the living. Only the Mountain-River Awl contains both yin and yang within itself as one.

"The Awl can trap anything in the world. I lured you out with it and put a tracking spell on you. Then, exactly as I expected, you brought out the Soul-Tempering Cauldron, and then the Merit Brush, where everyone could see. The most important hearthstone under the Soul-Tempering Cauldron is from the Three-Life Rock. As for where you found such a fragment...I don't even need to guess. The moment the Merit Brush appeared in the world, I found the Reincarnation Dial and put it in the Mountain-River Awl. How do you suppose that cauldron ended up in your hands so easily? Did you really think yourself so lucky that someone would just give you a pillow the moment you felt sleepy?"

"Mountain-River Awl... The Mountain-River Awl was in your hands all along? *You* were the one who planned for it to appear in Qingxi Village?"

"Can't you read? 'Mountain-River.' 'Mountain-River.' The thirty-six mountains begin with Kunlun Mountain. I inherited the Mountain God's power and an inherent connection to the ten thousand great mountains. Why would I fight you for something... that has always been in my hands?" Cold sweat dripped into Shen Wei's mouth. Unbothered, he licked his lips. "One more thing you might want to know. Remember the bait you used to lure me here? That wisp of Chaos you took from your own body? Where do you suppose it is now, after I sucked it away?"

His expression twisting into something nearly savage, Ghost Face's countenance went blue and then red. His hand lashed out and grasped the icicle in Shen Wei's chest. The blood drenching Shen Wei's robes stuck flesh and fabric together tightly. He was a tragic sight.

Ghost Face gave the icicle a brutal twist. "I couldn't care less." His breath came heavily as he leaned in close to Shen Wei's face. "I don't need to know anything. I can simply bleed you out until you can no longer maintain this human form. Then I can pull Kunlun's tendon out of you and consume you, one mouthful at a time, and ever after, there will be only *one* King of the Gui in the world. I. Will. Truly. Be. Unmatched."

Agony left Shen Wei unable to speak, but the mocking smile that seemed carved into the corner of his lips was still loud and clear: *You're welcome to try.*

Ghost Face pulled the icicle halfway out, only to fiercely thrust it back in. Shen Wei's body convulsed. At long last, he passed out and hung motionless, head dangling limply.

In a flash, Ghost Face vanished into the endless darkness.

URING THE ENTIRE confrontation, Ghost Face hadn't
so much as glanced at Lin Jing, probably assuming he and
his trivial abilities were beneath notice. Overwhelmed
with shock and fear, Lin Jing muttered reassurances to himself. "It'll
be okay. Amitabha. Everything'll definitely be okay."

Lin Jing craned his neck, trying to get a look at Shen Wei, who
was somewhat obscured by the Wangchuan waters. He found himself wishing that he could turn into a large turtle, able to swim and
hide at will.

After another furtive look at their surroundings, he called out
in the tiniest voice he could manage. "Shen-laoshi...? Shen-laoshi?"
There was no response. "Shen—"

Out of nowhere, a youchu appeared, baring its crooked teeth at
Lin Jing. Startled, Lin Jing instinctively leaned away and clamped
his mouth shut to hide his own tidy pearly whites, afraid that the
youchu might see them and become jealous. The youchu, which
Ghost Face had presumably sent to keep an eye on them, licked its
lips but ultimately didn't dare take a bite of the things it was meant
to guard. Instead, it circled Lin Jing a few times, eyes trained on him
like a hunter with prey locked in its sights.

Lin Jing took a deep breath and stared right back at it, trembling.
"Hey," he said. "Do you speak human?"

High-level youchu were intelligent and capable of conversing with humans. This one gave its cunning prey a wary look. "Shut up," it responded in the peculiar, hoarse voice of its kind.

Being able to communicate was a good start. Lin Jing sat on the ground and deliberately let out a sigh. "Now that the others have all run away, it's just the two of us here. If I shut up, won't you be lonely—aaah! Don't do that! Be civilized, please!" The youchu had come closer, its menacing shark-like teeth on full display. "I'll shut up!" Lin Jing cried. "I'll shut up! I'll shut up right now! Please believe me! Monks don't lie!"

The youchu withdrew its claws and teeth and slowly backed off to one side.

There was nothing Lin Jing could do. He gave the unconscious Shen Wei another anxious look, but his only real option was to force himself to calm down and silently chant the Great Compassion Mantra. The youchu, seeing that Lin Jing's eyes were now closed, assumed that he was finally settling down and dismissed him from its mind. It risked a glance up at Shen Wei, impaled on the ancient tree. The youchu whimpered and retreated a tiny bit further. Peace was finally restored to this place, thousands of chi below the Huangquan.

But then the youchu sensed something. Its head snapped up with a start. Lin Jing was exactly where he'd been before, still sitting with his eyes closed like he'd become a statue of a Buddha. Behind him, the Great Sealing Rock was wreathed in a warm white glow, as though responding to something. The youchu shot to its feet and tried to reach over the rock to grab Lin Jing's shoulder, but as its claws neared the white light, they crumbled to ash, as if they'd touched a blazing hot flame.

Lin Jing, the fake monk, was quick on the uptake. Seeing the howling, screaming youchu told him that this was an effective approach, so he inhaled deeply and began loudly reciting scriptures. The white light on the Sealing Rock glowed hotter and hotter, and the guard dog of a youchu jumped up and down, but it had no way of getting any closer. The halo of white light kept spreading, expansive enough now that it brushed against Shen Wei. An uneasy furrow creased Shen Wei's brow—the only sign that he was more than a hanging corpse.

The youchu's spiraling anxiety finally drove it to risk everything. It flung itself forward with a howl, willing to be reduced to coal if that meant it could rip the damned scripture-reciting monk apart. A crackling filled the air as its flesh and skin roasted, but the youchu held fast in spirit even as its body was reduced to ruin. Its mouth, burned down to nothing but teeth, gaped open. It lunged for Lin Jing's neck.

That was enough to finally disrupt Lin Jing's chanting. He closed his eyes and yelped, "Buddha! This disciple is close to surrendering his mortal body and ascending to the higher realm! Where did da-shixiong go? Save me! Shen-laoshi! Boss! Da-shixiong!"

He kept up this random yelling until long past when he'd expected those knife-like teeth to sink into his neck. Eventually, he cracked his eyes open, only to find that the youchu had hurriedly fled—as if it had been scared off.

Something prompted Lin Jing to look up. Eyes like icy pools met his. At some point in the commotion, Shen Wei had woken.

"Shen-laoshi?" Lin Jing tried to call out. There was a minute flicker in Shen Wei's gaze. "A-a-a-a-are you okay?"

Shen Wei struggled feebly against his bonds, making the chains around his limbs clink together. Even that tiny movement made the veins on his forehead stand out. Eventually, with great difficulty, he managed a quiet "...Mmh."

"Why are you here? How did that...um, that person? The one who looks like you? How did he get ahold of you?" Lin Jing asked.

Shen Wei closed his eyes, tilting his head back to rest it against the Ancient Merit Tree. It was as though he had no strength at all. "He attacked me from behind," he said mildly. "I could've dodged, but I was busy taking back the Chaos. I had to take the blow so that our efforts wouldn't all go to waste. It's fine—except that he stabbed me in the heart with this icicle made from frozen water of the Huangquan, so I'm unable to move at the moment."

Lin Jing wasn't yet aware of who exactly Shen Wei was, but nothing about this situation seemed fine in the slightest. Lin Jing gulped. "Then what should I do? Do you have any way of getting me down from this stupid rock so I can help you?"

There was a long moment of silence before Shen Wei said, "That 'stupid rock' behind you is the mark of the Great Houtu Seal, placed there by the Sovereign Wa herself."

This revelation frightened Lin Jing enough that he didn't dare lean on it again.

"Don't worry." Shen Wei chuckled. "That Chaos King of the Gui has enough to deal with right now. As long as I have Kunlun's divine tendon, he won't dare do anything to me. We're safe for the moment."

"No, no, let's figure out a way to save ourselves," Lin Jing quickly said. "No magical tendon can staunch your wound. If Director Zhao ever found out I just sat back and let you bleed like this, he'd make me the main course of this year's Lunar New Year's Eve dinner."

Shen Wei's gaze softened at the mention of Zhao Yunlan. After some thought, he said, "If you must try something, please continue reciting your scriptures. The Great Seal originated from Nüwa's merciful heart. If you're sincere, it might help you."

Lin Jing considered that. Since reciting scriptures was all he could really do just then anyway, he sat properly. In a booming voice, with crisp enunciation, he began chanting as though he was announcing the news. The effect was comedic enough to make Shen Wei burst into laughter. With no sound around them but the murmuring Wangchuan waters, he slowly started to listen. The lines of his brows and eyes, ruthless and stern from all the bloodshed, slowly started to soften.

The white light around the Great Sealing Rock gradually grew to an eye-searing brightness. Lin Jing truly was a proper disciple of the Bodhidharma line. Who else could've entered a meditative state so easily even under these conditions?

The ropes around his body slowly melted away in the pool of white light, but Lin Jing didn't even notice. Shen Wei was a bit shocked. Birds of a feather, it seemed, really did flock together. Everyone who'd gathered around Zhao Yunlan seemed to be a little like him, one way or another; for example, when fixated on something, he could focus his whole attention on it and forget everything else.

Guo Changcheng, meanwhile, had successfully managed to keep the families of the missing people in the police station, but the expected good news from Zhao Yunlan and the others wasn't forthcoming.

Close to midnight, Chu Shuzhi and Daqing finally returned, both looking worse for wear. All they'd managed to bring back with them were a few IDs, phones, and keys that had been scattered over the ground. It seemed that whatever they were facing, it only consumed living things. These lifeless belongings remained untouched.

The police station was still as bright as day, and in the meeting room that had been co-opted for relatives of the missing, chaos reigned. Chu Shuzhi held Daqing in one arm, pinching his brow tiredly with the other hand. He waved at Guo Changcheng, beckoned him into a small office, and shut the door.

Guo Changcheng had a bad feeling. Looking from Chu Shuzhi to Daqing, he said, "Chu-ge, where are Director Zhao and the others? Did you find Lin-dage? Zhu Hong-jie went to find you guys. Did you see her? Is there any sign at all of the missing people?"

Chu Shuzhi silently took a small evidence bag from his pocket and handed it over.

Accepting it, Guo Changcheng peered inside and saw only a handful of dust. He froze. "What is..."

"Bone ash."

The evidence bag hit the floor with a soft splat.

Chu Shuzhi gave a succinct summary of what had happened at the resort, then told Guo Changcheng, "Call headquarters immediately. Tell Wang Zheng to treat these people as disappearances for now. But a death is a death, and we won't be able to keep the truth under wraps for long. Tell her to think of a reasonable explanation we can give people."

In utter disbelief, Guo Changcheng asked, "A reasonable... explanation?" Chu Shuzhi seemed to be saying that he wanted Wang Zheng to think of how to cover up the truth.

After a silence, the Corpse King delicately said, "Under normal circumstances, we can only do DNA testing if there are remains to test. It's not possible with cremated remains, never mind *this*. There's not much we can do about it. Even if we gathered every speck of dust in the resort, it's impossible to tell the families which heap of dust was whose loved one."

"Then we at least need to have a culprit..."

Chu Shuzhi laughed helplessly. "Guo Changcheng, do you know who the Soul-Executing Emissary is?"

Guo Changcheng thought the Emissary was scary, but he had no real idea about his background. He shook his head.

"I'll be honest with you," Chu Shuzhi said. "My thousands of years of cultivation allow me to walk under the sun. All corpses and skeletons bow to my will, so those in the know flatter me with the title 'Corpse King.' The next level up for me would be a ba,[10] or a 'Corpse Immortal.' But even if I attain that level, if it weren't for Director Zhao, I'd still never dare approach someone like the Soul-Executing Emissary. At the bare minimum, I'd keep a good two kilometers away from him. Do you understand what I'm saying?" Chu Shuzhi paused, then continued, "We're dealing with someone who can catch the Soul-Executing Emissary off guard. Even if he only managed that by being sneaky, it means his power is at least on par with the Emissary's. Whoever this is, he's too powerful. This isn't something we can handle."

Guo Changcheng stared at him blankly, unable to accept what he was hearing. "What about their souls? If the victims' bodies are gone, there should still be souls, right? How could anyone born into this world just...just *disappear* like that for no reason?"

Daqing jumped from Chu Shuzhi's arms and sat on the desk. "The souls are still there." The other two both immediately turned toward him, but the black cat seemed distracted and didn't elaborate.

After waiting a while, Chu Shuzhi prompted him. "Daqing?"

And then, right before their eyes, the cat's body began to elongate slowly, his glossy fur melting away. As Guo Changcheng and Chu Shuzhi stared, mouths hanging open, he transformed into a young man whose hair fell all the way to his ankles! He was barefoot, clad in garments from some unknown era; really, it looked as though

---

10 Ba (魃) is a drought monster, sometimes believed to be a corpse that doesn't dry out after death.

he'd carelessly wrapped a length of cloth around himself...but none of that seemed important. Most shockingly, black fur had been replaced by pale skin; and while the cat had been tremendously fat, the beautiful youth before them was slim!

"D-Daqing?!" Chu Shuzhi blurted.

The lazy expression that crossed the young man's face was unmistakably feline. "Mhmm, yes." He spared Chu Shuzhi a glance. "It's me, your lord."

As he spoke, he jumped down from the table, landing without even the faintest sound. Every movement, every step, radiated felinity. Awestruck by the magic that had unfolded before them, Chu Shuzhi and Guo Changcheng both made way for him.

Daqing kept speaking. "I don't know who sealed away my memories. I still can't remember much from all those years ago. But when I went up Kunlun Mountain with Zhao Yunlan, the Great Divine Tree awoke something in me. Now I can take human form again. Even though transforming makes me hairless, and thus, hideous, I at least seem to be able to remember some things now."

Guo Changcheng and Chu Shuzhi, who were both hairless and, apparently, uglier than "hideous," wore the same peculiar expression.

"The Netherworld officially calls the things we ran into today 'youchu,' but more accurately, they're gui," Daqing said. "I'm not exactly sure where the gui are from, but I know they're linked to the demise of Fuxi and Nüwa. You heard Shen Wei. When the gui came into the world, not a single blade of grass survived in the Great Wild. But as far as I know, the gui don't have souls, so even though they drink blood and gnaw on bones, they don't eat mortals' souls because there's no benefit to it for them. I think what happened here must've been too sudden. All those people died before their time, so even though their bodies disappeared, their souls are still souls of the living. Since the Netherworld couldn't reach them in time, those frightened spirits probably ran off somewhere."

"Then I'm going to go find them!" Guo Changcheng said.

"Why?" Daqing asked, bewildered. "Losing souls is the Netherworld's problem, even if they aren't in the mood to care about that right now."

It took Guo Changcheng a while to think of what to say. "But... But I promised the families of the people who disappeared that I'd give them an explanation..."

"You won't be able to," Daqing said patiently. "Besides, they won't believe you."

"So I need to go find the victims' souls! If a person existed, they can't just disappear for no reason." Guo Changcheng was absolutely adamant on this point. "That... That's not right."

Chu Shuzhi scoffed. "There are plenty of things that aren't right. Do you think you can fix them all? How do you even plan on finding these souls?"

No answer occurred to Guo Changcheng for that. He gave it some thought, then looked down, embarrassed. But Chu Shuzhi didn't keep laughing at him. Instead, he pulled out a little bottle and threw it to him. "Cows' tears. They'll help open your third eye so you can see the souls of the living."

Guo Changcheng looked up in disbelief.

"Go take care of official business first. Call Wang Zheng and tell her to send someone to come help after she gets the official story sorted." A bit awkwardly, Chu Shuzhi avoided Guo Changcheng's too-warm gaze. "I need to look for Lin Jing either way, so you might as well come along. If you can find the souls, we take them with us. If you can't, then forget about it. Just don't give me any extra trouble."

"You two go ahead. I need to find Zhao Yunlan," Daqing said. "He's on his own, and I'm worried about him."

He took a few awkward steps as a human, but it didn't seem to occur to him to use the door. He leaped onto the windowsill, then had a thought. Turning back, he added, "If the kid's too naive and doesn't understand, please try to be understanding, Corpse King. Be very careful. We only just got our new office. We haven't even had a chance to renovate yet."

With that, he jumped out the window into the darkness, blinking out of view.

THE TEN KINGS were seated high, high above.

The hall was as blue as the sky; its height and depth were endless. There was always a vast expanse of stars hanging overhead, and just underfoot were the Eighteen Levels of Hell—tongue-pulling and hot oil and all—with three thousand impassable waters flowing endlessly around them. Anyone entering the hall was walking on solid ground, but it was as if that ground were unmarred glass. The ghosts below were starkly visible as they were skinned, as they passed through mountains of knives, and as they were fried in hot oil. The sight made it seem that anyone in the hall could fall through the floor into Hell at any moment.

Zhao Yunlan had asked the Magistrate to lead the way to the real Reincarnation Cycle, but the moment they reached the Netherworld, they were informed that the Ten Kings wished to see them. The Magistrate had no choice but to visit the Yanluo Courts first.

As soon as they set foot inside and got a look at the "welcoming display," the Magistrate's gaze flashed. The Eighteen Levels of Hell weren't ordinarily visible within the Courts. As a rule, they were only displayed as a warning when a ghost who had committed the most heinous crimes refused to obey.

Showing it to Zhao Yunlan like this was truly no way to treat a guest.

The Ten Yanluo Kings wore fierce expressions as they peered down from their pedestals high up on the walls. The dark lighting made them look like beasts baring vicious teeth. Zhu Hong, who had tagged along, stared down into the Hell of Tongue Ripping. She saw a slouched man bound to a pole, and as she watched, one ghoul restrained him while another forced his mouth open, reaching in with a dry, blueish hand. Startled, Zhu Hong grabbed Zhao Yunlan's arm. "D-don't go over there."

Zhao Yunlan pried her fingers open. "Wait for me outside."

Stone-faced, he marched forward. With every step, he felt like he was treading on the heads of the countless ghouls below. When he reached the center of the Great Hall, he stopped. That placed him directly above the Hell of Oil Cauldrons. Zhu Hong couldn't shake the feeling that Zhao Yunlan would be spattered with hot oil at any moment. She tried to follow but couldn't keep from glancing downward...just in time to see a long, soft tongue being yanked out of a man's mouth. It seemed as if the blood would surely splatter her face. Her stomach roiled. Finally, unable to bear it, she turned away.

Zhao Yunlan's frosty gaze swept across the Ten Yanluo Kings. Then he turned to the Magistrate cowering at his side. "Do you guys expect me to just stand here while we talk?"

His voice was deep and cold. Each word pierced the distressed cries rising up from the Eighteen Levels of Hell.

To the Magistrate, Zhao Yunlan no longer seemed like the Guardian. At this moment, he was far more like Kunlun-jun. The Qin'guang King might be certain that Kunlun-jun's spirit hadn't been awakened, but seeing Zhao Yunlan like this made the Magistrate tremble. He shot a look at the reapers. A pair of them darted out immediately, then came back with a chair as well as some tea.

Zhao Yunlan took his seat like an important lord, crossing his legs. Then he placed a hand against the teacup that was being offered to him and glanced at the reaper's pale face, so like papier-mâché. "I'll pass on the tea. I'm afraid the food from down here won't agree with my stomach. Now, you've put on your little show to intimidate me and kept up your appearances. But we're all very busy, so let's get to the point."

Ten voices spoke, one from each of the Ten Courts, layering into a unique harmony as they angrily denounced him. "Impudent young man!"

From the moment Ghost Face had stolen Shen Wei away right before his eyes, Zhao Yunlan had felt like a chunk of ice was weighing down on his heart. He'd felt completely detached from everything anyone said or did; none of it seemed real or consequential. Only now, after having been confronted with such an extreme sight, did his mind begin to clear. Belatedly, he felt his anger float to the surface, although no trace of it showed on his face.

Zhao Yunlan crossed his arms in front of his chest. Ghost Face had taken the Soul-Executing Emissary. Whether Ghost Face harmed the Emissary or the Emissary had gone to Ghost Face's side, it was bad news for the Netherworld. What was more, while there might not be a clear prognosis for the Great Seal, it clearly wasn't going to hold out for much longer. And yet even under these circumstances, the Ten Courts were still putting on such an unfriendly welcome, appearances be damned.

Years of experience working with the Netherworld told Zhao Yunlan that the dumbasses were obviously planning to ask something of him, but they were unwilling to swallow their pride to do so. Either that, or they saw no need to take a mortal like him seriously and had chosen the route of coercion and bribery.

Whatever the case, it meant he was under no obligation to be polite either.

He gave a cold laugh. "You'll all have to forgive the bad manners. My parents didn't raise me right, so this is just who I am."

As one, the reapers held their breaths. Some didn't understand the situation and thought this man was clearly there to start a fight. The Ten Yanluo Courts were where every soul came to be judged for the sins committed before and after death. Every last one, even the noblest aristocrat or most commanding general, stood upright as they walked in and lay flat as they left. The reapers had seen count-less souls cry out for their parents but had never seen arrogance to match this. He behaved as though he wouldn't inevitably face reincarnation sooner or later!

Enraged, the ensemble boomed again. "Zhao Yunlan!"

Zhao Yunlan didn't back down. "Sorry, but that's *'Guardian'* to you," he retorted.

At that moment, the ground beneath them started to shake—small tremors that quickly became fiercer and fiercer. They sent sand and pebbles flying everywhere inside the Yanluo Courts.

Zhao Yunlan looked down. In the Hell of Oil Cauldrons below his feet, boiling oil was sloshing over the sides of the vats. The ghouls that had looked so impressive were now running around like chickens with their heads cut off, trying to escape. In the Hell of Copper Pillars, cracks appeared on the pillars, and in the Hell of the Mountain of Knives, the blades were jumping up and down like shrews.

A reaper came bursting through the doors to the Ten Yanluo Courts. Falling to their knees, they cried, "Terrible news! The Great Seal... The Great Seal broke!"

Even as they spoke, the doors to the Halls were thrown wide-open. Everyone peered out, only to see the water in the Wangchuan

River boiling. All the ferrymen had abandoned their boats and taken uncertain refuge up on the Naihe Bridge, which shook precariously. The narrow Huangquan Road was already submerged beneath the rising water, and a massive black shadow was slowly approaching from below. But just as it was about to surface, it stopped. Lights as soft as fireflies began glowing on either side of the flooded Huangquan Road—pea-sized lights all in a row. Zhao Yunlan remembered the little oil lamps that had lined the road—the soul-guarding lamps.

As the soft light and the huge shadow faced off, another reaper staggered in. "Ghost City! Ghost City's gates have cracked! It's utter chaos! The violent ghosts are going to rebel!"

The Ten Kings, who always presented a united front, started to panic. They sounded very much like ten enormous ducks quacking noisily at one another.

Zhao Yunlan grabbed the Magistrate by the collar, jamming his gun under the man's chin. "Take me to see the Reincarnation Cycle right now or I'll shoot you in the head!"

"Director Zhao!" Zhu Hong screamed, unable to believe his fearlessness.

A lone Yanluo King spoke up. "Guardian, will you explain yourself?!"

This single voice, unsupported by the other nine, was thin and weak.

"Explain myself? Go fuck *your*self!" Zhao Yunlan sneered. "I've spent a long time holding myself back with you sons of bitches. Now move!"

"Guardian, please wait!" This time, all ten voices rang out together.

Behind him, Zhao Yunlan heard a huge clang. Glancing back, he realized that the portal to Hell had been closed at some point.

The hall that had been so dark was now brightly lit, revealing the Ten Kings for all to see. Exposed by the light, they seemed surprisingly normal, despite their slightly peculiar getups.

The mechanism on the wall began to turn. With a great noise of metal springs, a stone door opened in the wall, behind which was another door. The Ten Kings descended from their towering pedestals, each taking out a key that was always on their person. They opened ten doors, one after another, and behind them all lay a huge pond with an ephemeral air to it. It didn't seem as though they were even in the Netherworld anymore—this was more reminiscent of the Jade Pond.[11]

And there, in the pool, Zhao Yunlan saw a gigantic lamp. It was a giant version of the small oil lamps on the Huangquan Road, standing at least a dozen meters high. The Qin'guang King, who had opened the final door, turned to Zhao Yunlan. "I'll be honest with you now. This is the last of the Four Hallowed Artifacts, the Soul-Guarding Lamp."

Despite the Wangchuan River's turmoil, it was oddly peaceful thousands of zhang below the Huangquan, where the Great Seal was.

By this point, Lin Jing had escaped his bonds. He recited a water-repelling spell and circled around Shen Wei many times before climbing the Ancient Merit Tree. "Hold on, let me take a look. I must have a wire or something on me that I can use to pick the lock."

"No need," Shen Wei said calmly. "All you need to do is pull the icicle from my chest."

Lin Jing shuddered. "P-pull it out? Won't you…"

---

11   The Jade Pond (瑶池) is a mythical place in the Heavens where the Queen Mother of the West (西王母) resides.

"I'll be fine, but thank you."

Lin Jing's palms were a little sweaty. "You said it, Shen-laoshi, not me. If I fuck you up when pulling it out, I... I... Can you sign a waiver for me first?"

Shen Wei motioned for him to lean in closer. Confused, Lin Jing did as he asked.

Right by his ear, Shen Wei murmured, "You see, I'm actually..."

What Shen Wei said shocked Lin Jing so badly that his legs turned to jelly. He nearly fell right out of the tree. No longer daring to waste a moment, he respectfully grabbed hold of the icicle embedded in Shen Wei's chest. With a great shout, he yanked it free. There was a sound of tearing flesh as Shen Wei's torso was dragged forward along with the icicle, only to fall back upon hitting the limit of the chains securing his limbs.

Lin Jing broke out in a sympathetic icy sweat, but Shen Wei didn't make a sound. Once the great length of ice—a meter long—was fully removed from his chest, a powerful gout of blood followed, spraying Lin Jing's face when he couldn't dodge in time. Expression tight with panic, Lin Jing hurried to check on Shen Wei.

The pain of the extraction seemed to have been more than Shen Wei could bear. Hair was plastered to his forehead with cold sweat, and his gaze was empty and unfocused. Lin Jing, afraid he would faint again, reached out to pat his face but then remembered that this was the Soul-Executing Emissary. His extended hand couldn't quite make the landing. "Shen...um, my lord? Can you hear me? Just...just hold on. I'll try to get you down as soon as possible."

Blood loss had left Shen Wei's lips horribly dry and cracked. As he faded in and out of consciousness, they moved minutely. Voice faint and muffled, he called out, "Kunlun..."

"Hm? What?"

Shen Wei's gaze seemed lost for a while longer, then suddenly snapped back into perfect focus. "My apologies... Could you, ah, hand me that icicle?"

As he spoke, the brutal wound in his chest started to heal itself, little by little. The bloody hole in his shirt was soon the only remaining sign that he'd ever been hurt at all. Lin Jing hastily hefted the huge icicle with both hands. It was made of frozen water from the Wangchuan River, which likely explained why it seemed so much more piercingly cold than normal ice.

As Lin Jing handed it over to Shen Wei, the ice melted all at once into a wisp of smoke with a bloodred tinge. In the next moment, Shen Wei swallowed it. The deep cracks in his lips closed over one by one; light returned to his eyes. And then, with a few soft clinks, the chains binding his limbs gave way.

Lin Jing leaned in close. "My lord, are you all right now? What do we do? What about the youchu from before...and that guy with the mask?"

Shen Wei laughed lightly. "Oh, him? He's gone to investigate the scrap of Chaos that I captured. I also prepared a little surprise for him in front of the Yanluo Courts."

Although he didn't understand, Lin Jing still found himself shuddering. As he gave Shen Wei a sidelong look, it occurred to him that Shen-laoshi... No, that the *Soul-Executing Emissary* and the masked man, despite their similar appearance, were worlds apart when it came to intelligence.

Lin Jing thought of himself as pretty dumb. Shrewd, calculating people made him want to run and hide far away in case they sold him off without him even realizing while he was still helping to count the money.

Shen Wei said, "The waters of the Wangchuan River are above us. Swimming up, you'll reach the Huangquan Road. Yunlan is most likely in the Netherworld, so let's go find him. Start swimming and I'll follow. But don't mention anything about my whereabouts just yet."

"Oh," Lin Jing answered. He paused, but then couldn't help asking, "Why not?"

"If I appear, this play won't reach its conclusion, and then how would we redirect all the disaster to our enemies?"

Hearing this, Lin Jing started silently chanting scriptures. What had his boss been thinking, falling for someone who was as calculating as...as...a calculator? It was probably a mistake he'd regret forever.

Back in the Mortal Realm, it was already late at night. Chu Shuzhi and Guo Changcheng were searching the resort with flashlights, still stumbling now and then. Chu Shuzhi wore a tiny whistle around his neck, and as the two of them walked, the whistle blew all on its own at all sorts of pitches. It could evidently attract the souls of the dead.

Chu Shuzhi felt as though, having had Guo Changcheng following him around for so long, he had become enough of a pacifist to go become a monk. All the world's calamities had nothing to do with him. Day in and day out, he was emulating Lei Feng[12]—one day trying to find a runaway girl at the highway exit and searching for lost souls in the dead of night the next.

The whistle's pitch suddenly rose, a sound similar to that of the Chinese hwamei bird. Chu Shuzhi raised a hand to stop Guo Changcheng. The two of them stood in the middle of a neglected pathway, listening as the whistle grew clearer and clearer. The notes rose and fell, the sound dragging out as though it were some kind of guiding siren.

---

12   Lei Feng (雷锋) was a folk hero around the 1950s-1960s, touted by the state as a model of altruism.

Guo Changcheng opened his eyes wide. Thanks to the cows' tears he'd applied, he saw a young person approaching from the end of the road, following the sound of the whistle. He was wearing a delivery company uniform and looked a little lost.

"Is that person human or a..."

"A ghost," said Chu Shuzhi.

Guo Changcheng shivered instinctively, but the confusion on the young man's face wiped his fear away. Instead, his heart ached a little.

Reaching them, the young person gave them a weird look, running a hand over his hair. "Sirs, why are you still out here so late? It's so cold! You should hurry home."

"What about you?" Chu Shuzhi countered. "You should go back soon too."

The young man laughed. "You're right. The guard's already signed for the package I was delivering, and I don't need to collect any packages today, so I can go home a bit early."

Chu Shuzhi took a little bottle from his pocket, opened it, and held it out. "Get in. I'll take you home."

The young man froze. The smile on his face gradually faded. He seemed deep in thought for a moment, as though suddenly coming to a realization.

"What's your name?" asked Guo Changcheng.

The young man looked up slowly. Sounding confused, he said, "My name is... What *is* my name? I don't remember."

"I remember. I've seen your ID. Your name is Feng Dawei, born in 1989. You turn twenty-four this year. You have an older brother, right? I wrote it all down," said Guo Changcheng. He took a notebook from his bag and flipped it open for Feng Dawei to see. Each missing person's details were meticulously recorded. "Your brother said that if it turned out you were no longer among the living, he'd take care of your parents. They're very sad right now, but they'll be all right."

Feng Dawei's eyes suddenly filled with tears.

"Come inside," Guo Changcheng urged. "We'll send you off. You don't want to be out here when the sun rises. I've heard sunlight isn't good for you guys."

Lowering his head, Feng Dawei wiped at his tears. "I'm dead, aren't I?"

Guo Changcheng hesitated, then nodded.

"How did I die? Did someone kill me? If the murderer is caught, will we be avenged?"

Choked up, Guo Changcheng had no idea how to respond. Instead, it was Chu Shuzhi's low voice that answered. "No evildoer can escape. Don't worry."

For a long while, Feng Dawei stared down at the little bottle. "But how could I just...die? I-I wasn't done living..."

"Come in," said Chu Shuzhi. "Let's get you a better life in your next incarnation."

Feng Dawei laughed bitterly. "Next life? Forget about the next life—can you take a message to my parents and brother?"

Guo Changcheng hurriedly got his notebook back out and carefully wrote "Message to Pass Along" on Feng Dawei's page in his childish handwriting. "Go ahead."

With a sniffle, Feng Dawei began to talk. He said a whole bunch of random, useless things, and Guo Changcheng faithfully recorded every last word. Once they were finished, he showed Feng Dawei what he'd written. The young man read his own message aloud, following along with Guo Changcheng's finger on the page. Finally, he smiled, albeit with a little difficulty. "Okay. I can rest easy now—there's nothing more I can do anyway. Bro, you're a good person. Thank you."

Taking a deep breath, he suddenly swooped into Chu Shuzhi's bottle.

Chu Shuzhi closed the lid on it and put it in his pocket, then turned to Guo Changcheng. "Let's go find the next one."

Guo Changcheng followed. After a few steps, Chu Shuzhi suddenly spoke again, without even turning to look back at him. "You're doing great."

The tiniest compliment had always been able to make Guo Changcheng light up. This sudden praise made him glow like the peak of spring.

At that moment, a howling arose, uncomfortably close by. It turned out to be a few low-level gui that had remained in the Mortal Realm. The creatures launched themselves at the pair, jaws agape as they followed the smell of fresh blood and flesh.

Chu Shuzhi shoved Guo Changcheng behind him and brought his foot up in a sweeping horizontal kick. He struck the nearest gui in the chest with a low thud. The gui stumbled back a few steps and fell on its ass.

Three or four more gui grew bolder at once, despite seeing this. They rushed forward, shoulder to shoulder.

Chu Shuzhi pushed Guo Changcheng in the chest. "Stay away."

But before the Corpse King, who had been emulating Lei Feng for many days, could stretch his muscles and start to really show off, someone landed in front of him. It was a youth holding a long skewer, which he turned on the gui. He stabbed them swiftly and precisely, as if making tanghulu. In the blink of an eye, he had created a truly revolting barbecue stick of low-level youchu.

No one would have called the young man pretty. His appearance suggested that his parents hadn't put much effort into making him, but his smile radiated absolute sincerity. He withdrew his sharp skewer, wiped it on the ground, and then approached Chu Shuzhi. "Hey, friend, are you all right?"

Still somewhat stuck in his own edgy teenager phase, being around strangers always made Chu Shuzhi defensive. His brow furrowed as the young man walked closer. Fortunately, the stranger was observant. Seeing Chu Shuzhi's dark expression, he stopped and kept his distance—his friendly smiling never wavering. "I'm a rogue cultivator. I sensed something off around here, so I came to check things out. Don't misunderstand, bro."

Chu Shuzhi gave a slight nod, all cold arrogance. He turned and called to Guo Changcheng. "Xiao-Guo, let's go."

Guo Changcheng ran over at once, but the young man tagged along, uninvited. Perhaps seeing that Chu Shuzhi was wary and didn't like talking to people, he turned his attention to Guo Changcheng instead. "What were those monsters just now? Why aren't there any people here? Do you guys know what happened?"

This was more questions than Guo Changcheng was used to being asked all at once; it was easy for him to lose track of the order they'd been asked in, and once his brain got muddled, it was hard for him to think. "I'm not sure either," he replied with a timid look.

"Then what do you guys do?"

"We're police," Guo Changcheng said.

"Oh! Really?" Surprise flooded the young man's expression, but he started to chat with Guo Changcheng naturally.

Chu Shuzhi stayed silent and listened to them talk, not dropping his guard for a moment. Only a dumbass like Guo Changcheng would lower their guard when a friendly rogue cultivator appeared in a place like this.

The stranger had a knack for conversation. In just a few sentences, he realized that words didn't come easily for Guo Changcheng, so he changed his approach at once. Rather than asking question after question, he started chatting casually about the resort, periodically sneaking in a few questions about their backgrounds.

As they walked, they collected six or seven more souls. It wasn't long at all before they'd entirely filled two small bottles. In the darkness, the bottles glowed richly with different colors. Chu Shuzhi tucked them side by side in his fanny pack and got out another empty one.

The Corpse King had an extreme personality and was cold by nature; necromancy was a deviation from the norm to begin with, not accepted by the world. Chu Shuzhi was lonesome and arrogant, wholly unconcerned about his merits, so he never paid it any mind. He'd always thought "morality" was a facade, nothing but an excuse to hide behind. The purer and more beautiful something seemed, the darker it might be beneath.

Despite this cynical outlook on the world, he somehow managed to put up with Guo Changcheng. Maybe by now it was just habit.

Either way, looking at the soul bottles in his bag stirred an inexplicable feeling in his heart. It made him grumble that Guo Changcheng was being too kind for no reason, even as Chu Shuzhi followed him around to collect lost souls.

There were plenty of gui wandering around the little resort. The unfamiliar cultivator kept helping them clear out any youchu in their way. He was quick and merciless, raising Chu Shuzhi's guard even more. So when the cultivator started asking about the Soul-Guarding Order, the Corpse King naturally gave him a chilly response. "Sir, if something is none of your business, maybe you shouldn't be asking. Why be annoying for no reason?"

Guo Changcheng just laughed, embarrassed. "Sorry. Chu-ge is a very good person. He doesn't really mean it like it sounds. It's just that we have regulations..."

The easygoing cultivator nodded repeatedly. "Ha ha! No worries, it's my bad for asking too much. Sorry, bro. I have no filter. It must be annoying sometimes. You're not annoyed with me, are you, li'l bro?"

"How could I be?" Guo Changcheng immediately asked. "You've helped us so much! When we get back to the county, we'll treat you to dinner. You're a good person."

But just then, they passed by a little store. The young man's profile was facing the display window, and he was talking with a dazzling smile, but from the corner of his eye, Guo Changcheng happened to glimpse the reflection in the glass.

What he saw there shocked and alarmed him. This kind, warm friend's reflection was that of a monster Guo Changcheng had never seen before: pitch-black all over, with different heads constantly surging in and out of its shoulders. In the window, its mouth was opened savagely in Guo Changcheng's direction—a mouth bristling with fangs that resembled ancient torture devices.

The little baton in Guo Changcheng's pocket reacted before he could even make a sound. Flames erupted toward the kind-looking youth. Chu Shuzhi turned back, stunned, only to see Guo Changcheng just standing there helplessly. The kindhearted cultivator, however, had sprung back a good dozen meters, effortlessly landing on the roof of a house.

Chu Shuzhi knew Guo Changcheng couldn't control the baton; anything the contraption did was an instinctive reaction to his fear. Stuffing the glass bottle back into his bag, Chu Shuzhi narrowed his eyes and stared icily at the person on the rooftop. "What happened?"

The young man on the roof was no longer smiling. He looked down at Guo Changcheng. "Yeah, friend," he echoed. "What happened?"

Guo Changcheng stumbled over his words. "His... H-his... shadow..."

Chu Shuzhi turned on his flashlight. The cultivator's lonely shadow had nowhere to hide from the light, but no matter how carefully Chu Shuzhi looked, he didn't see anything wrong. The cultivator squatted on the roof, letting him look all he wanted. Calm and collected, he asked, "What's wrong with my shadow?"

With Chu Shuzhi giving him a confused expression, Guo Changcheng was at a loss for words.

The young man shook his head with a sigh. "My efforts have truly gone to waste. I've been helping you guys all this time, and I don't need thanks, but if I hadn't been quick just now, would I have died at this li'l bro's hands? Even though he seems so honest and kind?"

Chu Shuzhi's forehead creased. At that moment, the whistle around his neck went silent. Footsteps rustled in the distance, followed by the sound of heavy breathing. In the darkness, it was hair-raising. Goosebumps prickled to life all over Guo Changcheng's neck. And then a huge youchu's head burst up out of the ground, right between the cultivator and the two of them, coming face-to-face with Guo Changcheng.

It seemed that the Great Seal was straining more and more. The gui wandering the Mortal World drew closer and closer to the city and streets, following the scent of fresh flesh and blood. Meanwhile, in the county less than fifty kilometers away, people were still completely clueless.

THE QIN'GUANG KING'S expression was grave. "Guardian, haven't you realized? The Great Seal is broken. The Soul-Executing Emissary guarded it for so many years, but now we have no idea where he is, or even whether he still lives. The small lamps on the Huangquan Road can only buy us a bit of time. As things stand, it appears that the Netherworld will be the first to fall, followed by the Mortal Realm. Please calm yourself. I assure you, I'd never test you in this manner under less extraordinary circumstances. But now we should work as one to get through this catastrophe together."

They're offering the carrot after *the stick,* Zhao Yunlan thought.

He kept his face studiously blank as he released the Magistrate, but he didn't lower his gun. Taking another look at the ethereal Soul-Guarding Lamp, glowing with unearthly energy, he said, "What exactly would the Qin'guang King have me do?"

The Qin'guang King sighed. "The Soul-Guarding Lamp was formed from the body of the Mountain God of the Great Wild, Kunlun. It calms souls and drives away evil. It is the last and greatest protection the Four Pillars have, but..." Another sigh. "Guardian, please take a look."

As he spoke, he tried to lead Zhao Yunlan to the edge of the pool containing the lamp, but Zhao Yunlan didn't budge. The Qin'guang

King, feeling a little awkward under Zhao Yunlan's icy stare, gestured with his hands. In response, the Soul-Guarding Lamp slowly floated up out of the water and rotated toward them. It even tilted forward slightly, displaying its lack of wick.

"Having reached this point, let us lay our cards on the table," said the Qin'guang King. "It's true that this humble god has treated Kunlun-jun disrespectfully in the past. But please, on account of this one's lowly rank and tireless efforts to protect the Three Realms, show mercy."

The sudden change in how the Qin'guang King addressed Zhao Yunlan was a shock for Zhu Hong. She turned to Zhao Yunlan, but as usual, his face betrayed nothing.

When he replied, Zhao Yunlan's smile was laced with mockery. "I can't say you seem much more respectful now. Why did you keep the Magistrate from taking me to see the Reincarnation Cycle? And given how many secrets the Yanluo Kings know, how could you not know it was Shennong who sealed Kunlun's memory and powers? I want to find the Reincarnation Cycle that he left behind and awaken Kunlun's divine spirit. If I do, I might even be able to help you deal with that overbearing Ghost Face outside. So why stop me?"

The Qin'guang King wouldn't meet his gaze. "This humble god acted out of line..." he hedged.

"The problem isn't *how* you acted," Zhao Yunlan interrupted. "It's that you dared to do something you shouldn't have. You knew Kunlun's divine spirit hadn't awakened because the Soul-Guarding Lamp remained unlit, right?"

The Qin'guang King looked everywhere but at him. "This... This..."

"Even if it did awaken, a divine spirit that's been sealed in a mortal body for hundreds of lifetimes has probably lost most of its power. I'd guess it's pretty much useless, huh?"

Laughing awkwardly, the Qin'guang King replied, "How could the Mountain God say such a thing?"

Zhao Yunlan's smile didn't reach his eyes. "If you won't say it, I will. The Qin'guang King has been hinting that the Soul-Guarding Lamp was formed from 'my' body. You've been working your way up to saying that the lamp's wick was Kunlun-jun's heart's blood, haven't you? I think you brought me here planning to extract a vial of it from my heart. Well?"

Zhu Hong stood behind Zhao Yunlan silently, fixing the Qin'guang King with a hostile glower.

With these words, the last shred of civility was ripped away. The other Yanluo Kings landed before them; the flutter of their colorful robes in the air was like a flock of parrots swooping down. "It is our hope that the Mountain God's noble character will have you consider the bigger picture."

With only the barest hint of a smile, Zhao Yunlan looked back at them. Zhu Hong, on the other hand, exploded. The lower half of her body transformed into a giant snake's tail, coiling around Zhao Yunlan. The delicate corners of her eyes elongated to reveal a cold-blooded animal's vertical pupils. "Don't you know he's just a mortal?" she demanded.

Unfazed, Zhao Yunlan answered for them. "They're not blind. Of course they know. Besides, would they dare try to force my hand like this if I weren't mortal?"

Zhu Hong's scales were as red as blood; when she hissed in fury, her scarlet forked tongue flickered out. "Why not just say you want to take his life?!"

Zhao Yunlan snorted. "Just think how bad that would sound."

"All mortals age and die," chorused the Ten Kings. "It is a normal part of the Reincarnation Cycle."

That's right. It's nothing but a mortal body! Can't you give it up to save the world?

This time, Zhao Yunlan laughed loudly. As he did, the ground quaked ever more violently, and the shadow beneath the Wangchuan River struggled with increasing ferocity. The little lamps lining the Huangquan Road teetered, on the verge of falling. The violent ghosts that had escaped Ghost City were wreaking havoc everywhere, and some were trying to force their way into the halls of the Yanluo Courts. Ox-Head and Horse-Face, standing on either side, held the doors shut. "My lord, we can't hold them back much longer!"

Now Zhao Yunlan sighed. Softly, he said, "I'd just like to remind you all it's not wise to burn *all* your bridges at once."

Zhu Hong transformed the rest of the way into a giant python, her gleaming red scales bristling in rage. She lunged toward the Qin'guang King, the nearest of the ten, and tried to bite him. A few reapers rushed forward and shielded him with pitchforks and large blades.

The Qin'guang King pointed at Zhao Yunlan. "Seize him!"

A cold voice pierced the air. "Seize whom?"

A crowd of yao rushed in. Every last one was either a tribe leader or an elder. Fourth Uncle gave Zhu Hong a stern glance, but to her surprise, he said nothing.

Then Fourth Uncle, who had been born in the zodiac year that corresponded to his own tribe, stepped out from the crowd. He first bowed solemnly to Zhao Yunlan. "Mountain God, this humble yao was a fool who failed to recognize the grace of your presence."

Of course, since even the Crow tribe had known perfectly well whom Zhao Yunlan was the reincarnation of, it was hard to say whether the Snake tribe leader had truly been unaware or if he'd been feigning ignorance. Either way, Zhao Yunlan didn't call him out. He just nodded with a tiny smile.

Fourth Uncle continued in righteous tones. "The Netherworld controls the Reincarnation Cycle and has always been rude and arrogant to cultivators from all walks of life. We can forget everything else you've done, but the yao are deeply indebted to Kunlun-jun. No matter how incompetent we might be, we could never permit you to treat the reincarnation of the ancient god with such impudence!"

"What do the yao mean by this?" the Qin'guang King demanded.

The Crow tribe elder, who had so clearly severed her tribe from the other yao but was now back in the fray for some reason, had tagged along at the back of the crowd. Hoarsely, she said, "If there is blame to be assigned, it belongs to the Yanluo Kings' betrayal. They're too dishonest."

Fourth Uncle's brow furrowed. He hadn't wanted to be so blunt, and now that the quiet part had been said aloud, he didn't know how to proceed.

At this point, more voices piped up from the doorway. "Old man Yanluo, we all followed you up Kunlun Mountain in a collective bid to defeat the King of the Gui, but you stabbed all of us in the back. What do you have to say for yourselves?" It was the Three Pure Ones of Daoism speaking. "The Netherworld's shamelessness knows no bounds. We know now why you had us all gather atop Kunlun Mountain. You secretly put a mark on each of us to attract the Chaos within the Place of Great Disrespect when it spilled over. You ensured everyone would suffer together! If the Netherworld had even an ounce of conscience, wouldn't you have kept it securely underground?"

By now, everyone who was anyone seemed to be there, even the Arhats of the West and unaffiliated immortals from all the land.

The Qin'guang King was furious. "The Great Seal splintering is a catastrophe for all Three Realms! Why should the Netherworld bear the burden alone?!"

Saying that was like stirring up a nest of hornets. All the great immortals started to argue within the Yanluo Courts, yelling over each other. At that moment, the black shadow beneath the Wangchuan River rose dozens of meters. Every single oil lamp went dark at once. A scream rang out. "Gui!"

A small group of gui were the first to float out of the water. There weren't many of them, but their appearance jabbed right at everyone's tightly wound nerves. And then, as luck would have it, Ghost Face too appeared in the Wangchuan River.

In reality, the Great Seal was on the verge of collapse but had yet to truly break. The current uproar in the Netherworld was due entirely to the fact that Shen Wei had released the bit of Chaos he'd captured into the Yanluo Courts, feeding into Ghost Face's neurotic paranoia. Shen Wei's ambiguous comments under the Ancient Merit Tree had made Ghost Face immediately suspect that Shen Wei was conspiring to make use of that scrap of captured Chaos.

Ghost Face had tracked his own trail of Chaos there. The very instant he surfaced from the water and saw the scene onshore, he realized he'd been duped, but it was already too late to leave.

"Chaos King of the Gui!" someone yelled.

The Qin'guang King, who was almost surrounded, immediately took advantage of the situation. "Look! The King of the Gui has already emerged! Is now really the time to debate who's right and who's wrong?"

As if on cue, the choir of the Ten Kings rushed to harmonize with him. "If you can all still see the big picture here, then please, let's set aside our prejudices and band together to deal with the gui!"

In the blink of an eye, Ghost Face was surrounded. He shot several meters higher above the river and whistled. Countless gui answered his summons, bursting forth from the Wangchuan waters. The Chaos that could swallow everything formed a huge blockade behind them. The Yanluo Courts had become a battlefield, inside and out.

Worry for her fourth uncle made Zhu Hong try to join the other yao, but Zhao Yunlan held her back. "Take a good look at the class of fighters out there. Don't get underfoot, little girl."

A high-level gui on a killing spree suddenly came dangerously close to Zhao Yunlan. He fired off a shot, but the gui managed to dodge. He was just about to take aim again when a familiar bell rang behind him. Lin Jing, who had been missing for several days, unexpectedly appeared and tossed out several talismans marked with sauwastikas.[13]

The gui disappeared at once in a curl of black smoke.

Lin Jing dragged Zhao Yunlan toward the secret chamber that held the Soul-Guarding Lamp. "Heads are getting bashed in left and right! What are you two hanging around here for?"

Zhao Yunlan studied him, expression inscrutable. "Were you the one who yelled 'Chaos King of the Gui' just now?"

Lin Jing hesitated. "I tried to pitch my voice higher."

"Pitch your voice higher? I'd know your voice even if it were breaking." A storm cloud descended on Zhao Yunlan's face. "Shen Wei, get the fuck out here!"

In response, Shen Wei slowly slipped out from behind the chamber's massive stone door. He looked far more anxious now than he had a moment ago during all his scheming and plotting.

When Zhao Yunlan's gaze fell on the crusted blood on Shen Wei's chest, his fist clenched hard enough that veins popped out on the back of his hand. He looked like he wanted to hit Shen Wei.

---

13 The *sauwastika* (卍) is a Sanskrit symbol representing the auspicious footprints of the Buddha.

Instantaneously, Lin Jing reacted, grabbing Zhu Hong and covering her mouth as soon as Shen Wei appeared. Despite her confusion, he pulled her off to the side.

Zhao Yunlan stayed silent for a long time, and Shen Wei's anxiety grew by the second. Finally, Zhao Yunlan spoke. "Shen Wei."

Shen Wei was instantly reminded of Zhao Yunlan's exhausted words after he'd seen through Shen Wei's deception in the Great Divine Tree: *"If you keep doing this, I'll really be angry with you."* Panicked, Shen Wei took a step toward him.

"Stay over there," Zhao Yunlan said, voice very low. "Don't come over here yet. It's not time for you to reveal yourself."

As if frozen, Shen Wei stood stiffly in place.

Zhu Hong, who was still completely in the dark, turned to Lin Jing. "What does he mean, it's not time for him to reveal himself?" she asked blankly. "Why not?"

"Amitabha, don't worry about it," came Lin Jing's calm response. Zhu Hong shut her mouth.

Zhao Yunlan pointed at the bloody mess on Shen Wei's chest. "Does it hurt?"

Shen Wei began to nod, but he only made it as far as lowering his chin before pausing and quickly shaking his head. In the end, not knowing how to answer, he could only give Zhao Yunlan a pitiful look.

Sizing up the situation at once, Lin Jing asked, "How could it not hurt? He passed out twice from the pain."

Zhao Yunlan inhaled sharply, expression dark.

Lin Jing developed a sudden, keen interest in the ongoing battle. He tugged on Zhu Hong's arm and pointed. "Look, Benefactress, they're fighting."

"I hold the power of the mountains and rivers," Shen Wei hurried to explain. "So in truth, the Mountain-River Awl was always under my control. I arranged for it to appear near Qingxi Village to lure Ghost Face and place a mark on him. Then I tricked him into using the Soul-Tempering Cauldron to summon the Great Merit Brush, leading him to use the Three-Life Rock as the hearthstone for the cauldron on Kunlun Mountain. The only thing he had that was made from the Three-Life Rock was the Reincarnation Dial, and it, along with the Merit Brush, is connected to one of the corporeal souls of every living being. As long as he used the stone from the Reincarnation Dial as the hearthstone, the two would be connected through the Soul-Tempering Cauldron. Meanwhile, the Mountain-River Awl was the best 'lock'; through the mark I'd left on Ghost Face, the Awl locked onto both the Reincarnation Dial and the Merit Brush at the same time."

"That means this whole time, Ghost Face has been running around doing all this work for someone else's benefit. Even the Merit Brush I got then was a dupe, wasn't it? Which means you already held three of the Four Hallowed Artifacts in your hands," Zhao Yunlan said slowly. "And on the peak of Kunlun Mountain... When the Netherworld had gathered everyone there, you also left marks on them all, right? That way, as soon as the Chaos beneath the Seal began to leak out, everyone got a taste of it, so no one could escape unscathed—and they'd all think it was the Netherworld's doing."

Shen Wei opened his hand, revealing a long strand of hair on his palm. He waved, and the pitch-black hair Zhao Yunlan loved so much floated up before his eyes. A profoundly inauspicious black smoke seeped from it, identical to the Chaos that Ghost Face was collecting.

Reaching out, Shen Wei pinched the strand out of the air. Back in his palm, it broke into several pieces. He confessed his crimes freely.

"This is the mark. All along, Ghost Face had been challenging the relationship between you, me, and the Netherworld. Without a wick
in the Soul-Guarding Lamp, the Netherworld would descend into
panic if the Great Seal broke early, and they would undoubtedly try
to take your heart's blood by force. By that point, the Netherworld
and I would've inevitably fallen out, giving Ghost Face the opportunity to strengthen the gui to break out of the Great Seal. Therefore,
I knew he would try to collect the power of Chaos to falsely give the
Seal the appearance of breaking."

Zhao Yunlan nodded. "I should've realized when you split the
ground open at the resort. *You* are the keeper of the Great Seal.
If even I could tell that it was only a Ghost Army Summons, and
not the Great Seal actually shattering, how could you not know?
You knew from the very beginning that Ghost Face was up to no
good, but you still let him skewer you with an icicle. What is *wrong*
with you?"

Shen Wei said nothing.

"Don't play dead! Answer me!"

"At the time, I..." Shen Wei hesitated. Pitifully, he tried again. "I..."

Zhao Yunlan interrupted him. "As the keeper of the Seal, of
course you could tell whether it was really broken. That meant you
had to let him get the drop on you, and you had to go missing, all
so the Netherworld and everyone affected by the shards of Chaos
would be thrown into a frenzy. Along the way, I bet you made sure
to tell Ghost Face that he'd fallen for all your schemes. Given how
suspicious and paranoid he is, he would've thought that meant
something was up with the bit of Chaos you took. He would've *had*
to come check it out, running smack into the Netherworld officials
and various immortals out there, right? All your little redirects sure
worked out well for you, huh?"

Eavesdropping off to the side, Lin Jing finally understood. "So that's what happened," he muttered.

Zhao Yunlan gave a cold laugh. "My lord truly took everything into—"

Before he finished the sentence, Shen Wei disappeared. Zhao Yunlan had the unmistakable sense of someone invisibly drawing closer. Unseen hands pressed against the rocky wall on either side of his body. Then an icy hand closed around his fist. Still invisible, Shen Wei murmured in his ear. "I'm right here. If you're upset, then hit me. I won't evade it."

Though Zhao Yunlan flung his hand off, before he could walk away, Shen Wei grabbed him tightly, pinning him against the rough wall.

"Let go!" Zhao Yunlan demanded. He twisted to one side and pushed, only to hear Shen Wei let out a muffled noise of pain. Belatedly remembering Shen Wei's chest wound, Zhao Yunlan immediately stopped shoving and felt for Shen Wei's chest, touching the dried crust of blood on his clothes. "You—"

Shen Wei's hand closed over Zhao Yunlan's, pressing it into his chest.

Zhao Yunlan took a deep breath. He looked back at the lifeless Soul-Guarding Lamp, floating above the water, and his face went blank as he slowly pulled his hand from Shen Wei's grasp. He turned to Lin Jing and Zhu Hong. "The Soul-Executing Emissary doesn't miscalculate. He has everything under control, and the Great Seal is still holding up. We're done here. Let's go. We've got to put in overtime and write up a report."

Having been forced to witness his boss's continuing cold war with his spouse, Lin Jing felt incredibly awkward. He took his best stab at cracking a joke. "We just got back to work and we're already doing overtime? It'll be the Longtaitou Festival soon, so aren't we gonna get any gifts?"

"Sure," Zhao Yunlan said, not batting an eye. "Everyone's getting ten kilos of monk meat."

Lin Jing slapped himself in the face. "Amitabha, why did I say anything?"

Suddenly, Zhu Hong spoke up. "Director Zhao, I have to stay. My fourth uncle is still here."

"Oh." Zhao Yunlan considered that. It seemed reasonable, so he nodded. "Okay. Just keep your distance from the action and be careful."

Without a backward glance, he left with Lin Jing.

Zhu Hong watched them go. They worked well together, stealthily leaving the battlefield by skirting its edges and not drawing attention to themselves. Finally, she let out a breath of relief, then tentatively addressed the empty air beside her. "Lord Emissary...? Are you still there?"

"What is it?" asked a desolate male voice.

Zhu Hong was momentarily speechless, then jumped up. "Why are you still here?"

After a silence, Shen Wei quietly asked, "Where am I supposed to go?"

Incredulous, Zhu Hong said, "Why didn't you leave with them?"

Shen Wei fell silent again.

"Lord Emissary?" she called out. "Shen-laoshi? Hello? Hello, hello? Can you hear me? Are you still there?"

"He...probably doesn't want me to follow him." Shen Wei's voice came from below the Soul-Guarding Lamp. Zhu Hong couldn't help taking a few steps toward him, only to hear, "He said if I lied to him again, he'd be truly angry with me."

"You've *lied* to him?" she exclaimed, eyes wide and mouth agape. Then, without waiting for an answer, she shook the thought from her head. "No, never mind that. The point is, you believed him?"

Shen Wei, hiding behind the lamp, wasn't afraid of being seen. He allowed a hazy silhouette of himself to become visible. The look he gave Zhu Hong was a little lost.

Zhu Hong heaved a sigh. "Look, I'm not the brightest. I don't understand what you guys are plotting half the time. Those conspiracies all seem very cool, but Zhao Yunlan has threatened to make stew out of Daqing at least ninety-nine times, if not a hundred by now. And yet that stupid cat is still living his best life, isn't he? Just getting fatter all the time?"

In her wildest dreams, Zhu Hong never dared imagine being the one to teach the Soul-Executing Emissary a lesson like this— the Emissary, the love rival she couldn't win against. The thought both pleased her and made her jealous. "I arrived just in time to see Ghost Face drag you off, and I can tell you, he looked like he wanted to cut Ghost Face into a million pieces. After all these years around him, I can tell at a single glance if he's genuinely angry or if it's just his temper flaring up. Why do you think he's angry? Because you hid things from him? Because you lied to him? Shen Wei, I really think... Never mind, I'm not thinking about it, not that I dare to—but I mean, if you ran away from home and worried your mother sick, and she slapped you a couple of times after you were found, wouldn't you deserve that?"

Bewildered, Shen Wei just stared back at her. The two of them looked at each other for a while, and then Zhu Hong abruptly turned away. "Sorry," she said stiffly. "I forgot you don't have a mom."

"It's all right," said Shen Wei.

Zhu Hong had no idea how to respond. There was an awkward silence between them until, after a while, Shen Wei suddenly spoke again. "You... You care deeply for him, don't you?"

The question made Zhu Hong feel as if something had been stuffed into her heart. "Yeah," she mumbled.

"Then... Then why did you tell me all this?"

Zhu Hong rolled her eyes. "I just want you to stop upsetting him."

Confusion flickered across Shen Wei's face for just a second. He seemed somewhat distracted. His brows knit together, and the glittering water of the pool beneath the Soul-Guarding Lamp reflected in his eyes. Zhu Hong had just about concluded that his soul had drifted away when he finally looked back and nodded at her.

"You're right," he said sincerely. "Many thanks."

Standing up, Shen Wei made himself invisible once again. Zhu Hong heard his footsteps approach, and then he said, "Miss Zhu, please give me your hand."

Zhu Hong didn't know what he wanted but extended her hand anyway. As she watched, Shen Wei placed a palm-sized branch in it. The branch had two tiny buds of green. Such a small branch wasn't heavy, of course, but somehow Zhu Hong felt as if this unassuming twig contained an extraordinary weight.

"What is—"

"A branch from the Great Divine Tree on Kunlun Mountain," Shen Wei said. "In all the time since the world was first split, only Nüwa has ever taken a branch from the Great Divine Tree. She planted one of them thousands of zhang below the Huangquan, where it became the Ancient Merit Tree. This is the second branch. Take care of it."

Zhu Hong stumbled, nearly dropping it. She quickly clutched it in both hands and raised it to her eyes with reverence and awe.

She looked as though she wanted to place it on an altar and worship it.

"The branch of the Great Divine Tree failed to thrive when it was planted in the Place of Great Disrespect, most likely because the existence of the gui is anathema to it. Throughout all the years I've stood in Kunlun's stead, I've done my very best, but I've been unable to care for it well. Millennia have passed, and this branch's two small buds are all I have to show for my efforts. I've always regretted that deeply," Shen Wei said. "Your fourth uncle may not have the time to worry about you right now. Hide here and stay away from them. If you face danger, each bud will save your life once."

After a pause, Shen Wei continued, "If you don't use them, then once the dust settles, please plant it somewhere with beautiful mountains and flowing water."

He sounded as if he was leaving his last words. Zhu Hong asked, "Where are you going?"

"I'm going to pursue him."

"Does he still need to be pursued?" Zhu Hong set aside her confusion for a moment. Jealously, she said, "That bastard may have left easily, but now that his anger's burned away, he's probably full of regret and waiting for you just up ahead."

The invisible Shen Wei didn't respond. Perhaps he had already left.

Zhu Hong's guess was right on the money. Zhao Yunlan hadn't gone far at all. He'd found a hiding spot by the opening of the Huangquan Road, and there he squatted, a growing number of cigarette butts littering the ground at his feet.

Afraid of bearing the brunt of his anger, Lin Jing kept his distance. He was observing the fury of the battlefield with a pair of binoculars he'd scrounged from somewhere.

Zhao Yunlan had just lit his twelfth cigarette when a hand reached out from nowhere, snuffed it out, and snatched it from his mouth. Zhao Yunlan froze, then slowly turned to see Shen Wei standing there hesitantly, looking as though he wanted to say something but didn't know where to start.

Shen Wei looked frankly terrible. He was covered in blood. His glasses had long since fallen off somewhere. The hair on his forehead was a little long, brushing the bridge of his nose and nearly covering his eyes. All in all, he was a pathetic sight. He fidgeted with the cigarette he'd grabbed from Zhao Yunlan like a kid who was in trouble and was afraid to go home.

There was a long silence. Finally, Zhao Yunlan let out a resigned sigh and opened his arms. "Come here," he said, and Shen Wei pulled him into a tight embrace.

Even a dog would go blind, seeing this, Lin Jing thought to himself. He pretended to not exist.

Having decided to see no evil, Lin Jing could only focus on the battle. It was like the various tribes and factions had come to a tacit understanding and were using the many reapers of the Netherworld as cannon fodder, pushing them to the forefront where Ghost Face and the gui could see them. By that point, more than half of the reapers had been injured or killed.

Nevertheless, even tiny shards of Chaos were still tremendously harmful. Immortals and gui alike had to avoid the sharp edge of its destruction. Occasionally, someone was unable to evade it and was swallowed silently, leaving behind not even a single hair. After all, wasn't the whole point of Chaos to return everything to nothing?

As Lin Jing watched, the Qin'guang King was backed into a dire corner by a shard of Chaos. With a splash, he fell into the

Wangchuan River, where his huge sleeves pulled him to the surface and kept him afloat.

A vast net emerged from the surface of the water, lifting the Qin'guang King into the air. Sopping wet, he scrambled and stumbled onto the shore, only to see the best of each tribe standing in the positions of Fuxi's Bagua, setting up a huge array.

"Amitabha, what array is that?" Lin Jing murmured.

From behind him, Shen Wei's voice said, "That's Fuxi's Bagua Net."

Lin Jing was so startled that his hands shook, nearly dropping his binoculars.

Shen Wei kept talking. "The yao probably brought it. Legend says that Fuxi was born in the Eastern lands. Once he was elevated into a sage, Chiyou took over the Eastern lands, and after Chiyou came the wu and the yao. When Fuxi died, he left behind the Fuxi Bow and Bagua. The bow was taken by Houyi of the wu and eventually found its way into human hands. As for the Bagua Net, it's probably a closely guarded secret of the yao. Unsurprisingly, each race has a hidden trump card."

As the Bagua Net floated out of the water, the shard of Chaos seemed to retreat for the first time. Far overhead, the expression on Ghost Face's mask twisted.

A sudden golden light exploded from the Bagua Net. Lin Jing, shocked, exclaimed, "That's Buddha's Golden Seal that we worship in the west... The legendary final treasure to suppress evil and monsters at the end of time!"

Before the sound of his voice had even begun to fade, the golden light flooded the entire Netherworld. The little lamps on the Huangquan Road, having been extinguished at some point, were lit once more. This time, their flames were far brighter, as if a dragon of fire were snaking along the Huangquan Road, waving its tail.

The piece of Chaos, along with countless gui, was sucked into Fuxi's Bagua Net in an instant.

Shen Wei sighed softly. "Everything has settled. Let's go."

From the moment Fuxi's Bagua Net had appeared, the winners and losers had already been decided. The battle was over.

With a sound of acknowledgment, Lin Jing got to his feet. But a strange feeling still lurked in his heart—a sense that something was about to happen. Before leaving, he unthinkingly lifted his binoculars for a final look and got a crystal-clear view of the expression on Ghost Face's mask: the expression of someone laughing even though he wanted to cry.

An instant later, the mask split in two. The halves fell, revealing the face that was a gloomy mirror of Shen Wei's. Ghost Face's robe billowed like a flag in the wind, despite the still air.

"Very well," Lin Jing heard him say hoarsely. "You win. I can't beat you. You don't even deign to fight me... Very well."

Shen Wei stopped.

"You and I were born exactly the same. I don't understand how I was inferior to you. You're the solitary, noble Soul-Executing Emissary, while I'm the King of the Gui everyone wants to kill. That's all fine." Ghost Face gave a guttural laugh. "I merely hate that you're too despicable and cowardly to even fight me, instead choosing to humiliate me with these...these *ants*. You'll regret this! You think you've won without dirtying your hands? Yes, you'll regret this, my good brother."

Breaking into gales of laughter, Ghost Face's body suddenly grew vast—several dozens of meters, as tall as a mountain. From thousands of kilometers away, a muffled roar sounded deep beneath the ground. It rumbled like thunder as it rose to the surface.

Shen Wei's expression suddenly changed.

Ghost Face seemed nearly manic. Then, abruptly, he exploded; his body blew apart into tens of thousands of pieces. At the same moment, seemingly in response, Fuxi's Bagua Net, which contained the shard of Chaos, broke.

G UO CHANGCHENG clutched the little baton Zhao Yunlan
had given him in a death grip. He was still reeling from the
extreme terror of coming practically nose-to-nose with a
youchu—a youchu that, just a second ago, he had electrocuted into
a burnt pancake.

Not only that, but the youth who'd just been talking and laughing with them also turned out to be a monster. His reflection in the
glass showed a monster with a mouth that opened a full 180 degrees,
as if its head had split in half to reveal a scarlet tongue and a fanged
maw. Wandering through an empty resort to collect the souls of the
recently deceased sounded like a horror film in its own right, but
that was just setup—the main event was about to begin.

Chu Shuzhi sidestepped the shower of electrical sparks, which
didn't distinguish between friend and foe. He shoved his fanny
pack into Guo Changcheng's arms. "We went through a lot of work
collecting those, so hold on tight. Don't drop it."

Guo Changcheng's hands were shaking like he'd suddenly developed Parkinson's. All he could do was hug the bag tight to his chest.

"Are you afraid?" Chu Shuzhi asked seriously.

Ever honest, Guo Changcheng nodded so vigorously that he
looked like a chicken pecking at rice.

"Scared to death?" Chu Shuzhi continued. Guo Changcheng wiped his tears and kept on pecking. "That's good." There was zero sympathy in Chu Shuzhi's voice. "Keep it up."

That left Guo Changcheng speechless. Chu Shuzhi patted him firmly on the shoulder and adopted a creepy tone, pointing past him. "Look. What's that?"

Guo Changcheng looked where he was pointing and found himself staring straight into the eyes of a few youchu. With his fear primed by Chu Shuzhi, a bloodcurdling, inhuman scream exploded out of him. *"Ahhhhhhhhhh—!!!"*

The little group was burnt to a crisp. Chu Shuzhi gave Guo Changcheng a thumbs-up.

A moment later, moving with such speed he seemed to teleport, Chu Shuzhi vanished and reappeared on the roof of one of a row of small houses. He ripped his jacket open, exposing an arm that had turned a weird shade of blue. He wiggled his fingers, making his joints creak stiffly, then got out a piccolo carved from bone and began to play.

A string of eerie notes sounded as his fingers danced. The calm earth underfoot started to ripple and buckle, and the "dust" that had coated the ground of the resort drifted up into the air. The dust motes were quickly drawn to each other, and one by one, intact human skeletons took shape. Several of the skeletons took up positions by Guo Changcheng; the others threw themselves at the mysterious youth.

The "youth's" eyes had become completely red. He turned his gaze on Chu Shuzhi. "Corpse King."

The notes Chu Shuzhi was playing became sharper. As though he had issued a command, his bone soldiers started to attack. One skeleton's sharp phalanges thrust toward the youth's chest with lightning speed, only for him to vanish, ghost-like, on the spot. The skeleton's fingers punched five small holes into the ground.

Flickering back into view off to one side, the youth struck at the skeleton soldier. The skeleton was unable to avoid the heavy blow, and its skull shattered, sending fragments flying in all directions. But at the renewed sound of the piccolo, the bone shards pieced themselves back together. The restored skeleton stretched out its neck, throwing itself at the youth again.

Since the skeletons Chu Shuzhi had conjured were made of the ashes blanketing the resort and he could just keep rebuilding them, even being pulverized only slowed them down. Although they weren't very powerful, their attacks served to tangle the youth up. The moment he made a mistake, the skeletons' narrow phalanges could stab in deep.

The youth gave a cold laugh. "This would be one thing coming from anyone else. But don't you think it's funny that *you're* part of the Soul-Guarding Order? You, a criminal Corpse King surrounded by the stench of death? Back when you slaughtered people without batting an eye, bled them dry, and feasted on their corpses, were you putting on this act of being a good person?"

"I've already paid for my crimes," Chu Shuzhi said. He reflexively glanced at Guo Changcheng and saw that he was too busy trying to deal with the endless swarm of youchu to listen to the conversation. Inexplicably, Chu Shuzhi found himself sighing in relief. "And what do you think *you* are?" he countered.

The youth's lips quirked up. He decapitated a skeleton and stuffed the whole skull into his mouth. As he chewed, he said, "Me? We gui are part of the natural order." Then, abruptly, he recited, "'Guard the souls of the living, bring peace to the hearts of the dead, atone for crimes done in life, and complete the unfinished cycle.'"

Having rattled off the inscription on the back of the Soul-Guarding Order, he seized a skeleton and dismembered it, one limb at a time. Simply tightening his fist around the bones was enough to crush them. With another icy laugh, he said, "Whoever wrote *that* must've been a complete idiot!"

As a human, Guo Changcheng's unique status among his colleagues meant that when he'd started at the SID, he'd only signed a labor contract. Since he wasn't bound by the Order itself, he only vaguely knew about it and had never actually seen it. This was the first time he'd ever heard the entire Soul-Guarding Order...and it came from the mouth of this monster.

But for some reason, the words suddenly flooded his mind, pushing everything else out. He just stood there, frozen, and the baton in his hand also calmed down. A youchu hidden in a corner suddenly launched straight at him from its hiding spot. One of Chu Shuzhi's skeleton soldiers responded by doing something a human would do: it took a huge diagonal step and spread its arms wide, shielding Guo Changcheng with what few bones it still had left. The youchu smashed it to pieces, and Guo Changcheng scuttled backward and fell on his ass. He yelped and closed his eyes, holding the baton above his head. It went off just as the youchu's claws were about to brush against him.

Medium well.

Guo Changcheng struggled to catch his breath while the shattered skeleton gradually rebuilt itself. Slowly, it walked over to him. Despite knowing Chu Shuzhi had made the skeletons, Guo Changcheng couldn't suppress a shudder of fear when it extended a creepy, white-boned hand toward him. But in the next second, the hand came to rest on his head, as though comforting him. It patted his hair gently.

If a forensic scientist or other expert had been there, they might've been able to tell Guo Changcheng that this skeleton had belonged to a very young man, probably just over twenty years old.

The soul of the living, the heart of the dead—perhaps every corpse on the verge of turning to dust still held a fragment of a treasured memory.

For reasons Guo Changcheng didn't understand, the rims of his eyes suddenly stung.

The skeleton turned to face away from him, standing guard.

A sound like a muffled clap of thunder rang out. Guo Changcheng automatically glanced at the sky only to see that it was empty of the moon and stars. The sound of thunder continued, but no lightning split the darkness overhead. Then he realized that the "thunder" was coming from underground.

The skeleton soldiers all stopped in their tracks. Their teeth clacked in a strange harmony, as though they also knew how to fear and were shaking with it. Even the youchu on the ground were motionless. They lay down in different positions, ears pressed to the ground, listening to something.

Chu Shuzhi's instincts screamed at him that something was terribly wrong. He was a decisive fighter, and equally decisive when he fled. Without wasting his breath on explanations, he came flying down from the wall and grabbed Guo Changcheng by the collar. The wind crammed Guo Changcheng's scream back down his throat. A second later, Chu Shuzhi soared right back up and landed on the roof. Guo Changcheng couldn't help but look down, only to see that the ground seemed to have turned into a huge pool of marsh gas, so black that it was impossible to see the bottom. Thick smoke billowed within the cracks in the earth.

The weird youth who'd been troubling them suddenly ripped off his human skin, revealing the huge monster underneath: a high-level youchu. Following his lead, all the youchu's voices rose in unison, letting out a long wail toward the sky.

Without a single glance back or a pause for breath, Chu Shuzhi dragged Guo Changcheng to the entrance of the resort. He found their car, yanked the door open, and threw Guo Changcheng inside. He slammed his foot on the gas, and they were off like a shot.

Guo Changcheng was still fighting to breathe properly. "What was *that*?"

"I don't know," said Chu Shuzhi solemnly.

Still confused, Guo Changcheng asked, "Then why are we running?"

Chu Shuzhi drove as if the car were an airplane, rocketing along so fast that the entire frame shook. It seemed almost as though its wheels were no longer on the ground. In an eerie tone, he said, "If we don't run, you won't see tomorrow's sun, dumbass."

"Then what about Director Zhao and the others?" Guo Changcheng craned his neck, looking behind him. "Will they come back? I need to call them."

But as everyone knew, there was rarely cell signal during a disaster. Guo Changcheng couldn't even dial 110.

Chu Shuzhi spun the steering wheel, sending them into a giant turn. The tires gave an earsplitting screech.

The resort's location had been chosen for its scenic mountain background and the hot springs. This particular mountain rose about a thousand meters above sea level. For safety reasons, the road winding up it was closed at night. Chu Shuzhi rammed the car right through the barricade, driving desperately for the peak; escaping somewhere higher up seemed to be instinctual.

After managing to calm down slightly, he recalled that, back when Buzhou Mountain had fallen, all the races were said to have climbed a certain primordial mountain in search of protection. The fragments of legend lodged in his memory seemed to be guiding him.

Guo Changcheng peered out through the window. At the foot of the mountain, not a single light was on in the resort. It seemed like a yawning mouth waiting to swallow everything up.

Suddenly everything went blurry as sheets of rain cascaded down the glass. The pounding of the rain blended with some kind of furious roaring, thick with evil. Guo Changcheng shivered violently.

Fast as a tornado, Chu Shuzhi drove to the top of the mountain. The very peak was inaccessible by car; it was reachable only via a thin man-made stone path that led to an unsafe-looking little suspension bridge. It had railings, but it was slippery from the rain—it looked horribly treacherous. And there, at the very top, was a cave full of stalactites. During the day, you had to buy a ticket to enter, but now, in the dead of night, it was unattended.

"Bring your baton," Chu Shuzhi told Guo Changcheng. "There's food and water in the trunk. Take as much as you can. Director Zhao should have left a backup lighter there too. Let's go!"

They gathered everything together as quickly as possible. Guo Changcheng kept his head down and ran after Chu Shuzhi, so it wasn't until they were already inside the cave that he looked back and realized there was a cliff with a thousand-meter drop below the bridge's crude railings. His legs nearly turned to jelly. He couldn't even imagine how he'd managed to run across.

Chu Shuzhi found that he too had no signal. It was just the two of them, cut off from the world, accompanied only by the steady pitter-patter of the rain as they hid within the cave. He peeled off his drenched shirt and took a seat, half-naked. He waved away the food and water Guo Changcheng tried to push toward him and took a glance outside. "I'd say something major has happened," he muttered.

Throughout the night, the two of them took turns standing guard. Guo Changcheng got up in the second half of the night and insisted on taking his turn. It seemed unnecessary to Chu Shuzhi, but he looked at the little baton that never left Guo Changcheng's hand, and then he leaned against the frigid wall of the cave and closed his eyes.

Guo Changcheng forced himself to stay awake, keeping watch over the mouth of the cave. He sat upright, never loosening his grip on his baton.

Eventually, he felt that daybreak *had* to be approaching, but the sky to the east stayed stubbornly dark. The whistle around Chu Shuzhi's neck suddenly blew a few times, and Guo Changcheng rubbed his eyes firmly, switched the flashlight on, and dropped a few more cows' tears into his eyes. He peered outside and saw a silhouette floating in all the wind and rain. It seemed to be a young woman, clinging to the railings of the precarious little suspension bridge!

Chu Shuzhi had woken up at the first sound of the whistle. He looked outside. "Mmh. A young female ghost."

Guo Changcheng sat up straight, flipping his notebook open. "I recognize her. I saw her ID and the photo her family brought."

"Give me a bottle," said Chu Shuzhi.

Soul bottle in hand, the Corpse King walked out of the cave. But perhaps he had an air of ruthlessness about him and a somewhat cruel appearance. Before he could get near her, the girl began screaming as though she'd suffered some terrible shock. "Stay back! Don't come near me!"

Buffeted by the wind and rain, the railing creaked from her swinging. She looked dangerously close to falling off.

Chu Shuzhi had no choice but to stop in his tracks. He didn't know what the girl had seen before she died, but it seemed like it wasn't a pretty memory. Even as a ghost, she was frightened and skittish, like a bird startled by an arrow. Chu Shuzhi shot a look back at Guo Changcheng, who approached and carefully stepped onto the bridge.

The bridge was only meant to hold one person at a time, and was deathly slippery underfoot from the rain. Neither of them was particularly heavy, but Chu Shuzhi still felt like it was trembling and swaying under Guo Changcheng's footsteps.

They both stood sideways so Guo Changcheng could squeeze past, albeit with great difficulty. Then he took the bottle from Chu Shuzhi and tried to approach the floating girl. "Miss, please don't be scared. We're the police. Come down here to where I am. Let me take you back, all right?"

For a long time, Guo Changcheng stood in the wind and rain, getting drenched to the bone as he negotiated softly with the terrified girl. Finally, she let her guard down a little, accepting the reality of her death. Eyes on the bottle in Guo Changcheng's hand, she carefully began to climb down.

Guo Changcheng breathed out a sigh of relief...just as a roar came from the other side of the bridge. Freshly frightened, the girl clung to the cold metal railing. Every last hair on Guo Changcheng's body stood on end.

Chu Shuzhi curled his fingers as though drawing a bowstring back. A small bow made of rainwater materialized in front of him, and he slowly pulled out a yellow talisman for summoning thunder and chasing away evil. Rolling it into the shape of an arrow, he nocked it on the water bow.

Just as he was about to shoot, the surface of the bridge suddenly shook unnaturally. Chu Shuzhi paused, then saw Guo Changcheng stare past him, panic-stricken. An unspeakable smell of rot found only at the bottom of the Huangquan drifted by on the wind.

At last, the Corpse King broke out in a cold sweat.

Meanwhile, in the Netherworld, no one had been prepared for Ghost Face to blow himself up.

Shen Wei swept Zhao Yunlan into his arms. "Get down!"

There was a tremendous noise as the waters of the Wangchuan River erupted, forming a towering wall hundreds of meters high. It crashed back down like a tsunami, creating a huge vortex. Everyone with fast enough reflexes flew up to the top of the towering Yanluo Courts; everyone else was sucked into the ink-black Wangchuan.

Shortly thereafter, the entire Huangquan Road, the Naihe Bridge, and the Yanluo Courts themselves all shattered at once

The three men beat a hasty retreat, but Zhao Yunlan hesitated. "Zhu Hong's still there…"

Shen Wei grabbed him and pushed him along. "Don't worry, she'll make it. I gave her a branch from the Great Divine Tree."

They retreated out of Ghost City and had just reached the pagoda tree that stretched up to Antiques Street in Dragon City, connecting the yin and yang worlds, when they heard a loud meow. A black shadow flung itself into Zhao Yunlan's arms.

"Damn fatty, why are you still here?" demanded Zhao Yunlan.

Daqing screamed into his ear. "I've been looking for you all over the world! You heartless dick! I almost turned the entire Netherworld upside down trying to find you! What just happened? Was there a gas explosion at the Yanluo Courts?! Me-*fucking*-ow, I was scared to death!"

Before Zhao Yunlan could respond, Shen Wei seized both human and cat and threw them up the tree. "Catch up later! Hurry and get up there!" This last order was roared at Lin Jing, who immediately obeyed and scrambled after them.

Shen Wei brought up the rear, shaping three consecutive seals with his hands. The shadow pursuing them stopped in its tracks, as if it had hit an invisible wall. Shen Wei stumbled back a few steps, exhausted. He slumped heavily against the pagoda tree, fighting for breath. Icy sweat dampened his temples.

The black shadow was now held back underground, but it was like a rapid river restrained by mud and sand. It smashed relentlessly against the invisible seal, and with every blow, the sound that rang out was enough to make the earth tremble.

Zhao Yunlan grabbed Shen Wei's hand, all but dragging him up the tree. Shen Wei leaned against him, utterly drained. Once he finally caught his breath, the little group traversed the pagoda tree back to the Mortal Realm, where they found quite a welcoming committee. Wang Zheng, Sangzan, and many of the SID's night shift were all there, with both lao-Wu and lao-Li, the nighttime and daytime guards.

Lao-Li had a huge bone in his hand, probably thinking of using it as a weapon. Even the old man guarding the pagoda tree had left his little shop, observing them from the doorway.

There was a sudden squeal of a car's brakes as Zhao Yunlan's father drove onto the pedestrian street at great speed—but no, it wasn't his mortal dad. It was unmistakably Shennong's mortar.

The mortar made a beeline for Shen Wei. The first words out of his mouth sent everyone into an uproar. "Has the Seal broken completely?"

Zhao Yunlan's supportive grip on Shen Wei tightened.

Under the weight of all the confused, nervous, or undecipherable gazes, Shen Wei nodded. "The King of the Gui used himself to blow a hole in the Great Seal, but just now, I resealed the old Houtu Seal thrice on top of the fissure to keep it below ground. Besides that, the Soul-Executing Blade opened a substantial crevice at the resort. A little Chaos might leak through there, but it shouldn't be too serious."

"Nüwa disappeared thousands of years ago," Shennong's mortal said. "The old Houtu Seal has limited power. How long can you hold it?"

"No more than half a day," Shen Wei replied. His voice was very low.

At that point, Wang Zheng quietly spoke up. "What *is* the Great Seal?"

Gently tugging her arm, Sangzan raised a finger to his lips to tell her to stop talking. Sangzan might've only understood seventy or eighty percent of what was being said, but he had helped Zhao Yunlan research ancient secrets and heard bits and pieces about the topic at hand. By this point, he had pieced together about half of what was going on.

Shennong's mortal stared intently at Shen Wei. "What do you intend to do, Great Immortal?"

Unperturbed, Shen Wei met his gaze. Holding Zhao Yunlan's hand, he said, "I intend to keep the vow I made all those years ago."

After a moment of shock at his apparent serenity, the mortal looked down at Shen Wei and Zhao Yunlan's joined hands. A kaleidoscope of expressions crossed the mortal's face before he stiffly averted his eyes. He gave a dry cough and then asked, "How can I assist you?"

Shen Wei's gaze swept over everyone present, living and dead alike. "Long ago, Kunlun sealed the Four Pillars with the Four Hallowed

Artifacts. Since then, it has been known that on the day the Seal weakened, the Artifacts would manifest in the world in response to the calamity. All four are now in my hands, and I must once again seal the Four Pillars that hold the earth and sky in place. I hope everyone here can help me stabilize the foundation of the sealing ritual."

When he finished speaking, a vast Bagua appeared above Antiques Street. On it were the Four Symbols—shaoyin, taiyang, shaoyang, and taiyin [14]—pointing in their corresponding four directions: west, south, east, and north.

The long, slender Mountain-River Awl sprang from Shen Wei's palm first, growing until it once again looked as it had atop the great snowy mountain, jutting up like a great precipice. Upon reaching its full size, it took its position in the Black Tortoise position. It made a tremendous noise as it settled, and in response, an equally large sundial appeared, rotated, and then landed in the White Tiger position. The Merit Brush, carved from the Great Divine Tree, shot up into the sky and came to rest in the position of the Azure Dragon. Last to appear was the Soul-Guarding Lamp, lacking its wick and giving no light. Shen Wei pointed, and it landed in the position of the Vermilion Bird.

"Wait," Zhao Yunlan said. "Isn't the Soul-Guarding Lamp in the Yanluo Courts?"

"Earlier, I stayed behind and took it with me," replied Shen Wei. "The one in the Yanluo Courts is an illusion." He ducked his head slightly, as if feeling a trace of shame for his sneakiness. "Extreme times call for extreme measures. My apologies."

---

14 The Four Symbols (四象) represent the guardians of the four cardinal directions, and they are each associated with a series of things like colors or seasons. The four creatures are the White Tiger of the West (shaoyin), the Vermilion Bird of the South (taiyang), the Azure Dragon of the East (shaoyang), and the Black Tortoise of the North (taiyin).

Zhao Yunlan eyed him without a word.

Shen Wei drew one of Zhao Yunlan's hands close. "This will hurt a bit," he murmured. "Please bear with it."

Something pricked Zhao Yunlan's fingertip. A bead of blood formed, then flew straight into the Soul-Guarding Lamp, where it became a slender thread. And then Shen Wei took off the pendant he'd worn around his neck for so long, the one that he never removed for any reason. He opened it and carefully poured some of its precious contents out. A minuscule flame flew from his fingertip, landing precisely on the tip of the delicate wick formed of blood. A firefly-faint glow began to shine within the Lamp.

Shen Wei leaned down and sucked Zhao Yunlan's bleeding finger into his mouth.

"Wait, that's it?" Zhao Yunlan asked, dumbfounded. "Didn't that Yanluo King say he needed a whole vial of blood from my heart?"

"The ten fingers are linked to the heart," said Shen Wei. "The Soul-Guarding Lamp has lacked its wick for millennia. The Netherworld wanted something that would guarantee peace—something to keep the Lamp burning for thousands of generations. I, however, have only half a day to reseal the Four Pillars. A single drop from the tip of your finger is replacement enough."

Then Shen Wei addressed the crowd. "All those years ago, Kunlun-jun, the Mountain God of the Great Wild, sealed the Four Pillars. I was heir to the thirty-six mountains and rivers, but I was born in filth. I am unable to establish any connection with the Four Hallowed Artifacts, so I hope you will all lend me a hand. You'll have my deepest gratitude."

Having said that, he resumed his true appearance. He stood before them clad in the Soul-Executing Emissary's midnight robes, the full length of his hair spilling down around him. His innate demonic aura was unmistakable, as was his air of gentlemanly righteousness; a man at war with himself yet possessed of an elegance beyond compare.

No one could reject him.

Wang Zheng and Sangzan exchanged a glance, and together, they walked beneath the Mountain-River Awl. Daqing, holding his golden bell in his mouth, turned and prowled to the Ancient Merit Brush. Lao-Li, who had tied a string of tiny golden fried fish to the huge bone he carried, followed Daqing. Lin Jing got out a string of 108 Buddhist beads and stood beneath the Reincarnation Dial.

Shennong's mortar was about to take a step when Zhao Yunlan called out and stopped him. "Hey, um, you."

The mortar, wearing Zhao Yunlan's father's body, turned back. "Who?"

After a beat of silence, Zhao Yunlan said, "You've taken enough advantage of me. Do you think you're actually my father? Just come here for a sec so I can talk to you."

The mortar followed as Zhao Yunlan moved off to one side. "Please go ahead, Kunlun-jun."

With his back to the pagoda tree, Zhao Yunlan glanced at the ground. All seemed completely peaceful beneath the tree, not at all as though something impossibly vast was being held down. He was out of cigarettes, so he reached into his dad's pocket and claimed the packet he found there.

He lit up, then briefly stood in silence, wreathed in smoke. After a moment, he said, "Actually, I have a favor to ask of you."

"I am at Kunlun-jun's disposal," Shennong's mortar said quietly.

"No, I mean it," said Zhao Yunlan. "I'm my parents' only son. By all rights, I should take care of them in their old age and see them off. I never imagined I'd run out of time, but here we are. White-haired elders shouldn't have to see their black-haired children off. Think of a solution for me."

More moments passed before the mortar said, "I... I confess I don't understand what Kunlun-jun means to say."

Zhao Yunlan snorted. "Don't play dumb. I think you know exactly what I'm getting at."

Shennong's mortar took a long look at him. "So in the end, is the Soul-Executing Emissary only able to uphold his vow because you've agreed to accompany him into death?"

Casually blowing a smoke ring, Zhao Yunlan asked, "Do you think I'm selling my body?"

"My apologies. I misspoke." The mortar lowered his head. Finally, almost in a sigh, he said, "I understand."

Zhao Yunlan's eyes bored into his until the mortar continued, "Should Kunlun-jun no longer be in this world, I will leave your father's body and live on as 'Zhao Yunlan' for you. Please be at ease, Mountain God."

"Live well. Live like 'Zhao Yunlan.'" Zhao Yunlan gave his father's shoulder a disrespectful pat. "Enjoy the things you should enjoy, and whatever you need to do, do it well. Thank you." He stubbed out his half-finished cigarette and brushed past.

The mortar walked toward Lin Jing and the Reincarnation Dial, while Zhao Yunlan went to stand alone below the Soul-Guarding Lamp.

Zhao Yunlan laid a gentle hand on the Soul-Guarding Lamp. Uneven inscriptions were etched onto its surface, identical to those on the back of the Soul-Guarding Order. A strange feeling stirred within him, like the lamp really was connected to his flesh and blood. The flame seemed to miraculously flicker in time with his heart, as though two people were standing there: the person he'd been thousands of years ago and the person he was now, thousands of years later.

The passage of time had transformed everything.

Turning, Shen Wei looked at the old man from the general store who stood guard over the divide between yin and yang. The wrinkled old man led the whole crowd of night-shift ghosts from 4 Bright Avenue, forming a circle around the ritual. Then he raised his head and bowed to Shen Wei, just as people had in the ancient past. "I am old and have no other use," he said. "I will help guard you, Great Immortal."

Shen Wei nodded. Raising a finger, he wrote in the air, stroke by stroke, an ancient text from the time of gods and demons. The text itself seemed to hold power, flowing in the air like rippling water. Then Shen Wei brought his fingers together and struck the words forcefully with his palm. The strokes all dissipated at once, flying toward the four positions, where they landed on each person's brow.

At once, everyone could hear the spell, which had been passed down from the beginnings of the Great Wild. The weight of it was incomparable; the urge to bow down and worship spontaneously ignited in each and every heart.

Finally, Shen Wei glanced to the south and met Zhao Yunlan's gaze. A faint smile suddenly graced his lips, like a springtime flower bursting into bloom.

CHAPTER 23

I T WAS PITCH-BLACK in the halls of the Yanluo Courts. Zhu
Hong, unable to see a thing, wandered through the darkness,
completely lost. The only trace of light came from the branch
of the Great Divine Tree that Shen Wei had given her. Its soft white
light formed an invisible shield around her, completely separating
her from both the fearsome gui and the Chaos that threatened to
swallow everything. The tender buds seemed even greener than
before.

From behind her, someone urgently called her name. Zhu Hong
turned to see Fourth Uncle tucked into a crack in Yanluo Courts,
hidden carefully beneath a huge, familiar-looking scale—the Fuxi
Scale, one of their tribe's sacred objects.

It seemed he was injured badly enough that he was no longer able
to maintain his human form. A glimpse of vivid green beneath him
betrayed the presence of his tail.

Upon seeing her, Fourth Uncle addressed Zhu Hong sternly.
"What are you doing here? Why didn't you go with the Guardian
when he left? Doesn't your precious little life matter to you?!"

He assessed the situation outside and emerged from the crack
just long enough to coil his long tail around Zhu Hong and pull her
back into it with him. Traces of blood lingered around his mouth.

Pale with anger as he faced her, he snapped, "No other child in the whole tribe is as simpleminded as you! Don't you understand what danger is, you stupid girl? Don't you know to run?"

"I-I was worried about you..." Zhu Hong's voice faltered.

Fourth Uncle interrupted her in a chilly voice. "I don't need some little yao who can't even transform properly to worry about me."

As he spoke, he checked Zhu Hong over carefully, only to find that she didn't have so much as a scratch on her. Confused but relieved, he finally said, "I see luck was with you."

Zhu Hong held up the branch she was carrying. "The Soul-Executing Emissary gave this to me."

Fourth Uncle froze, then took the branch and examined it. "This... This is from the Great Divine Tree? Why would he give such a thing to just anyone? What did he say to you?"

"He told me to plant it somewhere nice if both buds survived."

Hearing that, Fourth Uncle's expression changed. "That sounds as though he's leaving his last words. The Great Seal is on the verge of breaking... Unless it already has?"

When Zhu Hong only gave him a confused glance, Fourth Uncle rapped lightly on her head and handed the branch back. "Fine, fine. Dumb people have dumb luck. Stow it safely away. It could wind up saving your life."

Zhu Hong nodded at once, then made a small sound of surprise. She held the branch up in front of his face. "Fourth Uncle, quick, look!"

At the bottom of the branch, which was about two fingers thick, some of the dry bark had been pushed aside to reveal a spot of bright, fresh green. The branch had grown a third bud!

"What's happening?" Zhu Hong gasped. "Didn't Shen Wei say that in tens of thousands of years, it only ever grew two buds?"

"The name 'Shen Wei' is not yours to speak." Fourth Uncle glared at her before continuing. "The Divine Tree atop Kunlun Mountain is as old as the Heavens and Earth. It's the beginning of all living things. Back when Nüwa borrowed a branch from the Great Divine Tree to guard the entrance of the Place of Great Disrespect, there was murder in her heart, so the tree she planted was dead before it could even live. I wonder if this branch sprouting a new bud out of nowhere means that someone's had a change of heart."

Despite being in the most dangerous place, the two snakes were relatively safe. Guo Changcheng and Chu Shuzhi, on the other hand, were still clinging to life up on the bridge.

Seeing Guo Changcheng's terrified expression, Chu Shuzhi fired his arrow without stopping to see what was behind him. The flying talisman summoned a bolt of lightning that came crashing down from the sky, piercing the gui beside Guo Changcheng. Then Chu Shuzhi spun around, whipping up a great curtain of rain with his arm, which was once again a bluish gray. The rainwater formed into a giant skull, about three meters in width, that nosedived to shield him.

Only then did Chu Shuzhi see what was behind him: the red-eyed monstrous youth who'd disguised himself in human skin and been revealed as a high-level gui. The "youth"—no, the gui—had swelled in size now, having absorbed the Chaos that had leaked from the cracks in the ground.

There had only ever been two Kings of the Gui. One had perished by blowing himself up while the other was hindered by Kunlun's divine tendon and Shennong's oath, becoming something that was not quite a god. The position was now vacant, and every high-level gui was frantic with the desire to claim it for their own.

With the Seal shattered, all the high-level gui were even more powerful than before. This one blocked Chu Shuzhi's giant skull with a raised arm; a pinch of his fingers shattered it back into raindrops that splashed everywhere. An immense force struck Chu Shuzhi in the chest, sending his scrawny body flying right off the bridge. He began to fall toward the distant ground below.

Guo Changcheng didn't stop to think. With no idea where he found the courage to act, he climbed over the railing and launched himself off the bridge toward Chu Shuzhi, as if committing suicide. The fanny pack he'd been clutching to his chest was left behind. The soul bottles it held all rolled out, scattering over the bridge's surface.

THE FOUR HALLOWED ARTIFACTS, connected by the ancient text, began to orbit around Shen Wei. Every single person helping to stabilize the ritual could feel the link between the ancient texts that Shen Wei had placed within them and the Four Hallowed Artifacts. Without thought or volition, they all followed along, silently chanting words they were unable to understand or read.

The ancient words seemed to stir something in lao-Li, who still held the huge bone he'd brought along. He looked down at the fat cat beside him, who was somehow both funny and unspeakably solemn. Listening to the tinkle of the cat bell, lao-Li suddenly spoke, his voice very low. "Three hundred years ago, there was someone who fell ill with an incurable sickness in his bones. The pain was excruciating. Death did not come to claim him, but living was unbearable. These days, he'd probably know it was bone cancer. His family decided to burn incense and pray to the gods..."

A violent shudder passed through Daqing. He looked up in disbelief.

Lao-Li's hair was snow white with age. He reached out a trembling hand to pet the black cat's head, just as he had countless times before. But this time, the cat avoided his touch.

This elderly man who'd kept silent watch over the entrance at 4 Bright Avenue, who seemed to have a weird obsession with bones, appeared to age ten years in an instant. His lips trembled before he finally continued.

"In the end, no god answered. The only one who came was a black cat with a fondness for fried fish. The man was incurably ill. He couldn't even go outside, so he was also extremely bored. The mere sight of any living thing was incredibly exciting for him. He saw the black cat as a blessing from the Heavens. It gave him a reason to live."

Lao-Li's eyes were damp, as if he was about to cry, but they were already too murky to shed a single tear. "Eventually, he realized his visitor was no ordinary cat but a divine creature, able to communicate between yin and yang, fly into the sky, and dive into the earth. Then one day, the cat accidentally entered the wine cellar and fell into a tub of alcohol. While drunk, the cat revealed the secret of the golden bell he wore around his neck. He said it was a gift from his old owner that held half of his spirit. It could regenerate flesh and bone, and even reverse the Reincarnation Cycle... That man was almost at the end of his life. His terror of death was driving him nearly out of his mind."

Icily, Daqing said, "So you tricked me for my bell and taught me a valuable lesson. Until then, this stupid cat didn't know to be wary of people. I heard you lived out your life and were eventually buried outside Shanghai Pass. You lived a few dozen extra years. How was it? How did it feel?"

"Like a lump in the throat," lao-Li said softly. "Like maggots in the bones.

"Hmph." Daqing turned away. "You poor thing. Why did you squirm your way into the Special Investigations Department?

An accomplished scholar guarding our doors and doing random chores—isn't that below your pay grade? Or did you hope to get something more from me?"

Lao-Li sank to his knees. Three hundred years later, he had been reincarnated, but he carried with him the poison buried in his bones from that other life. He stood at the door to 4 Bright Avenue as a nondescript guard, hoping for nothing more than to feed a few crispy fried fish to the ever-fatter black cat at the beginning and end of each workday. He'd expected to live out the rest of his life that way, and that his next life would be more of the same. But now, as the Merit Brush hung above his head, every single detail from the past flashed before his eyes, as fresh as if no time had passed at all.

Finally, lao-Li's murky tears fell.

The Merit Brush, which had been silent and unmoving all this time, slowly started to stir, as if it had heard something. It began to rotate around the circle; halfway around, it revealed its black and red tip.

At the same moment, the other symbols responded as well.

Wood begets fire. The Soul-Guarding Lamp began to glow with a brilliant light.

Fire begets metal. Even without sunlight, the shadows on the Reincarnation Dial started to move slowly and independently.

Metal begets water. The lines decorating the Mountain-River Awl glistened and flowed like they were alive.

The earth shook mightily, and the three ancient seals of the Great Houtu Seal broke at last. Thousands of zhang of brutality surged up out of the ground, as though hoping to consume the whole world.

All the shining lights of every city, village, tall bridge, and street were extinguished. The lights of the Mortal Realm were like a delicate mirage; as the north wind swept past, they all disappeared without a trace.

An unhurried voice chanted the sealing spell. "With the Three-Life Rock, seal the white mountain to the West."

Stone that is aged but not yet old.

Lin Jing and Shennong's mortar simultaneously felt an emptiness in their chests. The ancient text from before, along with the gold seal from the descendants of Bodhidharma and the breath of the descendants of Shennong, entered the Reincarnation Dial together. The Reincarnation Dial quickly turned three times clockwise and then three times counter-clockwise before disappearing in midair.

A huge sound came from the west, as though a gargantuan nail had been driven thousands of kilometers into the ground, forcing a crack in the curtains of black mist that covered the great earth. Once the tempestuous black mist was scattered, much of it seemed to miraculously dissipate.

"With the spirits of the mountains and rivers, seal the black waters to the north."

Water that is frozen but not yet cold.

"With the source of kindness and evil, seal the endless green to the east."

Body that is dead but not yet born.

One by one, three of the Hallowed Artifacts disappeared on the Bagua. Only the Soul-Guarding Lamp remained.

"With the soul of a deity, seal the great fire to the south."

Everything changed atop the Bagua. The Four Pillars had risen, and the Soul-Guarding Lamp moved to the very center.

Zhao Yunlan had no time to react before he felt the ancient text flow out of him; in that instant, his connection to the Soul-Guarding Lamp was severed. Arms slipped around him from behind. He turned to look and found Shen Wei standing there, already drawing him into a deep kiss.

The kiss was exquisitely tender at first, gentle and lingering. It wasn't until Zhao Yunlan felt something stream out of his heart, quick as lightning, that he realized what was happening.

He began to struggle for all he was worth, but Shen Wei's hands were like steel on the back of his head, impossible to escape. Zhao Yunlan's heart turned to ice. Every moment between them—the day he'd met Shen Wei, all that time spent getting to know him, *everything*, right to this very moment—flared before his eyes like light reflected on water. It was the sensation of his own memories being mercilessly wiped away, one by one.

Shen Wei's entire body burst into flames. As his long hair and robes ignited, he finally released his hold on Zhao Yunlan, who now lay unconscious. Shen Wei pushed him away through the air, and he landed in the arms of Shennong's mortar, who stared at Shen Wei in shock from a distance.

Shen Wei took one final, deep look at Zhao Yunlan. Then the fire engulfed him utterly, and he vanished.

In the end, he himself pushed away the one he had struggled so hard to hold; it was he who broke their oath to die together, after all his meticulous scheming to extract that promise.

If one doesn't die, doesn't perish, then one cannot become a god... He had truly been born a fool. Only now, as his road came to its end, in this moment between life and death, did understanding arrive like a bolt of lightning.

Somehow, in that instant, peace flooded Shen Wei's heart. At last, he felt worthy of the one he loved...

It was a shame that he would never see him again.

THE EARTH'S VIOLENT CONVULSIONS were even stronger down below the Huangquan.

Fourth Uncle kept Zhu Hong close, shielding her. His iron-hard scales flickered in and out of view beneath his skin as he protected her from the debris falling around them.

After a while, things finally calmed down underground. The heavy black mist, too thick for anyone to hope to find their way through, slowly and miraculously started to dissipate. The disheveled lucky survivors peeked out from various nooks and crannies, warily assessing their surroundings.

"Fourth Uncle, what is it?" Zhu Hong asked quietly.

Shushing her, Fourth Uncle cautiously extended his senses outward, only to hear her make a sudden sound of surprise. Turning back, Fourth Uncle saw the branch of the Great Divine Tree with its three tiny buds float slowly out of her hand. As it moved away, Zhu Hong immediately began to follow it.

Fourth Uncle pulled her back. "Wait! What are you doing?"

"Shen Wei saved me! I promised him I'd find a place to plant it properly. I can't be the one to lose a branch of the Great Divine Tree!" Beside herself with worry, Zhu Hong shook off Fourth Uncle's hand and ran after the branch like a newborn calf that didn't know enough to fear a tiger.

Zhu Hong was only a few hundred years old. She didn't know the ways of the world, and she'd never even heard of the Great Houtu Seal, so she didn't feel a sliver of fear. Fourth Uncle, on the other hand, could hardly just let her run off on her own. Transforming his tail into legs, he headed after her.

The branch flew until it was above the Wangchuan River. The black mist that had shrouded the river's surface was completely gone now, revealing the deep, cold water below. The branch hovered there and then plunged downward.

Zhu Hong instinctively feared the Wangchuan River, but she remembered the promise she'd made. Gritting her teeth, she became a snake and dove after the branch, slipping through Fourth Uncle's grasp. He had no choice but to follow.

As far as those watching were concerned, the two snakes were basically committing suicide. No one knew why the Chaos had temporarily retreated, never mind what the Great Seal's current condition might be. It was possible that the Chaos was just regrouping for another round of attacks. Anyone jumping into the Wangchuan right now was clearly courting death.

Following the branch of the Great Divine Tree, Zhu Hong and Fourth Uncle swam downward. Fourth Uncle, who *was* wise in the ways of the world, immediately recognized that the branch was headed toward the legendary Ancient Merit Tree—and as expected, the tall, withered tree soon came into view.

The Ancient Merit Tree had remained unchanged for tens of thousands of years, but now it extended a wizened branch. It waved gently up and down in the Wangchuan waters, stirring up the gentlest of waves as though welcoming something.

The branch of the Great Divine Tree came to rest beside the Ancient Merit Tree, sinking into the deepest dirt.

With incredible speed, it started to grow roots, then branches, and then leaves. Within only a few moments, it stood tall and lush, complementing the splendor of the Ancient Merit Tree at its side. Next, it reached out with its slim, tender tendrils, twining around the Ancient Merit Tree, which had been dead for tens of millennia. Zhu Hong's eyes widened in surprise at the sight of tiny buds growing from the Ancient Merit Tree's dead bark.

The two giant trees kept growing thicker and taller by the moment. In no time, they were thousands of zhang tall, their tips breaking the surface of the Wangchuan River. Their flourishing green canopies spread over what was left of the Yanluo Courts and then spread further still. From afar, the trees were furiously green, and so thick and dense that nothing was visible beyond them.

Back at the foot of the tree, Fourth Uncle's injuries had all miraculously healed. His gaze fell on the empty clearing behind the Ancient Merit Tree where the Sealing Rock of the Great Houtu Seal had once stood.

The Great Houtu Seal had fractured and disintegrated. Flames raged on the ground, shrouded in black mist and the cries of the gui. The Four Pillars had been restored to their original positions, and the new Seal was about to fall into place...

Aboveground, Wang Zheng suddenly murmured, "What's that sound...?"

"Must be the mountains." Shennong's mortar listened for a moment. "All ten thousand mountains crying together."

Wang Zheng's eyes widened. "Mountains can cry?"

"Yes," Shennong's mortar said gently. "Legend has it that the only time the ten thousand mountains cried out in one voice was when Pangu fell. They didn't make this kind of noise even when

Kunlun-jun's body turned into the Soul-Guarding Lamp—perhaps because at that point, the Mountain God hadn't truly and fully died."

For a long moment, Wang Zheng stood rooted to the spot before his meaning sank in. She'd never interacted all that much with Shen Wei or the Soul-Executing Emissary, so the wave of emotion she felt caught her off guard. Tears were streaming down her cheeks by the time she caught herself. For ghosts, weeping came at a cost, but she couldn't keep the tears from falling.

Sangzan sighed and pulled her into his arms.

And then, softly, a familiar voice said, "Silly girl, what are you crying about?"

Wang Zheng froze and looked down. At some point, Zhao Yunlan had opened his eyes, and now he was slowly getting to his feet.

Meeting his gaze, Wang Zheng had the sudden sense that something was...off. At a quick glance, he was the Zhao Yunlan she worked with every day, but when she looked more closely, he was somehow...different.

Her heart gave a sudden twinge. Had Shen Wei really taken away all of his memories?

But Shennong's mortar, after a few moments of observing Zhao Yunlan uncertainly, took three steps back and solemnly knelt in an elaborate formal bow. "Greetings to the Mountain God."

Zhao Yunlan—or rather, Kunlun-jun—folded his hands behind his back at first but then gave him a casual wave.

There was a swirl of light before Wang Zheng's eyes. The man who had just been wearing a rumpled trench coat was suddenly in a long green robe instead, exactly like the ephemeral figure who had once walked the Great Wild thousands of years ago.

"Back when my master forcefully suppressed the Mountain God's primordial spirit and sent you into the Reincarnation Cycle, he and the Lord Emissary agreed that the Emissary would live and die with the Great Seal," said Shennong's mortar. "Now another calamitous trial has come upon the Mortal Realm, the Great Houtu Seal has been broken, and the Soul-Executing Emissary has sacrificed himself for the Seal. All actions and consequences have fallen into place."

The blazing flames settled into a gentler orange that reflected warmly in Kunlun-jun's eyes. After a moment of silence, he quietly said, "I know."

"The Emissary became a god as a King of the Gui," continued the mortar. "He got what he wished for, and in the end, erased your..."

"Enough." Kunlun-jun didn't so much as look back. "I know all that too."

Shennong's mortar lowered his head respectfully. "When my master left this world, he tasked me with watching over the vow between him and the Emissary. Now... Now that the Mountain God has returned, this humble god has fulfilled his duties and can depart."

Kunlun-jun remained silent. He spread his hands, in which lay the scale Nüwa had left behind. It had once contained a small cycle of eleven years.

Shennong, what exactly did you want to tell me?

A faint noise from below startled everyone as if they were birds spooked by the sound of a bow. But it was only the ground underfoot stirring as a giant tree burst forth, bountifully crowned with lush green leaves. The leaves dripped with dew that seemed to have come from another world. As the dew drops fell, the cracks left by the breaking of the Great Seal slowly started to close over.

What was eternal?

Why did good and evil, right and wrong, have to exist at all?

What was life?

And what was death?

Kunlun-jun reached out, happening to catch a leaf falling from one of the branches. Abruptly, he asked, "Was it you who sent Guo Changcheng to the SID?"

Still with the utmost respect, Shennong's mortar said, "Yes. When my master was alive, he tasked me with finding someone whose third eye wasn't open, yet who could see through to the truth; someone quiet and unassuming, but blessed with great heaven-given merits."

"I see," Kunlun-jun said, quiet as a sigh. "I understand now. Thank you."

In that instant, Nüwa's scale turned into dust in his palm.

Unable to restrain himself any longer, Daqing asked, "What *exactly* is going on?"

Kunlun-jun took two steps forward, then sat cross-legged beneath the Soul-Guarding Lamp. Stroking the black cat's head, he said, "Don't worry. The Lamp is still lit."

Then, like an ancient statue of a god that had been silent for millennia, he shut his eyes as if meditating. Behind him, a pea-sized flame danced within the huge Soul-Guarding Lamp.

Guo Changcheng's tiny stun baton lay quiet. He had lost all capacity for fear or terror. His mind was empty of everything but the sight of Chu Shuzhi falling. He made a desperate grab and caught Chu Shuzhi's arm in both hands. Eyes squinched closed, he listened to the roar of the mountain wind whipping past.

But at that moment, Guo Changcheng realized with a start that he was no longer falling.

He immediately opened his eyes and saw that, because he'd knocked over the little fanny pack that Chu Shuzhi had given him, the soul bottles had tumbled out. When they'd knocked against the railings, their covers had all shattered. The souls he'd collected came pouring out all at once.

They didn't take human form; instead, they were clusters of brilliant light. Seven or eight souls, including the girl from the bridge, came together and formed a huge net that stretched down from the bridge. It caught them both…just barely.

Shocked, Chu Shuzhi grabbed hold of Guo Changcheng and leaped back up to the bridge, pushing off from the net. His foot brushed the railing as he leaped again and landed at the end of the bridge. He looked back at the net of souls, complex emotions passing over his face. "Thank you," he said. His voice was very low, and the words felt strange and unfamiliar in his mouth.

Next, after tossing Guo Changcheng into the cave behind him, he flung twelve talismans all at once. They hurtled toward the red-eyed gui, and divine thunder heeded the call, transforming the bridge into a high-voltage power grid.

The net of souls changed shape again, becoming a stream of lights that flew in a circle around Guo Changcheng.

A pale orange glow, like the gentlest flame, suddenly enveloped the unassuming Guo Changcheng. The souls around him seemed to sense something; they couldn't help but draw closer. Something like a voice stirred in Guo Changcheng's head, and words came spilling out of his mouth: "G-guard the souls of the living, bring peace to the hearts of the dead…"

From somewhere distant, a ray of light pierced all the darkness in the Mortal Realm. Weak at first, it gradually began to spread, covering the entire earth as though it had caught fire.

With a shriek, the red-eyed gui covered its eyes. It stumbled back several steps before it twisted and shriveled, melting to nothing under that brilliant light.

Chu Shuzhi turned to look at Guo Changcheng. For a moment, he had the feeling that Guo Changcheng himself had become a flame, miraculously flickering in perfect time with the fire covering the earth. Somewhat apprehensive, the Corpse King strode over to him. When he cautiously tried to reach into the flames surrounding Guo Changcheng, he felt only a peculiar warmth rather than scorching heat.

Unable to see the flames, Guo Changcheng kept chanting along with the voice in his heart. The second half flowed from his lips. "...Atone for crimes done in life, and...complete the unfinished cycle."

His voice overlapped with something within the vast earth, creating an unending resonance and echo. Chu Shuzhi, sensing something, looked up to see all the souls they hadn't found in the resort the previous night float up the mountain. One by one, they stopped before Guo Changcheng.

Guo Changcheng's notebook contained detailed descriptions of all the missing people in their families' words. Lining up, each soul found their own page. Some took up the pen and added "To so and so" on their page; others, upon laying eyes on their own names in that lopsided, childish writing, smiled peacefully, as though they had finally let go.

In the end, one at a time, they vanished into thin air and became countless points of light that flew skyward.

A sound like spring thunder rumbled in the distance. Where the sky had been covered in dark clouds, a tiny glimpse of white shone through. To the south, two vast trees burst up out of the ground. They towered over houses, then over skyscrapers, eventually dwarfing even mountains as they reached up into the sky.

Finally, only one of the souls that had gathered around Guo Changcheng remained. Touching down on the ground, it assumed the likeness of Feng Dawei, the delivery driver.

"Ge!" he called out to Chu Shuzhi and Guo Changcheng with excitement. "Thank you, guys. There really is a next life—I believe it now. Next time I'm reborn, I want to be my parents' son again, and my brother's brother. I want to live a good life and do lots of wonderful things to make up for this life."

With every word, Feng Dawei became more and more transparent. Finally, he splintered into shards of light and floated off into the endless Reincarnation Cycle.

The light building on Guo Changcheng had become blinding in its radiance. Now it suddenly broke away from him, soaring off like a meteor.

The Mountain God of the Great Wild, seated beneath the Soul-Guarding Lamp, seemed to sense something. His eyes snapped open as a ball of fire, bright as the morning sun, flew into the lamp. The flame within, which had been only the size of a pea, flared and shot up, now hundreds of meters tall.

Kunlun-jun got to his feet and pressed his hands against the Soul-Guarding Lamp. They glowed orange in the firelight. With his back to everyone, he stared into the flame. A trace of apprehension and anticipation flickered across his impassive face.

Gradually, a figure took shape in the flames and tumbled out into Kunlun-jun's embrace. He wasn't heavy, but catching him seemed to take all of Kunlun-jun's strength, causing the Mountain God to stumble. He and the person in his arms fell to the ground.

"Shen-laoshi!" Lin Jing yelped quietly, shocked.

The calm facade Kunlun-jun had worked so hard to maintain finally cracked. He held Shen Wei so tightly that his knuckles whitened.

Shen Wei suddenly began coughing as if he were choking. He reflexively angled his head to the side, leaning against Kunlun-jun. In the wake of a soft exhalation, tiny flames blazed at his brow and both shoulders, then disappeared into his body.

"Was...was that soul fire...? But how could the Chaos King of the Gui have soul fire?" asked Shennong's mortar, baffled. "Has a soulless being of great evil truly gained three ethereal and seven corporeal souls somehow? Could a gui have a soul?"

"The King of the Gui has become a god, and thus the gui now have souls." Kunlun-jun pressed a soft kiss to Shen Wei's brow. "Shennong's wish has finally come true. Thousands of years after his death, he has finally completed the true Reincarnation Cycle he always wanted."

"H-how...can that be possible...?" Shennong's mortar said in disbelief. "He... Didn't the Emissary sacrifice himself to the Soul-Guarding Lamp?"

Shen Wei's right hand was clenched tight, as though holding on to something. Kunlun-jun, sensing something familiar, gently took hold of his fist. Slowly, Shen Wei's fingers relaxed. A golden calming charm flew up from his palm, hovering before Kunlun-jun's eyes.

A sudden smile of recognition broke across Kunlun-jun's face. He had personally drawn that charm on the back of Shen Wei's hand when they'd first met in this life.

The calming charm flew into the Soul-Guarding Lamp, which slowly started to rise. Eventually it disappeared into the great south.

The new Four Pillars were now in place.

"You were the one constantly reminding me of Shennong's words," Kunlun-jun said, "and you were also the one who found the Lamp's true wick." Ever so carefully, he picked Shen Wei up in his arms. "So how do you not understand now?"

"The...the true wick...?"

"That kid, Guo Changcheng. He's the wick reincarnated." Kunlun-jun's voice was very low. "What's burning within the Soul-Guarding Lamp right now is all the merits earned by the wick over hundreds of lifetimes and reincarnations. That's why the Lamp returned Shen Wei to me."

As he spoke those words, the canopy of the tree that had grown taller than the mountains themselves turned into millions of water droplets, which dispersed to every corner of the earth. The ground that had been devastated by the destruction of the Great Seal was restored to how it had been; fresh green buds, so easily overlooked in early spring, burst from the soil. The mortals on earth would never even remember that such a dark calamity had ever occurred.

At last, the first ray of light pierced the dark clouds. A new day had dawned.

AFTERNOON SUNLIGHT slanted into the office. A humidifier pumped out soft white mist. The couch for visitors was occupied by a coat that had been flung there haphazardly and was now wrinkled—not that its owner cared.

The room's silence was broken only by the clacking of a keyboard. Zhao Yunlan was busy trying to edit a report, but the more he read, the more tightly his brows knit together. After a while, he picked up the intercom to the criminal investigation unit across the hall. The swearing started as soon as he opened his mouth. "Lin Jing, what's this bullshit you wrote? Get the fuck over here! Now!"

It took only thirty seconds for Lin Jing to get the fuck over there. "Heh heh, you asked for me, boss?"

Zhao Yunlan unleashed a tongue-lashing. "How many spelling mistakes did you make in this report? Just try to count them, you illiterate fool! Don't you care about improving yourself?! You're here all day, but do you do a shred of real work—" He broke off. "What are you doing?"

Lin Jing was in no mood to pay attention to the tongue-lashing. He inched closer, adjusting his camera angle. "C'mon, boss, say cheeeeeese—"

Zhao Yunlan did not say "cheese."

There was a click, and then Lin Jing excitedly showed Zhao Yunlan the selfie he'd taken of the two of them. Thanks to his position and angle, Lin Jing's face was so close to the camera that it looked like a huge pancake; meanwhile, Zhao Yunlan's foul expression and placement in the background made him look like a ghost haunting Lin Jing.

"You showed up in the picture!" Lin Jing was weirdly happy. "I thought primordial gods couldn't be photographed by mortal instruments... Wait, I get it. It's like with Shen-laoshi, right? This is just your physical manifestation in the Mortal Realm, and you can assume your original appearance whenever you want? Hey, can I take a picture with you looking like *that*? Just one?"

"Fuck off," Zhao Yunlan snarled.

As quickly as he'd arrived, Lin Jing fucked off again.

After less than five minutes of calm, there was a knock at the door and Zhu Hong walked in. "Director Zhao, I'd like to withdraw my letter of resignation."

Zhao Yunlan pointed toward his paper shredder with his chin. "Already done."

"Oh." There was a pause before Zhu Hong said, as though looking for something to talk about, "Then I need to take a day off tomorrow. It's the fifteenth of the lunar month."

"Got it." Zhao Yunlan didn't even look up. "Focus more on your cultivation from now on." When she didn't take the hint and leave, he finally spared her a glance. "Anything else?"

"There's something I can't help wondering about." Zhu Hong leaned forward, lowering her voice. "Why did the branch that Shen Wei gave me grow a third bud? What made the first two grow in the first place?"

The look on Zhao Yunlan's face suggested that he didn't want to answer. But Zhu Hong was a girl, and he was usually a *little* more polite to girls—especially ones he'd ruthlessly friend-zoned.

"The first bud sprouted when he swore that oath with Shennong. The second one grew when he upheld his oath, and the third was when he decided to..." Zhao Yunlan stopped. A shadow crossed his face. "The Reincarnation Cycle couldn't be created in the Place of Great Disrespect because the gui didn't have souls. The three buds on the branch of the Great Divine Tree reflected the fact that the King of the Gui had gained three ethereal souls. Since the King of the Gui is connected to the Reincarnation Cycle, Chaos is no longer just lifeless doom; as a result, the gui, who devoured anything and everything, have also disappeared. Understand?"

Zhu Hong thought about it. "That seems...very profound. Where did the gui go, though?"

"The gui are a physical manifestation of Chaos," Zhao Yunlan replied. "They're gone, but they're also everywhere."

"Everywhere like the ever-burning Soul-Guarding Lamp?"

"Mnh."

"Then what about you?" Zhu Hong asked. "Will you go back to Kunlun Mountain? Does the Soul-Guarding Order still exist?"

"I'm not going back." Zhao Yunlan copied a document onto his portable hard drive, then threw the drive to Zhu Hong. "Put the official government header on that for me and add the department stamp. Kunlun Mountain doesn't have the right conditions for cultivating the land and planting trees, so it's not like I can open a bed and breakfast there. What would be the point in going back? So I could spend my days with a bunch of dumbasses worshipping me? No way."

Zhu Hong caught the hard drive. "This all still feels a bit like a dream."

"Oh?"

"I had a crush on Kunlun-jun! I sure know how to pick them!"

Zhao Yunlan just stared at her.

"Oh, one more thing." Zhu Hong took a cardholder from her pocket and pulled out a hotel discount card. "I heard that you, O Great Immortal, can't return to your own home, so I'm giving you this. It gets you forty percent off, so you can stop spending all your pay to put a roof over your head. This is all I can do to help you."

Silently, Zhao Yunlan accepted the card before saying, "Fuck off."

No sooner had Zhao Yunlan gotten rid of Zhu Hong than Chu Shuzhi strolled in and got comfortable in a seat right in front of him, studying the real live Kunlun-jun as if watching a peep show.

Throwing his mouse down on the desk, Zhao Yunlan asked, "Haven't you people had enough?!"

"Just one question," Chu Shuzhi said.

Zhao Yunlan's temper flared. "I've never loved you! And yes, xiao-Guo is indeed the reincarnation of the Soul-Guarding Lamp's wick, okay? You can fuck off now!"

"So he has merits bestowed by the Heavens, just like Nüwa?"

"Always doing the same thing, always being the same person, day after day, for tens of thousands of years, keeping the lamp burning— is that any less worthy than the act of creating humanity? If you don't know what you're talking about, keep your mouth shut. Don't fucking embarrass me."

Chu Shuzhi gave that some thought. "In other words, xiao-Guo is the goodness missing from your heart?"

"Fuck! Off!"

Chu Shuzhi was ready enough to fuck off, but when he reached the door, he rested a hand on the doorframe and threw one last retort over his shoulder. "Ah, there's no one more ill-tempered than an unfulfilled old man who has to stay in a hotel instead of going home." He slammed the door and bolted like a rabbit.

"...Fuck," Zhao Yunlan muttered.

With nothing better to do, he killed time playing Minesweeper until the workday was finally over. But just as he was about to leave for the hotel, the door to his office was pushed open yet again. Daqing poked his head in. "Hey, someone's here for you."

Zhao Yunlan looked up in surprise. His blue-light glasses almost slipped down his nose. "I don't have any appointments..."

Daqing ignored him, turned in place, and then nudged the door open with his butt. Addressing the person behind him, he said, "Come on in, Shen-laoshi."

The expression on Zhao Yunlan's face clouded over at the speed of light. In a brisk, professional tone, he said, "Sir, if you have a crime to report, you'll have to do so at your local police station. We don't take cases directly."

It looked as if Shen Wei had come straight from teaching. His hands were still full of lesson plans. "Yunlan..."

"Excuse me, who are you? Don't call me that, I don't know you," Zhao Yunlan said, cutting him off. "Sorry, sir, I hit my head two days ago. I've got amnesia, and my thinking is still a little fuzzy. I'm in no shape to accept guests for a while. Please close the door for me on your way out. Thanks."

After the Soul-Guarding Lamp spat him out, Shen Wei had been comatose for an entire week. That whole time, Zhao Yunlan had stayed by his side, not even stepping away long enough to change clothes. But the moment Shen Wei woke up, Zhao Yunlan had immediately begun acting as though they were complete strangers, to the point of running away from home to avoid him.

Now, just as Shen Wei was about to say something, Zhao Yunlan's end-of-the-workday alarm rang. Zhao Yunlan grabbed his coat and bag and headed for the door. "You'll have to excuse me. I'm finished for the day."

Grabbing his wrist, Shen Wei called out, "...I'm sorry."

"Sorry?" Zhao Yunlan glanced at him. "Sorry for what? Deception? Or deception? Or maybe deception?"

Shen Wei was silent.

Off to one side, Daqing pretended to lick his paws. His eyes shone with excitement as he watched the drama unfold.

Zhao Yunlan tried and failed to pull his wrist from Shen Wei's grasp. "If there's anything else you need, just spit it out. I have a date at a hotel after work."

Shen Wei's grip tightened. He'd always been quick to act but slow to speak; after trying for a while, he only managed to repeat, "I'm sorry."

"It's fine, all right?" Zhao Yunlan snorted. "If apologies could fix things, why would we need the police? Why are you still hanging on to me? Do you want a salute and a handshake from Mr. Policeman or something?"

"Oho—!" Daqing spoke up, drawing out his words. "Rushing off to a hotel room..." Shen Wei skewered him with a look, and the cat hurriedly meowed out the rest. "...is something he wouldn't dare do even if you lent him a whole other spine."

Zhao Yunlan kept his mouth shut. *This treacherous little shit!*

By that point, the members of the criminal investigation unit across the hall had finished slowly gathering up their things and were ready to leave. Lin Jing was the first to cross the threshold. Confronted with this scene, he froze for a moment before saying,

"Oh, hello, Shen-laoshi. Here to ambush him after work? Excellent timing!"

Behind him, Chu Shuzhi clapped. "Perfect timing! High technical scores!"

Zhu Hong rattled off a hotel name and room number without looking up from the novel she was reading on her phone. "I also think ambushing him at night is a good idea. It's possible to compensate for emotional disharmony with physical intimacy."

In under twenty days, this girl's worldview seemed to have been shattered only for her to somehow cultivate a fascinating frame of mind that included the motto, "Loving someone means wanting to see him get railed."

Guo Changcheng was the last to come out. Locking the door, he politely said, "Hello, Shen-laoshi." Then, somewhat out of character, he continued despite not knowing the situation. "Don't be mad anymore, Director Zhao. When Shen-laoshi was still injured, you were worried out of your mind, right? You didn't even leave his bedside to rest."

All of his seniors looked back at him. As he gazed at them in confusion, they gave him a collective thumbs-up.

The utterly bewildered Guo Changcheng was unaware that he had offended his boss and was now facing an entire year of workplace bullying.

Zhao Yunlan still said nothing. *These treacherous little shits!*

In the blink of an eye, everyone dispersed. Only Daqing was left, daringly hanging back in hopes of seeing how things would unfold. But then lao-Li, who always got off work late, came in carrying a lunchbox. Even from a distance, the smell of dried fish filled the hallway. As lao-Li approached, Daqing swore, then circled Shen Wei's feet. "My lord, please give me a place to stay!"

Shen Wei took the key to Zhao Yunlan's apartment from his pocket and hung it on the cat's collar. Like a rocket shot from a bow, Daqing, despite his bulk, bolted out the hallway window and ran off.

Lao-Li saw this from a distance. Giving Shen Wei and Zhao Yunlan a helpless nod, he bent down and set the lunchbox by the door to the criminal investigation unit. "Tell Daqing to heat it up first before eating it tomorrow," he told Zhao Yunlan.

Having learned about Daqing and lao-Li's complicated past, Zhao Yunlan no longer knew how to face this person who had mistreated his cat in his absence. He just gave a blank-faced nod.

"It won't be crispy anymore," lao-Li sighed. A little forlorn, he left.

Finally it was only the two of them left in the hallway, illuminated by the last rays of the setting sun.

It was a while before Shen Wei quietly said, "You still won't forgive me?"

Zhao Yunlan looked away.

Slowly, Shen Wei released his hand. "Kunlun, I... I'll do anything you want.

The thing was, Zhao Yunlan wasn't really trying to get anything out of the situation. He couldn't bear to hit or yell at Shen Wei, but he also couldn't just let it go. Instead, he'd resorted to throwing a tantrum and running away from home.

He was passive aggression incarnate as he responded, "What are you saying, mister? Like I told you, I somehow got amnesia; I have to check my ID for my own name. Don't try to take advantage of my condition and trick me."

Shen Wei's lips were a little pale. Zhao Yunlan turned to leave, determined not to look back. But before he could even take a step, there was a noise behind him. He spun back around and saw Shen Wei kneeling on the floor.

"What are you *doing*?" Zhao Yunlan leaned over to pull him up. "What the hell is your problem? Get up!"

Shen Wei said nothing.

"Get up!" Zhao Yunlan demanded.

Shen Wei remained silent.

Finally, unable to get him to move, Zhao Yunlan plopped down on the floor beside him.

After a while, he poked Shen Wei. "Hey, it's practically sunset. The night shift's about to come out. Won't that be embarrassing for you, Lord Emissary?"

Almost under his breath, Shen Wei said, "Didn't you say you couldn't remember me?"

Zhao Yunlan huffed. "Yeah, who are you again?"

Shen Wei seized his hand in an iron grip, unwilling to budge.

After another stretch of silence, Zhao Yunlan said, "If Shennong hadn't had mercy and let my divine spirit out just before the Four Pillars were established, what would've happened to me? I would've forgotten everything once I woke up, just like everyone else, right? I never would've known that someone like you existed in the world. I guess everything related to you would've vanished too, right? And there I'd be, just wondering who had cleaned up my kitchen."

Shen Wei carefully glanced at him.

Zhao Yunlan sighed. "Shen Wei, all I really want to ask is this: How cruel is that heart of yours?"

Tentatively, Shen Wei reached out. When Zhao Yunlan didn't pull away, he inched closer, putting his arms around him. Millions of explanations seemed to come to mind, but he couldn't bring himself to voice any of them. He didn't want to mention them at all. Lips by Zhao Yunlan's ear, he said, for the third time, "I'm sorry. It was wrong of me."

It was as though, no matter how much pain Shen Wei was in, he felt no need to say a word about it—and could accept the blame regardless of what the truth was.

The scrap of fury lingering in Zhao Yunlan's heart guttered and died. Nothing of it remained, not even ash. His heart just felt a little sore.

Still wrapped in Shen Wei's arms, Zhao Yunlan helped him up. They walked outside, guided by the setting sun.

Shen Wei followed Zhao Yunlan. In a quiet voice filled with hope, he asked, "Going home?"

"Hotel," Zhao Yunlan answered.

The light left Shen Wei's eyes as he stopped dead in his tracks.

Zhao Yunlan sighed, then said a bit harshly, "I already paid for the room. Can't I stay another night?"

Completely lost, Shen Wei blinked and stared at him.

"Besides," Zhao Yunlan finished, "I didn't say you couldn't come with me."

BONUS
STORIES

ACASE FROM A SOUTHERN CITY landed in the SID's lap. Someone down there was keeping a ghoul as a pet, resulting in negative societal repercussions. Chu Shuzhi took Guo Changcheng on a business trip there, and the two of them were gone for over a month before they finally managed to resolve the issue.

Despite how long Guo Changcheng had been working at the SID, there'd been no notable improvement in his abilities. His colleagues sometimes wondered if he and Xiaomi, the newest member of the team, had been born in the same litter—Xiaomi being a year-old Samoyed puppy.

What the pup lacked in intelligence it made up for in appetite. It had been a stray that someone found and turned in to the police station near Bright Avenue, where it had stayed, unclaimed, for a month...during which time it had eaten the police department out of house and home. The cops had suspected the dog was there as some sort of scam. One thing led to another, culminating in Zhao Yunlan bringing it to 4 Bright Avenue to entertain Daqing.

Xiaomi ate and drank without a care in the world. Chu Shuzhi, before leaving to deal with the pet ghoul, had spent over a month teaching the pup to sit and shake hands, but when he got back, he realized that Xiaomi's brain was on a timed reset or something.

The dog's only two unlocked skills were once again grayed out and unavailable.

Guo Changcheng and Xiaomi's shared inability to learn new tricks seemed to hint at a mutual ancestor eight hundred years back.

Luckily, though, Guo Changcheng had a portable magical weapon.

The Netherworld had nearly been destroyed in the catastrophe with Chaos. In the aftermath, Shen Wei had almost single-handedly established a new system for the Netherworld. After that, although he rarely made an appearance or involved himself in its business, the Netherworld no longer dared show him even a hint of disrespect. The Soul-Executing Emissary, whom all Three Realms feared, was now even more powerful and venerated than before; naturally, this meant that collecting lost pieces of souls was effortless for him. All the pieces he collected went straight to Guo Changcheng's little stun baton to fuel the conversion of fear into power.

Once Chu Shuzhi returned to the office, he started watching stock reviews and scrutinizing the candlestick chart, leaving all the work to someone else. Guo Changcheng, on the other hand, patiently began filling out reimbursement forms and attaching receipts. It took him a long time, so when he went looking for Zhao Yunlan to get a signature, he found the office across the hall locked.

Zhao Yunlan was gone again.

Guo Changcheng ran a hand through his hair. "Director Zhao isn't here?"

Without looking up, Zhu Hong said, "Officially, he's off picking up the keys for our new office today and has to do a final inspection. Plus he's moving today—ugh, why does this always freeze up? I hope we have better internet in the new place."

Daqing, who was chasing Xiaomi all over the room, screeched to a halt upon hearing this explanation. He looked over and asked, "And *un*officially?"

Despite the trace of jealousy in Zhu Hong's tone, she clearly savored the words as she said, "He got fucked so hard that he can't get out of bed, duh."

Shock made Guo Changcheng tremble and miss his chair when he tried to sit. He nearly fell on his ass as it rolled away.

Zhu Hong gave him a bombastic side-eye. "Our boss is that fucking gay. What's there to be shocked about?" Then, changing the subject, she said, "Hey, how's the internet for you guys? The speed is really ticking me off today."

"It's pretty slow," Chu Shuzhi agreed.

Lin Jing, whose game was sucking up all the bandwidth, kept his mouth shut and tried not to draw attention to himself. But it didn't take long before Zhu Hong figured it out and gave him a good smack.

As punishment, Lin Jing's computer was disconnected from the internet. His only option was to choose from among the offline games on his computer, like *Plants vs. Zombies*...which earned him another smack, this time from Chu Shuzhi.

Head down on his table, Lin Jing sobbed. "I can't keep living like this."

"You're just too idle. Xiao-Guo, stop writing that report. He's got nothing to do, so give it to him."

Guo Changcheng looked at the teary-eyed Lin Jing with a good-natured chuckle. "It's okay, I'll do it."

Lin Jing flopped on the table and stole a glance at Guo Changcheng. A bit of time passed, and then he glanced at Guo Changcheng again. Guo Changcheng was quietly typing away. He was a slow but meticulous worker, so he looked extraordinarily calm.

Unable to help himself, Lin Jing stood up and reached across the desk to pluck a strand of hair from Guo Changcheng's head.

"Aiyou!" Guo Changcheng yelped, looking lost.

"I'm, uh…doing an experiment," Lin Jing laughed.

"His hair smells exactly like sheep's wool when it's burned," Chu Shuzhi said, not even looking over. "There's nothing different about it. It's just part of his meat sack. He gets one every time he reincarnates, so why would it be special? Shallow."

"How do you know what it smells like?" Lin Jing asked. "Did you already try burning it?"

Chu Shuzhi's silence said it all.

"Actually, I still don't get it." Lin Jing fiddled with the stolen strand. "How could such a fine young man be…" He sighed. "Xiao-Guo, do you feel there's anything unique about you? Something different from everyone else?"

Everyone was too afraid of disturbing Guo Changcheng's peaceful state of mind to dare mention the Soul-Guarding Lamp in front of him. Guo Changcheng, of course, wasn't sure what they were talking about. Confused, he asked, "Does being a little slower than everyone else count?"

"But…" Lin Jing paused. Guo Changcheng was the wick of the Soul-Guarding Lamp; Kunlun-jun had personally confirmed it. The wick had experienced countless brushes with adversity over hundreds of lifetimes, but his heart always remained unchanged. It had earned merits comparable to Nüwa's, yet Guo Changcheng himself was unlucky and didn't lead a particularly auspicious life. He remained quiet and toiled in obscurity, with all his merits going to the Soul-Guarding Lamp.

Lin Jing shut his mouth. If Guo Changcheng found out what he was, what would he think? If he knew that he had collected enough merits over his lifetimes that he should at least be obscenely wealthy, or should've even ascended to immortality, but could only be an ordinary mortal in the Reincarnation Cycle because of the Lamp... would he still be so peaceful and happy?

Someone whose third eye wasn't open, yet who could see through to the truth; someone quiet and unassuming, but blessed with great heaven-given merits. "But what?" Guo Changcheng was no less bewildered.

"Oh... I was just thinking, why was the plaque Kunlun-jun left behind called the 'Soul-Guarding Order'?" Lin Jing murmured. But before Guo Changcheng could work out what he'd said, Lin Jing continued, "Oh, right—what're you guys doing after work?"

"Oh, I'm bringing some stuff to Grandma Li," Guo Changcheng said. "The South Tibetan Education Action Team's summer program has started, so I'm going to help them make posters and pamphlets in the evening."

Lin Jing mindlessly toyed with his Buddhist prayer beads. "The Hinayana school of Buddhism was about cultivating for one's own deliverance, while Mahayana Buddhism is about cultivating toward the deliverance of all living things. I've always been curious, xiao-Guo—what are you cultivating toward with all that running around you do?"

"Cul...cultivating?" Guo Changcheng had no idea what he meant. "I don't know any cultivation."

"Then why help so many people unconditionally?" asked Zhu Hong.

"It's not like I have anything else to do..." Guo Changcheng was like a swan that had been scooped up out of the water. He extended his neck, a little lost, with no clue why everyone was suddenly showing him so much interest. If this were happening on a TV show, odds would be that he had some kind of terminal illness and was going to die soon. Fear made him stutter. "I'm j-just trying not to do harm. If there's anything I can help with, then I'll lend a hand. But most of the time I'm not really much help. I don't know how to do anything."

"I just remembered a quote." Chu Shuzhi had been silent for a while, but now he spoke up. "I saw it on a mural in an ancient tomb. There's no knowing how old it was, but it said, 'Filth resides in human hearts. Overthinking leads to bitterness, which begets anger and resentment. They do all that they should, as well as all they should not. But the greatest kindness is to do no evil, and that alone is enough to save the world.'"

That alone is enough to save the world...

The words seemed to float halfway across Dragon City until they came out of Zhao Yunlan's dad's—or rather, Shennong's mortar's—mouth. "Something's been nagging at me for the past few days."

Sitting back against the window, Zhao Yunlan had one leg lazily crossed over the other while he looked out over the central area of Dragon City University's campus. It seemed that exam season might be coming up; Shen Wei was surrounded by a gaggle of students bombarding him with questions. A smile lurked in Zhao Yunlan's eyes as he watched. Unconcerned, he asked, "Hmm? What was that?"

"Why was the wooden plaque the Mountain God left behind called the 'Soul-Guarding Order'?"

Zhao Yunlan glanced at him. "What do you think?"

Shennong's mortar thought about it, and then, carefully considering his words, he said, "I've heard it said that there are two kinds of people unafraid of death: the first is someone with a great obsession who walked on a path with no resentment or regrets; the other is someone who knows what lies on the other side of death.

The Soul-Guarding Lamp burned steadily over these past five thousand years. Now the old Reincarnation Cycle has broken and the new Reincarnation Cycle has been completed, aided by the King of the Gui's soul and the merits of the Soul-Guarding Lamp's wick. I wonder...was all of this the result of a colossal gamble by the great sages of old?"

Zhao Yunlan's lips quirked up, showing off his dimples. "If we'd had that kind of ability, why would we have died one by one? Shennong asked you to keep an eye on the Soul-Executing Emissary, and somehow you wound up becoming a conspiracy theorist instead?"

Even more confused now, Shennong's mortar asked, "Then why did the Mountain God leave behind the Soul-Guarding Lamp and Order? Why did my master release the Mountain God's memories and powers at that precise moment?"

"The instant Shen Wei decided to erase my memories, his oath to Shennong was fulfilled." Zhao Yunlan poured himself a cup of tea. "With the oath fulfilled, whatever power Shennong had over us automatically disappeared, so naturally I 'woke up.'"

"So...it was all a coincidence, then?"

Zhao Yunlan pondered for a moment. "I wouldn't say that."

The mortar's confusion just kept growing.

The way Zhao Yunlan glanced at him wasn't the look of a son looking at his father, but a gaze that pierced through their current identities and fell on the mortar itself.

In that moment, Zhao Yunlan suddenly seemed like the older of the two.

"Just wait," he said. "Maybe in another one or two thousand years, you'll understand. Explanations are no use. You have to experience it yourself. When you feel the call to sacrifice yourself, you'll understand some things you couldn't before. Whether it was the Soul-Guarding Lamp or Shennong's oath, back then, we only had a vague sense of the future. Perhaps it was going in a good direction, or perhaps..."

Shennong's mortar asked, "What if it didn't develop in a good direction?"

"Someone else once asked me that. If we died, new gods would naturally arise in the world. If we could serve as an example for them, our deaths wouldn't have been for nothing." The sound of familiar footsteps on the stairs told Zhao Yunlan that Shen Wei was approaching. Grabbing his trench coat from the back of the chair, he draped it over one arm and straightened up. He shot another glance at the mortar. "Aren't you one of the 'new gods' yourself?"

The mortar sat stock-still, but Shen Wei had already reached them. He gave the mortar a chilly but polite nod, then turned to Zhao Yunlan, expression immediately softening. "Are we leaving now? Have you two finished talking?"

"Mn," Zhao Yunlan answered. To Shennong's mortar, he said, "Drive carefully on the way back. Don't let my dad notice anything. Take care of his body."

Shennong's mortar stood up. With great respect, he said, "Thank you for your wisdom, Mountain God. In truth, I came to say good-bye today. Having carried out my mission, it would be inappropriate to continue occupying a mortal's body."

Zhao Yunlan was taken aback. "When are you leaving?"

"Today," the mortar said. "After taking Mr. Zhao back now."

"All right, then." Zhao Yunlan thought about it, then gave him a casual wave. "Take care. If you ever need anything, come find me."

Shen Wei and Zhao Yunlan went downstairs together, while Shennong's mortar stood at the window. Together, they ambled through campus toward the neighborhood across the street, as if taking a leisurely afternoon stroll.

Even further in the distance, in the green areas of the neighborhood, flowers on the large condo terraces quietly burst into bloom wherever they passed by. It struck the mortar then that spring had already arrived.

THE SPECIAL INVESTIGATIONS DEPARTMENT relocated from 4 Bright Avenue to 9 University Road, which was only one block away from Dragon City University.

Before leaving, Lin Jing, who was reluctant to part with their old office, took his DSLR camera and zoom lens around 4 Bright Avenue and photographed every last nook and cranny, right down to the cobwebs. Then he picked out the few pictures he was happy with and submitted them to a magazine as a series he called "Places of the Past."

The magazine's chief editor was so shocked when he saw the photos that he had to be hospitalized. He even called the police, accusing Lin Jing of "intentionally creating supernatural photos to terrorize people." It was a terrible look for the department, so Director Zhao had no choice but to quietly take care of it. Upon his return, he gave Lin Jing the beating of his life.

Life at 9 University Road settled back into a routine: eating, sleeping, and beating up Lin Jing.

The new office space was an appealing one. It had a little attic that got plenty of sunlight throughout the day, and there was a two-level basement. The lower basement housed the library while the upper basement had a mahjong table surrounded by a bunch of memorial tablets that gave the ghost employees somewhere to rest. They could even play a game of mahjong during bouts of insomnia.

With all the natural light the attic got, and thanks to a thick layer of sound-absorbing paint, one could go up there for a nice afternoon nap. Opening the window offered a lovely view of the front courtyard...or it would have, if a lovely view existed. Everyone had wildly different ideas about what to do with the space, so after it had been divided up for everyone to do their own thing, the result was the polar opposite of a cohesive whole.

As for the backyard, Zhao Yunlan claimed it entirely for himself. After a lifetime spent learning absolutely nothing about art, his taste was...rather unique. He vetoed the roses Zhu Hong liked, vetoed Chu Shuzhi's suggestion of vines, and vetoed Lin Jing's request for bodhi trees.

In the end, after careful consideration, he planted a garden full of vegetables, including bok choy, cherry tomatoes, pumpkin sprouts, pea shoots, xiangchun...a whole array of vegetables all next to each other. And in the center, like a bright moon shining among the stars, was one single slutty eggplant.

Zhao Yunlan said he eventually wanted to fill the back garden with napa cabbage and have a row of pickled cabbage and kimchi jars in the attic to snack on as they pleased.

Having heard his lofty aspirations, no one, human or ghost, had ever set foot in the garden again.

When Shen Wei finished teaching for the day, the sun was already due west, and it was still comfortably warm outside. It was just a leisurely five- or six-minute stroll from the university back to the new office, including waiting for traffic lights. Everyone at the SID had a copy of Shen-laoshi's class schedule, and they eagerly anticipated his daily arrival. Ever since their boss, Zhao Yunlan, had stopped fucking around, he'd been leading a peaceful life at the office—he barely even set foot outside the vicinity anymore! It was a death knell for the SID employees' opportunities to follow in their boss's previous footsteps and skip work or leave early. As a result, despite having moved, everyone felt that life was as difficult as ever.

But as long as Shen-laoshi came, he could get their boss to leave immediately. Shen-laoshi was the bugle call of early dismissal, and by extension, the symbol of happiness. As a result, he always received the warmest possible welcome. Countless greetings—"Hello, Shen-laoshi!" "Shen-laoshi, you've worked hard!"—would ring out, accompanied by fond gazes.

On this particular day, when Shen Wei arrived, everyone started to pack up their things out of habit. Only Lin Jing was still focused on work: he was tinkering with his new listening device. The bug was the size of a young girl's pinkie nail and looked similar to a fish scale. Apparently, the power of technology and magic combined was remarkable. The moment the bug stuck to something, it would turn invisible and start to eavesdrop.

Daqing was curled up on the stair railing. His black tail waved at Shen Wei. "He's upstairs in the attic."

"Mn, thank you." Shen Wei nodded, glancing over as he passed by. The railing was only half as wide as the cat's belly, making it seem like Daqing might roll right off at any moment. The words "Why don't you go somewhere roomier?" slipped out of Shen Wei's mouth. "Take care not to fall."

Daqing froze for a moment, then realized Shen Wei was calling him fat. He gave a yowl, fur standing on end. "I'm! Practicing! Yoga! What's wrong with practicing yoga? Is there a problem?"

Shen Wei gave his head a pat and then headed up the stairs, still smiling.

In a huff, Daqing lay back down on the railing. Further annoyance approached in the form of Lin Jing. "Daqing-gongzi, which yoga pose are you practicing right now?"

"...Cat Pose."

Following the precept of "monks don't lie," Lin Jing responded appropriately. "Ha ha ha ha ha ha!"

He earned two bloody claw marks on the face, and his bug flew out of his hand. It instantly stuck to something and vanished.

Ghost-like, lao-Li popped up out of nowhere and wordlessly handed over a cotton swab and band-aid, like a pet owner who'd come to deal with the mess their pet had made. The cat, however, didn't appreciate it. Without even a *hmph*, Daqing jumped down from the railing, stretched, and left.

Sometimes, relationships had the fragility of glass. Whatever kind it was, once it shattered, it could never be put back together— not even if one forgot...or even forgave.

It was best if a person stayed consistent, whether that meant being selfish to the end, even at the cost of hurting countless other people, or carefully cherishing someone else's feelings, however foolish the feelings might seem.

Shen Wei gently pushed the door to the attic open. There was a sofa bed up there, positioned for basking in the sun all day long. Zhao Yunlan had a throw blanket draped over his waist and a book in his hand, one finger tucked between the pages. Shen Wei walked over and bent to give him a light kiss.

Eyes still closed, Zhao Yunlan said, "Mn... You're finished with your classes?"

With a noise of acknowledgment, Shen Wei reached down to tug Zhao Yunlan up to a sitting position. "Wake up, it's getting late. If you sleep any longer you'll have a hard time falling asleep tonight."

Zhao Yunlan flopped across Shen Wei's thighs as if he lacked bones. Voice muffled, he said, "I didn't mean to fall asleep." Eyes cracked half-open, he shook the book—*Vegetable Planting Techniques*—that he was holding. "This book must be cursed. I've never even made it to the first chapter. The foreword alone knocks me out! Right now, I'm only on page eight, still in the introduction."

Shen Wei took the book and flipped through it. It turned out to be a textbook from an agricultural university, without a single centimeter of page space wasted. Even the illustrations were in black and white. There was no trace of entertainment to be found in its pages. Shen Wei said off-handedly, "Why are you reading this? You personally planted every seed out in the garden. If they're lucky, they might even cultivate into spirits one day. They're certainly not going to die."

Zhao Yunlan was stubborn. "No. Science and technology are the primary forces of production."

"Then you can keep studying your science and technology," said Shen Wei.

With a mischievous glint in his eye, Zhao Yunlan said, "The primary forces of production and I don't get along. I fall asleep as soon as I start reading it."

Looking down, Shen Wei saw that the sleepiness in Zhao Yunlan's dark eyes had evaporated. He was now looking at Shen Wei with something akin to a smile.

He wrapped his arms around Shen Wei's waist. "But if I can't keep reading, I won't be able to stop thinking about it. My mood will plummet, and if those bad moods last long enough, I'll get depressed!"

Shen Wei raised an eyebrow.

Zhao Yunlan carried on with his bullshit. "Did you know people living in Nordic regions have a high suicide rate? That means people who live in cold places are more susceptible to depression. Kunlun Mountain is covered in ice and snow year-round, and there aren't even any heaters there. I must have a genetic predisposition to depression."

"I apologize for my lack of insight."

"You must not love me anymore!" Zhao Yunlan exclaimed. "You fickle man!"

Shen Wei's head was starting to hurt. Rubbing his temples, he said, "Stop whining. What do you want?"

The smile Zhao Yunlan flashed him was full of pearly whites.

"I'll read it to you tonight at home." Shen Wei's voice was mild and resigned. "But you have to pay close attention. If it makes you sleepy, just go to sleep. You're not allowed to start anything." His earlobes were as red as those of a little wife being bullied and teased by a tyrant.

Zhao Yunlan grabbed Shen Wei by the collar and angrily pulled his head down. "Excuse me, can you drop the 'pure, innocent lamb' act? Shen Wei, babe, have I taken advantage of you even a single time...? Sure, I've always *intended* to, but I've never actually committed the crime!"

Shen Wei hurried to appease him. "Okay, okay, okay. Get up. Let's go home."

"I can't." Zhao Yunlan turned his face away, expressionless. "There's been too much strain on my lower back."

"Then shall I carry you?" Shen Wei offered, gentle and embarrassed.

Zhao Yunlan glanced at him and then stood up, all without a word. His back had magically stopped hurting, but his stomach felt sour instead.

The moment the pair left, everyone else scattered as well. Zhu Hong was first to leave, followed by Lin Jing. Chu Shuzhi, on the other hand, poured himself a cup of tea and didn't start to slowly gather his things until the stock market was closed for the day. But when he looked up, he saw that Guo Changcheng was still there. It was just the two of them at that point, and Guo Changcheng was like a backdrop, silently sitting and zoning out to the point that it seemed like his soul had fled.

"Why aren't you leaving?" Chu Shuzhi asked.

Guo Changcheng seemed to wake from a dream. He gave a great shudder, knocking over the hydroponic plant on his desk and drenching his entire workspace. Chu Shuzhi touched his own face subconsciously, worried that his cultivation had weakened to the point that his livor mortis was now visible and spooking the kid.

"I-I-I-I-I'm leaving now."

Chu Shuzhi studied him. "You...look nervous, and your expression is solemn. What, are you planning to go bomb a bunker?"

If Guo Changcheng had had dog ears, they would've undoubtedly been drooping.

Twenty minutes later, the two of them walked out of 9 University Road together. "So, your uncle set you up on a date," Chu Shuzhi said.

A tiny firework exploded out of Guo Changcheng's pocket.

Chu Shuzhi took a hasty step back. "Watch it. What are you so afraid of? Are you going on a date with the wicked witch?"

Afraid of setting fire to his own pants, Guo Changcheng took out his little baton and held it in his hands. Before he even reached his parking spot, the traffic controller at the intersection yelled, "What are you doing?! You can't set off fireworks in the city! Where's your sense of civic responsibility?"

Turning his head away, Chu Shuzhi said nothing and pretended not to know Guo Changcheng.

The Corpse King was cold and solitary. Aside from joking around with his few familiar acquaintances, he gave off an unapproachable air. As a result, he was constantly lonely and bored. Other than working on his cultivation, he had nothing to fill his free time, so he was never able to satisfy his hunger for gossip.

He suddenly found himself curious about human dates. A thought popped into his mind. Heroically, he said, "All right, stop setting off fireworks before you get a fine. How about this: I'll come along on your date and sit at the next table, pretending I'm just some random customer."

Guo Changcheng glanced at him, speechless. Was that the eagerness of a nosy auntie on Chu-ge's unsmiling face?

They arrived half an hour early. Chu Shuzhi had flipped through an entire old magazine before the girl made an appearance.

Right before Chu Shuzhi's eyes, Guo Changcheng froze into a human stick. To Chu Shuzhi's mind, it was a marvel, really. It had been many years since he'd last seen a mortal with such zombie potential.

Letting his gaze drift down, Chu Shuzhi noticed that Guo Changcheng's pants were still trembling uncontrollably, as if he were a quail sitting on shards of glass. It was just as well he'd confiscated Guo Changcheng's baton, otherwise the girl's smooth, straight hair would've been electrocuted into curls by now.

"Useless." Chu Shuzhi was frustrated on Guo Changcheng's behalf.

The girl was the amiable sort. She didn't immediately head for Weibo and make a post titled "My Exquisite Date." Out of consideration for Guo Changcheng's ineloquence, she valiantly tried to keep the conversation going, but he reacted as if it were a criminal interrogation. No matter what she asked him, he quivered and sent

SOS signals to Chu Shuzhi...who was pretending to be engrossed in the menu and flat-out rejecting the signals.

After the trembling had gone on for a solid ten minutes, the girl finally asked, "Are you...a little nervous, maybe?"

"A little" was putting it kindly. Guo Changcheng nodded, face and ears crimson.

The girl smiled. "Don't worry. We're just having a chat."

Guo Changcheng nodded again, no less red. He took a careful glance at her, then looked away uneasily.

When confronted with someone who couldn't carry on even a semblance of conversation, most people would just get up and leave. This girl, though, was a little interesting. Guo Changcheng seemed to have awoken some kind of protective urge in her.

"You really remind me of the Indian guy on *The Big Bang Theory*," she said cheerfully. "You're so cute. My aunt said you're a police officer. Is that true?"

Guo Changcheng buzzed like a mosquito. "Mn."

"Really! I never would have guessed! What happens when you run into a bad guy?"

After some thought, Guo Changcheng gave her an honest description of exactly how he would capture a "bad guy." He made a grabbing motion, then pretended to take out his "secret weapon." "Just like this. Then I'd say 'D-d-d-don't come near me,' and then they're captured."

The girl stared for a moment, then realized he must be joking. She burst into laughter. "Ha ha ha ha ha! You're so cute!"

Guo Changcheng clammed back up—it hadn't been a joke at all.

Chu Shuzhi watched coldly, resting his head in his hand. Reflecting on actual situations from work, he found that those memories seemed a bit endearing, not just foolish. But when he looked at the cheerful girl and the slightly spaced-out Guo Changcheng, and then down at his own watch, he suddenly found himself thinking that there was no point just sitting there on his own.

But somehow, the pair at the next table kept on chatting with no signs of stopping. Trying to be patient, Chu Shuzhi killed time on his phone for a while. Once his vision started blurring, he couldn't take it anymore. He called for the waiter. "I'd like to order."

The waiter hurried over, only for Chu Shuzhi to give his order in a dark, creepy voice. "Kung pao chicken. Rare. I want it to still be bloody."

The waiter was taken aback.

Guo Changcheng overheard and immediately turned to glance at Chu Shuzhi. Seeing the Corpse King's deathly expression, he realized he'd gotten too carried away.

He began racking his brains to figure out how to end the conversation, just for the girl to suddenly turn serious. "Oh, right," she said. "I actually wanted to say..." And then she paused, as if it was something difficult.

"What is it?

The girl looked down thoughtfully. "We've only just met, so I really shouldn't say this, but I like you quite a lot."

As he blushed like a stalk of red sorghum on the spot, Guo Changcheng's eyes nearly fell out of their sockets.

The girl continued, "There are some things I'd like to say up front. To be honest, I didn't want to come today. My aunt said you were a police officer, and I don't think I'd feel very at ease living with an officer who deals with crime. I'd be worried sick about you, day in and day out..." She sighed. "So I wanted to ask, are you really committed to this line of work?"

Guo Changcheng froze. Before he could respond, a hand descended on his shoulder and he was hauled up out of his seat.

"C-Chu-ge?"

The girl looked at Chu Shuzhi, utterly perplexed. Chu Shuzhi glanced at her, his smile not reaching his eyes, and then his gaze landed on Guo Changcheng. In an incredibly ambiguous tone, he said, "Going on a date behind my back? You really think you're hot shit now, huh?"

Guo Changcheng's mind boggled. *Wh-what?!*

The girl's eyes flew wide-open. She sat there in shock at the Corpse King's aura and the dramatic turn of events. Chu Shuzhi grabbed a few bills from Guo Changcheng's wallet, tucked them under a glass as payment, and stalked off with Guo Changcheng under his arm.

"What are you looking at? I did that for her own good. How dare she try to poach someone from Kunlun-jun? I'm astounded that the idea even crossed her mind." Chu Shuzhi stuffed Guo Changcheng into the car, then he stretched out his long legs. "Drive," he ordered. "Take me home first."

Guo Changcheng didn't say a word. Crimson-faced, he started the car.

On his crossbody bag, an invisible object shaped like a fish scale was sending signals.

The very next day, a rumor began to spread: "Chu-ge and xiao-Guo are dating! 9 University Road is full of gays!"

And what happened to whom? Lin Jing? The Lin Jing who just so happened to hear something he shouldn't have and spread the rumor?

Heh heh.

THE MOUNTAIN SPIRIT[15]

CUNNING TRAITORS prevail while loyal subjects are slandered.

Two key court officials, Wang and Zhang, found themselves framed by scoundrels. One was sentenced, along with his entire family, to execution while the other was sentenced to exile at the northern border. Righteous citizens from across the land rose up in fury.

One such person was known as "Master San." Master San, whose last name was Shen, was unpredictable and had a wild reputation. With his unparalleled qinggong skills,[16] he had never been defeated. From thousands of li away, Master San rushed to the rescue, managing to steal Lord Wang's widow and young son away from right under the henchmen's noses. Later, when Assistant Minister Zhang was on his way to join the army in the north, Master San spirited him away. After that, they were never heard from again. The henchmen papered all the streets and alleyways with wanted posters but never found even a trace of them.

---

15   The Mountain Spirit (山鬼) is a poem from Nine Songs (九歌), a collection of ancient poems. The poem is about a mountain goddess who yearns for her lover. Note: Shen Wei's original name, 嵬 is a combination of these two characters.

16   Qinggong (轻功) is a martial arts technique based on a real-life discipline for scaling vertical surfaces. Qinggong in wuxia and xianxia is often exaggerated, allowing practitioners to glide in the air, travel at miraculous speeds, run over water, and leap through trees or over buildings.

As a result, this incident grew into a legend, a story people loved to tell...

1

So MANY TORCHES burned on the mountainside that it looked as if the slope itself was ablaze. The constant sounds of people, horses, and dogs could drive one to panic.

The woman fled through the night, clutching her child in shaking hands. Her collar was already soaked in cold sweat, and the wind plastered it to her neck like a thin layer of ice. Her skin was half-frozen, and so was her heart. The blood pumping through her struggled to generate heat, but it wasn't nearly enough to warm chilled flesh or ease the pain of betrayal.

She stepped on a loose rock and lost her footing. As she slid down the mountain, a short, shrill scream escaped her. She closed her eyes, shielding the infant in her arms as best she could, and braced herself for a hard landing.

And then...a long, deftly placed bamboo stick stopped her forward momentum. The bamboo bowed as the woman was jerked to a halt. When it sprang back, she started to fall backward, but then the stick swung easily around behind her. With one light tap, she was steadied.

"Careful, now," someone said.

The hoarse voice belonged to a tall man dressed in rags. A small piece of wood hung around his neck like a dog's name tag, and a rusting wine jug was strapped to his waist. He looked tremendously disheveled, his face half-hidden by unbound hair. His eyes were half-shut, and he smelled of alcohol. It was hard to guess how old he was, but no matter his age, this was a disreputable way to look. He had a blade of grass in his mouth, the bamboo stick in his hands, and a rag-wrapped sword on his back. When he walked, his shoulders swayed, which somehow gave him an even more unreliable air, like someone who might start a fight or make trouble at any moment.

All told, he was the sort of man one would steer well clear of if encountering him on the street.

But this woman and her child were being hunted down on the mountain. He was the only person she could turn to, so what choice did she have? Nevertheless, she was sheltered, without connection to any of the rough people of the jianghu,[17] so fear still gripped her heart. When the man took a step toward her, she subconsciously held her child tighter and stepped back.

The man might've looked ready to start begging on the streets at any moment, but he was very perceptive. He immediately recognized her fear. Rather than approaching further, he extended his bamboo stick toward her and said, "Grab hold."

The woman gave him a careful glance and hesitantly grabbed the stick. It was roughly two meters long, and in the man's hand, it was like an extension of his arm. He could help her at any moment, but he could also use it to keep his distance so she wouldn't be uncomfortable. She tightened her grip on the bamboo, feeling a sense of safety well up in her heart. Stammering, she said, "H-hero... Shen."

"Just Shen San," the man said lazily. "I'm a nobody, not some hero. Despite appearances, ma'am, I won't hurt you for no reason. You don't have to worry."

"Shen... Master San." The woman's voice was very small. "Thank you for saving me and my son. I have no way to repay you for your enormous kindness..."

---

17 Jianghu (江湖 / "rivers and lakes") is a common setting for wuxia stories, featuring an under-ground society of martial artists, outlaws, and their associates, who self-govern and settle issues among themselves based on principles of strength and personal conviction.

"Mm." Shen San accepted her thanks but then said, "I'm just doing what I should. There's no need to repay me. In any case, I was sent by someone."

"My late husband... Before his death, we hosted an endless stream of guests. Now that our family is in ruins, plenty of people are ready to kick us while we're down. Not a single person in court spoke up. Whereas you, whom we've only met a single time..."

It might've been her nerves, but once she started speaking, she couldn't seem to stop. To Shen San, it was like having a weak bee buzzing by his ear, so annoying that it made his brain swell. But seeing how she trembled as she spoke, he couldn't exactly tell her to stop. He just stood and picked at his ears.

His gaze suddenly snapped into focus, and his swaying shoulders stilled. The woman was pulled forward mid-speech by the bamboo stick. A heartbeat later, a cold light flashed in front of her eyes. The sharp wind of a slashing sword cut at her cheeks, followed by a warm splash across her face. The smell of blood filled her nostrils. Startled, she cried out involuntarily.

On the ground before her lay a small corpse that looked both like a bird and a fox—a winged creature covered in gray fur. Despite having been cut in two, it still seemed to stare at them eerily with bloodred eyes.

"A thousand-li tracker. Do these people need to go to such extremes to hunt down a mother and child?" Shen San *hmph*ed, wiped his sword with the rag, and then nudged the little corpse with his foot. Extending a hand to the woman, he said, "Ma'am, let me see your child."

There was no room for discussion. He grabbed the swaddled infant and took a careful sniff, detecting a very faint fragrance—like incense and rouge—that grew more pungent as he leaned closer.

A couple of cries pierced the air. Seven or eight thousand-li trackers were circling overhead, their needle-sharp calls cutting through the night and carrying into the distance.

"The tracking scent is on you, and now these beasts have found their mark," Shen San said. "Go quickly!"

There was no way to know how many of the creatures her pursuer had. They came diving down, one after another—and one after another, Shen San cut them from the air. Their blood filled the sky like rain, but it and their cries all seemed to be drawing the pursuing troops closer and closer.

Shen San glanced at the woman and her child. Her legs might as well have been only an accessory to give her height for all the use they were. She'd need to install wheels to have a prayer of outrunning the mounted troops and their hounds. They couldn't run forever.

He came to a sudden stop. "Please forgive me, ma'am."

With those words, he bundled mother and son into a hidden cave. Taking the cloth the baby was swaddled in, he stuffed the woman's outer robe into it and shaped it into a human form. Looking back at the duo, he set down all the dried food he had on him, as well as his wine jug. "The dock is just twenty li to the south on the other side of this mountain. My friend should be waiting for you there with his boat. You can trust him. Once you cross the river, you'll be able to shake the hunters. Do you have somewhere to go in the south?"

Very quietly, the woman answered, "I have family from my mother's side I can go to."

"Mnh. I won't stick my rough, unrefined nose where it doesn't belong, then." Shen San nodded.

At that moment, he accidentally met the infant's gaze. Somehow, despite being on the run for half the night, the baby hadn't let out a single wail or made a fuss. He simply stared with black-bean eyes at the world in which he had only just arrived. He almost seemed a bit divine.

Intrigued, Shen San smiled at the little thing. It was then that the woman realized Shen San's own eyes were like stars.

Shen San removed the wooden plaque around his neck. The words "Soul-Guarding" were carved into the front, and on the back were four lines of mysterious text. The writing looked like something you'd find from a scam artist telling fortunes on the roadside.

He hung the plaque around the child's neck. "My mother said I was born with this and that it can turn calamities into blessings. She probably made it up, but I've lived this long with no major illness or injury. I'll give it to your little one for peace of mind."

The woman quickly stopped him. "Master San, what about you?"

"Those legless dumbasses can't catch me." Shen San gave a careless wave. "Stay hidden. I have my ways of escaping."

Alarmed, she called out, "Master San!"

But Master Shen San, carrying the fake swaddle, clasped his hands and gave mother and child a sloppy bow before disappearing into the night like a swallow. The thousand-li trackers gave chase at once, following the scent in his hands.

From all different directions, the bright flames of countless torches headed to the top of the mountain in pursuit. Armed soldiers blocked off all roads leading down from the peak, trapping Shen San. Surrounded by the howling wind, Shen San's gaze swept across the thousands of soldiers and horses that had chased him all the way to the mountaintop. With a light smile, in front of the gathered crowd, he jumped off the cliff.

2

IS RIGHT ARM FELT as though it had been twisted off. A cracking sensation and pain woke him. Shen San's first instinct was to struggle. As he opened his eyes, his dark, blurry vision was brightened by a person: someone wearing black robes, with water-smooth hair so long that it touched the ground. Man or woman, he couldn't tell; he only saw that their lashes, as dark as crow's feathers, were lowered.

An immortal, Shen San thought in a daze.

Feeling him move, the "immortal" spoke comfortingly beside his ear. "Your shoulder is dislocated. I have to put it back in place. Please bear with it."

Tch—a male *immortal.* Disappointed, Shen San sank back into unconsciousness.

Now, Master Shen San was in his prime. There was no way he would've let anyone force him into jumping off a cliff. Even as he'd leaped, he had an escape planned. The moment he was in the air, he shook out a bundle of string he had hidden in his sleeve. The string was as fine as a spider's web, and with it, he managed—just barely—to dangle from an old tree on the cliff. Hidden under the tree, he tossed his outer robe down. He'd filled it with a frame of branches, approximating a human shape well enough from a distance. It drew the pursuers' attention away from him.

His initial plan was to simply climb back up once the hunters had all left, but it was like they'd become part of the mountain. They kept on searching, and even set up cooking fires. They just wouldn't leave.

As a result, Master Shen San had hung from the cliff for an entire day and night. His right arm had gone completely numb, and the wind had nearly turned him into cured meat. It was unsustainable. Finally, he had no choice but to try to climb down with only one working arm. He periodically bumped into the side of the cliff, which would make him slide down a dozen meters. After a perilous journey, he reached the bottom, only to fall into a turbulent river. The water stole his last warm breath away and carried him off...somewhere.

It appeared someone had managed to fish him out of the river.

In his daze, Shen San felt as if someone was always staring at him. From time to time, an ice-cold hand would trace his face, from his hairline to his cheek and back again, and a fragrance as cold and clean as fresh snow would fill his nostrils. After a while, the sky grew dark, and the air grew heavy with humidity. Dew started to form. Nocturnal beasts began prowling in the valley.

A far-off roar startled him awake.

He realized he was in a small, thatched hut. He lay on a straw bed, soft and clean and very comfortable. All his joints were back where they should be, and his broken left leg was in a wooden splint. Ointment had been applied to all his wounds. He felt refreshed.

As soon as he stirred, a voice spoke from behind him. "You're awake. Drink some water."

Startled, Shen San pushed himself up from the bed with one hand, whipping around to see who'd spoken. He had been traveling around alone since the age of thirteen or fourteen, and his qing-gong was unparalleled—how else would he have had the guts to leap from such a tall cliff?—but he hadn't detected the other person's approach at all.

Finally getting a good look at him, Shen San saw a young man with a pale complexion. His eyes and brows were works of art, and with his lowered lashes, he seemed to carry a quiet serenity, as if sculpted from snow.

Shen San was immediately distracted. "You... Are you human, or..."

The young man looked up. "Mn?"

Those eyes were like nothing Shen San had ever seen. The corners might've been drawn with the stroke of a brush, but perhaps by a painter who wasn't quite a proper artist. This "brushstroke" held a hint of demonic energy—cold and eerie, making the souls of the beholder quiver.

As soon as their eyes met, the words "an immortal" died on Shen San's tongue. "...a yao?" he finished.

3

THIS "YAO-XIONG's" name was Wei. He had no last name. Master Shen San asked if his name meant "towering into the clouds, ever steadfast and unmoving," but Wei said it did not; it was just the combined characters for "mountain" and "ghost." It seemed no thought had been put into it at all.

Yao-xiong spoke little, and when he did, it was always softly. When he didn't want to speak, he would just smile. That smile must've been enchanted, because each time Shen San saw it, he felt as though the flowers on the mountain would burst into bloom, dripping with dew. It was a heart-stirring sight.

He was a good yao, his yao-xiong—elegant and kind. Since Shen San had a broken leg, his yao-xiong had taken him in to recover. Giving him shelter was gracious enough to begin with, but his yao-xiong also took the most attentive care of him, digging up a bunch of weird herbs to apply to his wounds every day. The herbs were very effective. The meals his yao-xiong prepared never contained rare or precious ingredients, but wild mountain herbs and game had their own unique flavors. There was a Go set in the little hut, each piece hand carved from stone; when they had nothing to do, they would play a game to pass the time.

Sometimes Shen San felt like he was no longer in the Mortal Realm, that he had instead fallen into some sort of ethereal, other-worldly place. Every morning, he woke to the sound of the wind brushing against the little bell at the window. When the bell chimed, it attracted flocks of birds that would chirp all at once in response.

The days were long but quiet. There were no sounds of horses and carts, no people's rights and wrongs, and no bloody jianghu fights. At night, the soft breeze became long and mild. When the moon was round, they would look down to see frost covering the whole ground. When it wasn't, they would look up to see the endless expanse of stars.

Shen San played countless games of Go with his yao-xiong under the huge plum blossom tree in the small yard. When not playing Go, they would chat about anything and everything while enjoying some wine that his yao-xiong said he had made himself. It was as mellow and rustic as his playing style in Go. It went down smoothly and would neither intoxicate you nor harm your health.

Yao-xiong might've simply grown out of the earth. He lived alone in this hidden corner of the mountain, a place so remote that even birds rarely passed by, yet he had everything he needed.

During Master Shen San's recovery, he frequently asked Yao-xiong what his original form was, but Yao-xiong only ever responded with a smile. It wasn't until Master Shen San had named every single plant he could think of, as if reciting a menu, that a thought suddenly struck him. "I've got it!"

Yao-xiong didn't look up from where he was pounding medicine. "I'm not a camellia, nor jasmine, nor azalea, nor a plum blossom."

"Oh, none of those flashy, commonplace flowers." Shen San seemed to smile. "You're a snowflake."[18]

Though Yao-xiong took such nonsense to be idle chatter, he still shook his head, exasperated. "Snowflakes melt the moment they land," he retorted readily. "Where would they get the time to cultivate? Come, it's time to change your dressings."

"Not all of them melt." Shen San lifted his injured leg and set it down flat with a little difficulty. As he removed the splint immobilizing it, he kept talking. "Last year, I went to the west at a friend's invitation. It's all mountains over there—mountains connected to mountains. Even in the middle of the year, the fierce winds at the peaks make it feel like the dead of winter. The snow there never melts. It covers the peaks year-round. I think you might be a snow spirit from the top of one of those mountains."

As his brain randomly retraced his travels through the mountains and sea, he started thinking about all sorts of bizarre tales. While his mind couldn't help wandering, Yao-xiong had already carefully applied fresh medicine and re-wrapped his leg. Yao-xiong's hands worked quickly, but his touch was extremely gentle. Shen San felt almost no pain.

When Shen San looked down, all he could see was the top of Yao-xiong's head and all that ink-black hair. Yao-xiong, half kneeling on the ground, was being so careful—he might not have been holding an unruly man's leg at all, with its thick skin and rough flesh, but a delicate, fragile heirloom. The tiny pot of boiling soup was emitting thin wisps of white steam and whistling faintly. The thatched hut was dry and clean inside, with clothes and bedding that smelled like fresh sunshine.

---

18 The Chinese word for "snowflake," when translated, "xuehua" (雪花), literally, means "snow flower," which makes it sound like it's a type of flower.

Wanderers of the jianghu had no career or family. They came and went in the wind and rain, like duckweed. A mere sip of warm congee was sometimes enough to make tears spring to their eyes.

Shen San was a wanderer among wanderers. His wanderings had brought him to the bottom of the cliff, and he'd come to this sudden stop at this small hut after being swept away by the torrential waters. Something stirred in his heart. Words burst from his lips. "Yao-xiong, you brought me back here and you've tended my wounds so carefully. If things go the way they usually do in books, I should be offering myself to you right about now."

Yao-xiong's hand quivered. The medicine bowl fell to the floor and smashed.

Shen San froze. "I'm just..."

Before the word "joking" could leave his mouth, Yao-xiong had picked up the broken pieces in a panic and fled.

The breeze from his passing made the little wind chime ring again and again. Much like the chatter of a gaggle of girls just leaving childhood behind, the sound was somehow both pleasant and annoying.

Eventually, Shen San came to a realization. He stared, dazed, eyes and mouth wide, at the half-open door of the thatched hut. Understanding dawned.

It was just like the stories: the scholar and the fox spirit, the lost traveler and the mountain spirit, Xu Xian and Bai Suzhen.[19]

He had met a male fox spirit, a male mountain spirit, a male snake.

A beautiful fruit that had fallen from the skies, perfectly sweet... but eating it resulted in a bit of a toothache.

---

19   The two protagonists from the Legend of the White Snake (白蛇传), one of China's most famous folktales. Xu Xian is a human scholar, while his lover, Bai Suzhen, is a white snake spirit who has cultivated human form. They fall in love, but must overcome ordeals and persecution to be together. Over centuries, the story has evolved from a tragedy to a love story.

4

EVER SINCE SHEN SAN'S NONSENSE had complicated everything with the specter of romance, the easy comfort they'd shared had faded. While playing Go, they tried to avoid looking at each other and just focus on the match instead. When they chatted, it felt—at least to Shen San—as if they had to search for things to talk about.

It was all very awkward.

But at the same time, his leg healed quickly. Shen San was a rough man, accustomed to cuts and stab wounds. The broken bone healed in well under the time it would take for ordinary folk, and then there were a few days of hobbling around after the splint came off. In no time, he was back to running and jumping easily. With his limbs all back in working order, there was no more reason for him to spend his days under someone else's roof. Besides, he still had things that had to be taken care of.

A day came when, as Yao-xiong watered the medicinal herbs in the garden behind the hut, Shen San packed up his things. He stood beneath the eaves, zoning out as he watched Yao-xiong busying him-self among the plants. When Yao-xiong turned, their eyes happened to meet, and they both froze.

Yao-xiong stood up. Surrounded by the herbs, he was first to speak. "Are you leaving?"

"Mnh," Shen San answered and then found himself wanting to explain further, even if it was unnecessary. "I was tasked with sending Lord Wang's widow and son across the river. I don't know how they're doing, so I need to check in on them. And after the Mid-Autumn Festival, Assistant Minister Zhang will be leaving for the northern border. We shared drinks once, so I must ensure he arrives safely."

Yao-xiong stood stone-still before finally opening his mouth. "I..."

You and I shared drinks once too.

"Hmm?"

"Nothing." Yao-xiong lowered his head. "Then we'll meet again."

The lives of the people of the jianghu were like grass. They never spoke of parting or leaving. Shen San looked down, adjusted the sword on his back, and walked across the courtyard. When he reached the gate, he suddenly stopped. He turned back to look at Yao-xiong, who was watching him go. "A great kindness should be repaid with action, not words. I'll remember everything you've done for me. Once I've dealt with those things, I'll come back and bring a couple jars of good wine with me, and then...then..."

His tongue, usually so nimble, failed him. Cold sweat broke out all over his back. As it evaporated, heat suffused his neck and then his ears, steaming him until he stammered. "Th-then, I-I'll be yours to command."

Yao-xiong seemed to laugh, but the sound was tinged with melancholy. Shen San gave him a searching glance, then took his leave.

He walked along the river for hundreds of meters before turning back to give the little thatched hut and its garden one last look from afar. As he walked, his legs felt heavy and there was an emptiness in his heart. He couldn't summon any real energy; even his heartbeat felt like it was just going through the motions. It was as if a rope lay around his neck, trying to drag him back to the place he was leaving behind.

Master Shen San, who could come and go without leaving any trace, was no longer decisive, unrestrained, and free. He now knew he had well and truly fallen for the yao's tricks. His very soul was held hostage.

He had to return.

5

AT THE END of the ninth lunar month, as autumn settled deep into the earth, the grass and trees withered.

Shen San's sword broke.

He'd had the blade forged by a random roadside blacksmith, and it wasn't worth much, so he wasn't especially upset to lose it. He just dug a hole and filled it with the corpses of the people who'd been hired to assassinate Assistant Minister Zhang. Then he stuck a wooden plank in the ground and wrote: "A hole full of shitty dogs. Signed, your grandpa Shen."

Finally, he stuck his broken sword in the ground by the plank, burying it right to the hilt. He couldn't have possibly shown more arrogance.

A few of his friends guided the terrified Assistant Minister Zhang away. When they saw Shen San's "masterpiece," they tried to talk him out of it. "Killing them is one thing, but why *this*? Are you trying to make trouble for yourself? How can you continue in the jianghu after this?"

"I'm not continuing." Shen San leisurely wrapped his hand, which he'd injured on the broken sword. He glanced southward, facing the fierce wind head-on. "I'm washing my hands of all this and retiring."

"Retiring? Retiring to where?"

"A paradise of peach blossoms," he said. "A cave filled with webs of desires."

That didn't sound anything like a proper retirement spot. But when his friends tried to ask what had gotten into him, Shen San had already demonstrated his ability to walk without leaving footprints. With a few leaps, he was gone.

He started his journey south in late autumn. By the time he reached his destination, the Mortal Realm was buried in snow.

Winter had arrived particularly early this year, and it was particularly cold as well. Frost crusted both banks of the Yangtze River. He was wanted by the palace and buffeted by the snow. He couldn't have been any more haggard. But despite all that, a warmth was nestled right by his heart, urging him to ride back with the speed of an arrow in flight.

In the depths of winter, coated in a layer of snow so fine it looked like salt and bearing the fine wine he had so carefully chosen, Shen San finally found the little valley where he'd convalesced. When his eyes fell on that little thatched hut, waves of flowers bloomed in his heart. He strode forward at once, but then remembered something. Retreating a bit, he faced the bitingly cold wind and dusted himself off, then scrubbed the mud from his pants with frigid water from the pond. The chill turned his fingers the red of cooked shrimp, but he still made sure to wash his face.

Unfortunately, with his hands so cold, he had little fine control over them. When he tried to shave with his small dagger, he accidentally cut his chin.

He hid this tiny blemish under his shirt collar and then made a show of strolling leisurely over to the hut. He had it all planned out: he would open the door, and when his eyes finally fell on the person within, he would smile and say, "I'm back. You can order me around as you please."

Just a short few hundred meters more. His heart was as soft as cooked tofu. Those words rolled around on his tongue at least a thousand times. How he would stand, what tone he would use, how he would smile... He had mentally rehearsed it all, until he could've done it in his sleep.

He reached the gate. But just as the words were about to leave his lips, Shen San suddenly saw that the garden was covered in ice and that snow had drifted over the frozen ground. The medicinal garden was strewn with sickly branches and leaves, all clumped in the mud.

His heart sank. All the warmth evaporated.

Yao-xiong was deeply fastidious. Had he been there, not a single fallen leaf would be lying in the garden. It was clear he'd been gone for a long time. The little garden was abandoned.

Dazed, Shen San stood at the entrance for a while before finally going in with his wine. He searched both inside and out. Everything, even the stone Go set, was covered in a layer of dust—everything but the wind chime, which still rang. All that had happened there might as well have been just a figment of his post-injury imagination.

With a puff of the icy wind, it all scattered like dust.

6

SHEN SAN SETTLED DOWN in the thatched hut. Clumsily, he cleared out the mud and snow in the yard and dusted everything inside the hut clean, then buried his wine jars beneath the plum blossom tree. After the bitter winter, the plum blossoms would bloom. They would carry moonlight within their petals, dusted delicately with frost.

He reinforced the hut with wood and stone, showing every sign that he intended to stay for a long time. Next he carved a sword out of wood, and every morning when the birds started chirping, he practiced with it. He spent his daylight hours hunting and fixing up the garden, and when the sun set, he slept.

Slowly, the ethereal little garden and hut that had seemed fit for an immortal came to seem more and more homely. The once-elegant garden of medicinal herbs was reborn as a vegetable garden. Shen San hung a row of cured meat and dried fruit beneath the wind chime. He brought so much life to the place that even when the chime sounded, it seemed to ring with the fragrance of living.

The only thing he couldn't bear to touch was the plum blossom tree by the entrance. That, he left to grow as it pleased.

In the blink of an eye, the plum blossoms had bloomed thrice and withered thrice. In the thatched hut, Shen San had played Go against himself for three years.

Shen San had fulfilled his promise, but the one he'd returned for never came back.

Finally, it seemed he couldn't wait any longer.

One evening, he washed the stone Go set and hung up the board. He put away the cured meat and dried fruit hanging in the window and packed up all the rest of his things before the sky turned dark. It added up to only enough for a small bundle, which he hung from his wooden sword. After hanging that on the door, he blew the lights out early and went to bed. It seemed he was about to go on a long journey.

Just after midnight, when the moon was barely hugging the plum blossom tree's branches, a black-robed man stepped out from the tree's shadows. He laid one ice-cold hand against the bundle, then passed through the door as silently as if he were a shadow himself.

It was the hut's owner, Yao-xiong Wei.

Three years earlier, when Shen San had left the mountain, Wei had followed him the whole time. Wei watched as he traveled great distances and faced constant danger, but also saw him at the height of his glory, his call never going unanswered. Wei had thought he would never come back. But somehow the man really did walk away from all that hustle and bustle and return. As a result, this mountain spirit who was never meant to see the light of day had been left with no choice but to hide himself, hoping Shen San would leave again in disappointment. He never imagined he'd be in hiding for over a thousand days and nights.

But...

Wei's long sleeves stirred up a light breeze. The highly skilled man, who would startle awake at the drop of a leaf, somehow fell into an even deeper sleep, as though his soul had left his body. Wei gently sat down next to him, the tip of a finger carefully tracing each of his features.

Stroking further downward, Wei's finger came to rest on the back of Shen San's hand, which he then cradled in his own. Barely audible, he called out, "Kunlun."

He had sworn never to meet Kunlun's reincarnations. He had already trespassed in caring for Shen San for over a month. Those dozens of days spent with him should've never happened. He shouldn't still be greedy for more.

It was just as well that the man had reached the end of his patience. He was finally going to leave.

The next day, as usual, Wei hid in the shadow of the plum blossom tree. He didn't emerge from his hiding spot until he had seen Shen San leave with his bundle and horse. After leaning against the gate in a daze for some time, feeling a void in his chest as if his heart had been cut out, he unearthed the wine Shen San had buried under the tree.

Perhaps Shen San had thought the wine Wei made wasn't strong enough; the wine he'd brought back was powerful liquor from the north. When Wei swallowed it, it felt like a fierce blaze had ripped him open from throat to chest. He so rarely traveled around the Mortal Realm that he had never really tasted strong mortal alcohol, and therefore wasn't aware of his own lack of tolerance. After only a few gulps, he was sliding down the plum blossom tree.

The great weight of an endless lifetime dragged him inexorably downward. Past and present blurred together; he could no longer count the number of times he had endured parting and death all alone. Reflecting on all these memories made his chest burn the same way the alcohol did.

There, beneath the plum blossom tree, Wei fell into a drunken stupor. He lay insensible for three days and three nights. On the fourth morning, when the sunlight stabbed his eyes, he had the sudden sense that something was off. He sat up and found he'd been taken inside the hut.

Just then, someone moved to block the morning light spilling in through the window. Shen San was there, observing him closely, arms crossed in front of his chest. Slowly, he said, "I only brought two jars of wine. How dare you drink and spill an entire jar while I was gone?"

Wei looked up at him in disbelief. He opened his mouth, but no words came out.

Didn't you leave...?

Somehow, Shen San seemed to hear his thoughts. "I went to buy salt on the other side of the mountain. The salt jars in the kitchen here were all nearly empty. It's not like I can make some appear out of thin air like you, Yao-xiong."

After saying all that, he seemed angry. He stood up wearily and walked out. Panicked, Wei also got to his feet, not even knowing if he wanted Shen San to leave or stay. With his brain still mush from his bout of drunkenness, the poor, lonely ghost finally followed his heart for once. He reached for Shen San. "Don't—"

Shen San's hand closed over Wei's pale wrist. "You've been here all along these last few years, haven't you? Somehow you could see me, but I couldn't see you."

Wei was speechless again.

"Oh." Shen San read the answer on his face. Expressionless, he pried Wei's fingers loose and flung his hand away.

Wei's heart turned to ice. As he watched, Shen San walked to the door, resting his hands on the doorframe, and then turned back. "So you really aren't human."

What could Wei possibly say? The panic and emotion flooding his eyes were as stark as ebony on pristine snow.

Shen San glared, then stalked out into the garden. But just when Wei thought he was really going to leave this time, there was a furious roar. Rushing outside to see what was happening, he found Shen San in a rage, battering at the plum blossom tree with his wooden sword. "Do I care?! Did I ever say I cared whether you were human or ghost or any other manner of monster?! I came back, just as I said I would, but you wouldn't see me for three years?! *Three years!* You piece of shit!"

"I..."

"I didn't say you could speak!"

"I'm...really not a plum blossom spirit. There's no use hitting the tree."

Shen San paused.

The tree, whose blossoms had just fallen, trembled in fear, and a heap of tender young leaves drifted to the ground.

7

I F HE WASN'T A plum blossom spirit, then what was he? Shen San never did find out. But to be fair, Wei had never tried to find out how many times Shen San had wet his pants as a kid or how many birds' nests he'd destroyed. There was no need to know everything about Wei's past either. So after their one-sided fight and Shen San's one-sided forgiveness, the two of them made a home together.

Yao-xiong enjoyed everything, however refined or crude it might be, as if it were sweet honey. He had no objections to Shen San's cured meat, dried fruit, or garden full of vegetables and fruit. When he had time, he even gave Shen San a hand with them.

Whenever Shen San went out to hunt or had to travel long distances to buy things, he always thought of the person waiting for him at home, which made his heart glow with warmth, like there was a little furnace inside. That warmth took the edge off the chill of the cruel world.

In time, this peaceful existence made Shen San feel as though he was losing his kung fu skills. He dedicated a significant part of each day to sword practice, but—perhaps because now there was some-one off to the side watching, distracting his mind and heart—his wooden sword somehow seemed heavier by the day. There were days when he simply lacked the energy to continue, but he didn't think much of it. So what if he didn't have enough energy? He was retired now. All he had to do was hunt, and his remaining skills were plenty good enough for that.

The two of them took their meals together and bedded down together, and in no time at all, a whole year had passed. New Year was approaching, and snow was once again falling north of the river.

Shen San disguised himself and traveled through the mountains to buy supplies at the nearest market. A snowfall was a good sign for the coming year, and the year that had just passed had been uncommonly peaceful. True, the emperor was as unreliable as ever, and true, corrupt officials continued to abuse their power, but at least the battles just past the borders had calmed down. It seemed the Heavens had rewarded the people with a smooth year, and much like grass growing on the cliffside, a tiny gust of spring wind was all it took for them to start to thrive once again.

The market was busier than in past years as well. Shen San's first step was to sell his hides and mountain delicacies, after which he went in search of good food and good fun. He wanted to empty his money pouch right back out again. It wasn't long before his horse was carrying all manner of New Year's goods and snacks. Finally, when he'd bought all they could possibly carry, he decided to head home. He bought a few sweets that his Yao-xiong liked, fresh off the stove and wrapped in thick wax paper. He tucked them inside his clothes, where they might stay warm until he got home if he rushed quickly enough. The woman selling the sweets smiled at how handsome he was and wrapped him a few extra white sugar cakes.

Shen San still had some copper coins, so he threw a handful to a beggar on the street. Then he spotted a little bookstore and decided to buy a few interesting books to take back to his Yao-xiong to help keep boredom at bay.

As he perused the store's wares, he stumbled across something unexpected at the bottom of the trunk: a heavily illustrated book called *Tales of a Bitten Peach.*[20] When he opened it, he froze. The detailed pictures and text left absolutely nothing to the imagination.

20 *Tales of a Bitten Peach* (分桃记) *references an ancient Chinese story about a duke and his male lover, who offered the duke a peach after taking a bite. Bitten peaches, like cut sleeves, can symbolize gay romance.*

Somehow, it had managed to shamelessly sneak its way into a pile of serious literary works, where it sat, unabashed, as if it had every right to be there.

The bookseller's eyes were keen. He came closer and murmured, "I see you're very discerning, sir. This is the only copy of this work."

Shen San burst out laughing. "This so-called 'work' is nothing but an insult to common decency." With a sweep of his sleeves, he left.

But less than ten minutes later, this "decent" individual was back. He pretended to pick through the books, looking very serious, then pulled *that* book out as quickly as a thief. He threw down a few coins and ran away with the book tucked close to his chest.

Carrying this secret, he raced all the way home through the heavy snow. He and his horse were both soaked with sweat when they arrived, and between that and the freezing cold, he started to shiver uncontrollably. Afraid that he'd take seriously ill, Wei rushed to get him a change of clothes and have him take a hot bath. Shen San, confident in his own health, paid this no mind. Instead, he chased Wei in circles, teasing him and feeding him the sweets. Shen San wanted his Yao-xiong to go to bed early so he could carefully study his new book.

But to his surprise, before he got the chance to study the essence of life, illness overcame him. That night, Shen San burned with a high fever. He'd traveled far and wide since his youth and yet hadn't been sick for many years. Now he lay dazed with fever, sweat pouring constantly from him. Wei cared for him without resting or sleeping. He took off Shen San's sweat-drenched clothes and wiped his body down.

It wasn't until the latter half of the night that Shen San's restlessness eased enough that he finally fell into a fitful sleep. Wei, afraid his fever would worsen, still didn't dare fall asleep himself. He lit an oil lamp and kept watch.

Keeping an eye on the rise and fall of Shen San's chest, he idly flipped through the books Shen San had brought back. His eyes flickered over the books' text, but he registered not a word. It seemed he was only leafing through them to pass the time...until, under Shen San's wet clothing, he found *Tales of a Bitten Peach*.

Wei took a casual look, turning five or six pages before he realized exactly what he was seeing. He flung it away, then glanced guiltily at Shen San, lying beside him. Shen San's face was a bit red, and he was completely out of it. When he showed no sign of waking, Wei held his breath for a while, restlessly smoothing his hands over the sheets.

Eventually he gathered his courage and picked up the book he had tossed aside. Cautiously turning just a few pages made him look like he was about to pass out. He kept reading, cheeks and ears flushing red. His blush deepened as his gaze landed on Shen San, then deepened more as he glanced back at the book, and still more again when he looked back at Master Shen San.

It wasn't even Lunar New Year yet, but he'd already donned auspicious red, fit for a wedding. Much like the snow falling outside the window, he was about to melt.

Shen San had fallen ill due to the cold entering his body. After a few days of careful care, he recovered, just in time for Lunar New Year's Eve. Once he'd shaken off his weariness from being sick and was once again alive and kicking, he discovered that his treasure was missing.

Only two people lived in the hut, and some stupid work of erotica could hardly cultivate a pair of legs for itself and run off. That left only one person who could've hidden it.

Yao-xiong's personality was as transparent as water. A single glance was all it took to see through him. He had only a few places to hide things, and Shen San could've found them all with his eyes closed. He sent Wei outside on the pretext of wanting a few pretty branches of plum blossoms. But while he was still rummaging through the chests and drawers, Yao-xiong suddenly returned, intending to ask Shen San where he should put the branches. Instead, he caught Shen San in the act of stealing the book back.

Startled, Shen San dropped the book.

In those few short days, Yao-xiong, who was pure as a blank sheet of paper, had read through it countless times, and the book's thread binding had already come loose. When the book hit the ground, its pages went flying, dusting the floor with elegance.

The two of them stared at each other. Shen San burst into laughter; his mortified Yao-xiong fled.

8

BUT LIFE WAS LIKE A DREAM. Beautiful days were as ephemeral as bubbles.

After Lunar New Year, Master Shen San's vitality faded like smoke. He was always sleepy and had less energy by the day.

One particular day, Wei had gone out and found some black and white stones, and now he sat in the garden, sanding them down into Go pieces. Shen San had terrible sportsmanship. When he lost, he'd want to take back his moves; when Wei refused, Shen San would throw the pieces at him. For all Shen San's famed prowess with weapons of assassination, not a single thrown stone ever hit his Yao-xiong, thanks to Wei's ability to appear and disappear as he pleased. The result, however, was that they'd lost many of the

Go pieces. At this point, they no longer even had enough to play a full game.

No matter how much Shen San slept, he never felt rested. Now, as he lazed in a sunbeam against the plum blossom tree, he abruptly said, "Yao-xiong, you don't have a past or a last name. Why don't you just take mine?"

Wei didn't say anything. He blew dust off the piece he was currently sanding, but the corner of his mouth quirked up.

"'Mountain' 'ghost' Wei. Such a carelessly chosen name, and a little spooky to boot. It's not a good name. We should change it."

"To what?"

"Mm...here. In this world, the mountains and seas are all connected, and lofty peaks stretch out endlessly. Why don't we add a few more strokes and make it a proper name? What do you think of this 'Wei'?" [21]

Shen...Wei.

Shen San jumped up. "I'll go write it down for you..."

Perhaps it was only that he'd gotten up too quickly, but before he even finished speaking, he stumbled. He reached out to put a hand against the plum blossom tree, but his limbs felt numb and weak. Black spots bloomed in his vision.

Maybe he'd never truly recovered from the terrible chill he'd taken around the New Year. Shen San recovered, then fell sick; fell sick, then recovered again. He never fully got better. Half of the lush garden was dedicated to medicinal herbs, but however many of them he ate, he never showed any signs of recovering.

---

21 The character for his current name, Wéi (嵬), is formed from the characters "mountain" (山 / shān) and "ghost" (鬼 / guǐ), while Shen San's suggestion, Wēi (巍), has the added character wei (委). Both characters mean large, tall, lofty, but 嵬 has a more uneven, craggy connotation while 巍 is more majestic and dignified.

This cycle continued for over half a year. Spring turned to summer, then to autumn, and then a harsh winter was nearly on their doorstep. The prolonged illness had stripped too much weight from Shen San's frame. His strength faded more and more. It was nearly Lunar New Year again before he was able to take a few steps outside.

This year, Yao-xiong adamantly refused to let him leave alone. For the first time, the two of them left the little hut deep in the mountains together, journeying to the village to purchase supplies. When they arrived, however, they found that the bustling market of past years was but a memory. All the nearby villages were deserted.

When they finally encountered someone—a fleeing refugee— they learned that war had broken out in the north. The emperor and his corrupt officials had escaped to the south in a panic, abandoning the capital itself. Battle, no matter where it occurred, endangered civilians, so people left their homes behind to seek safety elsewhere. But the Yellow River was flooded, and a drought was ravaging the south. Starvation and disease were rampant.

The short-lived prosperity of the previous year seemed to have been borrowed time. It had lasted long enough to give people a false sense of security, and then it shattered around them.

The pair went home empty-handed. Shen San's heart bore a crushing weight the entire way. As soon as he set foot inside the thatched hut, he threw up a mouthful of blood.

This time, he never got up again.

In his delirium, Shen San heard weeping close to his ear—and between the sobs, words. "Humans and ghosts don't belong together," and, "I should've never broken my oath and approached you."

Appalled, Shen San was struggling against his body's weakness for even a moment of clarity when he heard the yao say, "I should've never let myself harm you. I'm leaving."

Shen San somehow found the strength to reach out and grab the belt at Wei's waist. "Don't... Don't you *dare*. You started this. If you dare...dare to leave without warning... I'll...I'll dig out my heart... and boil it..."

That year, the Emperor Star[22] fell, and so did the country.

Deep in the mountains, alone between the vastness of the earth and sky, a solitary ghost stood heartbroken, with nowhere to go.

9

ON JINGZHE,[23] the snow along the sides of the streets melted. The bones it had hidden all winter lay bare to the shining sun.

After three days of unconsciousness, Shen San suddenly woke up. He looked at his Yao-xiong, who had been keeping watch over him, and smiled with bright eyes.

"I dreamed we were on a snowy mountain."

His yao forced a smile. "What mountain?"

"I think...Kunlun Mountain?" Shen San seemed to be staring off into the distance. He didn't see how Yao-xiong trembled violently at the word "Kunlun." He just kept speaking. "There was a tree on the mountain. Was that your original form? Did you transform from that tree?"

Wei...no, Shen Wei...seemed to choke on something. With difficulty, he said, "...No."

---

22 In traditional astrology, the North Star is known as the Emperor Star (紫薇星), and influences on it can represent both the fate of the emperor personally and significant outcomes for the nation as a whole.

23 Jingzhe (惊蛰), meaning "the startling awake of insects," is the third of the twenty-four traditional Chinese solar terms. Usually around early spring, when insects first leave winter hibernation, approximately March 5th–20th.

"I didn't think so. That tree looked ancient and rather ugly. You're actually the snow that covers Kunlun Mountain year-round, aren't you?" A smile broke over Shen San's face. "I never used to believe in gods and immortals, but I do now, a little... When I was younger, I had a wooden plaque that said 'Soul-Guarding.' My mom said I was born with it, and she told me to take good care of it. She was afraid I wouldn't live long without it. I never believed that, but a few years ago, I gave it to a tiny baby. Ever since then, my health's crumbled, year after year, and I'm at the end of my life. I brought it on myself by not listening to my elders. It has nothing to do with you."

His Yao-xiong's eyes were so red that they seemed about to bleed. Shen San gripped his hand lightly, giving it a shake. "Xiao-Wei, wait for me. Don't leave. Stay here in this garden. If there is a next life, I'll come find you again, okay?"

His Yao-xiong gave no reply.

"Okay?" Shen San tried again.

"...Mn."

It was enough. Shen San closed his eyes, satisfied. Merely speaking those few words had exhausted him. He couldn't have lifted even a single finger again.

You promised. This time, you'd better keep your promise, Yao-xiong.

With that final thought, he nestled into Shen Wei's arms. His fingers went slack.

He headed for the next life, eager to fulfill his promise.

10

VER THE NEXT TEN YEARS, Wei—*Shen Wei*—looked far and wide for Shen San's lost wooden plaque.

When he finally held the dusty wooden plaque in his hands, a light shone on it, as though it were divine.

Shen Wei leaped up into the clouds. From there, he saw a weak but identical light glowing in the Mortal Realm, as if it and the wooden plaque were echoing each other, connected despite the distance. Turning invisible, he followed the light.

It led him to a newborn boy. The infant's eyes hadn't opened yet, but the curve of his lips was already familiar.

Shen Wei reached out as if to touch the child's face but then seemed to remember something. Dejected, he withdrew his hand. He turned and morphed into flowing light, then flew toward the peak of Kunlun Mountain.

Sealed atop the mountain was a descendant of the mystic White Tiger who had been sleeping there for tens of thousands of years. Shen Wei hung the wooden plaque around the beast's neck, then gently stroked its head. He wiped away its early memories, leaving only those of its master, then undid the seal.

"You can protect him from now on."

And so, the Soul-Guarding Order came to be.

11

THE FIRST GUARDIAN had only one flaw: he just wouldn't settle down. At thirty years old, all his peers were married and close to having grandsons, but he was still frittering his life away, a silver-tongued flirt. He wandered the land, sometimes stirring up scandal. Every time his family inquired, the shameless thing would reply with, "I feel like I made a vow with someone in a previous life. I have to wait for them."

He held out for that vow from his previous life until his thirty-first year, when his mother fell ill. Nothing could cure her, and the end of her life was drawing near. On her deathbed, she held his hand and told him she could not rest easy.

Hearing that, he glanced out the window, as though someone would come for him at that very moment. But though he waited a long time, there was nothing outside but a branch of plum blossoms on the verge of withering and falling.

His heart dropped, as if he had lost something important. For a while, he was lost in a daze.

Finally, this lifelong bachelor relented. His family was delighted; they had long since found a suitable family for him and immediately sent someone to serve as matchmaker.

The celebrations were as joyous as could be. The bride, swathed in red silk, was elegant and dignified as she held his hand. She seemed to be quivering like a butterfly. Agitation gripped him, but for what reason he could not say. Sensing something, he suddenly turned and looked back—

But there was nothing to see except a courtyard full of guests, and nothing to hear except the sound of drums and gongs. What a beautiful, auspicious day.

"First, bow to the Heavens and Earth!"

12

IN THE YARD of the little thatched hut, there was one more jar of wine.

After witnessing a beautiful wedding, Shen Wei returned to the hut alone. He dug the wine out and drank it in celebration of the marriage.

He was still a lightweight. Even the thousands of arrows piercing his heart didn't keep him from falling drunk.

In his stupor, even as he forgot who and where he was, he seemed to find himself back at that day before the Reincarnation Cycle, when he had made his vow with Shennong. He seemed to hear that great sage sigh. "It's for your own good that I forbade you to see him."

13

IN TENS OF THOUSANDS OF YEARS, that was the only time he crossed the line.

It was nearly his undoing.

The Great Sage Shennong surely was great, glorious, and correct.

POCKET DIMENSION

1

"**T**HEN CLICK HERE, and then you just need to set a PIN." Zhao Yunlan started to pass the phone to Shen Wei, then changed his mind and held on to it. "Forget it, I'll set one for you. You can never think of anything new anyway."

Shen-laoshi was firmly set in his ways. Every last one of his passwords was set as the unit number of their home. He had absolutely no concept of cybersecurity.

"Good thing you don't have much money," Zhao Yunlan said.

At the day-to-day level, Comrade Shen Wei showed every sign that he really knew how to enjoy life. Having turned his attention from manipulating the Three Realms to eating, dressing, and living well, he was more than prepared for the task.

Looking at the bigger picture, however, it was clear that Shen Wei had never truly engaged with the world. In tumultuous times, he'd hole up somewhere on a mountain. In times of peace, he'd rent some random place and live there for a while. Despite all his years wandering around the Mortal Realm, he had no savings or assets, never mind real estate or housing. To this day, other than his salary card, he didn't have a single penny to his name.

As for all the famous mountains and rivers of the world, well, the government ran all of that now, and he certainly didn't get a cut of the tourism money.

"Here, let me teach you how to send red envelopes again." Zhao Yunlan hooked an arm over Shen Wei's shoulder, ruining his elegant pose. Under the pretext of teaching, he took Shen Wei's phone and sent himself a red envelope, and then, very pleased with himself, accepted it. "Congratulations are in order! This generation's final remaining antique has officially entered the age of mobile payment... Tch, not again."

His phone had started ringing before he'd even finished speaking. Zhao Yunlan glanced at it, but he didn't want to answer, so he put the phone face down. But the caller refused to give up. They called three times in a row before realizing he was ignoring them and calling his office landline. Zhao Yunlan stepped over the little sofa and poked Daqing, who was busy grooming himself. "Damn fatty, pick up the phone."

With Shen Wei there, Daqing didn't dare express his fury. He leaped onto the desk, tail swishing in outrage, and slapped the phone, pretending it was Zhao Yunlan's face. "Hello, Special Investigations... Huh? Ha ha... Good afternoon, sir... You're looking for Bureau Chief Zhao? I'm afraid he said he's not here at the moment."

Zhao Yunlan had a sinking feeling. He flipped his phone back over and saw that not all the calls had been from the same person—the last two were from his dad. All he could do was get up, head aching, and drag himself over to the desk. "Don't these monsters have anything better to do than pull strings through my dad?"

The Special Investigations Department in the Mortal Realm, otherwise known as "the Soul-Guarding Order," had always been a combined daycare and labor reform center.

Other than xiao-Guo, who was a mortal, and comrades like Wang Zheng and Sangzan, who had been taken in by the Guardian, everyone at the SID could be divided into two categories: those like Zhu Hong and Lin Jing, who had been sent by their elders or family to gain some practical experience, and those like Chu Shuzhi, who were there to serve out a sentence. Since the Soul-Guarding Order's original purpose was coordinating between the Three Realms and maintaining peace in the Mortal Realm, they often had to clean up after all kinds of violent monsters that were on the run in the Mortal Realm, all while following mortal laws and regulations.

It was a thankless job, and their boss was a mortal. Working under him didn't do their cultivation any good, so hardly anyone with actual skill had wanted to sign up.

But everything had changed now. The Great Seal had gone out with a bang, the Four Hallowed Artifacts had returned to their places, the new Reincarnation Cycle had been made complete, the King of the Gui had become a god, and Kunlun had returned. None of this was widely publicized, but it also wasn't a secret among those in the know in the Three Realms. Overnight, the tiresome job of working at the SID became a highly coveted golden post. Now *everyone* wanted to get their foot in the door so his immortal aura might rub off on them. Zhao Yunlan, annoyed beyond bearing, rejected every single applicant with the excuse of "there's a limit to how many names can fit on the Soul-Guarding Order."

The Order couldn't fit that many names, but the Special Investigations Department—an executive branch of the government—certainly could.

As a result, in order to have *some* kind of link to the Soul-Guarding Order, those with brains started to make use of their connections. Using their influence, they managed to have the Special Investigations Department in Dragon City changed into the

"Special Investigations Bureau Headquarters, with regional offices in various other cities." It all sounded very official.

Just like that, Director Zhao, who spent his days coasting by at 9 University Road, suddenly found himself with a new title: "Bureau Chief Zhao."

This year, for the first time since they'd been upgraded to be the Special Investigations Bureau, they were hiring. Zhao Yunlan, who'd been living a peaceful life caring for his vegetable garden, received orders to leave his little attic and properly oversee their expansion. New hires might not be able to enter the Soul-Guarding Order, but they would still fall under the umbrella of "regional offices."

Zhao Yunlan didn't want to hire just anyone—he'd maxed out his quota for employees without brains—and with their limited hands on deck in the main office, hiring on a large scale was unrealistic. With that in mind, for this first round they'd restricted the applicant pool by distributing a limited number of applications to the various yao tribes and cultivating sects so that they could oversee the initial round of vetting candidates.

The result? Venerable masters from all over had started showing off their skills...by finding ways to use them to acquire even a few more applications.

"Hello?" Zhao Yunlan picked up the phone lazily, then sighed. "Aren't you retired? Why are you worrying about this instead of organizing dances in the public square for middle-aged ladies?[24] Who reached out to you to get an in? Uh..."

Daqing's ears pricked up to listen in on the long, spirited lecture coming from the other end of the line. At first, Zhao Yunlan tried to

---

24 Plaza dancing (广场舞) is a trend where dancers, mostly middle-aged women, gather in public areas to perform group choreography to a variety of music.

interrupt and explain himself with "I didn't! I really didn't," but to no avail. He gave up and leaned against the desk, bored. His gaze traveled from the ceiling all the way to Shen-laoshi's clean, crisp sleeve. He was seriously starting to miss Shennong's mortar—at least that stupid Mr. Bowl hadn't fancied himself an orator.

This retired old comrade had recently been on the receiving end of many random visits. After discovering why, he was incensed. In the Year of Our Lord 2018, people would still go to all this trouble just to get more applications? What was the world coming to?

So here he was on the phone, giving Zhao Yunlan a thorough tongue-lashing.

Zhao Yunlan responded in the flat monotone of someone reciting scriptures. "Yes, I know... You're right... No, I'm not trying to use the situation for my own benefit. I really do have limited resources. If too many people apply, we won't be able to get to all of them... No, my morals haven't been corroded—we haven't had any acid rain in Dragon City... No, I don't spend all day being a smart aleck. I spend some time every day facing the wall in earnest self-reflection! Prevention is the best cure, really... If you don't believe me, ask Shen Wei!"

Someone knocked on his office door three times, and then Lin Jing, holding a calendar, poked his head in. He bowed to Shen Wei before saying, "Thank you, Shen-laoshi. Boss, it's the Dragon Boat Festival tomorrow. On behalf of all our colleagues, I'm here to ask if we're getting anything for the holiday."

Zhao Yunlan, with his phone tucked between his ear and his shoulder, had zero patience left. He pointed to the door. "Everyone's getting a notice on how to have a morally honest and frugal holiday. Out!"

Representative Lin was chased away, tail drooping.

He had barely left when Zhu Hong knocked and came in. "Thank you, Shen-laoshi. Bureau Chief Zhao, my fourth uncle asked me to invite you to dinner. A few yao tribe elders all want to pay you a visit." She sighed. "I'm just the messenger. I know they're really annoying. If you don't want to go, then don't. Don't feel obliged on my account."

Zhao Yunlan was close enough to Zhu Hong that he could turn her down without worrying about fake pleasantries, but the yao were family to Kunlun. He couldn't blatantly disrespect the yao elders. Zhao Yunlan could only give her a resigned wave.

Turning around, Zhu Hong nearly ran into Chu Shuzhi, who looked like he was in a hurry. He barely had time to nod at her. "Be careful," he told her, then added, "We've got a problem, lao-Zhao. Someone's messing with the application forms."

Shen Wei, who'd been engrossed in messing around with his phone, looked up. "What's wrong?"

When it came to the Special Investigations Bureau, Shen Wei never spoke up unless someone asked for his input. But this time, he took an interest because he'd been the one who helped make a kind of "watermark" on the applications. The Soul-Executing Emissary hadn't watched over the Great Seal for over five thousand years for nothing. He'd witnessed the rise and fall of all different tribes and clans and knew their ways. He himself was essentially a walking, talking archive of lost techniques... But since no one dared ask to buy the intellectual property from him, the "archive" was still very low on funds.

"There are still ten days left before the deadline," Chu Shuzhi said, "but we've already received more applications than we sent out—oh, right. Thank you, Shen-laoshi."

Shen Wei's brows knit together.

"Gather them all together. I want to take a look." Zhao Yunlan put down his phone and walked over. "Hey, by the way, what kind of secret code is 'Thank you, Shen-laoshi'? Why is everyone saying that when they come in?"

"Uh..." said Shen Wei.

"For the red envelopes he just sent us, of course," Chu Shuzhi said. "Our bonus for the Dragon Boat Festival, right?"

Zhao Yunlan grabbed Shen Wei's phone to find that, in the time he'd been wrapped up on a call, Shen Wei-tongxue had mastered the technique of mobile payments and diligently done some after-class practice. He'd been going down his contacts list and sending each person in the Special Investigations Bureau a red envelope.

It wasn't the kind where you sent it into the group chat for everyone to fight over—Zhao-laoshi hadn't reached that lesson yet. No, Shen Wei had sent each one individually, and had only made it halfway through his contacts before running out of money.

His Shen-laoshi viewed cash the same way he viewed in-game currency—and not even the kind you had to buy, but the kind the game gave you for free to start.

When Zhao Yunlan said nothing, Shen Wei gave him a quizzical look.

"It's fineeeee." Zhao Yunlan dragged the word out for one entire kilometer. Then, standing one kilometer away, he sent back a pained smile across the distance. "If you run out of money, I'll transfer you some more. Go on, finish sending the red envelopes. Ah...ha ha ha. You sure are a quick learner."

And so, everyone received a holiday bonus for that year's Dragon Boat Festival, sponsored by an anonymous Mr. Zhao. The Heavens themselves would've been moved by the gesture.

2

ALL THE APPLICATIONS that had raised concerns were stacked up in the basement. There were no lights down there, but it wasn't dark. The silvery glow of all the applications together was as bright as a row of incandescent bulbs.

Wang Zheng and Sangzan worked overtime throughout the day, and when Zhao Yunlan and the others came down the stairs, they had just finished separating the applications by different tribes and regions.

The application's design was a work of art. They'd been handed out in white envelopes secured with little seals, which had also been made by Shen Wei. The application belonged to whomever could open the seal. Even if someone else later managed to get their hands on it, that person's information wouldn't be recorded. It was a way of doing preliminary screening since it wasn't realistic to organize a written test. To start with, potential applicants were masters of different things and came from different backgrounds, so it wasn't fair to have them sit through a standardized theory exam. What was more, many who cultivated way out in the middle of nowhere couldn't read simplified Chinese.

Sangzan said, "Bureau Chief Zhao, taking the sum of the parts into consideration, we sent out 729 applications, and we have received more than 1,560 back."

"That big a difference?" Zhao Yunlan asked.

"Yes, what a splendid sight," Sangzan sighed.

In his years at the Special Investigations Bureau, Sangzan had been diligent and keen. Through industrious work and dedication, he now spoke Mandarin fluently, successfully getting rid of his "slutterer" moniker. But then he'd set an even higher goal for himself:

he'd started learning chengyu,[25] and was constantly trying to incorporate them into his everyday speech—and testing his colleagues' patience in a whole new way.

Zhao Yunlan was used to it by now. He automatically ignored all the proverbs and idioms in Sangzan's speech and gave him a wave. "Thanks for your hard work."

"How dare you say that; it was no trouble at all," Sangzan responded, smiling. "All I have is the coat on my back, so if I can help, this much is like a drop in the bucket."

For fuck's sake, Wang Zheng didn't even stop him! All she did was stand next to him and smile indulgently!

"Okay, as long as you're happy," said Zhao Yunlan, giving up. "Hurry up and clock out, you two."

The average person wouldn't be able to produce a knockoff of Shen Wei's anti-fraud watermark—especially not one so similar to the real thing. While Zhao Yunlan had been speaking with the couple, Shen Wei had already gone through all the applications in the pile.

"Shen-laoshi, what do you think?" Chu Shuzhi asked. "To be honest, I really can't figure out the difference."

Shen Wei didn't say anything. After some consideration, he suddenly waved his hand and rearranged them from the categories Wang Zheng and Sangzan had sorted them into. The glowing applications fluttered upward like butterflies. In a dazzling show of light, they fell neatly into two piles with a *whoosh*. One pile was noticeably higher.

---

25 *Chengyu (成语) are Chinese proverbs or idioms, usually based on quotes from literature or historical quotations and condensed to four characters. Educated people usually have a good chengyu vocabulary and are able to apply them with ease.*

Zhao Yunlan hiked up his pants and knelt, picking out a few from each pile to look at. He pointed at the taller pile. "These ones are all the same?"

Shen Wei nodded.

"Huh? Aren't they *all* the same?" Chu Shuzhi asked, completely mystified. "Isn't that why we can't tell if they're real or not?"

"No," said Shen Wei. "He's talking about the seal on each application."

It turned out that the seals on every application *looked* the same, but the methods of opening them varied. That meant they could get applicants with a variety of qualifications, and it would prevent applicants from sharing answers.

When the applications had been sent out, different seals were sent to different tribes. For instance, the Snake tribe was familiar with water, so it wouldn't make sense to force them to use the True Flames of Samadhi to open the seal.

While all the seals on the submitted applications had been opened, the tiny bit of aura lingering on them was enough for an examiner to see the problem: all the seals on the applications in the taller pile were identical. They had clearly all been copied from one original.

"When we sent out the applications, I made a record of where each one was sent," said Shen Wei. "We can see which tribe received the original of this one."

Chu Shuzhi's eyes bulged. "Hang on...! Each one of over 700 applications is different? And you kept a record of them all?"

"Yes." Shen Wei adjusted his glasses. "And...?"

The thought left Chu Shuzhi speechless. No wonder there'd been no mention of paying this consultant. With this kind of output, they would've had to auction off Kunlun-jun to cover the fee!

Now that they had a starting point, things were much easier. A check of Shen Wei's records revealed that the application in question had been sent to a yao tribe—specifically, the Water tribe of the South Sea.

Zhao Yunlan got up. "Tell Zhu Hong to call her fourth uncle."

Overall, there were four types of yao: those who flew, those who walked, those who swam, and those who'd cultivated from inanimate natural objects. From there, they further divided into individual tribes, each living in different areas.

Since Zhu Hong was from the Snake tribe, and their chief, Fourth Uncle, was both good at getting things done and fair in his dealings, the Snake tribe was said to be both privileged and capable. As a result, they were particularly respected. In just a few short years, they'd come out on top among all the yao. Whenever something came up, the yao turned to Fourth Uncle.

Fourth Uncle arrived at 9 University Road less than five minutes after receiving his niece's call, despite the scorching sun. After being given an overview of the situation, he first apologized to Kunlun-jun. He had too much shame to ask for more applications, so he turned, rolled up his sleeves, and personally set off to the South Sea to capture the barnacle responsible for the whole mess.

3

"ACTUALLY, THE MORE I think about it, the stranger this situation seems," Shen Wei said that night while slicing ham in the kitchen. "There are always those with stronger abilities than others. I can't say for certain that there's no one out there who could copy something I made, but that envelope was quite crude. A single touch would tell any true master that each seal was different. How could they be so stupid as to forge hundreds of copies of the same one?"

Zhao Yunlan leaned against the cabinet. Rather than helping out, he was making more work for Shen Wei: every time Shen Wei cut a slice of ham, Zhao Yunlan ate it right off the cutting board. "What if they used some sort of powerful artifact? None of the yao are what they used to be, but each tribe has its own long-standing history. Maybe someone has a fun toy that's been passed down through the generations."

Shen Wei finished slicing the ham. He paused and considered that notion, then turned to grab a ceramic plate. "But I can't think of anything that was..."

Anything powerful enough to duplicate a seal made by the Soul-Executing Emissary, a King of the Gui, but used on such a menial task? What kind of artifact could it be?

A Pangu-brand photocopier?

Shen Wei turned back with the plate for the ham, only to realize that the cutting board was empty.

When Shen Wei fell silent, Zhao Yunlan followed his gaze, hastily finished chewing, and swallowed the evidence. Then, the very picture of innocence, he stretched out his back.

"Isn't it salty?" Shen Wei inquired.

Zhao Yunlan was about to flee the kitchen to avoid punishment when his heart suddenly skipped a beat. Shen Wei looked up at the same moment. The two of them glanced southward.

"What was that?" Shen Wei asked.

"I don't know, but..." Zhao Yunlan squinted. "It feels like...the Three Sovereigns..." The phone cut him off. "Hello? Zhu Hong?"

"Lao-Zhao, something's happened to my fourth uncle!"

"Slow down and explain."

"You know how he went to the South Sea? My tribe just contacted me and said the lamp representing the chief's life has gone out! My uncle, he—"

"Calm down for a second," Zhao Yunlan said. "When a great yao dies, there's always some kind of portent to announce it. It wouldn't happen so quietly. Maybe there's been an accident that's blocking his connection to his lamp. Ask your tribe to bring the lamp here, and Shen Wei and I will go take a look."

There was no time for dinner now. Shen Wei hurriedly packed his half-prepared ingredients into the fridge. They'd just have to get takeout when they got back.

One of the Snake tribe's elders arrived promptly with Fourth Uncle's lamp of life. With it in hand, Shen Wei and Zhao Yunlan teleported straight to the South Sea.

The tourism boom in the South Sea meant that things had been steadily going downhill for the South Sea Water tribe. Young yao, drawn to the dazzling human world with its sunshine, beaches, and coconut trees, no longer did anything but wear floral shorts and fool around among the tourists. But when these tourists' vacations were over, *they* went back home and got back to work or school; the naive little yao, on the other hand, just moved on to the next wave of tourists and kept playing. As a result, they weren't learning a damn thing, and their cultivation was suffering too. Their shrimp veins and fish scales were now tanned from the sun.

Theoretically, if the Snake tribe chief was paying a personal visit, these good-for-nothing yao were supposed to welcome him with a banner and fanfare. Who'd lent them the courage to act out?

Were they so high on fresh water that their egos were now badly overinflated?

Either way, Zhao Yunlan couldn't figure it out.

When they arrived at the South Sea, Zhao Yunlan realized the local Water tribe was in total disarray. The yao in charge, upon hearing that Kunlun-jun and the King of the Gui were there, nearly peed their swim trunks. They knelt shirtless on the beach, kowtowing with their bare backs to the sky. Each of them had a huge letter inked on their back. Collectively, the message read "Our crimes are severe. Please punish us, O Great Immortal."

It was such a sight that the hermit crabs were too fearful to even dare poke their heads out.

"Oh, get up! What are you doing? If you have something to say, just say it. Don't embarrass me like this!" From his seat up on a cloud, Zhao Yunlan cringed at the sight. He and Shen Wei couldn't even get *off* the cloud—the beach was so packed that there was nowhere to set foot. "I don't get it. All this feudalistic nonsense has been buried for a hundred years, but it's still somehow alive and well here with you yao? Please go educate yourselves!"

The South Sea was rich in resources, and there were ample varieties of seafood...or rather, of the Water tribe. This was a mixed-species tribe, created when the chiefs of each of the tribes had banded together to form an alliance. The one in charge was a three-thousand-year-old sea turtle, and the second-in-command was a two-thousand-year-old sea cucumber.

The pair were truly a golden duo. Neither of them thought the other's explanations were too slow. Zhao Yunlan listened as they sobbed their way through the story, but by the time they were only halfway through, his soul had already made eight trips around the thirty-six great mountains. His gaze was distant. For the first time ever, he thought Guo Changcheng was actually a very bright child.

Shen Wei, thankfully, had the patience to pay proper attention. "You're saying that the elder in charge of keeping watch over the

South Sea's forbidden area didn't receive any applications, so he stole one and went into the forbidden area and made copies?"

The sea turtle in charge sighed. "Exactly. His original form is a barracuda. He sold the fake applications for money so he could sell betel nuts wholesale. He's already escaped to avoid punishment!"

"Never mind what he was trying to sell. Let's set that aside," Shen Wei said. "Can you tell us what your tribe keeps watch over? How were the applications copied?"

Looking pained, the sea cucumber replied, "My lord, none of us even dare approach the forbidden area other than the Barracuda tribe, who've always been the ones to stand watch. It's said that some sort of ancient artifact is sealed inside there. Oh, and I should mention that the great Snake tribe chief came here earlier. He was annoyed that we couldn't explain in more detail, so he decided to go see for himself. We didn't dare stop him! But soon after he entered, an earthquake shook the South Sea, and the great chief hasn't been seen since! We still don't know what's going on!"

Shen Wei glanced back at Zhao Yunlan, who roused himself from his daydreaming and stood up straight. "Right, then. That's enough bullshit. Lead the way."

By that point, it was late at night. The Dragon Boat Festival was still underway, and there was no sign of the moon. The ocean looked bottomless, but something seemed to be stirring in its depths—something restless and agitated, creating wave after wave in perfect time with Zhao Yunlan's heartbeat. Their little party was still a thousand kilometers away from their destination when the South Sea Water tribe leaders, who had gone pale from fright, stopped dead. Nothing could persuade them to proceed any further.

The second-in-command said, "It used to be that during holidays, we felt brave enough to visit the forbidden area and do a lap to check things out. But then that stupid fish touched something he shouldn't have, and ever since, the forbidden area has grown scarier by the day. At first, it didn't get too frightening until we got within just five kilometers, but now, even from hundreds of kilometers away, we can hardly breathe from terror...!"

As soon as he got those words out, his eyes rolled back in his skull. Unconscious now, he began to sink, as if deficient in both blood and qi. A black shadow flashed in Shen Wei's hand, and the Soul-Executing Blade materialized, extending several meters out. With the blade still sheathed, he fished the sea cucumber back out of the water.

The sea turtle was in no state of mind for further pleasantries. He bowed to Shen Wei from a safe distance, then resumed his original form, picked up his partner, and shot off like a torpedo.

Two shadows flew swiftly over the dark waves, heading for the forbidden area of the South Sea.

The closer they got, the calmer the water became. By the time they were eight kilometers out, the water's stillness was downright unnatural, as though a pair of invisible hands had stretched its surface taut. It was like a pool of dead water, unbroken by even a single ripple.

In no time at all, Zhao Yunlan and Shen Wei reached the center of the forbidden area and found themselves confronted by a peculiar vortex. Not quite two meters in diameter, it swirled with incredible speed, like a needle embedded right in the sea floor. Knives couldn't cut through water, but it was as though something had cut a circle around the vortex, separating the water within from the water without. The water inside swirled rapidly, but the water outside remained unmoving.

The barest wisp of black smoke—hardly noticeable—seemed to hang above the vortex. It echoed the Soul-Executing Blade in a way that said they shared one source.

"If this is something left behind by a sage from the era of Chaos, we might not get along," Shen Wei said. "Let's forget everything else. The traces I left all over that application awakened whatever is sealed here. With the seal already loose, Fourth Uncle's arrival only added fuel to the fire. The seal's probably done for. Do you have any recollection of what's behind it?"

Zhao Yunlan's brow furrowed in thought, but he shook his head. "I've never seen it, but..."

He broke off as something flashed inside his bag. It was Fourth Uncle's lamp of life—a small candle encased protectively in a dragon's pearl. It resembled a crystal light, and right now it was flashing like it was about to die. Its weak light cast a beam across the water's surface, pointing straight into the vortex.

With no warning, the dragon pearl disintegrated, and the dwindling flame gave a single flicker. Zhao Yunlan reflexively cupped his hand around it just as the vortex below them exploded. All the stars in the sky above suddenly seemed like dust blowing in the wind. Shen Wei pulled Zhao Yunlan into his arms at once, holding his long blade in front of them both.

In an instant, it became shockingly apparent that something was deeply wrong—he and Zhao Yunlan weren't actually touching, despite how close together they were. Shen Wei whipped his head around in shock. There was some sort of clear film in between them.

Zhao Yunlan said something, but the sound didn't penetrate the invisible barrier. Shen Wei read the words off Zhao Yunlan's lips. *"This bubble is..."*

Bubble?

Shen Wei looked around. Fourth Uncle's lamp of life was reflected everywhere, revealing what might've been infinite layers of clear film, like soap bubbles clustered together. Vague mirages flickered across the surfaces of the bubbles, reflecting both Shen Wei and Zhao Yunlan an endless number of times. It was a frightening sight.

Only a few short moments later, the two of them, each trapped in their own bubble, started to drift apart. As the distance between them grew, Shen Wei's eyes went red. Drawing his blade, he slashed at the bubble.

There was a boom as the Soul-Executing Blade, which could cut through anything in the world, sank into the mud. Countless eerie bubbles were shattered, only for even more to rise from the seabed. The ocean's surface began to roil with mountain-sized waves, roaring at a volume much like the sound when Pangu had first split apart Chaos.

The mountains shook, the sea rolled, and Shen Wei's sight went black.

4

WHEN ZHAO YUNLAN jolted awake, he was still holding the short candle of the lamp of life, with its pea-sized flame. He moved slightly and instantly froze in place. His expression was one of absolute shock.

Slowly, he looked down at his right foot—his *sprained* right foot.

Kunlun-jun's body couldn't be so much as scratched; heat and cold alike posed no threat. It had been six years since Zhao Yunlan's divine spirit was awakened, and he'd nearly forgotten even the sensation of a mosquito's bite. How had he managed to sprain his ankle here in the South Sea?

Well, this was new. He grimaced and probed at his ankle. Nothing seemed broken, so he took another ginger stab at moving. Bracing himself with a hand against the wall beside him, he stood up. As he did, he noticed that something else was off: his limbs felt heavy, as if they weren't his own. Kunlun-jun's ability to fly and pass through the ground, moving freely through any part of the Three Realms, had disappeared.

What was more, Clarity had stopped ticking, and the talismans in his wallet had all turned into ordinary paper and were completely unresponsive. He couldn't summon his whip. Even the Soul-Guarding Order, to which he was connected by blood, lay silently in his palm like any regular piece of wood.

Zhao Yunlan held up Fourth Uncle's lamp of life so he could glance around. Wherever he was, it was extremely desolate. As far as the eye could see, not a single streetlight was lit. Lopsided houses in varying states of disrepair lined the streets, and the air was thick with dust.

It was like an ancient ruin.

He took a few limping steps forward, then had to stop to dump sand out of his shoes. Every breath was a major effort that felt like inhaling needles. Waves of pain stabbed at his heart. In the old days, he might not have been the healthiest mortal around, but he hadn't had *this* many problems! Was he just out of practice?

Dragging the weight of his body along, Zhao Yunlan did a loop around the street. His cell phone had no signal, but when he looked, it still displayed the time.

8:45 p.m.

The ham he'd filched before dinner was barely enough to fill the gaps between his teeth. As the pain in his chest and sprained ankle eased, this mortal body began reminding him exactly what it was like to have stomach problems.

A meow came from somewhere. Zhao Yunlan looked up and saw a black cat jump from the withered tree next to him onto the nearest roof. It padded across the top of a dilapidated wall at a leisurely stroll, tail upright. There was no mistaking it: the cat looked like a much younger Daqing, with his neck and waist clearly defined, as Daqing's had been before he gained weight.

Out of sheer habit, Zhao Yunlan reached out to play with him, whistling in his direction like a pervert. The instant the cat looked over, dark green eyes flashing, Zhao Yunlan saw a paper talisman in his mouth.

But before he could get a good look, the world started spinning. The cat disappeared, and the streets twisted together, contorting as the ground fell out from under his feet. He landed heavily, freshly spraining his right ankle, which had finally stopped hurting.

Zhao Yunlan hissed a curse, then had a sudden thought. He got his phone out again and took another look at the time.

8:35 p.m.

It was now...ten minutes earlier?

Striding through the streets, Zhao Yunlan counted down the time on his phone. Ten minutes later, the black cat appeared again, jumping out from the same place in the same pose. This time, Zhao Yunlan didn't bother the bizarre little animal. Instead, he leaned against a corner and observed.

The cat, talisman in its mouth, took five steps...and once again, everything began to spin.

Zhao Yunlan was whisked right back to ten minutes earlier. Again.

This repeated two or three more times. Zhao Yunlan hit the point where he didn't want to stand up anymore—his shoe was too hard to take off.

This world was like a song on repeat—a song that was about ten minutes long, and didn't take up too much space, and yet he was stuck here as it repeated again and again.

He felt along the wall, then suddenly remembered the weird bubbles that had appeared when he and Shen Wei had been separated.

Bubbles... Time that kept looping...

Abruptly, Zhao Yunlan got to his feet again. After dumping the sand out of his shoes, he walked quickly through the streets. The moment the cat appeared, he tucked the lamp of life between his lips, jogged a few steps, and between putting his hands on the roof and making use of the low wall, he managed to leap up onto the rooftop. He scooped up the black cat, took the talisman from its mouth, and backflipped down toward the ground.

Before he even landed, the time loop reached its end. Zhao Yunlan immediately touched the life lamp's flame to the talisman, which caught fire. A noise rang out like something shattering. The black cat in his arms melted into smoke.

Zhao Yunlan stumbled a few steps before finding his footing. When he looked back up, he saw that he hadn't returned to that same starting point. Other things had changed in the street before him too: a streetlight was now on, there was far less dust in the air, and the tree was no longer barren. It boasted only a few leaves, but at least it was alive.

Dusting off his clothes, Zhao Yunlan said, "So that's what this is. Tch! Here I thought the South Sea actually had something precious, but it turns out it's just trouble."

It was common knowledge that time couldn't flow backward, and a person couldn't jump randomly within his own timeline. Within the same dimension, the laws of cause and effect were immutable.

Back before Kunlun-jun had been awakened, Zhao Yunlan had once traveled eleven years back to Renwu year—except he hadn't, not really. Shennong had just put an eleven-year mini-cycle into Nüwa's scale, creating a pocket dimension. It had been an illusion that was very similar to, but different from, reality. He had simply been inside that pocket dimension for a while.

When Fourth Uncle had given him Nüwa's scale, Zhao Yunlan had already unknowingly walked into that pocket dimension. Within it, time had reset when it finished its eleven years, so since Zhao Yunlan had been inside, he had gone back eleven years too. He hadn't returned to reality until Shen Wei broke that dimension with the Soul-Executing Blade.

The bubble that had separated him and Shen Wei just now was the same as that eleven-year cycle. Every bubble was a world set to repeat over and over for a certain span of time.

Some were simple and crude, repeating every ten minutes; some might seem incredibly real and complex, repeating only after thousands of years.

So this wasn't some kind of artifact. It was simply all the remains of the sages' attempts to create the Reincarnation Cycle. The waste from their experiments had been sealed in the South Sea all this time until the seal had first been disturbed by the King of the Gui and then accidentally smashed open by a great yao, leaving it exposed to the Mortal Realm.

Zhao Yunlan looked up at the streetlight. *I knew you wouldn't leave me any inheritance,* he thought. *Just a bunch of messes for me to clean up.*

At this point, there was no knowing where Shen Wei was, so there was no point in hoping for rescue by his blade. No, Zhao Yunlan was going to have to shatter each tiny, looping world from within.

It wasn't complicated. Every pocket dimension had a point that connected it to the real world, and that point was how Zhao Yunlan got in. Once that point was found and destroyed, the pocket dimension would collapse, unable to sustain itself.

For example, the connection point in that eleven-year cycle had been the mysterious *Record of Ancient Secrets*. Zhao Yunlan had owned a copy in the real world, and there was another copy in the little cycle. When he entered the cycle with the book, the two copies overlapped, connecting the pocket dimension and the real world. Illusion and reality intersected.

At the time, Zhao Yunlan had been desperate to know what Shen Wei was hiding from him, so he kept chasing after the book. It never crossed his mind to destroy it. But if he had burned *Record of Ancient Secrets* as soon as he got it in the little time loop, cause and effect within the pocket dimension would've contradicted cause and effect in the real world, and the alternate world would've disintegrated. He wouldn't have needed to wait for Shen Wei's blade at all.

If he had burned *Record of Ancient Secrets* in the little time loop, the book would've still been in his hands when he returned to reality instead of staying behind in the loop.

As for the *real Record of Ancient Secrets*...it might've been Shennong's mortar who had hidden it in the Special Investigations Department to begin with.

Currently, all these overlapping pocket dimensions were like bubbles. Zhao Yunlan was reflected within them, and each one would take something from him as the connection point between that dimension and the real world. The now-stopped Clarity, the lifeless talismans, the Soul-Guarding Order that was now just an ordinary piece of wood, the whip that couldn't be summoned...or even his powers as Kunlun.

And of course, Zhao Yunlan had no way of knowing what the connecting point in each world was, so he would have to feel them out individually and destroy them to shatter the dimension. Only then would that given thing return with him to the real world.

"So fucking annoying." Zhao Yunlan sighed. "If I'd known it was going to be like this, I would've just organized an exam."

It was all this tactless South Sea Water tribe's fault. When he got back, he'd eat a whole seafood feast.

5

ZHAO YUNLAN HAD no idea how long he'd been lingering in the countless pocket dimensions.

Initially, the worlds were all simple scenes: a dilapidated road, a dark city, the countryside, underwater... There were no people to be seen, and the loops ranged from ten minutes to three days. They were always based on something inconsequential he had.

But it wasn't long before the pocket dimensions became increasingly complex, not to mention larger and larger. Other people started to appear, including some people he knew. The world based off Clarity, for example, looped for an entire three years during the lifetime of Zhao Yunlan's previous incarnation at the beginning of the Republican Era.

Clarity had been passed down from the previous Guardian, who was his prior incarnation. He had been chasing down a demon that had kidnapped someone, taking them hostage. The watch had been smashed in the process.

The hostage was a kid from an orphanage, and someone claiming to be the orphanage director rushed over to collect the child; while he was at it, he offered the services of a watchmaker he knew to fix the watch. When the repaired watch was returned, it was able to communicate between the worlds of yin and yang. It had become Clarity.

Zhao Yunlan watched as his previous incarnation, who had looked identical to how he looked now, hurried to the orphanage in search of its director...only to find that the orphanage director was a short nun, not the man who had offered to fix the watch for him.

"Ah, Shen Wei." Zhao Yunlan caught up to his incarnation, contemplating the watch's origin. He chuckled, shaking his head. "You sneaky bastard."

As things progressed, the time loops grew ever longer. By the time they exceeded fifty years, Zhao Yunlan was no longer a bystander in these pocket dimensions. He found he was starting to get involved: always playing a certain role and following the pocket dimension's plot.

Not every dimension came straight from his memories. Some seemed like memories from a past life, but with subtle differences. Some were of bizarre worlds with just a few familiar segments flashing through them.

Zhao Yunlan rather liked the latter sort because in the course of the five thousand years he'd spent in the Reincarnation Cycle, he had very few memories of Shen Wei. When Zhao Yunlan occasionally managed to catch him, it was inevitably only a brief glimpse before Shen Wei disappeared again.

But in the fake worlds, Shen Wei was always right there at his side, playing different roles in his life. In those worlds, they spent a whole lifetime together until they both found their own connection items and broke out of the cycle... Meanwhile, the real Shen Wei's Soul-Executing Blade was indeed stuck in one of the worlds. But having the blade didn't mean Shen Wei dared use it; if he destroyed a pocket dimension from the outside, whatever had been copied would be trapped in that cycle forever, just like that *Record of Ancient Secrets*.

All in all, Zhao Yunlan escaped from eighty pocket dimensions. With each escape, the time would reset to 8:35 p.m.

It was as though he had experienced the lives of all living beings in an instant.

Fortunately, Kunlun-jun had already spent thousands of years in the Reincarnation Cycle, and despite living out lives in all these pocket dimensions, he still held his original mission firmly in mind.

At last, he arrived at the eighty-first dimension.

Eighty-one: a multiple of the auspicious number nine.

Zhao Yunlan had a feeling that this dimension was the last, but he could've hardly expected that *this* one would last ten thousand years. The endless passage of time made it impossibly close to the real world. He grew attached to it. Finally, after a series of ups and downs, he reached its end...but Zhao Yunlan still hadn't managed to identify the connection point.

Everything he had on him, right down to his spine and his heart's blood, had been shattered within different pocket dimensions. What could this one possibly be?

What was left...?

6

OH RIGHT. There was still *himself*.

People existed to serve the world around them.

The heart existed to serve its body.

7

WHEN ZHAO YUNLAN ESCAPED from the last pocket dimension, all ten thousand mountains exulted. Great waves seemed to descend from the very Heavens, and they parted before him as if imbued with consciousness, allowing him to rise through their midst.

He registered the shrill sound of a blade descending just before the Soul-Executing Blade manifested out of nowhere, seeming ready to carve the entire South Sea in two. Zhao Yunlan's eyes shot open. He reached down into the seething waves and grabbed the hand wielding the blade. "Shen Wei!"

The huge wave crashed down to reveal Shen Wei underneath. He looked even more bedraggled than Zhao Yunlan, and he didn't seem to have recovered from the endless time loops yet. For a while, he was completely motionless and silent.

"It's okay," Zhao Yunlan told him gently. "We're back."

A shudder tore through Shen Wei's body, and he fell into Zhao Yunlan's arms. The Soul-Executing Blade dropped from his exhausted hand and landed on the back of a large snake floating nearby.

Zhao Yunlan let out the breath he was holding. Thankfully, Fourth Uncle's lamp of life was still burning. The old bug was still alive. Zhu Hong could keep right on fooling around at the Special Investigations Bureau with no need to return to her tribe to succeed her uncle as chief.

8

"**H**UH? AH... AH! O-okay."

Bright and early back at 9 University Road, Guo Changcheng answered a call. His tone fluctuated dramatically, ranging from shock to utter confusion and finally to embarrassment. Now he was awkwardly saying, "There isn't anything I want, but thank you, boss. R-really, it's okay... N-no, not even from duty-free stores. Please don't worry about it, as long as you're happy... All right. Have fun. Have a good vacation..."

Before he'd even finished offering his well-wishes, Chu Shuzhi and Lin Jing both stood up, slapping the table. Daqing's fur erupted into a pom-pom.

"Was that lao-Zhao?" Chu Shuzhi demanded. "What's the meaning of this? What do you mean, 'Have a good vacation'?! What's his problem?"

"He ran off? He just ran off like that? Is there no justice in this world?" bawled Lin Jing.

Daqing jumped over from the couch. "The shameless bastard! Give me the phone!"

Guo Changcheng hesitantly set the receiver down. "H-he already hung up."

"Call him back!" Daqing roared. "If you can't reach him, call Shen-laoshi!"

To no one's surprise, Zhao Yunlan's phone was turned off with well-practiced ease.

But next, something unexpected happened...

Shen-laoshi stood barefoot on the beach. He had one hand on his collar and the other on his belt, and his face was red from the struggle. He'd rather die than "do as the Romans do" and change into swim trunks!

What *was* this abomination?! Such an insult to elegance!

Zhao Yunlan chased after him. "Just try it on once...! How can you know you don't like it if you don't give it a try? *I* think you'll like it! Shen Wei, xiao-Wei, babe... You always wear black. Don't you get tired? Maybe a whole new world will open up in front of you...! Hey! Okay, okay, you don't have to wear it! Don't jump into the sea!"

Shen Wei had been pursued right to the water's edge. As he stepped into the surf, his phone fell out of his pocket...at the precise moment that a call came through. It rang once as it plunged to its death, making the ultimate sacrifice.

The screen went black.

At 9 University Road, Guo Changcheng innocently announced, "Shen-laoshi hung up."

Daqing completely lost it. Utterly outraged, he yowled, "How could Shen-laoshi, with his beautiful face, betray us?!"

Guardian
- FIN -

CHARACTER & NAME GUIDE

CHARACTERS
AND ASSOCIATED FACTIONS

The identity of certain characters may be a spoiler; use this guide with caution on your first read of the novel.

MAIN CHARACTERS

Zhao Yunlan 赵云澜

TITLES: Director of the Special Investigations Department, Guardian to the Soul-Guarding Order 镇魂令主, Mountain God of the Great Wild 大荒山圣, Kunlun-jun 昆仑君

WEAPONS: Dagger, whip, paper talismans, gun

Zhao Yunlan was born with his third eye open, naturally able to see ghosts and supernatural creatures within the Mortal Realm. When he was ten years old, a black cat, Daqing, brought him the Soul-Guarding Order, which is how he became the Guardian. Later, with the help of his father at the Ministry of Public Security, he became the Director of the Special Investigations Department. Zhao Yunlan is the most recent reincarnation of Kunlun-jun, the Mountain God of the Great Wild.

He wears a watch named Clarity (明鉴) which has the ability to reflect supernatural presences even when they can't be seen with the naked eye. The name "Clarity" comes from its mirror-like quality and ability to show the truth.

Shen Wei 沈巍

TITLES: The Soul-Executing Emissary 斩魂使, King of the Gui 鬼王
WEAPON: Soul-Executing Blade
One of the two Chaos Kings of the Gui. He has been keeping an eye on Kunlun-jun and his reincarnations for thousands of years. This time around, he has assumed the identity of a university professor to watch over Zhao Yunlan. Well-mannered and gentle, he does his best to suppress the innate cruel nature of the gui within himself. Due to a promise he made to Kunlun-jun in the past, he became the Soul-Executing Emissary and the keeper of the Great Seal.

SPECIAL INVESTIGATIONS DEPARTMENT (SID)

A police department under the Ministry of Public Security that investigates supernatural crimes in the Mortal Realm, headed by Zhao Yunlan. This department works with local law enforcement but is not under their jurisdiction.

Chu Shuzhi 楚恕之

A Corpse King and stoic man of few words who had been inducted into the Soul-Guarding Order to serve a 300-year criminal sentence from the Netherworld. His grim demeanor intimidates Guo Changcheng.

Daqing 大庆

A talking, fat black cat, and the SID's mascot. Daqing has lived for thousands of years and is very knowledgeable about supernatural and mythological matters. He was the one who brought Zhao Yunlan the Soul-Guarding Order.

Guo Changcheng 郭长城

The new intern at the Special Investigations Department. An orphan brought up by extended family, his uncle was the one who secured him this job. A recent graduate from college, Guo Changcheng has a great fear of people and often finds it hard to interact with others, especially those in positions of authority, such as his boss. Despite this, he has a heart of gold and often donates his time and money to charities and to help those in need.

Lin Jing 林静

A Buddhist monk who doesn't always abide by the strict rules of his religion.

Zhu Hong 祝红

A dependable member of the Special Investigations Department. Zhu Hong is half human and half snake and can transform into her python form at will, except during a certain period each month when her tail is always visible.

Lao-Li 老李

The day-shift doorman at the Special Investigations Department who likes to collect bones. In one of his past lives, he stole Daqing's bell to heal himself of bone cancer.

SOUL-GUARDING ORDER

In addition to being head of the Special Investigations Department, Zhao Yunlan is also the Guardian, leader of the Soul-Guarding Order. This is an organization that has existed since ancient times and is responsible for overseeing supernatural matters in the Mortal Realm. The Guardian has authority over those who choose to enter the Order and possesses three special talismans with the words "Soul-Guarding" written on them.

Wang Zheng 汪徵

An employee of the HR Department at the Special Investigations Department. As a ghost, she cannot come in contact with sunlight. From the Hanga Tribe, she died hundreds of years ago and has now reunited with her boyfriend, Sangzan.

Sangzan 桑赞

The librarian at the Special Investigations Department. From the Hanga Tribe. After being freed from the Mountain-River Awl, he has now reunited with his girlfriend, Wang Zheng, at the SID. Currently doing his best to learn Mandarin.

NETHERWORLD

Ten Kings of the Yanluo Courts (Yanluo Kings) 十殿阎罗

The highest-ranking officials of the Netherworld, the Ten Kings are final arbiters who decide the fate of each soul based on their previous life's merits and sins. Each presides over a different Hell; these Hells are differentiated by types of crime.

Qin'guang King 秦广王

The head of the first level of Hell, and the leader of the Ten Kings.

The Magistrate 判官

A high-ranking official of the Netherworld who carries out the Yanluo Kings' orders and manages the reapers.

Reapers 阴差

Low-level Netherworld workers. They are essentially Netherworld law enforcement officers sent out on tasks and errands, including retrieving newly deceased souls and guiding them to the Netherworld.

OTHER

Ghost Face 鬼面

Also known as the "Ghost-Faced Figure," Ghost Face is the other King of the Gui. A mysterious masked figure who seems to be an enemy of the Soul-Executing Emissary.

Shennong's Medicine Mortar 神农药钵

A medicine mortar used by Shennong that managed to cultivate a human form over time. He has been living inside Zhao Yunlan's father's body, occasionally taking control of it. He was tasked by Shennong to keep an eye on Shen Wei to make sure he followed through with his oath of guarding the Great Seal and staying away from Kunlun's reincarnations.

LOCATIONS

DRAGON CITY: A fictional metropolis where most of the story takes place. It is home to Dragon City University and the Special Investigations Department.

SPRING HARBOR RESORT: A relaxing resort where Lin Jing investigates a life-lending case. When he doesn't return, the SID goes to look for him, which is when they discover that the Great Seal is starting to fall apart and Chaos is beginning to leak out.

THE NETHERWORLD 地府: Where the deceased go after death. Common Chinese folklore believes that when people die, their souls are collected by **reapers** (阴差) who lead them through the **Gates of the Netherworld** (鬼门关) and down the **Huangquan Road** (黄泉路). The souls then arrive at the **The Ten Courts of the Yanluo Kings** (十殿阎王), where they are judged for their merits and sins. If they committed too many sins, they are sent to the **Eighteen Levels of Hell** (十八层地狱), but if they have accumulated enough good deeds in life, they may move on to reincarnation. In order to reincarnate, these souls first have to walk the **Naihe Bridge** (奈何桥), which crosses over the **Wangchuan River** (忘川河), and drink the **Mengpo Soup** (孟婆汤). After drinking the soup, the soul forgets everything from its past life and is ready to move on to the next one.

HUANGQUAN 黄泉: Literally "Yellow Spring." In Chinese mythology, "Huangquan" is a word that can be used to describe the underworld itself, but can sometimes describe a part of the underworld or a literal, extremely deep body of water souls reach after death. In *Guardian*, it is used as a term for both the road to the underworld and a body of water within the underworld. Sometimes, "Huangquan" and "Wangchuan" are used interchangeably to refer to the same body of water.

GHOST CITY 鬼城: A liminal space where the dead who don't have to go to hell are sequestered before they reincarnate. Some are guilty souls who have been imprisoned here, while others are souls who are unwilling to move on. It is a dangerous place where no living beings should venture, as those hostile souls harbor an unimaginable thirst for energy from the living.

NAME GUIDE

DIMINUTIVES, NICKNAMES, AND NAME TAGS

A-: Friendly diminutive. Always a prefix. Usually for monosyllabic names, or one syllable out of a two-syllable name.
Example: a-Lan

DA-: A prefix meaning "eldest." Not always used literally—can be added to a name or other diminutive as a way to add respect.
Example: dage

XIAO-: A prefix meaning "small" or "youngest." When added to a name, it expresses affection. Example: xiao-Guo

LAO-: A prefix meaning "old." Usually added to a surname and used in informal contexts. Example: lao-Wu

-SHU: A suffix meaning "uncle." Used to refer to a respected older man, usually a generation above.

-XIONG: A suffix meaning "brother." A bit antiquated and not commonly used today. Similar to the usage of Ge.

-SHIXIONG: Older martial brother. For senior male members of one's own school or for the oldest male to share the same teacher.

GE: Older brother or older male friend. Usually used to refer to a close but respected man older than the speaker. Can be attached to a name as a suffix. Example: Chu-ge

JIE: Older sister or older female friend. Usually used to refer to a close but respected woman older than the speaker. Can be attached to a name as a suffix. Example: Zhu Hong-jie, jiejie

TONGXUE: A general term used to address a student by someone who is not close to them. Used in contexts where calling them by their full name would sound too blunt. Can also be attached to someone's name as a suffix. Example: Zhao-tongxue

LAOSHI: A term used to refer to any educator, often in deference. Can also be attached to someone's name as a suffix. Example: Shen-laoshi

These affixes can also be combined. Combinations include but are not limited to:

DAGE: Literally means eldest brother, but when used outside family, it is an informal address to insinuate respect and closeness with a male friend older than the speaker.

LAOGE: Literally means elderly brother. In common usage, it's similar to dage but even less formal and suggests a closer relationship. Usually refers to a significantly older man.

PRONUNCIATION GUIDE

Mandarin Chinese is the official state language of mainland China, and pinyin is the official system of romanization in which it is written. As Mandarin is a tonal language, pinyin uses diacritical marks (e.g., ā, á, ǎ, à) to indicate these tonal inflections. Most words use one of four tones, though some are a neutral tone. Furthermore, regional variance can change the way native Chinese speakers pronounce the same word. For those reasons and more, please consider the guide below a simplified introduction to pronunciation of select character names and sounds from the world of *Guardian*.

More resources are available at sevenseasdanmei.com

NOTE ON SPELLING: Romanized Mandarin Chinese words with identical spelling in pinyin—and even pronunciation—may well have different meanings. These words are more easily differentiated in written Chinese, which uses characters.

Zhènhún
zh as in john.
en as in understand.
h as in horse.
un as in when.
(juhn hwen)

Zhào Yúnlán

 zhao as in **jou**st.

 y as in **y**ou.

 un as in b**oon**.

 lan as in **l**eaf.

 an as in r**un**.

 (**jow yoon lahn**)

Shěn Wēi

 shen as in **shun**.

 wei as in **way**.

 (**shun way**)

Guō Chángchéng

 guo as in **Go**rdon.

 ch as in **ch**allenge.

 ang as in t**ongue**.

 ch as in **ch**allenge.

 eng as in **uh+ng**.

 (**gwo chahng chuhng**)

 NOTE: *The difference between ang and eng is that chang leans more toward ah-ng and eng leans more toward uh-ng.*

Dàqìng

 da as in **da**rling.

 q as in **ch**eap.

 ing as in **Eng**lish.

 (**da ching**)

Zhù Hóng
> **zh** as in **j**ohn.
> **u** as in f**oo**l.
> **ho** as in **ho**me.
> **ng** as in lo**ng**.
> (**joo hohng**)

Lín Jìng
> **lin** as in **lean**.
> **jing** as in **jing**le.
> (**leen jing**)

Wāng Zhēng
> **wa** as in **wa**nt.
> **ng** as in lo**ng**.
> **zh** as in **j**ohn.
> **eng** as in **uh+ng**.
> (**wahng juhng**)

Sāngzàn
> **sang** as in **sung**.
> **z** as in regar**ds**.
> **an** as in r**un**.
> (**sung zun**)

Nǚwā
> **nǚ** as in **new**.
> **wa** as in **was**.
> (**new wa**)

APPENDIX

GLOSSARY

GLOSSARY

While not required reading, this glossary is intended to offer further context to the many concepts and terms utilized throughout this novel and provide a starting point for learning more about the rich Chinese culture from which these stories were written.

China is home to dozens of cultures, and its history spans thousands of years. The provided definitions are not strictly universal across all these cultural groups, and this simplified overview is meant for new readers unfamiliar with the concepts. This glossary should not be considered a definitive source, especially for more complex ideas.

GENRES

Danmei

Danmei (耽美 / "indulgence in beauty") is a Chinese fiction genre focused on romanticized tales of love and attraction between men. It is analogous to the BL (boys' love) genre in Japanese media. The majority of well-known danmei writers are women writing for women, although all genders produce and enjoy the genre.

Webnovels

Webnovels are novels serialized by chapter online, and the websites that host them are considered spaces for indie and amateur writers. Many novels, dramas, comics, and animated shows produced in China are based on popular webnovels.

Guardian was first serialized on the website JJWXC.

FOLKLORE, MYTHOLOGY, AND RELIGION

In Chinese culture, lines between superstitious and folk beliefs may be blurred. Throughout history as different religions drift in and out of popularity, the people have adapted aspects of various religions into practices that better fit their local culture, sometimes mixing elements from several faiths to create something very different from the original religion. The lore in *Guardian* includes elements from Buddhism, Daoism, other folk religions, and local beliefs, and this is a good reflection on the belief system in China. It's quite common for someone to not be religious but still visit temples on special occasions or to pray for good luck. As such, though all definitions and explanations provided in this glossary may not be the only version out there, we've done our best to provide the most commonly accepted version that pertains to *Guardian*.

THE BOOK OF LIFE AND DEATH 生死簿: A book that keeps record of all living beings, how long they live, and all details of their lives. The Netherworld uses it to keep track of all souls and to know when it's time to collect a soul from the Mortal Realm.

BUDDHISM: The central belief of Buddhism is that life is a cycle of suffering and rebirth, only to be escaped by reaching enlightenment (nirvana). Buddhists believe in karma, that a person's actions will influence their fortune in this life and future lives. The teachings of the Buddha are known as the Middle Way and emphasize a practice that is neither extreme asceticism nor extreme indulgence.

CHAOS 混沌: The original state of all matter, which was shaped like an egg before Pangu hacked it open with his axe from the inside and created the world as we know it. In *Guardian*, Chaos is true "death," when everything returns to its most natural state.

GHOSTS 鬼: The spirits of deceased sentient creatures. Ghosts emit yin energy. They come in a variety of types: they can be malevolent or helpful, can retain their former personalities or be fully mindless, and can actively try to interact with the living world to achieve a goal or be little more than a remnant shadow of their former lives.

THE HEAVENS: In Chinese culture, the Heavens are a generic yet supreme power, universal and formless, that enforce order upon all matter, often manifesting as forces of nature. This power is not a place or a god, but even presides over gods.

MERITS 功德: Merits are "points" a person accumulates throughout their lifetime that determine their karma. The more good things one does, the more merits they accumulate. The more merits they have, the better their karma. In the end, their karma decides what they are reincarnated as in the next life.

PANGU 盘古: A primordial god who separated the clear from the turbid, forming Heaven and Earth out of the Chaos, thus creating the world.

SIX PATHS OF REINCARNATION/REINCARNATION CYCLE 六道轮回: The Six Paths of Reincarnation are six different realms of existence a soul may be reborn into: god, demi-god, human, animal, hungry ghost, and hell. The previous life's karma determines which realm they reincarnate into in the next life.

THIRD EYE 阴阳眼: An innate ability a person is naturally born with that allows them to see ghosts and other supernatural things in the Mortal Realm. This is sometimes described as one's third eye being open.

THREE ETHEREAL SOULS AND SEVEN CORPOREAL SOULS 三魂七魄: In traditional Chinese belief, humans possess two kinds of souls: ethereal souls (魂) represent the spirit and intellect and leave the body after death, whereas corporeal souls (魄) are earthbound and remain with the body of the deceased. Different traditions claim there are different numbers of each, but three ethereal souls and seven corporeal souls is common in Daoism.

THREE-LIFE ROCK 三生石: It's said that on the shore of the Wangchuan River, there is a large rock with two long markings going through it that divide the rock into three parts, representing the past life, the present life, and the future life.

THE THREE REALMS: Traditionally, the universe is divided into three realms: the Heavenly Realm, the Mortal Realm, and the Netherworld. The Heavenly Realm is where gods reside and rule, the Mortal Realm refers to the realm of the living, and the Netherworld refers to the realm of the dead. However, in *Guardian*, the gods do not live in the Heavenly Realm; they live in the Mortal Realm.

THE THREE SOVEREIGNS AND FIVE EMPERORS 三皇五帝
  THE THREE SOVEREIGNS
  FUXI 伏羲: One of the Three Sovereigns of ancient mythology, said to have the head of a human and the body of a snake. According to legend, Fuxi is Nüwa's brother or spouse (or both), as well as the ancestor to the humans who came after.

NÜWA 女娲: Also referred to as Sovereign Wa (娲皇). One of the Three Sovereigns of ancient mythology, with the head of a human and the body of a snake. She is best known for patching up the hole in the sky and for creating humans out of mud; therefore, she is known as the ancestor to all humans. After mending the sky, she turned into a layer of soil that lies upon the original ground, which the story refers to as Houtu.

SHENNONG 神农: One of the Three Sovereigns of ancient mythology, known in folk legends as the inventor of agriculture and herbal medicine.

THE FIVE EMPERORS: Five legendary emperors among the founding national rulers in Chinese tradition. The five emperors vary depending on source. The two mentioned in *Guardian* are the Flame Emperor (炎帝 / Yandi) and the Yellow Emperor (黄帝 / Huangdi), who ruled over the humans. Together, they are referred to as Yanhuang (炎黄). The name of the Yellow Emperor is Xuanyuan. The Flame and Yellow Emperors fought in a fierce battle with Chiyou, which they won.

CHIYOU 蚩尤: A god of war. In *Guardian*, he is the ancestor of the wu and yao. Having almost been defeated by the Flame and Yellow Emperors, he begged Kunlun-jun to take the wu and yao under his care by kowtowing each step up the mountain. While Kunlun-jun refused to see him, Daqing, a descendant of Chiyou, was unable to resist and licked the wound on Chiyou's forehead from kowtowing. As a result, Kunlun-jun had no choice but to accept the wu and yao.

HOUYI 后羿: Descendant of Chiyou. In *Guardian*, he gives himself the title of Emperor Jun, but in Chinese mythology, these are commonly recognized as two separate figures.

TRUE FLAMES OF SAMADHI 三昧真火: A concept of both Daoist and Buddhist origin. In *Guardian*, it refers to both a special fire that Zhao Yunlan manages to obtain from the Bi Fang bird, as well as the three soul fires every person possesses: one located on the top of their head, and another on each shoulder.

BAGUA 八卦: A set of eight trigrams forming an octagon that surrounds the taijitu, or yin-yang symbol. It is the Daoist representation of all things in the universe.

THREE WORMS 三尸: Sometimes translated as three corpses; a concept that exists in Daoism to explain human mortality. In *Guardian*, this shares attributes with the three poisons from Buddhism as the source of a human's greed, wrath, and delusion.

GONGGONG 共工: A god of water, son of Zhurong, descendant of the Flame Emperor. Gonggong fought Zhuanxu for power, and when he lost, rode atop the divine dragon and knocked over Buzhou Mountain in a rage.

ZHUANXU 颛顼: An emperor from Chinese mythology said to be the grandson of the Yellow Emperor. Zhuanxu fought Gonggong for power and won.

BUZHOU MOUNTAIN 不周山: A mythical mountain formed from the handle of Pangu's great axe. Said to be the path to the Heavens. After being knocked over by Gonggong and the Divine Dragon, the sky collapsed, causing endless calamity.

KUNLUN MOUNTAIN 昆仑山: A mountain formed from the head of Pangu's great axe. In *Guardian*, the very peak of Kunlun Mountain is the forbidden place of gods, where the Great Divine Tree grows.

PENGLAI MOUNTAIN 蓬莱山: A mythical mountain on an island to the east. In *Guardian*, Kunlun-jun raises it out of the ground as the earth flooded after Buzhou Mountain toppled.

HOUTU 后土: The Queen of the Earth in traditional mythology. 土 (tu) can mean "earth" or "soil." In *Guardian*, Houtu is the name Nüwa receives when she transforms into a layer of soil after dying, which separates the yin and yang, creating the Netherworld.

GENERAL CHINESE CULTURE

BIRTH CHART 生辰八字: A series of eight characters assigned to a person based on the Sexagenary Cycle (Tian Gan Di Zhi/Heavenly Stems, Earthly Branches). Two characters each are assigned according to their birth year, month, day, and hour, forming eight characters in total. It's thought that one's fate can be told from their birth chart. Usually, when one's birth chart is "too light," it means they have a hard life ahead, perhaps suffering illnesses or other traumatic events. And when one's birth chart is "too hard," one might cause other people who have "lighter" birth charts to die.

CHINESE CALENDAR: The traditional Chinese calendar is a combination of the lunar and solar calendars. Nowadays, it is more common to use the Gregorian calendar to keep track of dates. The Chinese calendar is more often used for traditional holidays (Lunar New Year, Mid-Autumn, etc.), and occasionally, people will keep track of their Chinese calendar birthday. Using the Chinese calendar is considered a little unusual—though perhaps more common with older people.

CINNABAR 朱砂: A red mineral pigment used for drawing paper talismans. A form of mercury sulfide, it's traditionally thought to have mind-calming effects and is effective for dispelling evil.

DAGENG 打更: In the times before clocks, this was the traditional system for telling time at night. A night watchman would walk around town with a gong or a woodblock, striking five times throughout the night, once every geng, or roughly every 2.4 hours.

DEATH RITUALS: After a person dies, their family will lay out food, burn incense, spirit money, and paper renditions of objects to help the dead in the Netherworld. There are specialty funeral stores that will sell various papier-mâché objects specifically for funerals. These offerings, especially spirit money, incense, and food, will be continuously offered after the deceased has died to pay respects.

YIN/YANG ENERGY 阴/阳气: Yin and yang is a concept in Chinese philosophy that describes the complementary interdependence of opposite/contrary forces. It can be applied to all forms of change and differences. Yang represents the sun, masculinity, and the living, while yin represents the shadows, femininity, and the dead, including spirits and ghosts. In fiction, imbalances between yin and yang energy in a person's body can act as the driving force for malevolent spirits that are seeking to replenish themselves of whichever they lack. Those with strong yang energy (e.g., men) are considered effective at warding off yin-natured supernatural beings (e.g., ghosts).

MEASUREMENTS

Measurements have changed during different periods of Chinese history, but these are what they are generally accepted as today. They are often only used as approximations and not to be taken literally. For example, something described as "thousands of zhang" is just very large.

- Cun 寸 - roughly 3 centimeters
- Chi 尺 - roughly ⅓ meter
- Zhang 丈 - roughly 3⅓ meters
- Li 里 = roughly 500 meters
- 10 cun = 1 chi
- 10 chi = 1 zhang
- 180 zhang = 1 li

GUARDIAN-SPECIFIC TERMINOLOGY

FOUR HALLOWED ARTIFACTS OF THE NETHERWORLD 幽冥四圣器: Within the fictional world of *Guardian*, these are four sacred artifacts that are said to be passed down since primordial times, related to a seal that affects the balance between yin and yang, reincarnation, and life and death. They include:

REINCARNATION DIAL 轮回晷: Made from pieces of the Three-Life Rock, with scales from a black fish from the Wangchuan River. One can use the Reincarnation Dial to give a portion of their life to an older person, thus shortening their own life.

MOUNTAIN-RIVER AWL 山河锥: A large, octagonal pillar, tapered at the bottom, that pierces into the ground in the sacred place of the Hanga Tribe. Formed from the spirits of tens of thousands of mountains and rivers, it can absorb and imprison spirits of the dead.

MERIT BRUSH 功德笔: A calligraphy brush made from a branch of the Ancient Merit Tree. It writes in both red and black ink. The red ink records merits and the black records sins. Using it, anyone is able to rewrite their merits and sins.

SOUL-GUARDING LAMP 镇魂灯: An oil lamp that calms souls and chases away evil. The wick was made of the blood from Kunlun-jun's heart; the lamp itself was made from Kunlun-jun's body.

THE GREAT SEAL 大封: Seals the gui inside the Place of Great Disrespect. It was first made by Fuxi, then fortified by Nüwa. After their deaths, Kunlun-jun was in charge of keeping watch over the Great Seal. After Kunlun-jun died, the responsibility fell to Shen Wei.

THE FOUR PILLARS 四柱: The Four Pillars hold up the sky and hold down the ground. The Four Hallowed Artifacts are used to seal and protect the Four Pillars. By destroying the Four Hallowed Artifacts, one could destroy the Four Pillars, and thus the world.

PLACE OF GREAT DISRESPECT 大不敬之地: Thousands of zhang below the Huangquan River, where the gui are imprisoned. It holds all the impurities in the ground left behind from when the earth was first formed.

GREAT DIVINE TREE 大神木: The ancient tree that grows at the peak of Kunlun Mountain.

ANCIENT MERIT TREE 功德古木: A tree that grew out of a branch of the Great Divine Tree that had been planted in the Place of Great Disrespect. It has no leaves, no flowers, and bears no fruit.

RACES

WU 巫族: Beings that existed around the times of creation along with humans and yao. They are descendants of Chiyou.

YAO 妖族: Animals or plants that have gained spiritual consciousness after years of absorbing the essences of Heaven and Earth from their surroundings. Especially high-level or long-lived yao are able to take on a human form after diligent cultivation. This concept is comparable to Japanese yokai, which is a loanword from the Chinese yao. Yao are not evil by nature but often come into conflict with humans for various reasons, one being that the modern world is not conducive to cultivating. Descendants of Chiyou.

HUMANS 人族: Beings created by Nüwa in the likeness of the gods. For the most part, humans rarely successfully achieve anything from cultivation.

GUI 鬼族: Beings of great evil imprisoned in the Place of Great Disrespect. The more humanlike and beautiful they are, the more powerful. The two most powerful gui are Shen Wei and Ghost Face, the Kings of the Gui. Youchu, appearing in vaguely humanoid forms with festering pustules, are the lowest type of gui.

GODS 神: Powerful deities that existed before humans.

▪ priest ▪

An internationally renowned author who writes for the novel serialization website, JJWXC, priest's books have inspired multimedia adaptations and been published in numerous languages around the world. priest is known for writing compelling drama that incorporates humor and creativity, and a grand sense of style that infuses her worldbuilding. Her works include *Stars of Chaos: Sha Po Lang*, *Guardian: Zhen Hun*, *Liu Yao: The Revitalization of Fuyao Sect*, *Mo Du (Silent Reading)*, and *Can Ci Pin (The Defective)*, among others.